The chopper's engine clanked and screamed

Grimaldi bellowed as he fought the stick. "We're going down!"

MacLeod burst apart like a water balloon, turning the cabin interior into a charnel house. Bolan could feel Smiley bleeding out in his arms. Chet was screaming hysterically. "You bastards! You bastards!"

The Devil had come for his due.

The helicopter soared over a sandy beach and spun nauseatingly. She skipped like a stone as one of her skids hit an outcropping. Grimaldi's voice was uncommonly desperate. "Brace for impact!"

The helicopter hit.

Other titles available in this series:

Code of Conflict	Season of Slaughter
Vengeance	Point of Betrayal
Executive Action	Ballistic Force
Killsport	Renegade
Conflagration	Survival Reflex
Storm Front	Path to War
War Season	Blood Dynasty
Evil Alliance	Ultimate Stakes
Scorched Earth	State of Evil
Deception	Force Lines
Destiny's Hour	Contagion Option
Power of the Lance	Hellfire Code
A Dying Evil	War Drums
Deep Treachery	Ripple Effect
War Load	Devil's Playground
Sworn Enemies	The Killing Rule
Dark Truth	Patriot Play
Breakaway	Appointment in Baghdad
Blood and Sand	Havana Five
Caged	The Judas Project
Sleepers	Plains of Fire
Strike and Retrieve	Colony of Evil
Age of War	Hard Passage
Line of Control	Interception
Breached	Cold War Reprise
Retaliation	Mission: Apocalypse
Pressure Point	Altered State
Silent Running	Killing Game
Stolen Arrows	Diplomacy Directive
Zero Option	Betrayed
Predator Paradise	Sabotage
Circle of Deception	Conflict Zone
Devil's Bargain	Blood Play
False Front	Desert Fallout
Lethal Tribute	Extraordinary Rendition

Don Pendleton's Mack Bolan®

Devil's Mark

A GOLD EAGLE BOOK FROM

WORLDWIDE®

TORONTO • NEW YORK • LONDON
AMSTERDAM • PARIS • SYDNEY • HAMBURG
STOCKHOLM • ATHENS • TOKYO • MILAN
MADRID • WARSAW • BUDAPEST • AUCKLAND

Recycling programs
for this product may
not exist in your area.

First edition December 2010

ISBN-13: 978-0-373-61541-4

Special thanks and acknowledgment to
Charles Rogers for his contribution to this work.

DEVIL'S MARK

Printed in U.S.A.

When bad men combine, the good must associate;
else they will fall one by one, an unpitied sacrifice in
a contemptible struggle.

—Edmund Burke
1729–1797
*Thoughts on the
Cause of the Present
Discontents*

Some forms of evil are more obvious than others.
My task—and that of my associates—is to take on
all comers until the puppetmaster is exposed.
Then I'll mete out my brand of justice—hell on Earth.

—Mack Bolan

CHAPTER ONE

Tijuana, Mexico

The three-car prisoner caravan wended its way through the potholed backstreets. Bolan rode shotgun in an unmarked, armored Bronco. It was 4:00 a.m., and the Tijuana back alleys still bustled in a sloggy way with drunken, bleary-eyed tourists either looking for a last, ugliest bit of action or staggering away from it. The dens of sin didn't bother to promote themselves with neon lights or pamphlet-waving hawkers pimping strip shows as on the main strip. Displaying the wares was frivolous excess at this time of night and in this part of town. It was old school Tijuana—graffitied brown adobe walls, an occasional bare bulb and small, dark doorways. If you were here and had money, you had already picked your perversion. You just walked through a door and the wares found you.

Bolan glanced back at "the package."

Prisoner Cuauhtemoc "Cuah" Nigris wasn't a happy man. Nigris was the last of the "Baja Barbacoas," a quartet of Mexican cartel contract killers who specialized in kidnapping their victims and slow-roasting them alive in a traditional Mexican open pit barbeque covered with maguey agave leaves. The fact that a man who had terrorized the Baja Peninsula from Tijuana to Cabo San Lucas, and was rumored to have eaten parts of his victims, had been reduced to the shivering cold sweats was cause for concern.

Then again, all three of Cuah's fellow accomplices had been caught, and despite the best efforts of the Mexican authorities, the three had been shot, poisoned and garroted while in custody, and adding insult to injury, they had all had their heads removed at some point before they went into the ground. Nigris was the last of his culinary killing quartet and, in desperation, had broken the cartel code of silence. He agreed to spill everything he knew about anything and everybody if they would only extradite him to the perceived safety of the United States.

Nigris flinched under Bolan's scrutiny.

Babysitting was one of Bolan's least favorite activities, particularly when the mark was a torturer and cannibal, but the powers that be in the Justice Department wanted Nigris, and they wanted him badly. He was a potential goldmine of information. Three of the four were dead. The Justice Department wanted some life insurance for Nigris and Hal Brognola had asked Mack Bolan to be the man's personal policy.

Bolan sized up the policyholder.

Cuah Nigris was a light heavyweight in size and stature. Gang tattoos crawled over most exposed surfaces of his body, including his shaved head. His almond-shaped eyes revealed his Aztec heritage, and at the moment they were flared wide in fear as he sat shackled hand and foot in the back of the SUV.

Policía Federal Preventiva agent Majandro "Mole" Le-Caesar sat next to him. The PFP agent was armed and armored and wearing black battle fatigues. His dark skin and brownish-red Afro betrayed a lot of African blood, and "Mole," the national chocolate sauce of Mexico, was a nickname he wore with pride. Bolan had liked the man immediately. LeCaesar in return regarded the mysterious American with the gravest of suspicion. It was a sign of how desperate things were getting that the PFP would allow an agent to go dark on an American prisoner transfer. LeCaesar kept the muzzle of his MP-5 jammed into Nigris's ribs and his eyes on the streets.

Bolan turned his attention to Agent Smiley.

It wasn't the most onerous task in the world.

Drug Enforcement Administration agent Cambrianna "Bree" Smiley was short and dark with big brown eyes, big cheekbones, big lips and pretty much a big everything packed into a small frame. She was a woman who looked good in body armor. The words *Mexican firecracker* came to mind except for the fact that she was Irish and happened to tan well. Just about every national law enforcement and intelligence agency in the world kept a few lookers on the roster. Certain situations worked best with a beautiful woman on the team, but Smiley was more than window dressing. She had done a tour in Afghanistan in 2007 with the DEA's Foreign-deployed Advisory and Support Teams, or FAST, and Bree Smiley won a reputation as a problem solver.

And in fact there was a significant problem on the U.S. border with Mexico. A problem so bad the President of the United States had turned Mack Bolan onto it, as well. Bolan was used to being an enigma to federal agents and their not liking it. Smiley was taking it better than most. She wouldn't admit it, but things had gotten spooky lately and she was secretly pleased to have the backup. Agent Smiley gave Bolan a lopsided grin without taking her eyes off the road. "You getting a good look, Blue Eyes?"

"Something is about to go down," Bolan said.

"Impossible." Smiley shook her head while constantly scanning the road ahead. "I planned this transfer. We sent out the decoy Cuah at 7:00 a.m. yesterday, under guard like he was the Mexican president himself. Our decoy is a ringer, and he reached the border and was delivered into custody without a hitch. No one knows about tonight's little excursion except people I trust with my life, and that includes Mole. No one knows our route except me, and if we're being tailed, then they're better than you and me both. Cuah Nigris is coming to America and he's going to sing like a bird for me."

Nigris whimpered in the backseat of the Bronco as they swung out of the red-light district and headed north for the border. Bolan's spine spoke to him and long ago he had learned to listen to it. "We're gonna get hit."

"No way." Bree's back went up. "I planned this op."

"And you planned it well," Bolan agreed. "But we're gonna get hit."

"And how do you figure that?"

"Because your skin is crawling just like mine." Bolan turned to the backseat. "You happy, Mole?"

LeCaesar shook his head. "No, *señor.* I am not happy. I have a bad feeling."

"What about you, Cuah?" Bolan asked.

Nigris moaned.

Bolan turned back to Smiley. "It's unanimous."

Smiley sighed. "And just who are you again?"

Bolan shrugged.

The woman's shoulders sagged. "Tell me you're Justice Department."

"I've been associated with the Justice Department," Bolan admitted.

"Associated?" Agent Smiley finally took her eyes off the road and quirked an eyebrow at Bolan. "Dude, you're kind of spooky."

Bolan shrugged. "I've been spooky—and scary, too."

"Okay, Carnac. You got me. I got a real bad feeling right about now." Smiley's voice sank an octave in irritation.

"So you tell me, Mr. Interdepartmental X-Files Liaison mystery man, you got any suggestions?"

Bolan unzipped the duffel between his feet and pulled out his current car gun. Agent Smiley's eyes flew wide. "Jesus…"

Even LeCaesar was impressed. *"¡Madre de Dios!"*

The SCAR-H—Special Forces Combat Assault Rifle–Heavy—was about as brutal as black rifles got. The stock was folded, the barrel had been lopped to thirteen inches for close-quarters combat and a 40 mm grenade launcher was slaved beneath the forestock. The accessory rails along the top and sides were loaded with an optical sight, a laser pointer and a Taser unit in case Nigris suddenly became restless. The magazine was stoked with .30-caliber tungsten-steel-core armor-piercing bullets. Bolan had ten more mags loaded with the same and a spread of grenades specially picked for just this situation. Bolan jacked an antiarmor round into the launcher.

"Nice end-of-the-world weapon you got there, slick."

Bolan checked the loads. "I was a Boy Scout."

Smiley's grin lit back up. "I was a Girl Scout!"

"I know." Bolan nodded. "I read your file."

"Okay, now you're getting creepy again."

Bolan scanned the streets of Tijuana. He had an intense dislike for fighting out of cars. They were bullet magnets. The window frames and your fellow passengers got in your way when you tried to shoot back, and if the bad guys had the balls it took only one or two enemy vehicles to run you off the road or pin you to a standstill and do you like Bonnie and Clyde. "You got a route B?"

"Route B, C and D," Smiley confirmed. "I got Z if it comes to it."

Bolan checked their lead vehicle. The caravan was in loose convoy. The lead unit was a block ahead and had four armed and armored DEA men inside. The tail unit was about a block behind and similarly loaded with a DEA Fast Reaction team. It would take a very good observer up in a helicopter or a string of spotters on rooftops to make the Nigris train as it wound its way through Tijuana for the border. "I want route X."

"I'm all ears," Smiley said.

"Tell A and B units to continue on primary route. If we're blown, I say you and I go random. Screw silent running. We go O.J. mode and run. Have Control call in a chopper and vector us to the nearest garage with a rooftop. We fly our asses out of here, deliver Cuah to San Diego Branch, and we're eating pancakes at the IHOP by dawn."

"Like the way you think, Tall, Dark and Spooky." Smiley cranked the wheel and thumbed her com unit. "Control, this is Vector 1. Suspect ambush. Breaking formation. Suggest Vector 2 and 3 continue primary route. I need a rooftop and helicopter extraction for package ASAP."

The DEA controlling agent was across the border in a communications van watching the transfer by satellite. "Copy that, Vector 1. Working up a route. Break east for highway. Vector 2 and 3 continue—"

"Here they come!" Bolan watched two black SUVs and a pickup come boiling out of a side street in his sideview mirror. He clicked his com unit. "Vector 3! Right behind you!"

The three black vehicles formed a wedge filling both lanes of the road and forcing vehicles off the road. The pickup formed the tip of the spear and the truck bed was packed with gunmen. Bolan hit the button on the sunroof. "Mole," Bolan said.

The *federale* didn't need to be told twice. Nigris

squeaked as LeCaesar shoved him to the floor of the Bronco and stepped on his neck to keep him there. The agent lowered his window and leaned out into the night with his submachine gun in hand. Bolan stood up in the sunroof. He unfolded his rifle's stock and shouldered the weapon. His eyes flared as a man in the back of the pickup leveled a green metal tube about a meter and a half long and sighted at Vector 3.

"Vector 3!" Bolan shouted into his com. "Rocket! Rocket! Rocket!"

Vector 3 went up on two wheels as the DEA driver cranked the wheel in desperate evasive action. LeCaesar's weapon chattered into life and sparks walked across the pickup's hood. Bolan flipped up his grenade launcher sight and took a second to aim. The weapon slammed against his shoulder as the grenade launcher belched 40 mm fire. The antiarmor round punched dead on into the pickup's gleaming grillwork. The windows blasted out as the shaped-charge warhead turned a significant section of the V-8 engine into molten metal and superheated gas that filled the cab with fire. The men in the truck bed screamed as the truck lifted up off its chassis and came down without front wheels. The truck flipped and men were smeared onto the road like insects. The SUV drivers floored it to escape the burning, tumbling hulk.

LeCaesar roared into the night as if he was at a Club Tijuana home game. "Goal! Goal! Goooal!" He punctuated each outburst of pleasure with a burst from his weapon. "C'mon, *cabrons!*"

Bolan put his sights on the closest SUV and burned half his mag into the grille. Steam blasted out from beneath the hood. Bolan raised his aim and put the other half into the driver's side windshield. The SUV instantly veered hard left and plowed into the brown adobe wall of a brothel.

The wall cracked. The SUV crumpled like an accordion, spewing glass and bits of body panel like shrapnel.

Bolan slapped in a fresh mag. The remaining SUV suddenly found that Vector 3 had three windows open and outraged DEA Fast Reaction men pumping rounds into them from their assault rifles. LeCaesar grinned up at Bolan. "Cartel pussies, they—"

Both men lurched in the window frames as Agent Smiley hit the gas. She shouted back at them. "Down! Down! Down!"

Bolan snaked down out of the sunroof. He reached over the seat and hauled LeCaesar back inside. He had half a heartbeat to ram his feet against the floorboards and slam his free hand against the roof as the brights from another pickup roared out of a side street and lit up Vector 1 like stalag lights. "Brace for impact!"

The cartel pickup hit them broadside.

Smiley swore and took a brutal head bounce that cracked her window. Nigris screamed. LeCaesar and the prisoner tumbled around the backseat like two rag dolls thrown in on spin cycle. Bolan gritted his teeth as glass from his shattered window flew in his face. He lost his grip on the roof, and blood spurted from his hand as it sheared away the dome light. His stomach lurched as the Bronco went up on two wheels. Smiley gasped as it landed on its side and Bolan landed on top of her. Grenades and spare mags were everywhere. A frag spun like a top on the edge of the center armrest. Bolan grabbed it. He was risking a burn if gasoline was leaking, but he could hear boots pounding the pavement. As bullets began rattling against the overturned truck he pulled the pin with a bloody hand and tossed the grenade up and out of the shattered passenger window. "Frag out!"

Someone outside yelled *¡Granada!* and the shouts

turned to screams as the grenade spewed shrapnel in all directions. LeCaesar crawled out the sunroof dragging a mewling Nigris with him. Bolan grabbed his rifle and a bandolier and helped push the prisoner's limp body out the sunroof. Smiley blinked and gasped. Bolan grabbed her and hauled her out of the Bronco. He reached back inside and pulled her carbine out of its rack.

"Smiley! You all right?" The agent stared at Bolan out of a mask of blood. Her left eyebrow was hanging off her face. Bolan held up his middle finger. "How many you see?"

"Screw you!" Smiley replied.

Bolan shoved her carbine into her arms. "You're gonna be all right!"

LeCaesar slapped Nigris forehand and back, but the killer seemed catatonic. Bolan didn't think it had much to do with the crash. LeCaesar made a terrible face as he tossed the prisoner across his shoulders like a sack of corn. The PFP agent was hurt. Bolan jacked a fresh grenade into his launcher. "Mole!"

"¡De nada!" Mole rose to his feet with a groan. "Go! Go! Go!"

Bolan looked up the street. A rocket attack had left Vector 2 a burning hulk. It didn't look as if anyone had gotten out. Behind them Vector 3 had left the last enemy SUV riddled like Swiss cheese. Bolan slung one of Smiley's arms over his shoulder and clicked his com unit. "Vector 3! We need you!"

"Copy that!"

"Control! This is Vector 1! Convoy under heavy attack! Vector 3 vehicle damaged! Package intact! Vector 2 is gone with all aboard! Repeat! Vector 2 is gone!"

"Copy that, Vector 1." The voice of the DEA controller in California was grim. "Helicopter inbound. Sending Vector 3 extraction route now!"

Vector 3 came roaring up the block victoriously. A dark blue Ford F-150 came screaming down the road to meet them. Instincts honed in battle on every continent on earth roared up and down Bolan's spine. "Vector 3! Abort! Take evasive action! Get out of here!"

"Negative Vector 1!" DEA agents sprouted out of the windows of Vector 3 and fire chattered from the muzzles of their carbines. They tore forward in an eight-cylinder, automatic-weapon jousting match. "We don't leave people behind!"

The enemy wasn't jousting. They were playing chicken, and Bolan's guts told him they weren't going to blink. Bolan dropped Smiley and brought up his rifle as the Ford flew by. Fire strobed from the muzzle and spent casings flew as he held the trigger down on full-auto, ripping the Ford's rear tires. Vector 3 realized a heartbeat too late what the Ford's intentions were. Vector 3 swerved at the last second, and the F-150 turned to meet them.

The vehicles collided head-on at a combined speed of over 100 mph.

The DEA men firing out of the windows of Vector 3 snapped like kindling from the impact. The assassin riding shotgun in the Ford flew through his windshield like a rocket of flesh and blood and plowed through Vector 3's windshield, as well. The two 4x4s bounced apart like mountain goat rams that had crippled each other with one apocalyptic hit. Both vehicles were crumpled like tin cans. Bolan's blood went cold as he reloaded and slapped his rifle's bolt into battery. No one was getting out of either vehicle. Drug muscle wasn't known for going kamikaze. Something was terribly wrong. "We gotta go. We gotta go now."

"Jesus…" Smiley used her carbine to lever herself up.

LeCaesar groaned beneath Nigris's deadweight.

"Give him to me."

LeCaesar snarled. Nigris was still officially his prisoner until he was handed over to U.S. authorities. "Go!"

Bolan clicked his com. "Control, this is Vector 1. All convoy vehicles disabled. Vector 3 is gone. Package intact. We need extraction now or nev—"

Two Mercury Grand Marquis, one black, one brown, both with tinted windows, cruised down the street. They weren't suicide sleds like the first wave of attack. They were cruising slow, prowling, the clean-up squad. "Bree, Mole, we got company."

"Jesus!" Smiley flipped her carbine's selector lever to full-auto. "How many of these guys are there?"

Too many, Bolan thought. He led his team down a side street as the two sedans slid around the burning hulk of Vector 2. They ducked down one narrow street and then another. The streets turned into alleys and barrios swiftly turned into unlighted, two-story adobes, huddled together with dirt for streets and lines of laundry stretched between them. The stars and a few strands of Christmas lights were the only light save occasional votive candles on stoops. Nigris squeaked as he tipped off LeCaesar's back and landed in a fetid puddle. The agent's weapon clattered as the man dropped to his hands and knees. Bolan kept an eye on the maze as Smiley dropped to a knee beside the Mexican agent. "You okay, amigo?"

LeCaesar mumbled in Spanish that it was nothing and he was fine. Then he threw up. Smiley wiped his chin and grimaced at the dark stain on her hand. "He got busted up in the crash. He's bleeding inside. We need to call—"

"We don't call anybody."

"What do you mean—"

"I mean all bets are off." Bolan turned off his com. "I don't trust anybody but you and him."

LeCaesar pushed himself to his knees and wiped blood from his chin. "The gringo is right. We trust no one."

Bolan cocked his head at Smiley. "How come she's not a gringa?"

LeCaesar rose with her help. "She's *mexicana honoraria*."

"How do I get to be an honorary Mexican?"

The agent flashed bloody teeth. "You have made progress tonight."

"Great. Can I have Cuah's keys?"

LeCaesar's smile fell from his face. "That man is a killer and a cannibal. I am not so sure that is a good idea."

"I don't want to carry him and you can't." Bolan shrugged. "Just his legs. So he can haul his own freight."

The agent looked at Smiley, who nodded. LeCaesar agreed. *"Sí."* He pulled a dog-tag chain bearing handcuff keys from beneath his armor.

Bolan unlocked Nigris's hobble and leaned in close. "Don't even think about it." Nigris whimpered. Bolan could smell the fear on him sweating through his clothes, and he didn't like it at all.

"Mole, I thought this guy was supposed to be a genuine badass."

"He is." LeCaesar didn't like it either. "Or at least he was."

Bolan hauled Nigris to his feet. "We need to find a vehicle."

LeCaesar grabbed Nigris by the scruff of the neck and jammed his weapon in his back. "The next main street is that way."

Headlights suddenly flared to brights as if on cue. The black sedan filled the narrow alleyway the way they had come. Smiley and LeCaesar opened up. Sparks walked across the Mercury's hood and bullets chipped glass. "They're armored!" Smiley shouted. Brights hit them from the other end of the alley and they were pinned between the rapidly closing bumpers. Bolan was out of antiarmor rounds for his grenade launcher.

Nigris broke free of LeCaesar and ran screaming down the alley, waving his arms. *"¡Maricon!"* the agent snarled, but he wasn't willing to shoot his suspect.

"Cuah!" Bolan roared.

The black sedan accelerated. Nigris froze like a deer and the vehicle ran him down. He flew ten feet and the Mercury followed, grinding him to paste beneath its wheels. Both sedans advanced, putting Bolan, Smiley and LeCaesar in the big squeeze. The two agents fired without effect. There was nowhere to go. Bolan pulled a high-explosive grenade. Most civilian vehicle armor jobs were armored in the windows and body panels. Only the highest end military and diplomatic vehicles' undersides were mine-proofed.

Bolan pulled the pin and went bowling for bad guys.

He counted down one second of fuse time and underhanded the grenade down the alley. It bounced beneath the bumper of the oncoming brown Mercury. The front of the Marquis lifted higher than any low-rider dared dream as the undercarriage was annihilated. "C'mon!"

Bolan was already charging. The sedan behind them roared with acceleration. The Executioner burned half his clip into the stricken Marquis's windshield from the hip-assault position. He leaped onto the hood and helped up his companions. "Go!" They slipped over the hood and down the trunk. Bolan turned toward the oncoming juggernaut and emptied his weapon into the windshield.

His rifle clacked open on a smoking empty chamber as the sedan hurtled in.

Bolan jumped.

The brown sedan beneath his boots disappeared backward and was replaced by a black one. Metal flew. The black Mercury slammed to a stop and Bolan landed on the hood. The occupants were barely discernable behind the tinted glass. He reloaded his rifle and began to fire into the driver's side point-blank. The twenty steel-core rounds bit into the armored glass, the last five punching through.

Bolan pulled his last frag, armed it and shoved the bomb through the coffee-cup-diameter hole his rifle rounds had dug.

The interior of the Mercury flashed yellow, then sprayed red; it filled with scything shrapnel with nowhere to go. Bolan reloaded his rifle, jumped down and clambered across the shattered vehicle. Smiley and LeCaesar were street side, and he trotted up and joined them. No cars were immediately in sight. Bolan took out his phone and made a called the Farm.

Back in Virginia, Aaron "the Bear" Kurtzman answered on the first ring. "Striker! Where are you? We've been monitoring the DEA com link. It's blowing up, and Tijuana looks like a war zone."

"We were made the second we left the safe house. We're down eight DEA men and we lost the package. We got our hats handed to us, Bear, and right now I got a *federale* in real bad shape. I need you to vector me to a hospital, and I don't want to meet bad guys, *federales* or anybody else on the way."

"That's going to be easier said than done. I have the real-time feed from the satellite the DEA is using. The streets are swarming with cops and soldiers. All Mexican police and federal frequencies are blowing up."

"I figured." Bolan glanced at a manhole. "Pull up a schematic of the Tijuana sewer system. I'm extracting underground."

"Interesting." Bolan could hear keys clicking on the Kurtzman's side. "Give me a minute."

"Copy that." Bolan broke cover and walked over to the manhole. It looked as if it hadn't been moved in years. It was baked into the street, and he didn't have time to wrestle with it. The Executioner pulled an offensive grenade from his bandolier, pulled the pin and dropped the bomb. "Fire in the hole!" He ran back to the car and slid across the hood to cover. The night flashed orange. People in their homes screamed and every dog in the neighborhood started barking. Bolan rose from cover followed by his battered team. The manhole cover was gone and the hole it had covered had been somewhat enlarged. "You got something for me, Bear?"

"Yeah, I'm not sure about sewer reception with your rig, so I'm just going to download the route to your phone. You'll be on your own until you surface."

"Copy that." Smoke rolled out of the hole but even the acrid smell of burned high explosive couldn't cover the septic stench that awaited them down in the darkness. Bolan watched as a dull green grid of lines began to scroll on the screen of his phone. His route suddenly highlighted in red. "Got it. Bree, Mole, c'mon."

Smiley and LeCaesar limped to the hole and both of them wrinkled their noses in unison.

"Shit," the DEA agent said.

"Mierda," LeCaesar echoed.

Bolan considered the evening's activities. Shit was right, and shit was all they had. "Let's go."

CHAPTER TWO

Bree Smiley wasn't smiling. She wouldn't be quirking her eyebrow at anyone anytime soon, either. Blood leaked down her cheek as the Mexican intern sewed her left eyebrow back onto her face. Despite the blood and swelling, the DEA agent's thoughts were clearly written on her face. She wasn't happy. Bolan leaned in the door frame with his left hand bandaged. "You did good, Smiley."

"We lost our prisoner and eight agents."

"You survived."

Smiley rolled an eye at the needle going in and out of her brow. "I got mutilated."

"Scars are sexy."

"Sicko." Bree snorted and the effort made her wince. "How's Mole?"

"He got tossed around pretty good in the crash. Busted ribs, his kidneys are bleeding. His left lung didn't deflate, but it's lacerated. Good news is the doctor doesn't want to operate. They were most worried about infection from our septic stroll down below. They taped him up, put him on antibiotics and sedated him. Rest is what he needs most."

Smiley looked around without moving her head. "Pretty swank digs for Tijuana. Your controller did good."

Bolan smiled. Kurtzman would be amused at being referred to as Bolan's "controller," but Smiley was right. He had chosen wisely. Hospital Angeles had been built by the Medical Tourism Corporation specifically to cater to patients visiting from the United States and Canada. It was pretty much medical colonialism, but Bolan wasn't complaining and he doubted LeCaesar would, either. It was a thoroughly modern facility, and the best treatment anyone who had been in a gunfight in Tijuana was likely to get.

"Where are the rest of my boys?" Smiley asked.

Bolan had made some calls. "They're at the morgue along with what's left of Cuah and the dead perps. Your men are being prepped for transport to the States. Cuah and company are staying here."

"What about you?"

Bolan shrugged. "What about me?"

"Well, Cuah's dead. What's the status of your liaison-observer apparatus now?"

"Status is I'm going to stick around for a while. Hope you don't mind."

Smiley was visibly relieved. "I was kind of hoping you'd say that. You know, if you hadn't been there Mole and I wouldn't have made it out alive."

"Yeah," Bolan agreed.

"Humble, too."

He shrugged.

The woman looked at Bolan sincerely through her bruises. "Thanks."

"No problem."

The intern dabbed away the remaining blood with a wipe and stepped back to admire his handiwork. "There."

"What's the prognosis?" Bolan asked.

"Twelve stitches." He gave Agent Smiley a sympathetic look. "There will be a scar."

"Scars are sexy." Bree regarded Bolan dryly. "Or so I'm told."

"Dr. Reyes suspects there may be concussion. It might be best if we kept you for observation until morning and scheduled you for an MRI. Do you—"

"Screw that."

"Mmm." The intern looked back and forth between Smiley and Bolan. "Somehow I suspected you would say that. Very well, I recommend you see your personal physician when you get back to the United States as soon as you can. If you experience nausea or dizziness before you return to the United States, come back here immediately."

"Right, thanks."

The intern took his clipboard, made some notes and left.

"Right." Smiley stood up, made an unhappy noise and sat back down again. "Jesus…"

"Take it slow."

"Shit."

"Listen, just—"

"No." Smiley looked past Bolan and rolled her eyes as if she couldn't catch a break. "We got trouble."

"What kind of trouble?"

"Inspector Federal Israel Raymondo Villaluz."

"Is here." Bolan gathered.

"Yup."

"Is he a problem?"

"Well, he did sign over Cuah Nigris to me and Mole. Quite reluctantly, I might add."

"And we lost Cuah." Bolan sighed. "Has he spotted you?"

"Not yet."

Bolan ushered Smiley to the opposite row of beds and pulled the privacy curtain. He peered out the crack between the sheets of fabric. Inspector Villaluz was as tall as Bolan but lankier. He wore gray slacks and a gray suit coat.

His dress shirt was starched blinding white and cinched at the throat with a turquoise and silver bola rather than a tie. He carried his Resistol straw cowboy hat in his hand. Pancho Villa himself would have admired the man's mustache. The five-fingered comb-over crawling across his balding was comical. Bolan made him pushing fifty and definitely old school *federale*. "Give me the low-down on Villaluz, quick."

"He's about as good as Tijuana *federales* get. I'm not saying he's clean. Word is he hasn't paid for a beer or a meal in Tijuana in twenty years, but word is also he isn't in anyone's pocket. He's a 'peace and quiet or I crack heads' kind of cop. That's his problem. He hasn't kissed his superiors' asses, and he hasn't bent over for the cartels. He'll never rise higher than inspector."

Bolan watched Villaluz squint around the observation-recovery ward. He was obviously looking for them. There was no tough-guy swagger or bluster about him. He smiled and spoke to a nurse who was clueless as to where Bolan and Smiley had gone. Bolan made Villaluz for a man who was polite until it was time to not be polite, and then relaxed and enjoyed the violence. "You got anything else?"

"He's also a gunfighter. Real Dirty Harry type. They call him in when things get rough."

"Oh, yeah?"

Smiley spread her hands. "His nickname on the street is Dos Armas."

Bolan smiled. "Two Guns?"

"Yup."

"I think I'd like him."

"Yeah, well, he isn't going to like you. After losing three of the Barbacoa Four in custody? The *federales* put

Villaluz and the team he got to pick himself in charge of babysitting Cuah."

The shit storm was definitely on the horizon. "And then his superiors forced him to hand Cuah over to us."

"You got it. Still want to meet him?" Smiley asked.

"Definitely."

"You know I knew you were going to say that."

Bolan shrugged. He pulled back the privacy curtain and made a show of solicitously examining Agent Smiley's wound. Within seconds heavy cowboy boots drummed the linoleum toward them and stopped. The soldier turned. Anger passed across Villaluz's face, but he was looking at Smiley's wound. Bolan noted that the Mexican agent didn't like seeing women hurt. Up close he noted the broken nose and scar tissue around the eyebrows that bespoke a former boxer. Villaluz spoke the easy, smoothly accented English of a man who had worked the U.S.-Mexican border all his life.

"Agent Smiley, allow me to express condolences on behalf of myself and the Agencia Federal de Investigación for the loss of your men."

"Thank you, Inspector."

The man seemed sincere. He turned sincerely cold as he gave Bolan a hard look. "I have not met your companion. He is with your DEA?"

Smiley threw one out blind. "He's associated with the Justice Department."

"Ah." Villaluz looked Bolan up and down again. "May I ask in what capacity?"

"I was called in to facilitate the transfer of Cuauhtemoc Nigris into U.S. custody," Bolan said.

A lot of rejoinders clearly occurred to Inspector Villaluz, but he kept it simple. "And?"

Bolan didn't bat an eye. "I failed."

It wasn't the obfuscation Villaluz had expected. "I see."

"Three of the Barbacoa Four died in Mexican custody," Bolan continued. "The fourth died in mine. You and I need to talk."

"Yes, I believe I would like that very much. Agent Smiley, I gather you want to stay close to Agente LeCaesar?"

"At least until some backup arrives. I owe him, and he made enemies tonight."

"Well, I will tell you, the food for the yanqui visitors in the cafeteria here is bad and the coffee is worse. The staff cafeteria is much better. I know many of the doctors and staff here. I will see about getting us something decent to eat. It is Sunday morning, I suspect they will have menudo."

They followed the inspector to the elevator and went up four floors. Villaluz spoke a few words to a nurse and took over a medical conference room covered with Aztec murals. Within moments steaming bowls of tripe soup, baskets of tortillas and urns of coffee appeared. Smiley tucked in like a she-hyena with manners. Bolan took her hunger as a good sign. They shared a few moments of quiet save for table noises. Out of pride Villaluz wouldn't bring even a despised guest to someplace he wouldn't eat in himself.

Villaluz regarded Bolan with hospitable suspicion. "You like menudo, *señor*?"

"You have to look for it in the United States, and look just as hard to find a good bowl."

"Ah." Villaluz had no problem believing one couldn't get decent menudo in the United States. "You prefer the broth red or green?"

Villaluz was playing chess. Bolan swiped a tortilla through his soup and wolfed it down. "Clear."

"Ah." The inspector nodded at the wisdom of the statement. "Simple is best."

"Inspector, I'm very concerned that the cartel knew our route."

"I am very concerned about that, as well." Villaluz let some reproach creep into his voice. "However, I was not consulted on Señor Nigris's extradition."

"I concede the point, and it's regrettable," Bolan said. "However, three of the Barbacoa Four died in Mexican federal custody. We only came in after Señor Nigris demanded extradition to the U.S. in exchange for his testimony."

"Yes." Villaluz eyed Bolan archly. "You acceded to the request of a known cannibal."

"Actually it was your Federal Investigation Agency that acceded to his request."

Villaluz's face soured. "I concede that point, and I assure you I find it regrettable as well."

"Inspector, I believe you and I are on the same side."

"No, actually you are both from the northern side."

Bolan sighed inwardly as he sought a way to salvage the situation. "You come with a very high reputation, Inspector Villaluz."

"Thank you." The inspector accepted the compliment, but it didn't seem to engender any sense of obligation on his part. "However, I am afraid I do not even know your name."

Bolan nodded toward Smiley and shook his head. "Neither does she."

Smiley shrugged helplessly. "It's true."

The inspector was momentarily caught off guard.

"But you can call me Cooper," Bolan said.

"Very well. Let me be direct. I believe you are some

sort of yanqui paramilitary, Señor Cooper. A specialist, brought in to help bring in Cuah Nigris alive. But by your own admission you have failed. Your mission is over, and I think it would be best if you filed your after-action report in the United States, or at the CIA station in Mexico City if you must remain within our borders. But I believe you will find that you have worn out your welcome in Tijuana. I think you must be a brave man, and skilled, but my superiors are not pleased with this evening's activity, and to be honest, neither am I."

"I can see how you might feel that way, Inspector. So let me be equally frank. An international DEA counternarcotics operation got compromised in the worst way possible. Our informant is dead, and so are eight veteran agents. As far as I'm concerned, my mission has just begun."

Villaluz's color began to rise. "Señor Cooper, you—"

Bolan threw his changeup. "However, as I said, you come with a very high reputation, and I realize we took over your operation, over your objections, and we dropped the ball. Fact is you walk heavy on the streets of Tijuana. I'm a yanqui of unknown origin, and you must suspect I have access to assets and resources you don't, and vice versa. I suggest we pool them."

Villaluz leaned back in his chair, remeasuring Bolan. "An intriguing offer, but I am not sure my superiors would approve."

"Then don't tell them."

Villaluz blinked.

Bolan pulled out a business card with nothing but a number on it. "They don't have to know. But if you call that number, you'll have access to all the resources I can provide toward the case of Cuah, whether I'm removed from the situation or not."

Villaluz took the card and stared at it warily. "My own…secret Uncle Sam?"

"Something like that." Bolan nodded. "Can I ask you a question?"

"Of course." Villaluz tucked the card away. "You may ask."

"Is my leaving town a suggestion or an order?"

The inspector considered. "It's a suggestion, for now, but do not expect much in the way of cooperation with the state or local authorities here in Tijuana."

"Fair enough."

"Let me say—" Villaluz frowned as his cell rang. "Forgive me."

Bolan watched the inspector's face as he took the call. He said very little, and Bolan could tell by Villaluz's body language it wasn't good news.

"You need some privacy?"

"No, thank you." The inspector thanked his caller and clicked his phone shut. "As you know, any good policeman has his own intelligence network."

"Of course."

"I, of course, have put my machine into motion listening for any aspect of the Cuah Nigris case."

Smiley pushed her plate away and stifled a belch with the back of her fist. "Cuah's dead."

"Yes, that is true, and now a woman I happen to know in the Tijuana's fire department dispatch has just informed me a fire has been reported at the city morgue. Does this not strike you as an interesting coincidence, Agent Smiley?"

Smiley pushed away from the table. "Let's go."

"No." Bolan rose and checked the loads in his Beretta. "We'll never get there in time to do any good."

Villaluz stood and broke open a heavy, snub-nosed Colt .38. "Your associate is right."

Bree drew her weapon. "So why are we drawing down, then?"

Bolan pushed his weapon's selector to 3-round burst mode. "If the bad guys just took care of loose ends in the morgue, then our main concern is keeping Mole alive."

Villaluz donned his cowboy hat and tipped it at Smiley. "And you, señorita."

"Oh, well, thanks." Smiley checked her pistol. "I should have thought of that."

"It's the brain damage." Bolan said.

"Hey!"

"Stay behind us. Stick close." Bolan nodded at Villaluz. "Inspector?"

"*Sí,* the observation ward is on the first floor." Bolan and Villaluz fell into formation as they left the medical conference room. Doctors and nurses scattered to get out of the way of the two large, armed and grim-faced men as they strode down the hall. Smiley had to run to keep pace. "Hey! Wait up!"

A braver than average nurse stepped toward them as they entered neonatology. "Sirs, this area is—"

Villaluz held up his badge. Bolan held up his gun. "Staff elevator, where?"

The nurse gawked and pointed to the door down the corridor. Smiley caught her breath as they reached the elevators and Bolan punched the button. "How likely do you figure?" she asked.

The inspector scowled. "Agent Smiley, there have been two gunfights in Mexican hospitals this year. After what has happened this night nothing would surprise me." The elevator pinged and they stepped inside the car. Bolan glanced at the Colt Marshall in Villaluz's hand. "Heard they call you Two Gun on the street."

The inspector lifted his coat to reveal an identical

revolver in a cross-draw holster. "It is faster to draw a second gun than to reload the first. It is perhaps the most important thing my father ever taught me."

Bolan nodded. Villaluz Senior sounded like a man to be reckoned with.

Villaluz smirked at the machine pistol in Bolan's hand. "Yanquis and their big guns…"

The elevator door opened to the sound of screaming. Doctors and nurses were running in different directions down the halls. A worst-case scenario came through the wide double doors that led into the observation ward. Six Hispanic males walked in three by three. All six wore trench coats, which were open, revealing body armor. All four men carried submachine guns. For just a second before the doors swung shut, Bolan saw the dead bodies littering the floor, testifying to the fact that civilian casualties weren't a problem for the enemy. A crowd of doctors and nurses stampeded down the corridor like sheep before a pack of wolves.

"Everybody down!" Bolan roared and fired a 3-round burst into the ceiling.

"*¡Todos abajo!*" Villaluz thundered.

Medical professionals hugged walls, hugged the floor or threw themselves over counters or through open doors. A few still ran willy-nilly in blind and deaf panic. Bolan brought his Beretta 93-R on line in both hands. "They're wearing armor!"

"*Sí!*" Villaluz shouted. He held his .38 one-handed in front of himself like an old-style target shooter and shouldered a scurrying intern to the floor. Smiley dropped to a knee between Bolan and the inspector.

The killers shouted and swore in defiance. Everyone's weapon ripped into life at once. There was nowhere to run and no cover to be had.

Observation, Records and Receiving turned into the OK Corral as Team Bolan went for the head shots.

Bolan's first triburst collapsed a killer's face. Another gunner screamed as Villaluz's pistol erupted and shot his ear off. The screaming stopped as the inspector's second shot slammed through the man's septum and blasted apart his brainpan. Both dead men had the decency to collapse into their compatriots behind them and spoil their aim. Long bursts ripped into the ceiling lights, and half the corridor went dark. Smiley's auto-pistol cut loose as fast as she could pull the trigger. She caught mostly shoulder, but it was enough for Bolan and Villaluz's cross fire to crush the third killer's skull beyond recognition. Bolan's next triburst tore out a killer's trachea, and two huddling nurses screamed as they were struck by the arterial spray. Villaluz clicked on empty and slapped leather for his second gun. Smiley's Glock cracked on like clockwork and another gunner fell. The inspector raised iron, and the last hard-man staggered beneath a full broadside from Bolan and company.

The battle was over in a matter of heartbeats.

Smiley rose and ejected her spent mag. "Jesus, that was—Jesus!"

Fresh screams ripped through surgery as the double doors flew open beneath the boots of two more killers. Bolan's burst scattered the skull of one, but then the Beretta slammed open on empty. Villaluz punched a shot into one armored shoulder and clicked on empty. Both men simultaneously shoved Smiley to the floor and dropped to a knee. The action made both men's pant legs ride up and expose the ankle holsters they wore. Bolan's snub-nosed Centennial revolver rose up in his hand. Villaluz leveled a tiny, antique Colt .32. Bolan felt the wind whip of bullets passing close to his head as he and the inspector's revolvers spit fire.

The killer collapsed to the floor with his face cratered into a bloody moonscape.

Smiley pushed herself up snarling. "God...damn it!"

Bolan and Villaluz rose and swiftly reloaded. The Executioner eyed the inspector's cocktail-sized hideaway weapon. "So how come they don't call you Three Gun?"

"Before tonight—" Villaluz let out a long shaky breath as he reloaded his menagerie of metal "—I have never had to pull the third one."

Bolan considered leaving. Sirens sounded in the distance. The Hospital Angeles fire suppression system finally made up its tiny silicon mind about the gun smoke in the air and recessed sprinkler heads deployed out of the ceiling and brought on the rain. The goat-screw trifecta was complete as a baker's dozen of armed and soggy security guards roared through the surgery doors, guns drawn, telling everyone to get down a day late and a dollar short.

CHAPTER THREE

FIA Headquarters, Tijuana

The shit storm of recrimination was long, enduring and heartfelt. La Agencia Federal de Investigación wasn't happy and its collective, bureaucratic brain blindly pinned the tail on Mack Bolan as the donkey of its discontent. They threatened him with incarceration, litigation and deportation. Bolan weathered the storm. He had operated in Mexico before, and he had a few friends who owed him. Bolan called in markers, and the Tijuana FIA chief's jaw dropped as Bolan handed him the phone saying, "He wants to talk to you." It ended with stern warnings to behave himself in future. Bolan walked out of FIA Tijuana station a free man but all chances of further cooperation with local law were shot.

Bolan was radioactive in Tijuana.

The only people who would touch him would be the bad guys. Bolan walked out feeling a bit naked, as well. His Beretta 93-R machine pistol and his snub-nosed, 9 mm Smith had been confiscated. Both weapons were hard to come by, and both were probably about to become some cartel member's prize possessions as soon as the FIA evidence people could process them, declare them destroyed, then sell them on the black market.

Something was going to have to be done about that.

Bolan had a full war load in the CIA safe house, but

he didn't want to go there until he was sure he didn't have any tails, and he suspected he had a lot of them.

Bree Smiley walked beside him, livid beneath her bruises and stitches. "Sons of bitches. See if the Mexicans ever get reciprocity again on my—"

Bolan lifted his chin. "There's our reciprocity right there."

"*¡Hola, amigo, muchacha!*" Inspector Villaluz leaned against a gleaming black Toyota Tundra pickup and tipped his hat at them. "How was your visit?"

"We're pretty much persona non grata," Bolan said.

"Ah, yes." The inspector held open the door for Smiley. She climbed in the back. Villaluz gave Bolan a solicitous grin. "So, they…ripped you a new rectum?" He savored the American colloquialism.

"They tried."

"To be honest I was quite surprised to see you both walk out of the agency without shackles or escorts."

"They forced me to make some phone calls," Bolan admitted.

"I cannot imagine what that might mean."

Bolan sized up Villaluz. Cop. Gunfighter. Corrupt, but brave, and honorable by his own lights. Bolan rolled the dice. "It means that card I gave you means something."

Villaluz looked meditative as he pulled out into traffic. "So how do you feel? Are you hungry?"

Bolan patted the empty place where his Beretta should have been. "Actually, I'm feeling a little light."

"Ah." Villaluz nodded. "I think I can do something about that."

"Lunch wouldn't hurt either. Where do you recommend?"

"Mexicali," Villaluz answered.

Bolan consulted his mental map. Mexicali was more than a hundred miles due east of Tijuana. "Why Mexicali?"

"Why?" Villaluz smiled happily. "They have the best Chinese food in all of Mexico!"

"And to see who follows us," Bolan concluded.

"That, too."

"And because I'm feeling light."

Villaluz shrugged.

"You sure your superiors are going to approve?"

"I am getting you out of Tijuana, and I am keeping an eye on you," the inspector replied.

"And reporting our every move?" Bolan surmised.

"Well…" Villaluz pursed his lips judiciously. "As I believe the situation requires."

Bolan nodded. The inspector wanted the guys who had taken down Cuah Nigris, and he was willing to play both ends against the middle when it came to Bolan and his own superiors. They both knew Bolan and Smiley would be the fall guys if it went sour. It was a situation the soldier was willing to accept. "Fair enough."

Villaluz pulled onto Highway D2 heading east. It was Sunday, and most people were heading the other way for home. The brown landscape was lined with shrines. They were constructed out of tombstones, piles of bricks or adobe, and covered with collages of curled photos, dried-up postcards of the Virgin Mary, desiccated garlands of flowers and spent votive candles. They were shrines to the dead. Most Mexican roadsides were dotted with them, but here along the border they were mostly shrines to the murdered. Along the D2 they marched like dominoes to the horizon and were a testament to the endemic violence that convulsed the country.

They made good time. Traffic wasn't bad, and the inspector liked to drive fast. The only things that slowed them were the military and police checkpoints. Villaluz could have breezed through them on his FIA inspector's badge but he stopped at each checkpoint and chatted up the men manning them. Bolan watched as the inspector pressed flesh and clapped shoulders. He seemed to know most of the uniforms by name, and all seemed eager to bask in the inspector's reputation and machismo. Villaluz was dropping a net of lookouts and informants behind them on the road to Mexicali.

Bolan eased his seat back. "He's good."

"Mole worships the ground he walks on. Even the dirtiest cops do. The cartel street thugs respect him, and the cartel jefes in Tijuana have a hands-off policy. He doesn't mess with them and they don't mess with him."

"He's messing with them now."

"He's sticking his neck way out on this one, and that is uncharacteristic." Smiley shook her head. "Cuah and the Barbacoa Four all going down while in custody has him riled up. As far as he's concerned, someone has crossed the line, and now he's going to cross it, as well."

"There's going to be a war soon."

"Soon? Buddy, last night was World War III. I can't wait to see what you consider a real war."

"Stick around."

Villaluz hopped back into his truck and peeled out with screaming tires to the cheers of the khaki-clad *federales*. Bolan brought up the million-dollar question. "You ever seen the cartels attack like that?"

"I have seen them brazen, bold and reckless," the inspector said.

"You ever seen them suicidal? You ever seen them go kamikaze?"

The inspector pushed in the cigarette lighter in the dash and took his time lighting a Montana cigarette.

"You've seen this before tonight, haven't you," Bolan stated.

The usually loquacious Villaluz examined the glowing end of his cigarette. "Yes."

"How long has this been going on?"

"The taking of heads as a terror tactic is not new among the Mexican crime syndicates. I have seen them behave—what is the English idiom—crazy-brave to prove themselves. But ruthlessly willing to die, to sacrifice themselves to kill their target, that was, as you said, kamikaze. That is new."

Bolan shot the inspector a shrewd look. "That's not what bothers you the most."

"No, it is not. What bothers me most," the inspector continued, "is the code of silence."

"All criminal gangs have it," Bolan said.

"That is correct," the inspector agreed. "The Italian mafia calls it omertà, in Mexico it is simply called *silencio*, but as you say, in all cultures, it is basically the same. If you are a member, you do not talk."

"And?"

"I have never seen such a *silencio* as I have seen now. Cartel men talk about a code of honor, but in the end? They do not have one. That much money, that much drugs? They betray one another all the time. Now I fear there is some new player in the game, and his *silencio* is absolute. All of the Barbacoa Four died in custody, three in ours, and finally Cuah in yours. That is just the tip of the iceberg. Many have died in federal custody and witness protection, and whoever is doing this? He takes the heads of his enemies, and he takes the heads of his own fallen. No one is talking. You saw Cuah Nigris. He was wetting himself in fear, like a dog. What does it take to inspire such fear in a known sociopath?"

It was an ugly question and Bolan didn't have an immediate answer.

Smiley spoke from the backseat. "The DEA fears that al Qaeda has somehow infiltrated one or more of the border cartels."

Villaluz snorted. "I wish that was the case."

Bolan raised an eyebrow but waited for Villaluz to elaborate.

Smiley was less circumspect. "That's a hell of a thing to say."

"It is the truth, Agent Smiley. I am sure terrorists from the Middle East with money could pay the cartels to smuggle men and materials across the border. But a bunch of foreigners taking over the streets of Tijuana? With an iron *silencio*? Forgive me, *señorita*, but I was born here. I have been a policeman all my adult life. I promise you, getting Mexican gangsters to get behind Muslim sharia law and sacrificing their lives unflinchingly in the name of the Holy Koran? I do not find it credible. Something else is going on."

Bolan found himself on the same page as the inspector. "What do you think?"

"I do not know." Villaluz stared into the smog clouding Mexicali city in the distance. He suddenly perked up as they hit the city limits. "Let us get onto business."

"The Barbacoa Four?" Smiley asked.

"No, the best Mongolian Barbecue in Mexico." Villaluz roared into town as if he owned it, and now he whipped through the checkpoints with a flash of his badge. He drove to the famous intersection of Avenida Madero and Calle Megar and took a turn into La Chinesca, Mexicali's famous Chinatown. The buildings were a mix of old and new, but most had Chinese flourishes like pagoda accents and painted doors. What La Chinesca had more than anything was restaurants. They crowded every street, each one declaring in Spanish, Cantonese and English that they served the *auténtico* Chinese-Mexican cuisine.

Bolan had never seen so many Chinese people dressed like cowboys in his life.

Villaluz pulled down an alley and rolled up the windows against the flies and the rotting stench of the offal littering the ground from all the butchering going on to fuel over a hundred restaurants in less than four city blocks. The feral cats and dogs were some of the fattest Bolan had ever seen. He smiled at the inspector. "You were born here."

The inspector grinned back. "You are a very astute man. I was born in Mexicali, but as you may suspect, particularly for a man of my age, when I was coming up through the ranks, if you had ambition, Tijuana was the only place to be. But this is where I grew up. Right across the street. When I was a boy, you could cut the line between La Chinesca and the rest of Mexicali with a knife, and we were always fighting the Chinese gangs."

"What's the tong situation like here?" Bolan asked.

"A very good question. Up until the 1950s Chinese actually outnumbered Mexicans in this city. The tongs controlled the opium trade, prostitution and gambling. Now they are a small minority, and, as you might imagine, Mexican brown heroin pushed out China white in the 1980s and the tong control with it. The cartels have pushed the Chinese out of almost all organized crime except that which the Chinese commit against one another. Though they do a brisk business in specialty Chinese brothels, gun-running and gambling."

"What kind of gambling?"

"Mostly dog and cock fighting." Villaluz shook his head ruefully. "The Chinese have a ferocious reputation."

"Oh?"

"Oh, *sí,* if you challenge them? They have a special stipulation."

Smiley gave Villaluz a leery look. "What's that?"

"That if their animal wins? They get to cook and eat yours."

"That's sick," Smiley stated.

"Oh, some of the restaurants in La Chinesca specialize in fighting-dog meat. Many people, both Mexican and Chinese, believe if you eat moo shu pit bull it increases your virility, and machismo."

Smiley stared at a badly drawn graffito of a dog on the back door of the building. "No. Oh, hell no. Tell me we're not."

"We are. There is someone I think we should talk to." Villaluz gave Smiley a serious look. "*Señorita*, I strongly recommend you order the shark fin tacos with hoisin sauce."

Bolan opened his door and the side-street abattoir stench was almost overpowering. He gave Smiley a hand over an expansive puddle while Villaluz banged on the door. A pudgy little Chinese man in an apron and a paper hat opened the door with a cleaver in his hand. He and Villaluz exchanged a few words, and suddenly the man was all smiles and ushered them in. Smiley closed her eyes as they walked through the kitchen past meat hanging on hooks that clearly wasn't beef, pork or chicken. Both Chinese and Mexicans labored over prepping ingredients for the Sunday dinner crowd and takeout rush. They pushed through the kitchen door out into the restaurant. The decor was half Mexican rancho and half Mandarin splendor. It was just about noon on Sunday, and the place wasn't open for business yet. The chef led them to a booth in the back where a man sat with a bottle sipping Patrón Silver tequila.

Bolan was pretty sure he had never seen a Chinese

man dressed for a square dance before. The man wore a taupe-colored Stetson hat and a pink, yoked cowboy shirt. His attempt at a beard and mustache was worse than Villaluz's. Most of the Chinese people Bolan knew avoided the sun, but this man was deeply tanned and had crow's feet around his eyes. The man's sleeves were rolled up, and the calluses covering his knuckles bespoke long and intensive martial arts practice. He paused for the barest of moments as he took in the state of Agent Smiley's face and then nodded at the inspector.

Villaluz made a graceful gesture with his hand. "Señor Cooper, Señorita Smiley, allow me to introduce Señor Juan-Waldemar Wang."

Bolan shook his head. "That's a mouthful."

Wang threw back his head and laughed. "You have no idea, GI." Wang spoke his English with a southwestern twang. "So you can just call me J.W."

"You speak excellent English, J.W."

"Texas A&M, business. Take a load off."

Everyone took a seat. Wang made a vague gesture at the chef and a waiter with shot glasses and beers appeared almost instantaneously. Wang didn't appear to believe in frivolous excesses like lime or salt. He raised his glass. *"Salud."*

Everyone drank. The smooth tequila blossomed into warmth in Bolan's stomach and he chased it with a slug from a sweating bottle of Pacífico beer. Bolan motioned for another round of shots and raised his. *"Gan bei."*

Wang drank to the traditional Chinese toast "dry glass" and grinned. "Check out the culture on Cooper!" Bolan shrugged.

Wang looked Bolan up and down with renewed interest. "So my old buddy Israel is FIA, the señorita is DEA, what does that make you *muchacho?"*

"Concerned citizen?" Bolan ventured.

"Well, what's concerning you today, Citizen Cooper?"

"Milanesas?" Bolan asked.

Wang sighed happily at Bolan's request for fried, breaded steak. "Oh, we got that, and oh! And I have surprise delicacy!" Smiley squirmed visibly in her chair. Wang fired off a rapid string of orders in Cantonese, and the waiter and the chef made for the kitchen at the double. "What else is concerning you, Cooper?"

"Silencio."

Wang leaned back in the booth in thought. "Well, you know we inscrutable Chinese practically invented the concept."

"True, and as the inspector pointed out earlier, by comparison cartel guys talk about silence a hell of a lot more than they practice it."

"They're a bit loose-lipped compared to some," Wang conceded. "What's that to me?"

"Well, in Tijuana the *silencio* is starting to get enviable even by Chinese standards."

"I've heard that."

"How's it here in Mexicali?"

Wang smiled as the waiter staggered over beneath a mountain of plates and a bucket of beer on ice. "Ah."

The plates of beans, rice and tortillas and fried steaks were plentiful; however, the biggest point of interest were the heaping plates of fire-roasted red mezcal worms. Smiley eyed the mystery-meat milanesas with suspicion. She regarded the roasted caterpillars in open horror. Wang was throwing the gringos an open culinary challenge. Villaluz sighed with pleasure at the seasonal Mexican delicacy and dived in with aplomb. Bolan followed suit.

Bolan squeezed a wedge of lemon over his milanesa

and tucked in. Despite the fact that it was delicious, he privately hoped no canine gladiator had given its life for it. Bolan finished his beer and the waiter stopped just short of doing a baseball slide to fetch him a fresh one. Bolan and the inspector ate heartily and waited politely for Wang to pick up the ball again. Smiley picked at her beans and rice.

"Well, speaking of *silencio*," Wang stated, "I expect it might sound like something of a contradiction, but it's gotten a tad more violent and more silent here in ol' Mexicali."

The inspector speared himself another steak from the pile. "It is the same in Tijuana."

"It's my experience," Bolan said, "that Mexico isn't a very quiet place, and when it does get quiet it means something very bad is about to happen."

"That's pretty astute there, Coop."

Villaluz polished off his beer. "My friend is feeling somewhat light."

"Well, I reckon if I were him I'd want to go heeled." Wang pushed away from the table. "Follow me."

Bolan, Smiley and Villaluz followed Wang back into the kitchen and down the stairs into the cellar. Sacks of beans, rice and flour formed pyramids that nearly brushed the ceiling. Wang went to a steel security door and punched in a code.

Bolan stepped into the candy store.

Small arms of all descriptions were racked on the walls and covered tables. Wooden crates of weapons were palleted in piles like the beans and rice next door. "So what can I do you for?" Wang asked proudly.

"Tell me a story," Bolan said.

Wang chewed his lip for a moment in thought. "I'll tell you a story about the old days. Most yanquis don't know it, but the Chinese tongs used to run a lot of the crime on the border. When the U.S. had their anti-Chinese movements in the 1800s, many Chinese moved south across the border. In the end the Mexicans had their own night of the long-knives, but we still stayed. People still wanted opium and a place to do it. Men wanted Chinese prostitutes and places to do them. Mexico until recently was never the land of gunfighters the U.S. was, so if you wanted someone dead and didn't have men of your own? A tong hatchet man was a good bet."

"And then you got pushed out."

"Yep, in the 1980s Mexican brown heroin became cheap, plentiful and of higher quality than ever before. Our China white couldn't compete. Cocaine was the other drug of choice, and we were not a natural conduit for it. The Chinese criminal web in Mexico contracted. But if there is one thing we Chinese have it's worldwide connections. Mexican criminals have always gotten most of their weapons by stealing them or buying them black market from the Mexican military or smuggling them in from the United States. However, we Chinese have always been a secondary, shadow-conduit. AK-47s and light support weapons to revolutionaries in the south. PRC, Taiwanese and Philippine knockoffs of MAC-10s, Uzis and M-16s to the drug cartels. We Chinese never cared, business was business."

"And what's your relationship with the cartels?" Bolan probed.

"For the most part we have always had a wary truce with the cartels. We are a source of guns, and the Chinese laundries these days launder money into Asian offshore banks in the Pacific."

"And now?" Bolan asked.

"Now?" J.W. frowned. "Now, things are…"

"Beginning to take an alarming turn?" Bolan suggested.

Wang walked over to a crate and opened it with a small crowbar. "You know what those are."

Bolan looked at a dozen AK-47s packed in straw. "Kalashnikovs."

"You betcha. Weapon of the people. Used to be every cartel asshole wearing a Che Guevara T-shirt had to have one. I couldn't keep them in stock. Now? Now I can hardly give them away. The cartels took the high hat and consider them peasant weapons, used by barefoot illiterate assholes. Now they want M-4 carbines like your boys use. The weapons of the world conquerors."

Bolan was aware of this. "And?"

Wang pulled a pistol out from under his jacket. "You know what this is?"

Bolan eyed the large, uniformly gray, space-gun-looking Belgian weapon. "FN Five-seveN."

"No, it's a *mata policias.*"

"Cop killer."

Wang nodded. "Every Mexican criminal wants one of these. Now me? I'm a .45-caliber man, give me that 12.5 mm slug any day. But the little 5.7 mm rounds this baby squirts out? Rumor is they slide right through bulletproof vests. The U.S. war on drugs? Well, in Mexico it's starting to look like a civil war. The cops are arming up, the government is sending in the army, and the bad guys want a solution to all these assholes in body armor. They love the *mata policia,* and they all want that Belgian carbine that fires the same cartridge. But you know what the problem is?"

"Supply and demand," Bolan stated.

"That's right. Belgian guns have always been expensive, and trying to smuggle Belgian guns into Mexico, well, that's a very interesting proposition. It takes a U.S. buyer.

Five-seveNs are legal up north, but it throws in another middleman. If a U.S. citizen buys five or ten or fifty of them, he risks attracting a lot of unwanted attention, so the price goes way up. So they only come in at a very slow drip. They're also status symbols. I heard of them going for 10k a pop down here on the border and the supply just cannot meet the demand."

"So what's the solution?"

"From an economic standpoint?" Wang reached into an already opened crate and pulled out another pistol. "The solution is this."

The weapon looked like any one of a dozen 9 mm service pistols from around the world made of black metal and wearing black plastic grips. It was the Chinese QSZ-92 service pistol, and the only thing unique about it was the proprietary cartridge if fired.

Wang regarded the pistol. "Oh, I'll admit it's not as sexy as the Five-seveN. It's no race gun, but the 5.8 mm cartridge it fires has the pedigree. Needle-pointed steel-core bullet? Check. Magnum velocity? Check. And—"

Smiley stared at the pistol as if it were a snake. "And half the price of a Five-seveN."

"Try less than a tenth," Bolan said. "And you don't have to smuggle it across the U.S. border. You just pay off any customs official from Ensenada to Acapulco and he can bring them in by the container vessel." Bolan smiled at Wang without an ounce of warmth. "How many are you bringing in this year, Wang? Hundreds? Thousands? You going to bring in Chinese Type 05 submachine guns in the same caliber, as well?"

Wang frowned. "Therein lies the problem."

"What would that be?"

"I don't want to."

Bolan was mildly surprised. "Oh?"

"Oh, I'm telling you, my cousin in Hong Kong has them ready to go. He thinks we should market them locally as *asesinos chinos.*"

"Chinese assassins?"

"Yeah, my cousin earned his degree in marketing. He's good. He wants to sell them from Tijuana to Matamoros, one end of the border to the other, from sea to shining sea." Wang laid the weapon back in the crate. "Every punk on the street will want one."

"And be able to afford one," Smiley added bitterly. "You'll make a killing."

"You bet we would, but kill who?"

Wang turned to the inspector. "Forgive me, my friend, but the Chinese philosophy has always been to pay off the police and then get out of the way and let the Mexican criminals kill each other."

Villaluz's eyes narrowed but he reserved comment.

"Now it's different. Now it's war. The cartels aren't just killing one another. They are killing policemen, soldiers, mayors, judges and journalists. They are taking over whole towns. Parts of whole states. The days of paying off police and politicians in Mexico is almost over. Now it's simpler, and cheaper, to kill them. I was born in Mexico. I'm a Mexican citizen. My family is here. My business is here, and I reckon I just don't want to live in a narco-state."

Bolan had to admit that for a tong gunrunner who pit-fought animals and ate them J. W. Wang was a somewhat surprising man of conscience. He still kept his voice hard. "So what are you going to do about it?"

"I don't know." Wang looked Bolan straight in the eye. "What would you like me to do about it?"

"Go to war," Bolan said. He looked around at the crates of armament. "What else have you got?"

CHAPTER FOUR

Bolan sat shotgun in Wang's black BMW 7 series sedan. An exploratory tap of his knuckles on the body panels upon entry told Bolan the car was armored. Wang pointed to the corner across the street. "You see that guy?"

Bolan looked through the tinted window. A man as big as Bolan stood outside a barbershop on the La Chinesca street corner as if he owned it. He wore mirrored blue aviator sunglasses and a blue-and-white team Cruz Azul soccer team warm-up jacket. His black hair was pulled straight back into a short ponytail. He had zipped open the front of his jacket in the heat, and gang tattoos crawled up out of his wifebeater from his chest to his neck. By the way he was standing and occasionally adjusting his jacket, Bolan could tell he was armed. He reeked Mexican gangster, but there was something about the vibe he was throwing off that the Executioner didn't like. Great minds thought alike, and Smiley shook her head in the backseat. "There's something hinky about that guy, and more than just the fact that he's a scumbag."

"Who is he?" Bolan asked.

Wang made an unhappy noise. "It took some time to find out, but his name's Balthazar Gomez. He used to be a *sicario* for the Valencia Cartel."

Smiley shook her head again. *Sicarios* were cartel enforcers and hit men. "No one 'used to be' a *sicario*, you just end up in jail or dead."

Bolan mulled over other inconsistencies. The Valencia Cartel had merged with the west coast branch of the Federation Cartel. They were enemies of the Tijuana and the Gulf cartels and didn't have any friends in the north. Valencia operated out of the state of Michoacán, which left their boy Balthazar about fifteen hundred miles away from home. "Definitely something hinky about him."

"The boy is positively anomalous." Wang nodded.

Bolan liked what he saw less and less by the second. "So what's he doing hanging around in La Chinesca?"

Wang frowned mightily. "He's waiting for me to pay him."

Smiley leaned in between the seats. "Pay him for what?"

Wang squirmed in his seat slightly. "He wants his taste."

Bolan looked at the man, and he didn't like what he saw there either. "You telling me he's leaning on you?"

Wang squirmed even more. He might be a Mexican citizen who had been educated in the United States, but he was also Chinese and he knew he was losing face. "Yeah."

"Who's he working for?"

Wang stopped short of hanging his head in shame. "I don't know."

Villaluz had been taking all this in with increasing unease. "Forgive me, J.W. We have known each other for a very long time. You know I respect you, but I must ask. Why haven't you killed this man?"

Wang turned his face away to look out his window into the middle distance. "Because I'm afraid."

"Who does he work for?" Bolan repeated.

"I don't know. All I know is that he's *hombre marcado*."

"A marked man?" Bolan asked.

"Yeah."

"You know even in Spanish that usually means a dead man."

"I know!" Wang became increasingly agitated. "But that's not what it means now."

"What does it mean now?"

"It means he bears the mark," Wang stated.

"The mark of what?" Bolan probed.

"I don't know."

Bolan looked at the Chinese gangster and realized Wang was genuinely afraid of Balthazar Gomez. "Tell me what you do know."

"I know you don't mess with marked men."

"Or what?"

"The first three *hombres marcados* I heard about in Mexicali showed up at Tijuana cartel–controlled operations or fronts and demanded tribute. Of course they got killed and killed ugly."

"And then?"

"And then? Within a day the men who killed them were dead. Their families were dead. Their immediate friends were dead. Their business associates were dead. Everyone's head got taken, including the heads of the dead marked men in the morgue. The cartel capos who ran the killers got anonymous messages. *Silencio*, and pay. Two didn't pay and they and their families and friends ended up just like their *sicarios*. The third one paid. The bosses of the two who didn't got the same message. *Silencio*. Pay. There were a number of slaughters up the chain of command before they paid."

"These marked men are always out of towners?"

"Always," Wang affirmed. "As far as I've heard."

"And they're not taking over anyone's territory or operations?"

"No, they just demand a taste."

"And no one knows who's running them?" Bolan asked.

"No."

"And now you've got an *hombre marcado* in La Chinesca demanding tribute from you."

"Yeah."

Bolan nodded and flung open his door. "Right."

"Wait!" Wang cried, spewing a stream of very agitated Spanish, Cantonese and American profanity in Bolan's wake.

"Here we go," Smiley said.

Villaluz drew both revolvers. "This should be very interesting," he opined happily.

Cars slammed to screeching standstills as Bolan strode across the street straight at Balthazar Gomez. "Hey! Balthazar!"

Nearby citizens of La Chinesca scattered in all directions. The former *sicario* sneered behind sunglasses as Bolan reached the curb. "White boy? You—"

"White man," Bolan corrected him. Balthazar Gomez's sunglasses snapped at the bridge and his nose flattened beneath Bolan's fist. The soldier opened his hand, which made a sound like a frying pan slamming into a side of meat as he slapped teeth out of the marked man's mouth. Gomez staggered backward. He clawed beneath his sweat jacket and came out with an FN Five-seveN pistol. Bolan snatched the weapon out of his opponent's hand and beat him with it. More teeth flew as Bolan returned Gomez's gun forehand and back across his jaw.

Bolan tucked the gun away and had to give Gomez credit for still being upright.

The Executioner gave him no mercy.

Gomez flung a palsied punch in Bolan's direction. The soldier grabbed the arm and violently spun his sparring partner into a hip throw and projected him through the barbershop window. Glass shattered into flying shards. Chinese barbers shrieked and fled. Abandoned Mexican and Chinese customers in various states of midcoif cringed and jerked in their barber chairs. Bolan stepped over the sill through broken glass and into the carnage. Gomez was dazedly climbing up a shuddering patron's legs. The big American grabbed him and flung him against the back wall. The wall-length mirror cracked. Balthazar sank into a sink, and the basin ripped halfway out of the wall. Bolan closed both fists and delivered a series of rights and lefts.

He stepped back, and Gomez fell forward, flopping out of the sink with his face beaten and his seat sodden. He mewled slightly as he was dragged out of the barbershop by his ponytail. Bolan whistled through his teeth, and Wang's BMW bolted across the intersection and stopped in a shriek of rubber. Villaluz and Smiley emerged as Wang popped the trunk. The inspector grabbed the *sicario*'s legs and between them, he and Bolan heaved Balthazar into the trunk while Smiley covered the intersection with one of Wang's Chinese pistols. Villaluz handcuffed their perp and zip-tied his ankles with riot cuffs. Bolan slammed the trunk shut and everyone jumped back into the car as people on the street gasped and pointed.

"Drive!" Bolan ordered.

Wang was seriously unhappy. "Where?" he snarled.

Villaluz began speaking in fast and furious Spanish. Wang shook his head fatilistically as he put the pedal down and the BMW lunged back into traffic.

Bolan drew a Chinese pistol and laid it in his lap. "Where're we headed, Inspector?"

"A place I know and no one else in this car does, including the one in the trunk. Assuming you trust me, Señor Cooper, we will be safe."

"You don't get it!" Wang growled. "No one is safe from the marked men! They find you! No matter where you go! No matter where you hide! It doesn't matter who your *patron* is or who is protecting you! You're dead!"

Bolan's voice was as cold as the grave. "Just drive. Go where the inspector tells you."

Wang muttered, but he slammed through the gears and through traffic. In minutes they were out of La Chinesca, out of Mexicali and heading into the desert. Bolan watched as brown mountains clawed upward and the uglier and uglier roads kept creeping down toward sea level. "Laguna Salada?"

The inspector laughed. "You have been here before."

Bolan had walked the vast emptiness of the Sahara and Gobi deserts. Laguna Salada couldn't be described as a big empty. It had too many features of interest and too much character, but it was a big piece of brown solitude and Bolan watched it unfold before him. The Laguna Salada was a desert basin bounded by the Sierra Cucapah and the Sierra Juárez ranges. In wet years it was actually an inland fishing ground and bloomed like a rose. In dry years the saline watershed was salt desert and dunes where NASA had sent astronauts to train and Hollywood had filmed Westerns and WWII North African battle scenes. Depending on the weather, it was an off-road racing mecca, a land-speed record racecourse for land and water vehicles, an amateur astronomer haven, and Mexico's UFO and extra-terrestrial sighting ground zero.

Most of the time it was a fair chunk of sere-brown solitude.

Bolan had to admit there were worse places in Mexico to deliberately get lost. "You got a place out here?"

"I know of a place out here." Villaluz kept giving directions, and they slowly began to move out of the flats into the brown humps and hills that led into the Sierra Juárez.

A lot of things were bothering Wang, and he picked the least of his problems to avoid thinking about the major ones. The BMW bucked and slammed across road that was little more than cart path. "You know what this is doing to my alignment, old man!"

Villaluz put his hands to his breast innocently. "I did suggest we take my Tundra, but you insisted on your sedan."

Wang muttered something that sizzled in Cantonese.

Smiley looked about at the brutal landscape. "We should have packed a picnic basket."

"God provides," Villaluz assured piously.

It was Villaluz who provided, and what he provided was a goat ranch. The land was too hard for cows and sheep. It was too hard for BMW 7 series sedans, as well. They took a left turn into a box canyon that was nearly invisible from the road and came to a halt outside a cubist adobe. Steam tea-kettled out from under the hood.

Bolan got out and examined the inspector's redoubt. It was pueblo-style and used the rock face of the soaring brown cliffs as the back wall. The few windows were little more than firing slits. Bolan made most of it for original Yuman Indian construction. The satellite dish, prefab shed to the side and corrugated tin lean-to/garage with camouflage netting for a door were more recent. The small cottonwood corral for shearing and slaughtering was open and currently empty, though a few incredibly shabby-looking, random goats stared at the newcomers in slow, square-pupiled incredulousness from various vantages around the pueblo.

A donkey stood in the shade of the satellite dish and looked at the newcomers with little enthusiasm. Bolan noted the clumps of boulders and tombstone-sized shards of rock all around. Looking backward, the approach was flat save for the ugly dips and bumps that had had their way with the BMW's suspension. The pueblo was defensible, at least by Old West or possibly the conquistador's standards and the approach was a nice killing ground. Bolan couldn't immediately see the bolt-hole, but he knew it had to be there.

"Nice," Bolan acknowledged.

Villaluz sighed happily. "I am one-quarter Yuman Indian. My ancestors once lived here."

Smiley took in the pueblo and clearly wondered about the state of the facilities. "Little slice of heaven," she observed dryly.

Wang kicked his driver's side tire in anger. No one was ever going to tow his beautiful black vehicle out of the Laguna Salada. "Fuck!" he opined.

Villaluz cupped his hands over his mouth. "Fausto!" His voice boomed off the box canyon walls. "Fausto!"

Long moments passed before Fausto shambled out of the pueblo. He looked like Charles Bronson might have had he lived to be a hundred. His denim jeans and cowboy boots looked about as old and faded as he did. His cotton shirt was bleached blinding white. A red headband held back his shoulder-length gray hair. His face was a sun-raddled baseball mitt with two eyes a nose and a mouth. Duct tape held his cowboy boots together. The old man carried a Mexican army surplus M-1 Garand loosely in both hands. The weapon was missing a great deal of finish, and the stock was chipped and dinged but the metal and the wood gleamed with oil.

Fausto took in the panorama of interlopers stonily and finally turned his gaze on Villaluz. "Israel."

"Fausto!"

Fausto's features glacially moved into the semblance of a smile. *"Che, amigo."* He looked back at the unexpected guests. "Yanquis?"

"Sí." The inspector nodded.

Fausto contemplated this weird and wonderful turn of events. "Trouble?"

"Sí." The inspector nodded.

"Ah." Fausto turned and headed back into the pueblo. Villaluz nodded for them to follow. Bolan popped the trunk, and he and Villaluz manhandled Gomez out of the trunk. The man blinked dazedly in the glare and nearly toppled over. Villaluz produced a switchblade and cut the riot cuffs on his ankles. Gomez shuffled under the inspector's direction on feet stupid from lack of circulation. Bolan and Smiley grabbed gear bags heavy with ordnance. Wang spent a few mournful moments gazing at his stricken vehicle before his shoulders sagged and he grabbed some gear and followed suit.

Bolan had eaten well the past twenty-four hours, but his stomach rumbled as he entered the brown cube of the pueblo. A pot of pinto beans and bacon loaded with chilies bubbled over the hearth. They dropped their gear, and all took seats around a table made out of two sawhorses and planks. Villaluz shoved Gomez in a corner. Bolan put a Chinese pistol on the table and sat facing him. Fausto put out earthenware plates and began slopping beans and bacon and put out corn tortillas that had been steaming in a pan in the coals. Fausto gave Villaluz a questioning glance and the inspector nodded. The old man took up a clay pot and began splashing liquid into the mismatched coffee mugs around the table.

Bolan peered at the fresh pulque and smiled at Fausto. *"Tlachiquero?"*

Fausto nodded. *Tlachiqueros* were men who harvested the juice of the maguey plant and made pulque. Tequila and mezcal were distilled liquors from the same plant. Pulque was simply fermented like beer, had roughly the same alcohol content and was as ancient as the Aztecs. Villaluz clapped Fausto on the shoulder. *"Tlachiquero? Ranchero? Pistolero?* Fausto does it all. He is a—" Villaluz savored the English euphemism "—jack of all trades."

Fausto favored Bolan with a smile. "You like pulque, *señor?"*

"In the United States all you can get is the urine-in-a-can brands at the *super mercado.* But fresh made is always a pleasure."

Fausto cackled like a rooster with a herniated testicle as Bolan poured back his pulque, keeping the grimace off his face. Pulque was definitely an acquired taste, and could charitably be described as milky-, musty- and sour-tasting all at the same time. But most of its manufacture across northern Mexico was an artisanal industry, and Fausto had definitely put the time and love into his trade.

Smiley and Wang shuddered down a sip each. Villaluz hit his mug with gusto. Fausto gave Gomez his attention for the first time. "Who is this man?"

"He was trying to lean on our friend Wang," Bolan said.

Fausto took an ancient buck knife out of his pocket and flipped it open with a snap of his wrist. The blade had been sharpened so many times it was starting to resemble a scalpel. He looked to the inspector. "You want I should cut him?"

Gomez flinched but barely.

The inspector held out his mug for more pulque and measured Gomez. "Not just yet."

The ride through Laguna Salada hadn't done the beaten man any favors. "Perhaps he'd like a little something to cut the dust," Bolan suggested.

"A waste," Fausto proclaimed.

"He won't talk with a dry throat," Bolan replied.

Gomez drummed his heels on the floor and thrashed as Fausto pried open his mouth with fingers like cold chisels. Fausto poured a mug's worth of pulque down the *sicario's* throat. Gomez gagged and sputtered, and the old man treated him to another.

Bolan finished his meal, then rose. "I'm going to make a call. Keep our buddy Balthazar hydrated." The Executioner scooped up a Chinese assault rifle from one of the bags and stepped outside. He owned one of the latest satellite phones in existence, but in the box canyon he just wasn't getting full bars. Bolan pulled on a faded Boston Red Sox cap and took a hike out of the canyon. He squatted in the shade of a stand of mesquite trees and got a signal.

Aaron Kurtzman's craggy face appeared on his touch screen. "Striker! Where are you?"

"Laguna Salada," Bolan answered.

Kurtzman frowned for just a moment as he searched the massive database that was his mind. "What are you doing there?"

Bolan scanned his phone's camera back toward the pueblo. "Hanging at the goat ranch with Fausto, drinking pulque. You?"

"Mostly worrying about you. You got a sitrep for me?"

Bolan gave Kurtzman the condensed version, and the

computer expert began rapidly tapping keys on his end as he began pulling up CIA, FBI, DEA and NSA files. His craggy brow rearranged itself in question. "Running scared doesn't fit this Wang fellow's file."

"Well, Wang isn't typical tong, but he walks with heavy machismo around Mexicali. You're right, it isn't normal, and the cartel guys aren't acting normal, either. You capture cartel guys, and they usually start making threats or get all sullen."

"Well, I'm looking at your boy Balthazar's file and it pretty much jibes with what Wang told you. Cuah Nigris was pretty much a sociopath who found his niche. Balthazar Gomez is about as professional as cartel guys get short of being ex-military. He was a genuine A1 *sicario* down in Michoacán for the Valencia Cartel. Seven kills directly associated with him but no convictions. Half a dozen more suspected."

"Give me a timeline."

"Last word on him is that he was picked up by the police in a general sweep six months ago in the state capital, Morelia. They couldn't pin anything on him and let him go. Then he drops off the planet. His next known appearance is you grabbing him in La Chinesca this morning."

"So who's he working for?"

"That is the million-dollar question. Cartel guys betray one another all the time, but it's almost always because of power grab or a rivalry within the cartel. For a *sicario* to leave one cartel and go work for another is almost unheard-of. For one, it would be an immediate death sentence from the people you betrayed, and even if another cartel used you, you'd never be trusted."

"And yet our boy Balthazar is a thousand miles from home demanding a taste out of the Mexicali tongs, working for we don't know who."

"It is a conundrum," Kurtzman admitted. "And you say Wang says that most of these marked men are out-of-towners?"

"Out-of-staters," Bolan confirmed. "And as far as he knows, all of them bear Balthazar's MO."

"Hmm." Kurtzman mulled that over. "A genuine inter-cartel foreign legion."

Bolan smiled. "That's pretty perceptive, Bear."

"We try," he agreed.

"I might be tempted to call it an intercartel group of untouchables."

Kurtzman grinned in appreciation. "Even better, considering this new 'marked-man' status going around."

"So who's running them?"

"That is the question," Kurtzman replied.

"You got anything new on the street and hospital fights in Tijuana?"

"Well, half of the victims have already been cremated and all of them were missing their heads. There's not much to go on except the most basic of forensic evidence."

Bolan rose to his feet. "All right, do what you can. I'll get back to you."

Kurtzman grew concerned. "What's up?"

Bolan watched the rooster tails of dust rising in the distance from multiple vehicles. "Company."

CHAPTER FIVE

"We've got company," Bolan announced as he strode into the pueblo. Two pulque jars lay on their sides empty and a third was open. Fausto seemed to be matching the prisoner mug for mug. The difference was Fausto was still flint eyed. Balthazar Gomez was hammered out of his gourd and babbling. Bolan was mildly disturbed to see that the Valencia Cartel's #1 *sicario* was crying. "What's his problem?"

Villaluz, Wang and Fausto were all frowning as Gomez babbled in Mexican slang Bolan couldn't follow.

Villaluz shook his head. "He keeps going on about La Bestia and how we're all dead."

Warnings began spider-crawling up Bolan's spine. "The Beast?"

"Yes, he—"

The Executioner stalked across the room. "La Bestia?" Gomez jerked as if he'd been jabbed with a cattle prod. "The Beast?" Bolan shouted. Gomez howled as Bolan grabbed him by the hair and hurled him prone.

Smiley shouted in alarm. "Coop!"

The cop, the gunrunner and the old rancher watched with cold-eyed interest.

Bolan checked Gomez's right hand and wrist. He was covered with tattoos, but Bolan wasn't finding what he suspected. "The mark!" he demanded. *"¡La Marca de la Bestia! ¿Dónde?"*

Gomez moaned.

Bolan ripped away his prisoner's wifebeater. Tattoos of naked women, crosses and gang signs crawled all over his flesh. The soldier found what he was looking for behind Gomez's right ear. Bolan let out a long breath. Smiley peered over his shoulder and made an unhappy noise. "Oh, hell no. Tell me that isn't what I think it is."

The ex–Valencia Cartel *sicario* had 666 tattooed behind his ear.

Balthazar Gomez bore the Mark of the Beast.

Villaluz and Fausto crossed themselves in unison.

"So…" Wang's Texas drawl shook as he spoke. "This's like, some kind of satanic shit or somethin?"

"Yeah," Bolan affirmed.

Gomez shuddered like a squid and babbled.

Bolan's blood was cold in his veins. "What's he saying now?"

Villaluz looked down on Gomez as if a giant, pulsing, gangrenous spider had dropped into their midst. "He says no one can escape the Beast. He bears the mark, he is his, and now so are we."

Smiley was a little pale. "How the hell did they find us? We went dark, and I searched Gomez personally. He isn't wired up."

"I do not like it," Villaluz agreed. "If we had been followed from Tijuana, my contacts would have told me, and we switched cars in Mexicali." He turned a vaguely suspicious eye on Wang. "J.W.?"

Wang looked hurt. "Aw, hell, Iz, you tell me how! I didn't know I was kidnapping Balthazar today until Coop here beat the crap out of him and threw him in my trunk, much less anything about a road trip to a goat ranch."

Bolan eyed the stricken BMW baking in the sun outside. "What about your car?"

"My guys sweep it for GPS and bombs every morning and every night."

"Yeah?" Smiley said. "So how did they find us?"

Wang glared defiantly. "Maybe there's some kind of leak up north? Maybe someone bought some DEA agents?"

Smiley bristled.

Bolan cut short the speculation. "It doesn't matter," he stated. "Right now the cavalry is coming, it isn't ours and I don't think it's a rescue. It's a cleaning job. Kill everyone and take their heads." Bolan rose from the quivering mass that was Balthazar Gomez. "Better gear up. We've got about five minutes."

Bolan went to a bag and began to pull weapons. The Chinese QBZ-95 assault rifles were black, stubby, ugly weapons and not one of his particular favorites, but beggars couldn't be choosers. "Don't suppose you've got grenades, Wang?"

The gunrunner finally had something to smile about. "This is Mexico, amigo. The wise man goes nowhere without something that goes boom."

Bolan took in the duffel full of what looked like dull green, minifootballs on sticks with fins. They were PRC 70 mm rifle grenades. "How many you got?"

"Twelve."

"How many rifles we got?"

"Six, one for each of us plus two spares," Wang replied.

"You come prepared. What's the range on these bad boys?" Bolan asked.

"Seventy-five meters, but I'd wait until sixty, fifty would be better."

Bolan took out a grenade and clicked it onto the muzzle. "Load up every weapon, and keep handing them to me when I start firing."

Wang was mildly outraged. "What, you're gonna hog them all?"

"You ever fired a rifle grenade?"

"Hell, yes. I play with all my toys before I sell them."

"Ever fired one in anger?"

Wang had no response to that.

Bolan nodded. "Load them all, and when I start firing keep handing them to me."

He looked at Fausto and his M-1. "Is he any good with that Garand?"

"He can hit an ant in the ass at eight hundred meters," Villaluz announced.

Fausto smiled shyly and patted his rifle. "Six hundred." He took out a pair of wire-rimmed glasses and perched them on the end of his nose. "Seven-fifty?"

"Good man," Bolan said. "I'm going to grenade them as they come in range. I want everyone else to hold fire except Fausto. Fausto, you just do what comes natural whenever you feel it."

The old man took an ancient canvas bandolier full of clips off the back of his chair and walked to one of the slit windows. He shoved a handful of sunflower seeds into his mouth and began cracking seeds and spitting shells as he peered toward the mouth of the canyon. Bolan got the distinct impression this wasn't the first time Fausto had defended Fort Goat.

"Bree, how about being my grenade wench?"

Smiley grinned, and despite the tan skin and black hair he could see the Irish smiling in her eyes. "I'm your girl!"

Bolan gave her the basic rundown, and Smiley started loading clips and clicking grenades on muzzles. Wang and Villaluz began emptying gear bags, laying spare clips, extra pistols and hand grenades on the table. Villaluz glanced down at Gomez and took the precaution of binding his ankles together. The gangster shuddered on the adobe floor. "La Bestia…La Bestia…he comes…for us all…"

"Shut him up," Bolan ordered.

Gomez earned himself a strip of duct tape across the mouth. He blew snot over his gag and shook.

Villaluz shot Bolan a look. "This is not right."

"No." Bolan's skin was crawling as it had the other night on the streets of Tijuana before the attack. "No, it's not." He stepped to the door with a grenade-mounted rifle in hand. "I'm going to step outside. I'll need a bucket brigade. Keep them coming."

Bolan stepped out of the pueblo and the Mexican sun hit him like a hammer. He gazed out at the canyon mouth. It was around 1:00 p.m., and heat baked everything. The salt flats in the distance were one vast kiln of shimmering mirages, a promise of the water that turned the plains into a lake in the good years. Bolan glanced at the enemy's trajectory as they came in. The road was defensive, as well. It had wrecked the BMW, and it turned and twisted away from the main track a hundred yards from the entrance to the canyon. It would funnel the enemy straight in. Bolan started to suspect this little box canyon had fought off Aztecs, conquistadors and cowboys as well as *federales* and drug lords in its time.

Bolan lifted his binoculars. He made it eight vehicles, SUVs of various makes, 4x4s and all either black, dark blue or dark green with tinted windows. They were bee-lining for the hidden box canyon like the outriders of the apocalypse.

The soldier eyed the canyon mouth once more. "Fire at will, Fausto!"

"*Sí, señor!* I wait for the good shot! As you!"

Bolan's heart sank at the sound of a turboprop engine somewhere out above the salt flats. "Bree! Take this!" Bolan tossed his weapon back.

"Fausto! Give me your gun!"

Smiley caught the grenade-loaded assault rifle. Fausto made an unhappy noise, but the Garand sailed out of the slit window like a harpoon at Bolan. He caught it and strode out to the goat corral. A red-and-white Beechcraft Twin Bonanza broke the canyon rim and soared over to take a good look at the pueblo. Bolan snapped the rifle to his shoulder, and the ancient weapon bucked in his hands as he tracked and fired. The Bonanza dived. The Garand spoke five more times, then pinged as it racked open on empty and spit out the empty 8-round clip. The aircraft sailed out of sight over the mountain rim.

Bolan tossed the empty Garand back behind him. "Feed me!" He caught the grenade-mounted assault rifle that came looping over his shoulder.

"Well, that was effective," Smiley commented.

"The plane is their spotter, and all they spotted was one man with a rifle, and I want them to come in a rush."

"Oh."

Chickens squawked and scattered as he took over the shade of the low adobe wall. Vehicles filled the mouth of the box canyon. The lead was a black Hummer H3T pickup that filled the single lane dirt path. The other seven 4x4s bounced and bucked like broncos over the bumps and ruts to either side. Fausto's rifle began cracking in slow, aimed semiauto fire. The Hummer slowed and stopped as the other seven vehicles surged on. No gunmen hung out the windows or the sunroofs. They came on as if they intended to ram the pueblo. Bolan had scoped the approach with the eyes of a trained sniper. A tumbleweed beyond Wang's beleaguered BMW was Bolan's marker. He waited for the enemy to reach the magic sixty-meter mark. A gunmetal Chevy Suburban was first across the finish line.

Bolan sent him the big payoff straight from the People's Republic of China with love.

The stubby assault rifle slammed against Bolan's shoulder as the 70 mm rifle grenade spigotted off the muzzle and spiraled in straight and true. The elongated green football of the warhead punched through the Suburban's windshield and turned its interior into a blast furnace. Bolan flicked his selector switch to full-auto as he swept his assault weapon onto a Toyota Landcruiser and burned all thirty rounds from the magazine into the windshield. It cracked and raddled but didn't break. Bolan tossed the smoking, empty weapon behind him as the Suburban smoldered and died.

"Feed me!"

Bolan didn't even have to look back. Another grenade-mounted assault rifle fell into his hands as if he was running a timing pattern. He put his front sight on the Landcruiser and squeezed the trigger. The Toyota went up like a torch as shrapnel tore open its gas tank and super-heated gas and molten metal detonated it. The RAV4 next to it went up on two wheels from the blast. Bolan burned his mag into the windshield. The RAV wasn't armored, and the bullets swarmed through the glass. The driver died and the RAV rolled ugly. Bolan tossed his exhausted weapon back.

"Feed me!"

The bucket brigade sent another grenaded weapon into the Executioner's arms. He aimed and fired, and a Ford Bronco burst apart like a beer can full of firecrackers. He put thirty rounds into a Lincoln Navigator, but it came on with a total disregard for life and limb.

"Feed me!"

Bolan caught his next weapon and cracked the Navigator open like an egg. There were only two vehicles left, but they were uncomfortably close. A Porsche Cayenne wasn't a typical suicide sled, but the Porsche came on with its gears grinding and its engine snarling like a panther. Bolan's rifle brutally bucked against his shoulder as it slammed its two-pound payload airborne. The Porsche managed to crumple, expand and burst into flames all at the same time. Bolan dropped to a knee as flaming Porsche parts peppered the pueblo.

"Feed m—" Bolan rose as an ancient Ford F-150 came on like the Devil himself was on its heels. "Smiley! J.W.! Hammer him!" The old Ford's straight eight engine roared like a dinosaur, and it thundered in at ramming speed. Bolan emptied his clip into it.

Rifle grenades thudded right and left. The Ford went sky-high. Bolan dropped prone. The low adobe wall cracked and spit orange dust as something very heavy with a lot of pepper behind it crashed against it. A smoking steel bumper scythed overhead and slammed into the pueblo. Bolan waited as bits of truck rained down and popped up as the last of the scrap metal clattered to the ground. "Feed me."

Bolan caught a rifle and gazed across the sea of burning hulks. Gravel crunched behind him as the rest of the team emerged. The box canyon was an automotive graveyard in which most of the occupants had unwillingly been cremated. Tortured metal popped and ticked. The F-150's fiery demise had happened at nearly point-blank range, and it had liberally sprayed Wang's BMW with burning gasoline and flying auto parts. The luxury sedan was just starting to burn in earnest. Only the RAV-4 wasn't burning, but it lay on its back with a broken spine. The windshield was gone, and the two bullet-riddled passengers in front hung motionless and broken by their seatbelts.

Fausto clapped Bolan on the shoulder and cackled happily. The ancient redoubt of his ancestors had survived another siege. *"¡Bueno!"*

Wang stared inconsolably at his burning BMW. "Fuck."

Shell-shocked goats and chickens staggered about, making odd noises.

Smiley and Villaluz fanned out on either side of Bolan, their rifles at the ready.

Bolan eyes went beyond the smoldering SUVs and coolly observed the command vehicle. The Hummer H3T held position near the mouth of the canyon, its engine running, black paint gleaming. The tinted windshield stared at Bolan in opaque hostility. "What's the max range on these bad boys, J.W.?"

"Like I said, maximum effective range is seventy-five meters," Wang said. "They'll go a might farther but, it's all Kentucky windage after that."

"Mmm." Bolan nodded. He snapped up his weapon, took a moment to raise his sight about a foot over the top of the Hummer and fired. The 70 mm munition spiraled off across the canyon. It fell about fifteen meters short and another ten wide. Red desert dust vomited upward in a column as it detonated, and shrapnel sparkled off the Hummer's sides. The staring match continued. The range was too long for rifle grenades, but for a rifle it was spitting distance. Bolan peered down his sights. "Let him have it."

The rifle rattled as the Executioner held down the trigger. Smiley, Wang and Villaluz added their weight of shot on full-auto, as well. Fausto's big rifle boomed as he joined the fusillade. The Hummer suddenly looked as if it were in a wind-tunnel full of fireflies. Sparks streaked off the grille and hood and glass chips erupted in geysers from the windshield. But the Hummer just wasn't affected by the Chinese assault rifle rounds. Fausto's big bullets didn't seem to bother it much either. The big, black 4x4 was armored up well beyond normal levels of executive protection.

Everyone's rifle racked open on empty nearly at the same time.

Bolan slapped a fresh magazine into his weapon. The dark Hummer just sat there observing them with what seemed to be impassive evil.

Smiley shook her head as she reloaded. "Whoever these guys are, they're really starting to creep me out."

"Feed me," Bolan said. Smiley went to the doorway and scooped one of the two remaining grenade-mounted weapons. Bolan nodded and took it. "Go check on Balthazar. Sit on him, and keep the last grenade for yourself. Nuke anything that gets past me."

"What are you going to do?"

"I'm going for a walk to see if our friends out there talk, run or let me get close enough to blow them up."

Bolan nodded at Fausto. "Get back in your window. Cover the canyon mouth and keep an eye on the rims. J.W., Inspector, you're with me, but fan out wide. If the doors on that truck open up and hardmen come out, I want them in a cross fire."

Bolan went for a walk.

The rutted, pitted dirt path up to the pueblo was like the yellow brick road as it wove between the burning carcasses of cars that were sending the nasty black smoke of burning oil, upholstery and human flesh a hundred feet into the sky. Blackened bits of metal, glass and rubber littered the canyon floor. The sides of the canyon were littered with boulders and rock falls. Wang and the inspector moved swiftly from cover to cover. Bolan walked straight down the middle toward his impending appointment with his rifle at port arms. At ninety yards he began considering the shot. He could discern nothing through the tinted windshield, but he sure as hell felt himself being scrutinized and the scrutiny was decidedly unfriendly. At eighty yards Bolan's finger slid onto his trigger. It didn't matter if the man behind the glass was Satan's favorite son and his pickup was armored up to endangered diplomat levels. No windshield was going to withstand two pounds of Chinese shaped charge warhead.

And Bolan was getting tired of playing defense.

At eighty-five yards all-terrain tires buzz-sawed into the dust in Reverse, and the Hummer suddenly shot backward the way it had come. Whoever was driving was good. He kept it in Reverse at an engine-burning twenty-five miles per hour and kept it on the path even as it bounced. Bolan watched as the Hummer disappeared in its own dust cloud.

"Inspector?"

"*¿Sí?*"

"Let's get license plates on any vehicle that's still legible, then let's take a look at the people in that flipped over RAV. Photos, fingerprints, anything we can work up real quick. J.W.? Fade back and spell Bree on Balthazar. Send her out. I want her agent's eye and take on everything we find. Tell Fausto I want to move out of here in half an hour, and tell him I'm hoping he has a plan."

"You betcha."

Villaluz came out of cover and began snapping photos of the nearest hulk with his cell phone. Bolan did a lap around the Lincoln doing the same, but he suspected it wouldn't do much good. He found blackened bodies and black rifles that had been blackened further. He didn't find any plates and knew they had been removed. It would be hours before the wrecks were safe enough to prowl through, and Bolan didn't have much hope of finding any VINs inside. Bolan ambled over the RAV and slung his rifle. He drew a pistol and squatted beside the driver's shattered window. A Mexican man with a head covered with more ink than hair hung in his harness. About ten of Bolan's rounds had gone through his chest. Bolan pushed back the man's ear and scowled at the 666 tattoocd there.

Villaluz was doing the same on the passenger side. "I have a marked man, amigo."

"Same here." Bolan went through his corpse's pockets but all he found was ammo and enough knives to justify the word fetish. "You know we lit them up like the Fourth of July and they still kept coming."

"Yes, I noticed."

Bolan stood and waited for Smiley to bring the small forensics kit they had packed. "You ever seen that kind of zeal here in Mexico?"

"To be honest, no. One hears of such stories, but only during the Mexican Revolution. Men charging the cannons and the Gatling guns." Villaluz rose up creakily and looked at Bolan over the RAV's chassis. "But I will tell you, I am not as young as I once was, and like many men my age, more and more I find myself watching the History Channel on cable TV." Villaluz shrugged. "I swear, like senility, it is unavoidable."

Bolan let the man talk.

"And one sees many such stories on the History Channel. The kamikazes of the Japanese Air Force. The juramentado, oath takers during the Moro Wars in the Philippines. The assassins of ancient Persia during the Crusades. All with a single trait in common."

"Fanaticism," Bolan said. It was something he had run into too many times before.

"Yes, fanatics," the inspector agreed. "Utterly willing to die in the attempt to kill the enemies of their god or emperor."

"And our fanatics all bear the mark of the beast."

"Yes, and I will tell you something else. This is Mexico. We have you yanquis beat on occultism. Santeria, Aztec worship, voodoo, even satanism. I have seen it all. But these cultists are mostly interested in orgies, drugs and playing dress-up. Once in a great while their foolishness gets someone killed. But I tell you, they do not load up into SUVs by the bushel and make suicide assaults on pueblos in the Laguna Salada they have no business knowing about."

"So what do you think?"

"I do not know what to think. All I can tell you is that this situation is new, anomalous, and, as Señorita Bree said, it is beginning to…creep me out. To be honest? I will tell you. I am scared."

Bolan regarded Villaluz over the RAV. It took a lot for a man like him to say something like that. The Executioner wasn't scared. He had seen things far darker than this. But this situation was promising to get darker still, and he was willing to admit to being profoundly troubled. "We have to get Balthazar Gomez to the States."

"We are in agreement. However we are in a box canyon without transportation."

"I'm really hoping Fausto has something up his sleeve."

Villaluz smiled very tiredly. "I could tell you stories about the cornucopia of things Fausto has had up his sleeves."

"Over beer and shots, in the States, on me."

Villaluz unconsciously put a hand on the RAV's fender to steady himself. "I will look forward to that."

Bolan read the man like a book. Inspector Israel Villaluz was a genuine tough guy who had earned his rep the hard way. But he was a tough guy well past middle age, who watched the History Channel, drove the streets of Tijuana in his gleaming Toyota Tundra and let his reputation make punks shake. Long ago he had learned to love quiet, and that was what he insisted on in his jurisdiction. He had been in two very bad and bloody gun battles within twenty-four hours, and somehow the Antichrist had shoved his nose into it. Villaluz was tired and genuinely scared. His gas tank was on E and he was mostly running on pride and professionalism. "Let's head in—"

Bolan's head snapped around.

Villaluz cocked his head. "What is it, amigo?"

Bolan unscrewed the grenade from his rifle. It didn't have the range or accuracy for an antiaircraft weapon. "The plane."

The Bonanza flashed by the canyon mouth and stood on a wingtip as it banked in hard.

"¡Madre de Dios!" Villaluz raised his rifle.

Bolan was already firing, but the Chinese bullets were small and thin. The Bonanza's fuselage was sloped like a shark, and it had two engines rather than one. It roared overhead twenty yards off the deck. People in the pueblo were firing. Bolan and Villaluz were instantly eclipsed inside the dust maelstrom that churned up in its passage. The Executioner squinted, swung around and fired his rifle dry. Despite the dust his eyes flared as the plane maintained its course. Villaluz had mentioned the kamikaze. The proverb "Speak of the Devil and he will come" flashed through Bolan's mind. The soldier shoved Villaluz to the dirt and dropped down beside him.

The pueblo disappeared as it was hit by five thousand pounds of plane and 130 gallons of aviation fuel at two hundred miles per hour.

The canyon walls shook with the impact. Bolan hugged the RAV as chunks of shattered and smoking clay, varying in size from fists to engine blocks, thudded back to earth. Villaluz rose to his knees whispering. *"Madre de Dios... Madre de Dios...Madre de..."*

Bolan rose and clicked the grenade back onto the muzzle of his rifle. The pueblo was gone. Adobe was an excellent building material except that it was brittle. The ancient Native Americans had built well but they had never envisioned an aerial suicide attack. The Bonanza's death dive had shattered the pueblo like a hammer. There was nothing but smoking and burning rubble, and no pile was more than three feet high. Villaluz staggered toward the ruins. Bolan strode toward Wang's car. The flames had burned out and he opened the trunk. They hadn't emptied everything. Bolan rummaged and found six spare mags for the rifles, a machete and four one-liter bottles of water. "Inspector."

Villaluz turned very slowly away from the ruins. "You may call me Israel."

"Thanks." Bolan eyed the sky and the canyon mouth. There was still an armored Hummer out there and possibly up to five hardmen in Satan's service inside. "Israel, we've got to start walking."

CHAPTER SIX

The Laguna Salada was about nine yards below sea level, girded on both sides by mountains. It happened to be dry at the moment. Bolan and Villaluz were slowly being roasted alive, and they had gone through three of their four liters of water. Bolan had hoped they might run into naturalists or outdoor adventure types in all-terrain vehicles. He would settle for a UFO sighting. If something didn't come along soon, he would have to settle for making a phone call he didn't want to.

Bolan settled for the sound of nearby gunfire. He took the last water bottle and handed it to the inspector. "Drink your fill. Get frosty."

Villaluz gulped down half and handed over the bottle with a gasp. "What do you think?"

Bolan cocked his head and listened to the sounds echoing off the hillsides as he slowly killed the rest of the bottle. "I make it close to a dozen weapons. Pretty sure at least one if not two are Chinese QBZs like ours. And that sounds like the Hummer." Bolan lifted his chin at a deeper, slower, aimed "crack!" "One is definitely Fausto and his M-1."

Villaluz's sagging frame seemed to reinflate with the news. "Fausto is a fox, and nearly as hard to kill. He never told me about it, but I knew he would never put himself in a box that didn't have a back door."

Bolan reached into his gear bag and gave Villaluz three

of the spare magazines. Villaluz stuffed his pockets. "How do you want to play it?"

"We have one rifle grenade left. I say we sneak up behind the Hummer, blow it to hell, and between us and our friends we put any dismounted hardmen into a cross fire."

"As good a plan as any, amigo."

Bolan frowned.

"You are troubled?"

"Rather disturbed, actually," Bolan said. "If the plane radioed in before they suicided, then the bad guys would know they flew over two riflemen. That's us."

"And yet it is our friends who find themselves attacked once more."

"Right, you and me are on foot, in the desert, with no way to go except out of the canyon. We wouldn't be that hard to find. But Fausto's place got hit hard. Nothing but rubble. There must be a maze of canyons farther back in the hills, and Fausto must have had a secret way into them. Question is, how in the hell would the bad guys know anyone survived much less be able to track them? I haven't seen or heard another aircraft, and I'm currently dubious about the bad guys having a military quality observation satellite looking down on the Laguna."

Villaluz spit dryly and tapped behind his right ear. "We have a saying in Mexico, *El Diablo toma el cuidado sus los propios.*"

"The Devil takes care of his own." They crept along the foothills until they saw the Hummer parked about four hundred yards out in the flats facing an arroyo. The front doors were open and two men were firing through the open windows, using the armored door panels for cover. Two more men fired from flanking positions in the rocks to either side. Bolan dialed Smiley on his phone.

She was breathless and the gunfire was loud and right next to her.

"Christ, Coop! We thought you were dead!"

"Same here. You all intact?"

"Yeah, for the most part. There was a covered-up cavern in the back of Fausto's place. He cracked it open while you were doing your forensics. I was about to come join you when Wang spotted the plane. Fausto yelled for us to follow him. We went through. The cave was only about thirty feet long, and we got a bit singed but it led to a maze of canyons. Fausto knows them all like old friends. We hiked a few hours and I thought it would be best to stay dark."

"Good idea."

"Yeah, but those guys in the Hummer were waiting for us the minute we stuck our heads out of the hills."

"Funny how they keep doing that."

"Funny as a crutch, Coop."

"Well, me and Israel are sneaking up on their six. That make you happy?"

"Happy as a schoolgirl."

"How many hostiles?" Bolan asked.

"I count five, and I think there's still one in the truck, but be careful, one of these guys is a sniper."

"Let me guess—we lost Gomez."

Smiley's voice dropped an octave. "Let's just say if they want to take Gomez's head right now they could pretty much do it with a spoon."

Bolan thought that over. These guys were cartel gunners, or at least they used to be—they were ready to commit suicide for their cause, and their first impulse had been to kill one of their own in custody even if it let Smiley, Wang and Fausto drop and return fire. Bolan's thoughts weren't happy.

"Change of plan. I want the guy in the truck, but I don't think that's going to happen. So I'm going to take the sniper alive."

"Christ, Coop—"

"Even if this guy is ex-Mexican military, a sniper is a sniper. They're pros, and less susceptible to occult influence, real or imaginary."

"How are you going to get him?"

"Israel is going to light up the Hummer, and then I'm going to take the sniper when he tries to do something about it."

The inspector raised an eyebrow. "Oh?"

"Yeah." Bolan tossed him the grenade-mounted weapon. "Get close. All you have to do is point and pull the trigger. On my signal."

"Jesus," Smiley said over the line.

"Very well," Villaluz said.

Bolan scanned the flats. He eyed a very suspicious clump of hummocks and rock that was probably a tiny island when the Laguna was full. It was five hundred yards from Smiley's position and about a hundred east and back of the truck. The position was ideally suited to get the shooter out of range of the team's Chinese assault rifles and give him a little elevation on the ravine his targets were using for cover. "Bree, on my signal, raise a ruckus."

"You got it."

Bolan and Villaluz began to creep through the mesquite. The soldier began to flank wide left behind the dry-docked little island. Occasional shots came from the truck and the men around it. The sniper was waiting for his next shot. The bad guys hadn't rushed Smiley's position, and Bolan had a feeling they were waiting for someone to arrive. He moved out into the flats, and cover was getting harder and harder to find. The only advantage he had was that his enemy had no known reason to look in his direction. Bolan worked his way about fifty yards behind the sniper's position and spoke quietly into his phone.

"Now."

He saw Villaluz rise up from behind a rat's nest of tumbleweeds about forty yards from the Hummer and begin to fire. The rifle grenade spun into the Hummer's truck bed and detonated. The vehicle's armored cabin rippled with the overpressure of superheated gas and molten metal. Smoke and fire blasted out of the two open doors and enveloped the two men using them for cover.

Smiley and her crew opened fire.

Bolan broke into a run.

Salt crust and sand crunched beneath his boots, but the noise of the firefight more than covered it. Three quick rounds cracked from the sniper's hide. Bolan flew up the eroded edge of the dry isle. A chunk of slick rock the size of a grave formed a natural thirty degree ramp. Bolan ran up the rock. The entire mound was barely five yards by four. Two scraggly mesquite trees shaded the sniper. Two close boulders formed a natural firing slit for him. The sniper wore khaki cargo pants, an olive-drab T-shirt, and a desert camouflage bandana on his head. He lay prone behind a scoped German G-3 rifle resting on a bipod. Where Bolan's Chinese weapon was short, black and stubby, the G-3 was big, black and bulky and threw lead roughly the same size as Fausto's relic.

Bolan wanted the sniper, and he wanted his rifle.

Snipers spent hours, days, even weeks sneaking up on their targets, and that much time hiding made their ears almost always as good as their eyes. Their survival instincts were even better. But this sniper had just seen his ride home blow up on a column of fire, and he had been distracted for a fatal, precious second.

Bolan's boots left the slick rock ramp and he went airborne.

The sniper sensed him.

The Executioner was interested to note that the sniper had the wherewithal to know he would never be able to bring his big rifle to bear. He abandoned the weapon, rolled over and his hand flew for the pistol holstered on his thigh. Bolan dropped to the ground, and the sniper screamed as the soldier's boot landed on his wrist and snapped it in mid-draw. Bolan pressed a knee on the sniper's chest and shoved the muzzle of his weapon into the man's mouth. The sniper's face went white with shock, but the message was clear.

Bolan spoke into his phone. "Sniper subdued. Everyone. Status?"

Smiley came back first. "We're okay. We took out the far flanker, but we're real low on ammo."

Villaluz came back over the open line. "Hummer destroyed. All occupants dead. I killed the flanker on this side."

Bolan nodded. "J.W.?"

"Right here, Coop. You got the sniper?"

Bolan gazed down on his captive. The man was Mexican, with a medium wiry build. His crew-cut hair was regulation, but his short Vandyke beard, mustache and gold earring weren't. His face had gone gray with the nausea of broken bones, and his eyes were screwed up with pain. "Yeah, I got him. Ask Fausto what the plan is."

Bolan listened to Spanish fire back and forth on the speakerphone.

"Okay," Wang came back. "Fausto suggests we find ourselves a spot of shade and wait out the worst of the sun. Then he knows a dude who might rent us some donkeys about fifteen klicks north of here. Then he says there's an airstrip about another fifteen klicks north from there. Fausto wants to know, if he can get us there, can you arrange a plane?"

"Tell him I can arrange a plane."

Wang said something in Spanish on his end and laughed. "Fausto says he figured that."

"Tell Fausto he's the man."

"Fausto says he knows."

Bolan smiled wearily. "One more thing, J.W."

"What's that, Coop?"

"Israel took us into the desert, and the bastards still found us. They kamikazied the pueblo, and they still found you hours later."

"Yeah, that shit is kind of freaking me out, actually," Wang admitted.

"We have another prisoner, and I want to stay dark and get gone. Your turn. Pick a place. Make it random as hell, but someplace in Mexico, and wherever we go tell whoever helps us they should expect to get visited by Old Scratch himself."

"Jesus, Coop, you—"

"You can say no. No hard feelings."

"I got an idea or two."

"Good." Bolan stripped the sniper of his weapons and gear. The man flinched as Bolan folded his ear forward. Bolan grimly noted the 666 the sniper bore there. "Get up, you're going to walk."

The sniper glared defiantly.

Bolan stared down implacably.

"You can walk with one broken arm or two. You decide."

The sniper decided to walk.

Bolan made a phone call.

THE LANDING STRIP was about three hundred yards of salt flat that someone occasionally took the time to keep clear, and a small adobe well of brackish water. The nicest thing that could be said about it was that Jack Grimaldi had a Cessna Skyknight parked on it. A tarp had been pulled over one wing to form an awning, and six lawn chairs had been arranged beneath it around a large, stainless-steel cooler. The ace pilot sat in the shade drinking a Pepsi, smoking a cigar and running a rag over his MAC-10 submachine gun. Grimaldi gave the approaching desert caravan a cheery wave with the rag. "Come on in! The water's fine!"

Bolan's little band and their prisoner took their ease beneath the wing as the sun very reluctantly began to set. Stony Man Farm's premier pilot was drinking pop, but he'd brought beer and sandwiches for his passengers. Bolan made introductions all around and finally came to Wang. "Jack, meet J.W. He's going to tell you our next destination, and even I don't want to know about it until we get there."

Grimaldi just grinned. "No problem." He pointed toward a laptop connected to a satellite rig on one of the chairs. A power cord snaked up into the cabin. The two men wandered off.

Bolan took a seat and opened the laptop. Villaluz sat the enemy sniper in a chair next to him and kept the muzzle of his rifle against the back of his head. Aaron Kurtzman popped up on the screen immediately. "What have you got?"

"I want you to run a set of prints for me. I doubt that Interpol or the FBI will have anything. Have you-know-who hack Mexican military records." The sniper flinched in his chair and cradled his broken wrist. Bolan took out his satellite phone. Quite possibly it was the most powerful phone on Earth, and it had applications commercial

software companies hadn't dreamed of yet. Bolan pulled
up the finger-printing app and then wiped the screen clean.
The touch screen turned white.

"Give me your hand."

The sniper made a fist.

Bolan's hand closed around the man's wrist like a vise.
He dug his thumb into the sniper's ulnar nerve like a cold
chisel and the hand spasmed open. "Israel, on the screen,
starting with the thumb."

Villaluz took the sniper's thumb and pressed it onto
the screen. The screen made a noise like a camera and an
expanded, blown-up picture of the thumbprint filled the
screen. The screen went white again and Villaluz finished
off the fingers. The sniper sagged back sweating into his
chair.

"Give him a beer," Bolan said.

The sniper greedily sucked at the Dos Equis he was
offered. Bolan dialed a special number.

"Sending now," Bolan told Kurtzman.

The computer expert nodded. "Got it. Routing it to you-
know-who."

Back in Virginia, Stony Man Farm's hacker in residence, Akira Tokaido, was undoubtedly breaking into
Mexican Military records with the ease of a schoolboy
scaling a chain-link fence whose only defense was a sign
that said Keep Out. "What happened to Gomez?" Kurtzman asked.

"He got his head blown off. We buried him." Bolan
looked long and hard at his captive. "Who do I have
now?"

The sniper glared back with renewed courage.

Information began scrolling across the laptop before
Bolan. "Corporal Raldes Ayala." Ayala went boneless in
his chair as Kurtzman read his résumé. "Mexican Army

Light Infantry, Military Region X, Yucatán, Military Zone 34a, Quintana Roo. He attended the Western Hemisphere Institute for Security Cooperation in the counter-drug program in 2009, returned to his unit and made sniper specialist. This year he qualified for training in the Mexican Special Forces Airmobile Group."

"And then he disappeared."

"You guessed it. Six months ago."

A lot of dangerous individuals had gone missing in Mexico in the past six months and then begun reappearing in the most unusual places. Bolan raised a critical eyebrow. "You AWOL, Ayala?"

The sniper wouldn't meet Bolan's eyes.

Grimaldi and Wang came back. The ace pilot eyed the prisoner and then cracked himself another soda. "Okay, J.W. gave me a destination and I've figured out a flight plan."

Bolan held up a warning hand.

Grimaldi grinned. "It's all on the QT. No one knows but J.W. and me, and we aren't talking. This plane and everything I brought with it was swept for bugs before it crossed the border."

"Good enough. Israel, Bree." The American Fed and the Mexican cop followed Bolan a few yards away from the plane. "Bree, I know this was your operation." He looked to the inspector. "Then it became yours."

Villaluz waved his hand like he was brushing away flies. "I believe this has been your operation from start to finish."

Smiley regarded Bolan wryly. "What he said."

"So I want to stay dark a little while longer, any objections?"

Smiley shook her head. "I'm beginning to wonder if

I'll still have a job when I get back stateside, but what the hell. I can't remember the last time I had this much fun."

"Thanks." Bolan nodded at the inspector. "Israel?"

"I will see this thing through with you, amigo."

"Then I need to ask you two for one more favor."

The two cops looked at Bolan expectantly.

"I want Corporal Ayala debugged."

Smiley shook her head. "I knew I was going to get the shitty job."

Villaluz sighed stoically.

Bolan nodded. "I want a full cavity search and then make him throw up. After that I want you to check every square inch of him, look for any suspicious lumps."

Smiley gave Bolan a leery look. "And if we find one?"

"Call me. I'll take care of any necessary surgery."

Agent Smiley managed to be alarmed and relieved at the same time. She gave Bolan a sidelong look. "Coop?"

"Yeah?"

"You buying all this?"

"All what?"

"You know…Satan."

"The bad guys seem to buying into it, and so far it isn't pretty."

"Yeah, but…" Smiley blushed with embarrassment.

"Do I believe in the devil?" Bolan finished.

"Yeah."

"Do you?"

"Well, I was raised Southern Baptist. We sure heard about him a lot growing up, but as for a genuine goat-headed guy reaching into the hearts of men…I don't know. If you'd asked me forty-eight hours ago, my answer would have been no."

Smiley looked to the inspector. "What about you?"

Villaluz drew himself up with great dignity. "I am a trained inspector and a twenty-year veteran of La Agencia Federal de Investigación." He regarded Smiley with dead seriousness. "I have absolute faith El Diablo exists."

CHAPTER SEVEN

Wherever the devil was, he didn't appear to be inhabiting either end of Corporal Ayala's digestive tract. And while the sniper might or might not have El Diablo in his heart, he didn't seem to have him under his skin. Corporal Raldes Ayala was DEA and FIA certified bug free. Bolan was really hoping that was good news. If it wasn't, then it might come down to silver bullets, crosses and pentagrams of protection. He looked out the copilot window. The sun had set. To his left the Baja Peninsula was a long purple finger with the occasional light constellation of a town. To his right the Pacific Ocean was a vast black expanse. Grimaldi was paralleling the coast and heading south. Bolan noted they were starting to descend. He looked at his watch and did a little math with time, landmass and airspeed. "Ciudad Constitutión?"

"Man…" Grimaldi grinned. "And J.W. and I thought we were so subtle."

Bolan craned around to look at Wang. "Who do we have waiting for us?"

"No one yet. I figured I'd wait and make a call after we hit the ground. Keep our getaway as clean as possible."

Bolan looked back to Villaluz and the prisoner. "How's he doing?"

"His arm needs to be set. Soon."

Grimaldi flew over Magdalena Bay and banked over the small coastal town into the Ciudad Constitución Airport.

It was more of an airfield than an airport, but it was a step up from the airstrip back in the Laguna. The touchdown was feather light, and Grimaldi taxied the Cessna around the field and into a large arc of corrugated tin that served as an individual aircraft shelter. Everyone got out except Ayala and Villaluz. Ayala stayed in the back of the cabin bound and gagged. The inspector kept one revolver pointed at the corporal's midriff and another at his head. Everyone else stretched out the kinks, except Grimaldi. He bounced out of the plane as if he'd just spent the day at the spa. He spoke for a few moments with a man who wandered out of the shack with a clipboard. The pilot produced some documents.

Wang walked over to a bank of phones outside the shack and fed one some coins. After a few moments he began to speak in Cantonese. Bolan stretched. The ocean breeze was a blessing after the shimmering oven of the Laguna Salada. He'd caught a few Zs on the flight down, but he was really hoping for a bed and few hours' sleep.

Wang walked over.

"Okay, we got a ride coming and a place to stay. I arranged for someone to come by and set our boy Ayala's arm, and to bring enough morphine to keep him quiet and content for a while."

"Good enough."

There was nothing to do but hurry up and wait. Grimaldi took a walk around the hangars and admired airplanes. Smiley curled up in a chair beneath the shack's awning. Bolan and Wang stood guard. Half an hour later a long, black Lincoln Town Car with gleaming chrome rolled majestically onto the tarmac. Smiley came back from her catnap, yawning, with one hand vaguely going toward her pistol. The Lincoln flashed its lights and ground to a halt.

"Very Sopranos," Smiley opined.

Bolan watched the driver emerge beneath the field lights. He was tall, two inches taller than Bolan, with even broader shoulders. Dirty blond hair fell around his face in a shag cut off at the jawline. He was bad-boy handsome with the jaw of a wolf and amber eyes that only accentuated the lupine comparison. His cultivated five-o'clock shadow was a work of manscaping art in and of itself. The man wore a lot of black silk and even more Italian gray wool. Bolan pegged him for professional bodyguard though he seemed too good-looking for the job.

"World's most dangerous supermodel?" Smiley suggested.

Bolan smiled. He also noted the man was carrying beneath his right arm, but as he opened and closed the door he appeared to be right handed. The man regarded everyone except Smiley with open suspicion and barely concealed hostility. He spoke with a slight Southern drawl. "Name's Chet. Let's hit it."

Smiley gave Bolan a concealed nudge and walked up to Chet. "Hey handsome."

"Well, hey yourself." Chet leaned in with a leer. He looked right past Smiley's stitches and bruises and liked what he saw. "If you need someone to kiss that and make it better, you let me know."

The agent reached a hand up to Chet's face. "You are good-looking."

Chet shot her a killer grin. "Well, some people have—"

Smiley grabbed Chet's right ear, pulled his head down and had a look-see.

Chet reared up out of her grip and his right hand shot back behind his right hip. He was carrying in a small-of-the-back holster. It made Bolan wonder what Chet had under his right arm. Chet was appalled, but he didn't clear leather on Smiley. He slapped a hand reflexively to his tweaked ear and took a step back. "What the hell, shortstuff!"

The woman grinned back at Bolan. "He's clean."

"What the—" Chet flushed. He looked hard at Wang and then even harder at Bolan. "You in charge, slick?"

Bolan glanced around at his companions. "First among equals?"

Chet took a step forward and used his two inches to look down his excellent nose at Bolan. "Yeah? Well, while you're here in Constitución, I'm in charge. Got it?"

Bolan smiled amiably. "I hear what you're saying."

Chet took that as an affirmation. Bolan decided to let him keep it until it was time to take it away.

"Let's not dawdle." Chet jerked his head at his long, black ride. "The lady's waiting."

Bolan shot a look at Wang, who shrugged. Bolan pulled Grimaldi aside as everyone else went back to the plane and began to unload gear and the prisoner. "Jack, I don't know where we're going. I want you to stay near the airfield. Keep the plane prepped and ready to go, and while you're at it see about renting a second plane, and a helicopter if you can. We may be coming back in a hurry, and we may need options. Keep an eye out for any incoming private flights."

"I'll chat up the hangar chief, spread a little discretionary income around and see about setting up an intelligence network of my own. If an airplane full of evil lands, you'll be the first to know."

"You coming, slick?" Chet snarled.

Grimaldi grinned bemusedly. "He called you slick."

"I'll contact you when I know where we're holing up." Bolan grabbed his gear, walked to the car and slid into the back with Villaluz, the prisoner sandwiched between them. The tires spit gravel as Chet peeled out. The Lincoln didn't have the usual luxury sedan suspension. Bolan figured it was a VIP protection job, tightened, armored, and up-engined. "BPS?" Bolan asked.

Chet deigned to peer at Bolan in the rearview mirror. "It started out that way."

BPS was Lincoln automotive's Ballistic Protection Series. Bolan was thinking the Town Car might have spent some time in a custom armor shop. "Yours?"

"Naw." Faint amusement crossed Chet's face in the mirror. "But I insisted on it."

Bolan nodded sincerely. "Nice."

Chet almost smiled but seemed to remember he was in charge and didn't like Bolan. "You just relax and leave the driving to me."

Bolan relaxed. The Town Car was a plush ride with leg and elbowroom to spare. Chet took them through the business section of town and straight to the beach and the dappled waters of Magdalena Bay. The bay was the world's number-one breeding ground for migrating gray whales but it was off-season, and the bay was bereft of the thirty-six ton leviathans. Chet parked by the pier and slid out. His yellow wolf eyes glared about at every dark shadow, and his hand hovered around his hip. He walked over to the boat slip and spoke a few words in Spanish to someone Bolan couldn't see.

"The squid fishermen all came back about an hour ago," he told Bolan. "Other than that there's been no activity on the pier. Let's go."

Bolan and crew hustled their prisoner and gear onto a gleaming white cigarette boat. Chet got behind the wheel and took the vessel out of the harbor with familiar ease. Once away from the pier Chet shoved the throttles forward and the boat began to slice across the bay like a knife. Bolan leaned toward Wang. "So what are you thinking?"

"Well, first off, Chinese devils can't cross open or moving water. I'm figurin' the white devil can't neither."

"Good thinking."

Wang glanced back at the twin diesels. "And if he can, I'm thinkin' he can't match a thousand horsepower." He nodded at the gear bags. "Or our firepower."

"He hasn't yet," Bolan agreed. He watched a chain of barrier islands approaching. "Though you've got to admit his persistence has been admirable."

"Actually find it troubling, myself."

Bolan watched the islands. Only a few had lights, and they were scattered. The inspector had tried getting them lost in the desert, and Wang was trying a deserted island.

Wang lifted his chin at Chet's back and spoke below the roar of the diesels. "So what do you make of Handsome Boy over there?"

"I haven't figured him out yet. He's security of some stripe. I like his taste in cars. He can handle a boat." Bolan watched Chet bring the boat in to a little wooden pier lit by a couple of bare bulbs. "If things go the way they did in Tijuana and Laguna Salada, we're going to find out how good he is real fast."

Headlights winked and shone through the dunes, and the sound of engines in low gear filled the night. A pair of open, ex-army jeeps ground up to the pier. The men who drove them might as well have had "Chinese gangster" tattooed on their foreheads. They carried themselves like secret service agents, dressed like bankers and used too much product to make their flat-topped hair geometric. They cradled their semiautomatic Super 90 shotguns like they were gentling wild animals that might bolt any moment. They passed a few words with Wang and everyone began to pile into the jeeps. The island roads were little more than sand paths. Sea grass and dunes gave way to cardon cactus, palms and boojum trees. They crossed from the bay to the Pacific side of the island in about five minutes and pulled up in front of a modest Spanish-style mansion. A vintage Volkswagen "Acapulco" Thing sat parked on the sand drive with the canvas top down.

A hauntingly beautiful Chinese woman stood on the brick-and-sand portico with two more rubber-stamped tong thugs and a pair of black-and-tan Dobermans flanking her. Her hair was blue-black beneath the porch lights and fell in a single raven fall down to her waist. She looked like the heroine out of a Chinese historical epic, except that a Mexican print sarong clad her hips and she wore a pale pink men's dress shirt that Bolan immediately made as belonging to Chet. She smiled warmly at Wang and stepped forward to put her hands in his. Her voice was a smoky alto. "Cousin, my home is yours."

"Cousin," Wang said as he waved at the entourage, "you know Inspector Israel Villaluz by name and reputation. This is DEA Agent Smiley, and Mr. Cooper. My friends, may I present my cousin, Miss Sarah Tsui."

"You are all welcome."

The woman glanced at Ayala. "This is the man who has given you offense."

"He's the one," Wang said, scowling.

"I will have someone see to him." Sarah Tsui gave her cousin's hand a squeeze. "Tell me what is happening, if it is permitted."

Wang gave his cousin the short version, starting with Inspector Villaluz and company showing up at the restaurant in Mexicali and finishing with the battles in Laguna

Salada. He didn't leave out how the untraceable was being traced or the fact that Satan was hot on their heels.

Chet just about burst a gasket.

"Damn it, Sarah! I told you bringing them here was a bad idea!"

Tsui flinched slightly at the outburst but held her ground. "Val, Juan is family."

Bolan shook his head. Bodyguards shouldn't speak familiarly with their beautiful clients much less call them by their first name. He wondered why she called him Val. Bolan couldn't fault his advice. Sarah Tsui didn't need this kind of trouble.

"Fine then!" Chet loomed over his client. "Baby, your cousin can stay! But the FIA, the DEA, mystery slick and Satan need to take the boat back to the coast and get the hell back to the border."

Bolan took a step forward. "I think that's the lady's decision."

The guard dogs growled low in their throats. Tsui spoke with quiet authority. "Highlander, MacLeod, sit."

The dogs sat.

Chet whirled and stalked forward in a thunderstorm of outrage. "You remember who's in charge here, slick?"

"Me." Bolan stood relaxed and ready. "You got a problem with that?"

Chet was beyond fast. He was sudden. He cleared leather in a heartbeat. Bolan didn't bother yanking iron. While Chet drew, Bolan stepped in and hit him with a right hand lead. Chet's bluesteel revolver fell from nerveless fingers to the sand. His knees buckled and he sat down hard on the brick drive; his eyes rolled. Bolan teed up, took a step forward and gave the Chet an uppercut that laid him out flat on his back blinking up at the stars.

Tsui gasped, while the rest of the gangsters watched impassively.

Highlander and MacLeod wagged their tails excitedly.

Bolan dropped to a knee and relieved Chet of his weapons.

The man was packing heavy. His weapon of choice appeared to be a medium frame, four-inch .357 Magnum pistol with a bobbed hammer and custom rosewood grips cut to his hand. Bolan unloaded it and noted the glass-slick smoothness of the Smith's moving parts. Bolan had seen its like before. It was the weapon of a gunfighter. The piece would kick like a mule, but it was built for snake-strike speed in the quick draw and its Magnum caliber was an instant fight stopper. It was an interesting choice for a bodyguard and not a bad one. Chet was carrying three speed loaders in a shoulder rig beneath his right arm. He also had a Walther PPK in an ankle rig and a butterfly knife in his back pocket.

Bolan took Chet's wallet as he stirred and tried to sit up.

The soldier spoke quietly. "Next time you draw down on me I'll kill you."

Chet glowered from beneath his brows. "Fair enough."

"Who's in charge?" Bolan asked.

Chet sighed defeatedly. "Well, I suppose that would be you."

Bolan looked at Chet's Louisiana driver's license. "Chesterfield Valerie Brashear?" He raised a sympathetic eyebrow. "That's one doozy of a handle."

"Yeah, I know," Chet admitted ruefully. "Only in the South." He clambered back to his feet, rubbed his jaw and stuck out his hand. "Guys call me Chet. Girls call me Val.

Only doctors, lawyers and policemen call me Mr. Brashear and I try to avoid them as much as possible."

Bolan shook hands and gave Chet back his iron. He tucked his weapons away and went and opened the front door. "Well, I just got my ass kicked in front of my client. I need a beer."

CHAPTER EIGHT

"Enabling GPS tracking." Bolan touched the icon for the Global Positioning System on his phone and the application went active. But instead of going across the cell signal, Bolan's phone shot the GPS information heavenward from the island and bounced it off a U.S. military satellite and back down to the Cuidad Constitución Airport.

Jack Grimaldi's voice came back almost instantly. "I have you, Striker."

"Copy that." Bolan disabled the GPS.

"And I have both a seaplane and a chopper at our disposal."

"Copy that. Striker out." Bolan cut the line and glanced at the timer app. It had been just less than six seconds of exposure, and Bolan had a very hard time believing Mexican cartel men would have the resources to break into an NSA satellite feed, much less crack a Farm-encrypted transmission. He was fairly certain that the only person who knew Mack Bolan's current location was Jack Grimaldi.

And possibly the Devil...

Bolan shrugged the thought away. He had seen some very strange things in his War Everlasting, but he wasn't quite ready to accept demonic forces just yet. Others weren't so certain. Inspector Villaluz had pulled out the silver cross from beneath his shirt and wore it openly on his chest. Chinese feng shui mirrors had appeared throughout

Sarah Tsui's house to repel evil. Bolan was putting more faith in Tsui's men and their semiautomatic shotguns in repelling boarders when and if they came calling. If they did they would be coming for Ayala.

Bolan looked over at the prisoner.

One of Miss Tsui's armed retainers by the name of Qu knew something about Chinese medicine. He had skillfully set Corporal Ayala's wrist, rubbed it with a foul-smelling herbal liniment, forced him to gargle down some even fouler-smelling herbal tea, splinted his arm and shot him full of morphine. Ayala smelled like a compost heap and was resting bound but comfortably on a couch. Qu had rubbed some other kind of home-brewed liniment on Chet's lumped jaw, and the swelling had started going down almost immediately.

Qu had taken a look at Bolan's scarred and callused right fist and winked approvingly.

Tsui's man Gao had fired up a Chinese Army mess-sized wok and fed the masses beef and bell peppers with cabbage. Tsui had excused herself and gone to bed. Chet waited a discreet fifteen minutes and then followed her. Qu and crew and the dogs were doing perimeter duty outside. Smiley and Villaluz were exchanging cop-talk out on the deck.

Bolan had a great deal more faith in German Army ordnance than that of the People's Republic of China. He had adopted Ayala's G-3 A-3 rifle and he began field-stripping and cleaning it. "So, J.W., what's the deal?"

Wang looked up from his beer. "What's the deal with what?"

Bolan removed the bolt assembly. "This island for starters."

"There're twelve houses on it. Vacation homes. Most people come here to see the whales, sport fish and see the desert blooming. There's a growing college spring break trade, but we're here in the off-season."

Bolan stuck his key chain photon light in the action and peered down the barrel. By all indications Corporal Ayala had been taking loving care of his weapon. "Why is Miss Tsui here in the off-season?"

Wang's shrug had a slight sense of hopelessness about it. "She likes the heat. She likes being alone."

Bolan looked up from the G-3's trigger assembly. "What's your relationship with her?"

Wang flinched. He looked away, and then he met Bolan's gaze. "I love her."

Bolan decided the quickest course out of the emotional minefield was to walk straight through it. Bolan began applying PRC cleaning fluid and lubricant to various rifle parts. "And?"

"And we've been on again, off again." He stared into the middle distance. "I've asked her to marry me."

Bolan nodded. When she called him cousin, it was a Chinese honorific and Bolan was pretty sure it cut Wang to the bone. He began reassembling the rifle. "And now?"

Wang's voice was bleak. "And now we're friends."

"Friends enough for her to take on our troubles?" Bolan pinned the trigger assembly and the buttstock back on the rifle.

"We're here, aren't we?" Wang gritted his teeth. "You wanted a place no one knew about! You wanted obscurity. No one would ever guess I would come down here!"

Bolan loaded a magazine. The rifle clacked as he slapped the bolt off the stop, and it rammed a fresh full-metal-jacketed bullet into the chamber. "What's the deal with Chet?"

"Sarah is a wealthy Chinese woman in Mexico. After the second attempted kidnapping she wanted extra security."

Wang's face grew bleaker. "I think she chose him more for the picture on his Web site than his résumé."

"How has that worked out?"

"There've been two more attempts. They were amateurs, one level above street punks, but I'll give the guy credit. Chet was outnumbered and outgunned both times and both times he slaughtered them. Hell, you saw him." Wang shook his head grudgingly. "That man is rattlesnake fast."

"They're sharing a bed."

Wang stared glumly out the window into the night. "Yeah…"

"What else do you know about him?"

The gunrunner got up and pulled a laptop out of his gear bag. He clicked a few keys on it and pulled up a file. The laptop slid across the table in front of Bolan, who raised a speculative eyebrow at the wealth of information. "Little obsessive, don't you think?"

"Yeah, well, the son of a bitch is a *gwailo* guarding a Chinese national treasure, ain't he?"

Gwailo literally translated to *ghost man,* and had been a typical Chinese deprecatory description for Caucasians and their charming complexions for hundreds of years. Bolan could well imagine the local tong elements were none-to-happy about Miss Tsui and her blond gigolo-bodyguard.

Bolan read Brashear's biography.

It was a typical story of a man who couldn't keep it in his pants, literally and figuratively, but it made for interesting reading. Brashear had been born in Port Eads, Louisiana, the Pelican State's southernmost point and where the Mississippi met the sea. He was the son of a deputy sheriff, but Port Eads didn't have much going for it except fishing fleets. His first five years out of high school were murky except for a few minor brushes with the law. A judge had suggested military service and he had joined the National Guard with the 773rd Military Police Battalion. That was in 2003 and he had almost instantly been sent to Iraq. There were disciplinary actions on his record, almost all for being out of uniform, literally, with superior female officers while on duty. He'd also earned the Bronze Star for bravery. An IED roadside explosion had perforated his eardrum and earned him a Purple Heart and an honorable discharge. Brashear had moved to Los Angeles. He tried his hand at acting and modeling, and got a few jobs. To make ends meet he'd taken a job as a private detective with the Espy Security Services.

Bolan had heard of them. They had a somewhat sordid and shifty reputation, but they also had a reputation for results. Brashear had worked cases successfully for them for four years until suddenly leaving the agency. Wang had no info on why but Bolan could guess. Brashear had parlayed P.I., war hero and hunk into a professional body-guard career, and security jobs were lucrative and plentiful south of the border.

Kurtzman could get him more later, but Bolan figured he had Brashear's number.

Smiley and the inspector came in off the deck. Qu brought in the dogs and Bolan nodded in approval. You kept guard dogs out during the day to guard the premises and brought them in at night as your first line of detection and defense. The matching Dobermans sat at attention by the fireplace and regarded the human proceedings with immense gravity. Bolan addressed Highlander and MacLeod with equal seriousness. "Hello, guys."

Highlander and MacLeod thumped their tails on the floor in unison.

They seemed to like Bolan.

Bolan rose, stretched and took up the clean and

reassembled rifle. "We sleep in shifts. Bree and I will take the first watch."

"You and the *señorita* have been nonstop for nearly fifty hours," Villaluz stated. "If you wish, J.W. and I will take the first watch."

Smiley shot a hopeful glance at Bolan. He felt his own fatigue lying on him like a weight. "Good enough." He shouldered the sniper rifle and glanced at his watch. "Bree and I will spell you in four hours."

Bolan went to the bathroom and stripped out of his sweat-stained shirt and splashed water on his face. He looked up at a soft knock at the door. "Yeah, Smiley?"

The woman was blushing slightly as she stuck her head in. "How did you know it was me?"

Bolan toweled off and looked at his watch. "Actually you're a little early."

The agent frowned. "What does that mean?"

"Yes, you can sleep in my room."

Smiley was beet red. "Listen, I don't normally—"

"It's dark, it's late, things are getting creepy and you don't much like the idea of sleeping alone in a strange bed."

"Something like that," Smiley admitted.

"The buddy system." Bolan nodded. "It works for all of us."

Smiley looked at Bolan askance. "I hope you don't have any ideas about—"

"The only thing on my mind is rack time."

"Thanks." Smiley looked longingly at the bathtub. "God, I wish."

"I can't afford to have anyone naked and soapy if the other shoe drops. Maybe tomorrow if things stay clear."

Smiley sighed.

Bolan went to the guest room Tsui had designated as his.

It overlooked the beach approach to the house. He propped his sniper rifle near the window, arranged the rest of his weapons within easy reach and then turned off the light and sprawled out on the bed. Smiley came in five minutes later, distributed her weapons to her own satisfaction and spooned into Bolan. She was still slightly damp from doing as much as could be done with a washcloth. She sighed as Bolan draped an arm around her. "I must smell like a pig."

Bolan stuck his nose in her hair and breathed. "No, you smell like a woman who's been in three gunfights, went hiking in the desert and hasn't bathed in three days."

Smiley poked Bolan in the ribs. "You *are* a pig." Her voice grew very quiet. "So what do you think?"

"Suicidal Satanists that can find you wherever you go? That's a new one. Even on me."

"So what do we do?"

"For the moment? Sleep."

Smiley sighed and snuggled in closer. Her breathing slowed. Within sixty seconds she was sleeping the sleep of the just, or at least the Justice Department and the genuinely exhausted.

Bolan closed his eyes and joined her.

BOLAN AWOKE to a scream. He and Smiley had taken the second watch and let Wang and the inspector take the third. Dawn was filtering through the curtains. Bolan rolled up bare-chested out of Smiley's arms with a "Chinese assassin" filling either hand. Smiley blurted out a half-awake "What?" and fell off the bed, clawing for her pistol on the nightstand. Downstairs Qu and crew were shouting in Cantonese. Villaluz was shouting in Spanish, Corporal Ayala was screaming in it. Highlander and MacLeod joined the choir of mayhem, barking and snarling in full berserker mode downstairs. Despite the Tower of Babel–like confusion of tongues no guns were going off. Most of the shouting and barking seemed to be either of alarm or accusation rather than imminent attack.

"On my six!" Bolan hissed.

Smiley was up with her pistol held in both hands.

Bolan kicked open the door. Chet was pounding down the hall wearing nothing but bikini-briefs but wielding a gleaming silver-and-black Winchester Coastal Marine pump shotgun. He fell into formation with Bolan and Smiley as they approached the stairs. Bolan paused and shouted for the most sensible human downstairs. "Israel!"

"Cooper!" the inspector shouted up. "Clear!"

Everyone but the dogs quieted as Bolan came down the stairs. They were lunging against the sliding glass door and spewing froth from their mouths. "Highlander! MacLeod!" Bolan shouted. The Dobermans slammed their butts to the carpet and vibrated at attention. Since Bolan had clocked Chet the night before, the dogs seemed to regard him as the alpha male.

"What's going on?" Bolan asked. Sarah Tsui leaned against the kitchen counter. She used one hand to hold herself up and Chet's PPK hung forgotten in the other. "Miss Tsui?"

Chet pushed past Bolan. "Baby! What's wrong?" Tsui fell into Chet's arms in a faint. Everyone began shouting in Cantonese and Spanish and pointing fingers.

Bolan shouted at parade ground decibels. *"Hey!"*

The humans promptly shut up. Highlander and Mac-Leod leaped to their feet, clearly hoping Bolan was going to sic them on someone. Bolan spoke quietly. "Chet, put Miss Tsui on the couch. Elevate her legs."

Chet scooped up the woman. Ayala yelped as Chet

shoved him off the couch with one foot and laid out Tsui and put cushions beneath her knees.

Bolan turned to the inspector. "Israel? What's going on?"

Villaluz gave Bolan a sheepish look. "Forgive me, I fell asleep." He looked accusingly at Wang and the tong crew. "These gangsters took the opportunity to gamble."

Wang reddened beneath his tan. Dice and wads of cash lay on the kitchen floor.

Bolan resisted rolling his eyes. He turned to Qu and simply stretched his hands out in silent question. Qu pointed outside to the deck. Tsui spoke hoarsely from the couch. "I came down to have coffee and watch the sunrise from the deck. It is a ritual of mine, but then I saw…it." Tsui looked like she might faint again.

Bolan stepped through the sliding glass door and out onto the deck. He froze as he looked down at the beach. "J.W., tell Qu to go to my room and bring me my rifle and my phone." Bolan tucked his pistols into his waistband front and back, and Qu appeared at his side with the sniper rifle. Bolan pushed the big rifle's selector to full-auto. Smiley, the inspector, Chet and Wang stepped out onto the deck bristling with armament.

Smiley's voice was barely a whisper. "Jesus…"

Villaluz crossed himself. *"Madre de Dios…"*

"God…damn," Chet said. "You weren't lying, were you?"

Qu said something in Cantonese that Bolan thought might be a prayer to his ancestors.

"Chet," Bolan said, "go inside. Release the dogs. Stay with Miss Tsui and Ayala. J.W., stay on the deck and cover us with a rifle. Bree, Israel, you're with me."

Chet went inside and seconds later Highlander and Mac-Leod charged out and sailed across the deck railing. They hit the dunes running. Bolan slowly followed them with his rifle at the ready. Smiley and the inspector moved out to flank him on either side. Qu followed without being asked. The dogs padded about growling and sniffing and snarling, but they didn't seem to perceive any current threat.

Bolan approached the abomination.

The dogs had driven off the seagulls, but they had been at it, and they circled and flapped around the dunes cawing in indignation about their interrupted meal. The body had been crucified. The desecrated corpse hung upside down from a 4x4 post sunk in the sand. Barbed wire secured the feet to the post and the hands to the crossbeam rather than nails. A pentagram was painted on the victim's chest and there was a ragged gaping hole in the middle of it where the heart had once resided. The body was naked, caked with dirt, scavenged and fish-pale from blood loss but Bolan recognized the build and the tattoos on the neck and forearms.

It was Balthazar Gomez.

"Bree."

"Yeah?"

"You said Ayala blew Balthazar's head off. Was his head completely gone when you buried him?"

Smiley looked at Balthazar's crucified corpse and was looking pretty green around the gills. "No, mostly just the top of it. Someone's been…at him…since."

"This look familiar at all to you, Israel?"

"Only in nightmare, my friend," Villaluz said.

Bolan scanned the surroundings. Smiley and the inspector went into cop mode and did the same. There was no blood trail but then again it looked like Gomez had been drained dry. There were no footprints. It was as if someone had crucified the man and then thrown him into the sand like a lawn dart from the sea. Qu walked to the beach, looked both ways, made a circle and came walking back shaking his head. His face was calm but his hands were white-knuckled around his shotgun.

Ayala was screaming inside the house. Someone had to have been inattentive and he had gotten a glimpse down in the dunes of what his own fate might be. Qu shrilled imprecations at his men and shook his fist.

Villaluz peered at the body very closely. "The head was taken cleanly. With a single blow."

"Coop?" Smiley asked.

"Yeah?"

"Get us out of here."

"We're gone." Bolan took out his phone stroked his presets and dialed Grimaldi. He watched the icon dial and dial and dial. He clicked another app and shot for the satellite that would put him in touch with Stony Man Farm. Bolan frowned at his phone.

"What is it?" Smiley asked.

"Either Satan has turned off my service," Bolan said, "or we're being jammed across all frequencies."

CHAPTER NINE

"We get off the damn island!" Chet snarled. "We take the boat and we get off now!"

Bolan summoned patience. "They're waiting for that."

Coffee cups jumped as Chet slammed his fist down on the dining table. "I know you got a job to do, but so do I!"

Bolan sighed. "The boat's on the other side of the island. There are ten empty houses and half a dozen hills on the way. There could be snipers anywhere."

"Yeah? Well?" Chet shook back his hair, sat back down and looked significantly at the Dobermans. "The dogs ain't smelled nuthin."

Chet had a point. Highlander and MacLeod had been outside and off leash. They'd charged off into the hills and come back wagging their tails and expecting steak. It was a good point and it bothered Bolan.

"Chet, that boat is our only way off the island and the enemy knows it. I'm betting they're waiting offshore."

"Waiting hell!" Chet stabbed a finger at Bolan. "You saw that hoodoo down in the dunes!"

"I saw it," Bolan acknowledged. "We all saw it."

Chet waved a dismissing hand. "So just what're you supposing, slick?"

They were back to "slick."

Chet continued his tirade. "We bunker ourselves up

here? Board up the windows *Night of the Living Dead* style? We all know how that ended."

"That's exactly what I'm suggesting. We don't leave this house until we've taken their best shot and put a dent in them or my people come."

Everyone was watching the two bulls of the woods lock horns.

Smiley raised her hand like she was in school. "Coop?"

"Yeah."

"Point of Parliamentary Procedure?"

"Go ahead."

"Me, the inspector and J.W., we all went dark on your say-so. The only people who know we're here are your people."

"That's right."

"But our only link with your people is your pilot Jack."

"That's right."

"And he's gone dark like us."

"Right."

"So if he doesn't hear from us, how soon until he makes a move?"

Honesty was the best course. "He knows where we are, but I told him I would contact him first. That was twenty-four hours ago. He knows we've gone dark. At forty-eight hours he'll start wondering."

Chet rolled his eyes. "So when do the Feds send him in?"

Bolan stayed with honesty. "He's not under the direct authority of the federal government."

Chet's face went blank. "And just what does that mean?"

"It means the Feds won't be sending him in anytime

soon." Bolan shrugged. "On the other hand, Jack's impulsive and quite fond of me."

Smiley pushed. "So how soon?"

"He and I have been in this situation before. When I don't contact him tomorrow and he can't contact me—" Bolan tilted his head at the curtained sliding glass door "—he'll put a float plane on the beach or drop a chopper in the sand by dawn."

"So that's it." Chet shook his head again. "We gotta survive tonight."

"That's about it."

"Slick, you suck."

"You and Miss Tsui want to go? Go. If anyone wants to go with you, they can go. You can each take one loaded gun. I'm going to need everything else."

Chet's face went wolf. "Now you listen here—"

Smiley shot her hand up. "I'm with Coop."

Miss Tsui raised her hand. "I am also."

Qu and crew saluted like Roman centurions in unison.

Wang nodded. "I'm with Coop, too."

Villaluz sighed at Chet in sympathy. *"Vaya con Dios, amigo."*

Bolan looked over at Highlander and MacLeod. "Boys?"

The dogs thumped their tails on the floor.

They liked Bolan.

"There you have it." Bolan nodded at Chet. "You're free to go. You can take the motorcycle in the garage. I may need the rest of the vehicles."

"Well, damn it." Chet leaned back in his chair, folded his arms across his chest and scowled at nothing in particular. He turned his wolf eyes on Bolan in all seriousness. "Tell you what, slick."

Bolan figured he'd tomahawk the pistol already in his hand under the table into Chet's face and then hurl him to the dogs. "What's that, Chet?"

Chet smiled sadly. "Give you a choice, slick. You want me to stay here, I will, and I'll follow your orders. To the letter." He took a long look at Miss Tsui and then back to Bolan. "But on your say so, I'll make for the boat. If I make it off this rock and make it to the mainland, I'll go straight to your buddy at the airport and tell him you, Miss Tsui and all and sundry need evac ASAP."

Bolan saw past the supermodel who couldn't keep it in his pants when it came to clients, suspects or superior officers and saw the man who had won a Bronze Star in Iraq for heroic and meritorious service. "Rather have you here. Come nightfall I got a feeling I'm going to need every swinging dick."

"You got it."

"But if it comes to it…"

"What's that?"

Bolan nodded. "Be ready to make your run."

Wang shifted in his seat unhappily. "So that's it then. A siege."

"We take whoever or whatever comes tonight and teach them a lesson." Bolan leaned back in his chair. "Who's with me?"

Everyone was with him except the tong men until Wang explained it to them in Cantonese, then they were full-on in, as well. Bolan glanced back at the Dobermans. Come the dark the dogs would be crucial in a siege. "Boys?"

Highlander and MacLeod thumped their tails on the floor in agreement.

"Miss Tsui, have your man Gao make a mess of food now, as well as coffee, and a lot of it. Come nightfall I want this house blacked out so I need blankets over the windows.

I want the front door and the interior garage barricaded."
Bolan looked at the sliding glass door and deck outside.
"That's our weak point. So we're going to need a line of
defense inside. Have Qu and the rest of his men take the
wheelbarrow and start bringing up loads of sand. I want
every pillow case, suitcase, cushion cover, anything that
can make an improvised sand bag filled."

Tsui started giving orders and her men hopped to it.

Bolan looked out at the two barbecues out on the deck.
"Chet, get me the propane tank from the gas barbecue,
then start up some coals in the Weber."

Chet rose. "There's a spare tank in the garage, as
well."

"Get that one, too."

Chet waggled his eyebrows. "Gonna have us some good
old-timey redneck fun with the propane, boss?"

"Something like that." Bolan grinned.

THE OLD-TIMEY red-neck fun was on. Bolan sweltered
beneath the deck. He was covered with sand and bat shit
but he was satisfied with what he had wrought.

"Take up the slack!" Bolan shouted. Chet's PPK was
cocked, locked and duct-taped to a support post. Bolan had
tied kitchen twine around the trigger and the twine grew
taut as Chet pulled his end of the twine through the hole
in the floor Bolan had drilled.

Chet's muffled voice called from above. "It's taut!"

"You behind the couch?" Bolan called.

"Yeah!"

"Pull!"

The twine jerked. The little pocket automatic pistol went
"pop!" A bullet smacked into the support beam three feet
in front of it. "Good! Let go of the line!" The line went
slack. As the day faded Bolan peered through the PPK's

sights. They were still dead on but he gave the grips another two wraps of tape anyway. He uncocked the gun and crawled forward. He pushed a twenty-pound barbecue tank in front of the bullet hole in the target post. The problem was that, unlike in the movies, gas tanks didn't automatically blow up when you shot them. Bolan was hedging his bets.

He placed a two-gallon tin of gasoline in front of the tank.

"Israel! Is it ready?"

"Coming!" the inspector shouted. Villaluz crouched beside the edge of the deck and threw Bolan a BBQ mitt. He reached up and brought down a slightly smoking coffee can with a pair of tongs. "It is half past seven now, I suspect they will last perhaps eight hours."

Bolan took the can of charcoal lumps and put it in the sand next to the propane and away from the gas. Eight hours smolder time. Come three or three-thirty he couldn't count on a clean ignition. He'd just have to deal with that when the time came. Bolan crawled back, checked the knot of the PPK's trigger and then recocked the pistol. He emerged from the sweaty, bat-befouled belly of his homemade fuel-air bomb and closed his eyes as the ocean breeze hit him. He took the beer Villaluz handed down gratefully and wiped the sweating, ice-cold bottle across his brow. Qu and Zong nodded as they trudged by pushing another wheelbarrow load of sand.

Chet leaned over the rail. "You think they're gonna hit us tonight?"

Bolan looked out at the abomination in the dunes smothered with fighting seagulls. "That was supposed to make us panic and run. We didn't. Tonight's their last window of opportunity on this island before the cavalry comes."

"So what do you think?"

"What do you think of Qu and his boys?" Bolan countered.

"They're tough enough. They're armed for bear, and you wouldn't want to meet 'em in a dark alley." Chet scowled toward the surf. "But they aren't soldiers." He looked at Bolan honestly. "What about your crew?"

"Bree is a very talented DEA agent but her gunfighting has been learned on the job in the past seventy-two hours. Villaluz is a gunfighter, but not a soldier. J.W. loves guns, but he's a criminal who got into his first firefight two days ago." Bolan shook his head. "Plus I don't speak Cantonese, so any orders I give Qu and the gang have to go through him."

"Yep." Chet leaned on the rail. "Guess that leaves you and me the only straight-shooting soldier boys on this one."

"And Highlander and MacLeod."

"Yeah, and the dogs."

"By the way, what's their attack command?"

Chet shot a wary look back at the open door and spoke quietly. "The command is 'attack.'"

"Original." Bolan watched the sun as it started to set.

"Listen, I was talking to J.W. about when they attacked you at the pueblo. This all is gonna be a whole lot for not much if they go all-out on us again."

"Chet, I don't have any antiaircraft weapons." Bolan took a long pull on his beer. "But dropping a plane into a pueblo no one's ever heard of in the middle of the desert is one thing. It could be years before anyone finds that wreck. Doing it on a resort island is going to draw immediate heat. I'm betting they don't go to the well twice on that tactic tonight."

"Well, I guess that's some kind of consolation."

"Listen," Bolan said.

"Uh-huh?"

"You said you had your job and I had mine. You're right. Your first responsibility is Miss Tsui's safety. I still think the enemy is holding offshore. I still think we get hit come sundown. You might think about getting your client out of here. Not to the boat but someplace on the island. A cave, a culvert, it doesn't matter. I don't think the bad guys care about you. It's Ayala they want, and my crew that's given them offense."

"That's a mighty kind offer." Chet held his gleaming shotgun up into the dying light of the sun. "But I think me, my client and old painless here feel a whole hell of a lot safer with you."

"Fair enough. Let's go rig the garage."

BOLAN WAITED in darkness. Normally the night was his friend. It was when he did his best damage. It didn't feel friendly this night. The enemy owned it, and the enemy was out there. Bolan could feel it. So could the dogs. First Highlander and then MacLeod growled low in their throats and tensed. "Good boys." Bolan said quietly. "Everyone... get ready."

People shifted in their positions and gripped their weapons more tightly throughout the house. Bolan's internal clock told him it was around 2:30 a.m. The only sound was dim noise of the two jeeps in the garage running in Neutral.

Bolan sat on low stool in the middle of his revetment. Three couches had been pushed into a U-shape in the middle of the room. Their cushions had been stripped of stuffing and filled with sand. Tsui was a woman of extensive luggage, and most of it sat on the couches filled with sand as well. It looked like some little kids had built a fort while their parents were gone, but two or three feet of sand was one of the best bullet stops in the world, and it would form a nice bunker if Bolan had to go final option and pull his twine.

The dogs growled again, vibrating and fixated on the dunes outside like pointers. "Stay." Bolan rose up and walked to the window. It was blacked out with blankets and quilts, but he had cut a few thin slits to see out of. Bolan was the only person who had shown up on this one with night-vision gear and he had given his spare pair to Chet. Bolan didn't need night vision to see what was going on. The flickering orange glow outside told him. He peered out and confirmed it.

Out in the dunes the crucified corpse of Balthazar was burning like a torch.

A low, slobbering moan almost below human register howled out by the beach. It was as if the sound of a dying wolverine had been sent through a voice scrambler. Even Bolan felt the hairs on his arm stand up. Smiley started in her firing position as the moan was cut by a scream like a rabbit being killed. "Goddamn it! If they start playing Black Sabbath backward…"

"Cooper!" Villaluz whispered. "What do you see?"

Bolan didn't answer. It was just as well he was the only one looking out. Gomez's body was twisting and jerking on the crucifix with far more abandon than any normal dead body exposed to fire had a right too. Gomez, headless and heartless, was writhing on Satan's Cross like the damned writhing in hell.

Bolan smiled coldly.

The Wizard of Oz had nothing on these guys. This was Vegas level smoke and mirrors, and it was a diversion. Another horrid moan echoed through the dunes and hellish screams answered. Chet stage-whispered from the foyer right on cue. "Boss! I think we got movement out front!"

"Everyone hang tight. Bree, Chet, take up your twine. Don't pull until I say so unless the house is breached. Got it?"

"Copy that," Smiley said.

"You got it, boss."

Bolan went upstairs into the guest bedroom that overlooked the front drive. He carefully scanned through the slit in the blackout curtain. There were far too many boulders and large rock formations close to the house for his liking, but any landscaping would've required a bulldozer. Bolan had another idea for the enemy out in the dark. He caught motion as a gunman scurried from one piece of cover to another. The enemy was already within the thirty-yard mark. Bolan called softly down the stairs. "J.W., hit it."

Wang pressed the button on the automatic-garage-door remote. "Smoke in the hole!"

The garage doors and window had been taped shut, and the two jeeps had been idling for six hours filling the space with exhaust fumes with no place to go. The double doors rose and a forked cloud of poisonous fog roiled out of the garage like a living thing. Overpressure pushed it forward and the breeze off the ocean kept it moving. Car exhaust was heavier than air and the house was built on a rise. The roiling cloud expanded down the drive and began crawling among the rocks like something out of a horror movie. Men began hacking and choking and rising up from cover against their will.

"J.W.!" Bolan shouted. "Now!"

Wang hit the front floodlights and Qu and crew came out of cover. Blankets had been draped across the porch railing to conceal them, and the convertible VW Thing had been parked in front and its boxy interior filled with sand to provide cover. The four tong men had been dutifully lying on the porch since sundown. They rose up now and their semiautomatic shotguns began booming like broadsides of cannon from the days of wooden ships. The assassins had the choice of standing and fighting or staying crouched behind cover and sucking lethal levels of carbon monoxide. Most stood, and were cut down almost instantly by buckshot as they gagged and wept and tried to aim their rifles.

Bolan shouted back down the stairs. "Everyone hold position!" He held his fire and scanned the night beyond, waiting for the outliers, the light support weapons and snipers he knew had to be lurking.

An enemy rose up out of the rocks beyond the cloud with the almost ubiquitous four-feet of tube and rocket perched over his shoulder. Bolan's rifle was a thunderclap in the bedroom. The bullet hit the would-be rocketeer like a thunderbolt and spun him to the ground. Bolan tracked for his next target. Men at the fringe of the cloud were taking better aim with their rifles, and the Executioner laid his hand of wrath upon them. His rifle was a precision weapon, the range was short, and between the floodlights and his night-vision goggles even the men firing from far back in the shadows might as well have been standing up in broad daylight. Men fell crumpled to the sand never to rise again. Those few who still had breath in their bodies lost it as the cloud continued to billow and creep through the rocks like the Angel of Death.

Bolan dropped his seventh man and suddenly the island was absolutely silent. The sound effects from the beach had stopped. The toxic cloud quickly began breaking up and dispersing upon the ocean breeze.

Bolan waited for the big fat hit.

Someone began hurling thunderbolts far harder than Bolan's and one hell of a lot faster. Bolan hurled himself to the floor as a .50-caliber machine gun lit up the night and lit up the room he was in at eight rounds per second. Bolan crawled into the hallway and slid down the stairs. "Be ready!" he shouted. "They're coming in hard! Get Qu back in!"

The .50-caliber gun hammered the house. Adobe was a bullet-resistant substance but not bulletproof. It was also brittle, and given time one-and-half-inch long, full-metal-jacketed bullets could pound the walls into broken pottery. Qu and crew scurried off the porch. Bolan watched as they piled through the door one short. "Qu! Where's Gao?" Qu paused briefly from shucking fresh shells into his smoking shotgun to draw his thumb across his throat. Gao hadn't made it.

A second .50-caliber weapon opened up from the beach and put the house in a cross fire. Windows shattered and tracers tore through the blackout curtains and drew red lines through every room in the house. The makeshift fortifications began bleeding rivers of sand. Headlights shone in harsh shafts through the shredded curtains in both the front and back of the house. Vehicles were coming, and firing as they came. Bolan moved to the front of the house as the hammering continued. He risked a look out a shattered window and saw a military-style jeep rolling forward. It was dripping with gunmen, and one stood up in the bed behind the heavy machine gun. Men jogged two by two on either side of the vehicle.

"J.W.! Chet! On my signal! Bree, stay on the deck charge!" Bolan waited until the vehicle reached the drive. "J.W.! Now!"

Wang hit the garage door remote and the doors of the three-car garage began to close. The enemy wasn't having a method of egress closed off and the men on foot charged forward and physically stopped the door. The garage unit noticed the resistance and went back into opening mode. The jeep rolled forward almost to the doorway and began firing its Fifty into the garage entry to the house.

"Jesus!" Chet shouted. The refrigerator had been pushed against the door, and he was prone on the kitchen tiles behind a beanbag chair filled with sand. A volley of .50-caliber bullets were still whizzing all around him. "God-damn it, Coop!"

"Now!"

Chet pulled the twine. Bolan had been so satisfied with his bomb beneath the deck he had set another one under the five steps that led down into the garage. The pop of the Chinese pistol was lost in the enemy fusillade.

The house shook on its foundations with the detonation. The back blast disintegrated the door and nearly tipped the refrigerator onto Chet. The garage naturally funneled most of it the other way. A sheet of fire blasted across the jeep and the men in and around it.

"Chet! Israel! Go! Go! Go!"

Chet grabbed his shotgun, jumped up and pushed over the refrigerator. Villaluz pushed past him with a revolver in either hand. Bolan was pretty sure the carbon monoxide had been flushed out.

"Cooper!" Smiley called. "They're right on top of us!"

Bolan baseball-slid into the sand-sofa revetment. "Wait for it!"

The higher crack of rifle fire had joined the Fifty out front. It sounded like the boys coming up the beach were similar numbers to the ones who had hit the front.

Smiley's voice rose urgently. "Cooper!"

"Wait for it!"

A bullet smashed through a suitcase inches from Bolan's head and sprayed him with stinging sand.

"Coop!"

Timbers cracked. Bolan had a taken a saw to a section of deck and left it barely capable of supporting its own weight. Something had fallen through. Bolan's eyes flared as he heard a dim shout over the shooting. *"Scheiße!"*

"Now!" Bolan roared. Smiley yanked, and he heard the PPK pop underneath the deck. "Again!"

More boots hit the deck outside. Smiley's voice went up toward panic as she manically yanked the twine. "It's not working!"

"Again!" Bolan ordered. "Again!" There were only six rounds in the gun. "Ag—"

The house shook again as the deck and everyone on it went sky-high. The blackout blankets flew inside like flaming ghosts as they rode the blast wave. Smiley grabbed Bolan for dear life. The leather couches scorched with the heat, but they stoically refused to move an inch and the heat washed over and around them. Highlander and MacLeod howled, but Wang had them out in the interior hall, which was arguably the safest place in the house.

Bolan rose up, rifle in hand, and yawned against the ringing in his ears. Glass crunched beneath his boots. Out in the garage Bolan heard a pistol shot, and a second one a moment later. "Chet! Sitrep!"

"The inspector put down two men who were still twitching! The front seems clear!"

"Hold position!" Bolan pulled his night-vision goggles back down. "J.W.! Kill the lights!"

Darkness dropped over the house like a blanket. A jeep restarted as Bolan stood over the crater where the deck had been. Gears ground. Only the driver was still in the vehicle. The windshield was blown out, the guy looked like he was in pretty bad shape. The jeep lurched in Reverse. "Stop!" Bolan yelled.

The jeep surged backward in the sand.

He put a round into the hood as the vehicle surged forward.

The driver dived out of the still-moving jeep and rolled behind a dune clutching a rifle.

"Highlander!" Bolan shouted. "MacLeod!" The two dogs came bounding into the battle zone. Bolan pointed into the night. "Attack! Attack!"

The two dogs soared over the bomb crater and shot silently into the night like black, canine comets. "Everyone hold position!" Bolan jumped down into the scorched sand and followed. Almost instantly he heard a scream of agony. Just as instantly the sound was strangled off, leaving only the sound of the surf, smoldering wood and dogs savaging something.

Bolan came around the dune and found Highlander attached to the driver's throat and MacLeod's snout buried in his thigh. Both dogs yanked and whipped themselves against the flesh their fangs were buried in. The driver's dead body moved like a sack of rags beneath the dogs fury. Highlander and MacLeod weren't guard dogs. They were killers.

"Highlander, MacLeod, come!" They very reluctantly left their kill and came over wagging their tails at Bolan. "Good boys."

Bolan found no papers or ID on the body. The face was bruised, cut and flash burned and would bear reexamining in the morning. Bolan retrieved the dead man's rifle and trotted back to the jeep. Any normal enemy would be in full retreat by now, but Bolan still had no grasp on who his enemy was. If the situation were reversed, now would be the time Bolan would attack again with anything he had left.

The soldier drove back to the house and parked the jeep in the blast crater. Like a lot of MPs, Chet had spent a lot of time in gun jeeps and he and Bolan got the machine gun dismounted and remounted on the tripod stowed in the back. They got the gun covering the dunes and then backed the other jeep into the empty slot in the still-smoking garage, and now they had a heavy machine gun covering both approaches. Bolan put Chet and Villaluz on front gun detail. Bolan would take the back.

He stopped in the long entry hall and opened the closet. Corporal Ayala blinked up at him and quivered. Bolan snapped his muzzle inches from Ayala's face. *"Sprechen Sie Deutsch?"*

Corporal Ayala goggled up at Bolan in uncomprehending terror. He whimpered as Bolan slammed the door shut. He was sure of only two things. Ayala was scared out his mind and he didn't speak German.

CHAPTER TEN

"Germans?" Chet managed to tone down his usual scorn to open disbelief. "Boss, I thought we were fighting Satan, not the Huns."

"The guy who went through that section of deck we weakened," Bolan said, "yelled in German when he fell."

"All right, but you sure it was German? I mean there were a lot of guns going off and a lot of yelling goin' on. You even speak German?"

"Let's just say I've had a few choice German words directed at me in my time."

"You know?" Smiley grinned. "I bet you have."

Everyone laughed. Despite the gravity of the situation and losing Gao, even the Chinese were in fairly good spirits. There was no getting around the fact that they had taken it to the enemy but good. No further attacks had come in the night. Come the dawn Bolan had given everyone jobs, and his sniper rifle and a big Fifty had covered each task. Everyone sat on bullet-riddled sandbags in what was left of the kitchen and drank cold coffee. "Israel?"

Villaluz had gone detective on the corpses. "We accounted for twenty-seven. The deceased out in the rocks, with a few exceptions, all appear to be Latino. Those who reached the house were all badly burned, so a determination is difficult. All bore the mark of the beast, at least all did who were not too badly burned to find it."

"What about the jeep driver?"

Villaluz shrugged in a very Mexican manner. "He could be Caucasian. Then again, a great many Mexicans can pass for yanquis, and he was burned, cut with glass and—" the inspector sighed sadly "—savaged by dogs."

Bolan nodded. "Qu?"

Qu ran a hand over his shaved head. He looked at Bolan as he spoke Cantonese.

Wang translated. "Qu says he, Zong and Peng have looked at the bodies carefully. They do not believe they have seen any of these men in town, much less upon the island before. He wants to know if you want the bodies burned, buried or weighted and sunk into the ocean."

"Hold off on that. Bree?"

"To a man they were all armed with Russian manufactured AK-74 rifles. The black market is swollen with them. Most were mounted with aftermarket optics and tactical lights. I suspect the jeeps are ex-Mexican military. You could buy them anywhere. The .50 calibers are definitely Mexican military, and I'd bet anything they're stolen. I can't believe they had gun jeeps in place. They had to ferry them across somehow. When we get back to the mainland, Israel and I will chat up the harbor master."

Bolan had done some investigating of his own. He'd found no evidence of the sound and magic department. He suspected they had to have used wires to manipulate Gomez's body on the cross, but the killer's corpse was in such bad shape it was impossible to tell. Bolan had done a long-range patrol with the dogs and was fairly certain there were no enemy gunners currently on the island, but communications were still being jammed, and that was a neat trick however they were doing it. "Chet?"

"We're low on personal ammo, but not critical. But there's good news if we want we got more AKs than we

Get FREE BOOKS and a FREE GIFT when you play the...

LAS VEGAS GAME

Just scratch off the gold box with a coin. Then check below to see the gifts you get!

YES!
I have scratched off the gold box. Please send me my **2 FREE BOOKS** and **gift for which I qualify.** I understand that I am under no obligation to purchase any books as explained on the back of this card.

366 ADL E4CE   **166 ADL E4CE**

FIRST NAME   LAST NAME

ADDRESS

APT.#   CITY

STATE/PROV.   ZIP/POSTAL CODE

7	7	7	Worth TWO FREE BOOKS plus a BONUS Mystery Gift!
🍒	🍒	🍒	Worth TWO FREE BOOKS!
🔔	🔔	♣	TRY AGAIN!

Offer limited to one per household and not valid to current subscribers of Gold Eagle® books. All orders subject to approval. Please allow 4 to 6 weeks for delivery.

Your Privacy—Worldwide Library is committed to protecting your privacy. Our privacy policy is available online at www.ReaderService.com or upon request from the Reader Service. From time to time we make our lists of customers available to reputable third parties who may have a product or service of interest to you. If you would prefer for us not to share your name and address, please check here ☐—**Help us get it right**—We strive for accurate, respectful and relevant communications. To clarify or modify your communication preferences, visit us at www.ReaderService.com/consumerschoice.

▼ DETACH AND MAIL CARD TODAY! ▼

© 2009 WORLDWIDE LIBRARY. Printed in Canada.
® and ™ are trademarks owned and used by the trademark owner and/or its licensee.

The Reader Service — Here's how it works:

Accepting your 2 free books and free gift (gift valued at approximately $5.00) places you under no obligation to buy anything. You may keep the books and gift and return the shipping statement marked "cancel." If you do not cancel, about a month later we'll send you 6 additional books and bill you just $31.94* — that's a savings of 24% off the cover price of all 6 books! And there's no extra charge for shipping! You may cancel at any time, but if you choose to continue, every other month we'll send you 6 more books, which you may either purchase at the discount price or return to us and cancel your subscription.

*Terms and prices subject to change without notice. Price does not include applicable taxes. Sales tax applicable in N.Y. Canadian residents will be charged applicable provincial taxes and GST. Offer not vaid in Quebec. Credit or debit balances in a customer's account(s) may be offset by any other outstanding balance owed by or to the customer. Offer available while quantities last.

BUSINESS REPLY MAIL

FIRST-CLASS MAIL   PERMIT NO. 717   BUFFALO, NY

POSTAGE WILL BE PAID BY ADDRESSEE

THE READER SERVICE
PO BOX 1867
BUFFALO NY 14240-9952

If offer card is missing write to: The Reader Service, P.O. Box 1867, Buffalo NY 14240-1867

NO POSTAGE
NECESSARY
IF MAILED
IN THE
UNITED STATES

know what to do with. The Fifties have about a belt and half of ammo between them, and we've got an RPG with three rockets and enough undamaged Russian night-vision gear to put eyes on all of us." Chet shot his trademark smile. "Hell, except for the fact that we're out of propane and down a man I say we're almost in better shape for the siege than we were last night."

Bolan was pretty much in agreement.

"Germans?" Wang asked. "Really?"

"These guys are mostly drug muscle and some ex-Mexican military types. I'll give them their new can-do attitude, but their equipment and their tactics and approach? Someone is arming and organizing these guys. I'm looking for an outside player."

"Besides Old Scratch?" Chet asked.

Bolan smiled wearily. "We'll work our way up the food chain to him." He suddenly looked up.

Everyone looked at him expectantly.

"Rotors," Bolan said. "Everyone gear up." The sound of rotors became distinctly audible. Bolan picked up the RPG-7 and checked the rocket. Chet got on the house Fifty. Everyone else grabbed rifles and made ready. Bolan strode to the edge of the deck crater. A white Bell 205 civilian helicopter swooped low over the house and pulled a screaming U-turn by the shore and stood in place hovering. Bolan looked at the chopper through the RPG's optical sight. Jack Grimaldi stared back at him through a pair of binoculars. Bolan lowered his rocket launcher. "Our ride is here. We take nothing but guns and the clothes on our back."

Grimaldi set the chopper on the beach and hopped out with his submachine gun in hand.

Smiley glanced at the corpses strewed all about. "What about them?"

"We have no time. If someone is going to come and collect that many heads, then so be it. I'll try to get a satellite watching the island by nightfall. Get Ayala and Gao ready for transport. Chet, you and me remount the Fifties on the jeeps. We drive down to the beach in style."

The team moved quickly. They loaded the jeeps and drove in caravan down to the beach with Bolan and Chet on the big guns. No one messed with them. Bolan jumped down and shook hands with his best friend. "Jack."

Grimaldi grinned. "Didn't hear from you. Figured I'd drop in."

"Glad you did. Communications are being jammed."

"I noticed that about a klick from the island."

"How many does this bucket of yours hold?"

"Two crew and up to eight passengers."

"We got ten humans including you, guns and gear, a corpse and two big dogs."

Grimaldi considered this weird and wonderful turn of events. "Gonna have to lighten up." Bolan followed the pilot and between them they unbolted all the seats, removed the doors, threw out the toolbox and every nonessential thing that wasn't nailed down.

"Load up!" Bolan called.

Ayala was injured so they bound him up in the copilot seat. Everyone piled into the cleared cabin and held on to whatever they could. Smiley threw one arm around MacLeod and one around Bolan. The helicopter thundered, whined and shook as it lifted laboriously out of the sand. The Bell wobbled precariously out over the water.

"We're still too heavy!" Grimaldi shouted back.

Bolan slid the .50-caliber machine gun out the door and into the ocean.

"More!" Grimaldi shouted.

"How about the RPG?" Chet suggested.

"No!" Bolan said. "I want to hold on to that, for now!"

Wang said something to Qu, who nodded at Zong and Peng. Gao's blanket-wrapped body was unceremoniously buried at sea.

"Jesus…" Smiley muttered.

Chet shook his head. "They aren't sentimental, are they!"

Villaluz crossed himself.

The helicopter started gaining altitude and Grimaldi began skirting the island rather than crossing over it. Highlander and MacLeod might have been the first Dobermans to have stuck their heads out of a moving helicopter over the ocean. Their ears flapped in the rotor wash, and their tongues lolled in wind-drunk canine bliss. Smiley grinned at the sight and squeezed Bolan tighter.

She screamed as Wang exploded like a blood bag loaded full of firecrackers. Gore flew everywhere. Bolan snarled as a fist-sized hole punched up through the floor of the cabin between his boots and ripped a hole in the roof. Qu howled as something took his hand off at the wrist and blew a chunk out of the door frame behind him. Arterial spray hosed the cabin. The helicopter lurched, and the turbines made an ugly grinding noise as something went wrong in the engine compartment above.

"We're hit!" Grimaldi shouted.

Blood sprayed Bolan's face like a geyser and Smiley gasped in shock. There was another hole in the cabin floor, and everything from midthigh to knee on the agent's left leg was shreds and strings. Bolan grimaced and tried to put pressure on the hemorrhaging wound. "Jack, get us out of here!"

Villaluz pointed at the ocean below. *"¡Narcos submergibles!"*

Bolan cast a quick glance out the tilting helicopter's door and saw two slightly darker blue lozenge-shaped craft in the blue water below. He guessed they were about twenty yards long. Men stood on top of them with impossibly large rifles firing up at the chopper. They were narco smuggling submersibles, probably products of Colombia's illicit mangrove swamp shipyards. Normally they were used to transport up to fifteen tons of cocaine at a run. There was no reason whatsoever they shouldn't be used to transport Satan's scumbags and their ordnance. Blood squirted between Bolan's fingers as he desperately tried to keep Smiley's life in her body.

Peng's stomach burst open, and he toppled out of the cabin and fell, ribboning gore to the ocean below. Grimaldi veered desperately for shore. The enemy fire followed.

Chet shouted in despair. "Cooper!"

Bolan looked over. Tsui lay in Chet's arms with a hole in her chest the size of a softball. "Cooper!"

Smiley was white-faced with shock and blood loss as she whispered. "Cooper…"

The chopper's engine clanked and screamed. Grimaldi bellowed as he fought the stick. "We're going down!"

MacLeod burst like a water balloon. The cabin interior was a charnel house. Bolan could feel Smiley bleeding out in his arms. Chet was screaming hysterically. "You bastards! You bastards!"

The Devil had come for his due.

The helicopter soared over sandy beach and spun nauseatingly. It skipped like a stone as one of its skids hit an outcropping. Grimaldi's voice was uncommonly desperate. "Brace for impact!"

The helicopter hit.

Only Grimaldi and Ayala were belted in. Everyone else kept moving after the impact and they were tossed like clothes in a dryer. The chopper slewed through sand on its nose. Bolan went airborne out the door, sailed a good fifteen feet and found himself out over the water. He landed in about four feet of surf and came up spitting sand and seawater. There was no telltale nausea of broken bones, and he could walk. He slogged out of the surf.

The chopper sat upright but tilted on its twisted skid. Bolan limped to the wreck. Highlander staggered across the sand toward Bolan whimpering piteously. Qu rolled out of the cabin grasping his spurting stump. Bolan ignored the walking wounded and climbed into the cabin.

Zong's face was missing and what was beneath it had cracked like an egg. Smiley's face was ghost-white and slack in death. Inspector Villaluz's left arm hung at a worse angle than Ayala's, but he still had a pistol in his good hand. He was looking at Smiley and weeping. Chet Brashear lay gasping and blinking up at the cabin ceiling, covered with everyone's blood but his own, he outwardly appeared unharmed. Tsui's body was folded in two and jammed between the pilot and copilot seats. Peng's had been thrown clear, but the flight had left him little more than stuff on a rock a few yards away. Grimaldi was groaning and shaking his head in the pilot's seat. Ayala had broken into a fresh bout of screaming.

Bolan began triage.

He took off his watch and cinched the Velcro strap in a tourniquet around Qu's wrist and shoved a pistol in the tong man's hand. "Israel, we gotta go!" Villaluz still stared at Smiley's body and wept like a child. "Inspector!" Villaluz blinked into awareness and Bolan helped ease him out of the cabin. The soldier tore off both sleeves of his shirt and bound the inspector's arm across his chest.

Grimaldi spilled out of the cockpit and sat down in the sand. He stared at the stricken aircraft and then shook his head at Bolan in dazed sadness. "Sorry. That wasn't my best landing...."

"Get Ayala!"

Bolan turned at the sound of fresh sobbing. Chet was up and it was horrific to see him trying to untangle Tsui's crushed body from beneath the cockpit seats. "Chet, we gotta go."

"We can't!" Chet sobbed. "Those Satan sons of bitches! You know what they'll do! We—"

"We leave them as they lie!" Bolan stated with a steely gaze.

"You son of a bitch." Chet glared murder, but he left Tsui and scooped up a blood-covered rifle. "You son of a bitch."

"Save it for the enemy." Bolan scanned the shoreline. "They'll be along presently." He picked up the RPG. The glass in the optic was a spiderweb of cracks, and there was a significant ding in the exhaust cone but it was otherwise intact. Bolan detached the optical unit and flipped up the iron sights. "We're out of here."

Villaluz and Ayala both had broken collarbones and they leaned on each other like drunks. Bolan and Chet limped beneath the weight of their armament. Qu carried the two spare rockets under his good arm. Highlander followed with his head and tail hanging miserably.

Chet pulled up as they left the beach and moved into the rocks. "We can't just leave them like that!"

Bolan didn't have time for this. "Chet..."

"Goddamn it! You saw what they do to their own! God knows what they'll do with Bree's and Sarah's bodies! They'll do some kind of—"

Bolan brought up the RPG and spun. He stared down the iron sight and squeezed the RPG's trigger. The rocket whooshed from the tube and drew a line of gray smoke into the hulk of the helicopter. The antitank rocket detonated and ignited the leaking aircraft fuel. The ruptured tanks blew and spewed burning fuel in all directions. Bree Smiley, Sarah Tsui and Zong's funeral pyre sent choking black smoke into the sky.

"Jesus…" Chet breathed.

Bolan lowered his smoking launch tube. "That's the best I can do. You want to say some words? You got about ten seconds."

Villaluz raised his good hand and made the cross in the air. *"Cenizas a las cenizas, polvo a sacar el polvo."*

"Ashes to ashes," Grimaldi said.

Chet's eyes streamed as he watched the chopper burn. "Dust to dust."

"Amen," Bolan finished. "They killed our friends. They killed our dog. I say we get some payback."

CHAPTER ELEVEN

Bolan scanned the dock. The island was small, but his team had been brutalized. While the beachfront property was heartbreakingly beautiful, the interior of the island was like a real bad patch of the planet Mars. The overland trek had been hell. It had taken an hour and half in the worst of the afternoon heat. Injuries and endless battle had taken their toll. Villaluz, Qu and Ayala were gray-faced with shock, fatigue and dehydration. Bolan, Grimaldi and Chet had been forced to threaten them, beg them, remind them of what they had lost and half carry them this far. They were done. The only thing keeping Chet moving was his unwillingness to fail in front of Bolan. Every time they stopped, Highlander flopped into any available shade and panted like each breath was his last. Bolan wanted to join him.

But there was work to do, and payback was owed.

The sun was just starting to set. The cigarette boat sat at the dock just as they had left it. Bolan was sure there was a bomb on it, and even if there wasn't, the antimatériel rifles the enemy were using were at least .50 caliber and would chop the boat and everyone in it to pieces. Bolan considered. The maximum effective range would be about 1800 meters, but the enemy would want to be a lot closer. Call it a thousand. Bolan gazed across the Pacific with Grimaldi's binoculars. The sun was setting and dappling the water with a million winking reflections, and the enemy submersibles were camouflaged and barely broke the surface.

Bolan handed Grimaldi the binoculars. "Jack?"

The Stony Man pilot peered out across the ocean and instantly pointed. "There, about twelve hundred yards out, past the buoy."

"Right." Bolan stripped off his shirt and kicked off his boots. He tucked one Chinese assassin pistol under the front of his belt and one in the back. "I'm going to backtrack about a thousand yards down the beach, swim out beyond them and come up from behind. I'll be going slow. Figure forty-five minutes."

"Got it." Grimaldi nodded.

"I'm going with you," Chet stated.

"Oh?" Bolan asked.

"I was on the swim team in high school. I got my letterman's jacket and went to regionals. I swim like a fish."

"All right." Bolan moved back through the rocks. Chet hopped out of his boots and tossed away his shirt and ran after him.

"The plan is this," Bolan said. "We swim up behind the nearest submersible, we take it, sink the other one, then pick up our people and head for the mainland."

"Sounds simple enough."

"Most of these submersibles have a crew of four, who switch off two by two in shifts to make the two-thousand-mile run up from Colombia, but since these guys are transporting troops instead of coke there could be a lot more."

"Well, we did account for twenty-seven of them already," Chet said hopefully.

"We did that," Bolan agreed.

Chet's brow furrowed. "So if they inserted by sub, how did they get the gun jeeps across?"

"Don't know." Bolan smiled coldly. "Let's go ask them."

The soldier slid into the water and began a slow breast-stroke with his head barely above the water. The water by the shore was sweat-warm but quickly cooled with depth. Chet fell into stroke behind him. Bolan counted strokes and kicked out into the deep water of the Bahía Magdalena. After a thousand strokes Bolan could hear Chet gasping, but the soldier kept pushing out toward the first buoy. Chet showed up a minute later and clung to the buoy. His eyes glared out of the curtain of long hair falling across his face.

"Don't you worry about me!" he gasped.

"I'm not. You'll either make it or you'll drown," Bolan said. "If you drown, I expect you take one for the team and do it quietly."

"Son of a bitch…" Chet muttered.

Bolan kicked away and began the second leg of their journey. His shoulders and hips were beginning to burn, but he grimly churned on with his agonizingly slow stealth pace, barely making a ripple in the water and even less noise with his passage. He couldn't see the submersibles yet, but as he counted his second thousand yards he circled back toward land to come up behind them. A swell was starting to come up with the evening tide. Bolan was well aware of the fact that with the tide coming up and the sun going down, it was perfectly possible for him to miss the enemy submersibles altogether. He looked back. Chet was over a hundred yards back and had been forced to roll onto his side and adopt a survival stroke. It was all up to Jack Grimaldi.

The Stony Man pilot came through.

Bolan heard the distant pop of gunfire from the island. Twelve hundred meters was a ridiculous range for an AK-74 even with an optical sight, but the pilot managed to attract the enemy's attention. About four hundred yards away in the swell, the muzzle-blast of the enemy antimatériel rifles lit up like orange flares. Bolan angled in. He switched to a more aggressive breaststroke but still kept his head above the water. The closer submersible loomed ahead like a small whale in the water. Two men knelt upon the shallowly sloping deck. One man was the spotter and held a powerful set of binoculars. The second man held a Barrett M82A2 bullpup antimatériel rifle across his shoulder like a bazooka. Both men focused their attention shoreward. At thirty yards Bolan dived below the water. The submersible had a single screw, and its diving planes and rudder were all below the waterline to keep its exposed top featureless. Bolan swam up to the vessel and took hold of the fin-shaped starboard diving plane. He drew the Chinese pistol from below his belt and pulled himself halfway up out of the water along the submersible's sloping stern. He lay along the fiberglass hull and took the pistol in both hands. The two men were spotting and shooting and talking in Spanish. Bolan waited for a momentary lull in the musketry and conversation. "Freeze."

Neither man did.

The shooter spun, but he was carrying twenty-six pounds of ordnance over his shoulder and snap-shooting wasn't the big Barrett's forte. Bolan put three rounds through the sniper's chest, and the man fell back with his giant rifle for a pillow. The spotter shouted wildly as he dropped his binoculars and clawed for the pistol strapped to his thigh. Bolan double-tapped him through the heart. The spotter went limp and slid off the hull into the water. The Executioner dropped his pistol and heaved himself onto the hull. He had heartbeats before the other submersible responded to the pistol shots. He rolled the sniper off the hull and heaved the behemoth Barrett across his own shoulder.

There were water spots on the optic lenses, but the other submersible zoomed into Bolan's vision. They had a similar two-man sniper team on the other craft. They'd spotted Bolan and taken a dim view of him and his activities. The soldier fired first. The Barrett's shoulder yoke slammed into him like the kick from a mule. His shot tore through the prone enemy sniper and sprayed the other submersible's deck and the spotter with gore. The sniper slid into water one way and his rifle the other. If the spotter had been smart, he would have dived for the water, as well. Instead he tried to unsling his rifle. Bolan's second round clanged off the enemy hull in a shower of sparks and skipped through the spotter's face and out the back of his head.

A man stuck his head up out of the open hatch two yards away from Bolan. The man happened to have a handgun. The Executioner tried to bring the giant Barrett to bear but he knew he would never make it. Chet's .357 slammed from starboard and the crown of the crewman's skull flew like a divot.

"Sorry I'm late, boss."

"Get below! Secure the ship!"

Chet scrambled out of the water and headed down the hatch. Bolan put his sights on the enemy hull a foot below the waterline and grit his teeth as he began firing the .50-caliber rifle as fast as he could pull the trigger. The big Barrett boomed eight times, then racked open on empty. Bolan dropped the spent mag and tore a fresh one from the dead sniper's bandolier. The enemy submersible was turning. Bolan waited until it was stern on and again began firing just below the waterline. Bolan emptied all ten rounds into the enemy engine compartment, reloaded and began again. He felt like he was being trampled by a horse, but he kept firing until the third magazine was spent and the overheating weapon oozed smoke from an empty chamber. The stern of the enemy craft was cratered like the moon and oozing black diesel smoke.

"Chet!" Bolan unslung the antimatériel weapon and shouted past ringing ears as he drew his pistol. "Chet!"

"Yeah!" Chet's voice came up the hatch. "One hostile down!"

"Coming down! The other craft looks dead in the wat—"

The enemy submersible blew like a powder keg. Chet's head popped up out of the hatch. "What the hell was that? Secondary explosion?"

"Possibly." Bolan scowled in the fading light. "But I'm betting the bad guys just scuttled themselves with all hands."

"Christ, these guys are seriously creepy." Chet ducked back down. Bolan stood up and waved his arms. Back on the beach Grimaldi fired three rounds methodically to acknowledge. Bolan followed Chet below. The first crewman Chet had shot lay in a heap leaking the contents of his cranium all over the place. Chet had sprayed the second crewman's brains all over the port hull. The interior was incredibly hot and cramped. A grown man couldn't stand up in the compartment. A long trip would be agonizing, but Bolan had to admit if the enemy was lacking anything it sure as hell wasn't motivation. Bolan was also betting that these craft had come upon the island from a much closer location than Colombia. Bolan counted a dozen rolled sleeping mats along the hull walls. Chet pointed at a waterproof case the size of a large piece of luggage by the engine compartment. "The guy I shot down here was going for that."

Bolan made his way to the case. The latches were unlocked. He flipped it open and looked at about thirty pounds of C-4 high explosive.

"Man." Chet shook his head. "They really did do themselves, didn't they?"

"You think you can pilot this thing?"

Chet made his way forward and looked at the controls. "Looks simple enough. They're using a commercial GPS rig for navigating. You'll have to guide me into the dock with a visual."

"Get us underway," Bolan said. "Let's get our people."

Sinaloa, Mexico

BOLAN LOOKED at the lights of Mazatlán through his binoculars. It was 2:00 a.m. Chet regretted losing his Lincoln, but they had all rejected the idea of returning to Ciudad Constitución. Nothing good was waiting for them there. They'd left the Bahía Magdalena and headed south into open water. At the submersible's cruising speed of eleven miles per hour, it had taken them eighteen hours to round the Baja Peninsula and another twenty to reach the mainland coast. It hadn't been a pleasurable ride. The submersible had been designed for concealment not comfort. Villaluz's shoulder had been dislocated rather than broken, but both he and Ayala were in a lot of pain. They had kept Qu's stump from festering, but he needed medical attention ASAP. They had cleaned up the interior as best they could, but between dried blood and brains, unwashed bodies, dog and constant ninety-degree-plus heat the interior smelled like a zoo. Chet and Grimaldi had spelled each other at the helm. Chet called up from behind the controls. "You want me to bring us in?"

Bolan considered the city lights.

He had swept the submersible for bugs as best he could and maintained a communication blackout. However, so far the Beast had found them everywhere they had gone despite every precaution. Mazatlán might be Mexico's number-one vacation destination, but it was also one of Mexico's busiest ports and smuggling centers. The Beast would have assets here and he'd had nearly two days to set something up while Bolan and crew had putted across the Pacific. Bolan was giving good odds there was a trap waiting for them in Mexico's Pacific Pearl.

"Yeah, take us in," Bolan called. "Jack, bring the Barrett, the RPG and all the spare rockets and ammo for both." If they met with evil by land or sea, Bolan intended to give them a broadside they could take to hell with them.

"Hey, boss!" Chet called. "Qu's squawking about something!"

Bolan hunched his way back down into the stink of the hold. Qu took a knee before him. His stump had bled through another set of dressings. Qu raised his good hand up to the side of his face with the thumb and little finger out in the universal telephone signal. He shrugged at Bolan in question.

Bolan nodded. "What the hell."

Chet bristled. "You're gonna let him make a call?"

"I'm going to let everyone make a call. We haven't gotten jack with the silent running routine. We might as well pull in every friend or favor we got in this one. You want to drop a dime, do it now. I can't guarantee what's going to happen when we hit the beach."

Bolan took out his sat and phoned home. It was 2:15 a.m. Kurtzman answered halfway through the first ring. "Striker!"

"Hey, Bear."

"A whole lot of people want a sitrep, Striker, myself included."

"I'm in a commandeered narco submersible holding off the beach in Mazatlán."

"Okay…"

"Bear, it isn't good."

"How bad is it?"

"Agent Smiley is dead."

Kurtzman was quiet for a moment. "That's going to go over like a French kiss at a family reunion. DEA is already spinning up the perfect shit-storm. This is going to send them right over the edge."

"J.W. is dead."

Bolan could almost hear Kurtzman shaking his head. "The Mexican tong isn't going to like that."

"Yeah, research a woman named Sarah Tsui. She's dead, too, and the Hong Kong triads are going to like that even less."

"Tell me the inspector is still alive."

"Inspector Villaluz is busted up but still salty. My team is down to four effectives, including a Doberman."

The silence on the other side of the line was profoundly appalled. "You got any good news?"

"Ayala is still alive, but I'm in doubt whether he's worth the price we paid." Bolan took a long breath in the fetid air of the hold and let it out. "We're banged up bad, Bear, and whoever the Beast is, he's got our number. We tried it my way, Inspector Villaluz's way and the tong way. We can't shake this satanic son of a bitch off us. I'm presently holding a half-mile off the coast. I feel no joy in Mazatlán."

Kurtzman spoke carefully. "We could extract you, Striker. We could bring you in."

"I keep hearing 'you can't escape the Beast,' Bear. He found us in Tijuana despite Bree Smiley's best efforts, and she lived up to her rep. He found us in the worst part of the Laguna Salada. He found us on an island in Baja. I'll be damned before I let this Beast son of a bitch track us to the Farm."

Kurtzman's voice grew increasingly disturbed. "You're not buying this 'Beast' stuff, are you?"

"All I'm saying, Bear, is that I can't shake him. If I can't shake him, I'm sure as hell not leading him home."

"Give me the short version of what I've missed."

Bolan gave him a condensed version of everything that had happened so far along with pertinent points and people he wanted researched.

"So what are you going to do?" Kurtzman asked.

"If I can't shake him, then I'm just going to have to fight my way up the food chain and take him out."

"What do you need?"

"I need guns and gear, Bear. I need multiple war loads in multiple safe houses. Have cutouts deliver the gear and then have them get the hell away and have them stay away."

"You want me to alert Able and Phoenix?" Kurtzman asked, suggesting that the Farm's two action teams join the fight. "I can have them there in forty-eight hours."

Bolan knew that given the situation, the men of Stony Man Farm would come with or without permission and destroy half of Mexico in their wake.

"No. I don't want the Farm or any Farm personnel involved yet."

"Yet?"

"If I go down, they're batting clean-up. The Beast goes down no matter what. But I'm going to do it with assets on hand if I can."

"All right. Hal won't like it. The President won't like it. I don't like it. Able and Phoenix are going to put me on the shitlist when they find out I kept it from them. But it's your show."

"Yeah, it is."

"Keep one thing in mind."

"What's that?"

"I expect intel at every possible opportunity. If you go dark for more than a week, I tell the boys and it's their show. They rescue your ass or avenge it."

"Done," Bolan said. "Like I said, I need ordnance in Mazatlán, and I need it yesterday."

"What, you think I've just been listening to you flap your gums?"

Bolan smiled tiredly. "Me and the boys are about to hit the beach. Assuming we get past the sand alive, we're going to pick a random location. I'll call you from there."

"Copy that, Striker."

"Striker out." Bolan touched his phone off. Chet, Qu and Villaluz were still speaking into theirs. Highlander was a haggard matted mess, but he thumped his tail on the floor at Bolan hopefully.

The soldier nodded at Chet. "Take us in when you're done. We'll guide you in from up top."

"Copy that, boss."

Bolan grinned at Highlander. "Want to go for a walk, boy?"

Highlander vaulted up the open hatch like a jack-in-the-box. Bolan followed the dog and stood up in the hatch. Highlander stood on the prow and aimed his entire body landward like a pointer. "Hard to starboard, Mr. Brashear," Bolan called. He brought his binoculars up to his eyes. "Full speed ahead."

CHAPTER TWELVE

Playa Vista Resort, Mazatlán

Bolan looked up at a knock on the door. It was a rhythmic series of taps, but it wasn't Morse code. Qu recognized it and jumped to attention. He looked at Bolan eagerly. The team had spent the past three days eating, sleeping, reequipping and waiting for Armageddon. It hadn't come yet. Bolan nodded at Qu, who answered the door. Bolan began to understand the nature of Qu's phone call the other day.

The Chinese man filling the door frame was six feet tall and built like an Olympic swimmer. Bolan knew his pinstripe, tropical wool Savile Row suit cost thousands, and it fit the man's frame absolutely perfectly. He had a Superman haircut right down to the loose "S" curl perfectly falling across his brow. The epicanthic fold of his eyes made him look like he was observing the world with a permanent, sleepy disdain. The eyes widened a bare fraction to take in Qu's bandaged stump. The two men passed a few words in Cantonese. Qu was deferential in the extreme.

Qu and his crew were Mexican tong muscle and as tough as they came.

The new guy was a triad assassin straight out of Hong Kong and a stone cold killer of men. He gave Qu a barely perceptible nod. Qu nodded at the non-Chinese in the room and spoke the only word of English Bolan had heard out of him by way of introduction. "Mr. Zhong Fangyu."

Zhong turned his hawklike gaze on Bolan. "You are Mr. Cooper."

Bolan could tell Zhong had learned his English from U.K. speakers. "I am. This is Mr. Chet Brashear, and—"

The man looked at Chet in open scorn. "I am aware of him."

Chet bristled. "Hey!"

Zhong ignored the outburst.

Sarah Tsui was dead, and Bolan suspected Qu had let his personal feelings for Chet make for a less-than-glowing after-action report on the man. Bolan thought he himself might have fared a little better. Despite his haughty reserve, Zhong was clearly trying to size up Bolan. The killer and the warrior regarded each other. "Miss Tsui belonged to a family of some importance in Hong Kong," Zhong said.

Bolan nodded. "She was a great lady."

"Hmm." Zhong nodded imperceptibly. "Mr. Wang was a man of some importance in Mexico."

"He fought most bravely. I miss both him and his skills."

Zhong gave another infinitesimal nod of acknowledgment. "A reckoning is required. I require you to tell me everything you know regarding this situation."

"Require?" Chet thrust out his jaw. "Just who the hell do you think you are?"

"You were retained in the capacity of…?" Zhong let the question hang accusingly. "Bodyguard, was it? You should stick to the job you failed at and leave other matters to your betters."

Chet's eyes flared and his lips skinned back from his teeth. "Yeah, well, fang you too, you son of a bitch."

Zhong Fangyu turned his full attention on Chet. "Come here and say that."

Chet grinned.

"Don't do it," Bolan cautioned.

Chet stepped forward thrusting out his jaw again taunt-ingly. "I don't know what kind of Jackie Chan shit you think you know but—" Chet's left hand rocketed out of nowhere. It was a gorgeous to behold sucker-punch sped by gunfighter-fast reflexes. If you blinked you would have missed it.

Zhong caught Chet's wrist inches before the blow hit his chin.

Chet blinked. "What the—"

Zhong gave Chet the slightest of smiles and raised one eyebrow bemusedly. "You're quick."

Zhong squeezed.

Chet roared in agony and dropped to his knees. Zhong's fingertips were arranged in a mantis-claw on his adver-sary's inner wrist. Chet's hand fluttered like an epileptic bird as Zhong mercilessly dug his fingers in and played the arteries, nerve bundles and the spaces between Chet's wrist bones like piano keys. He spoke to Chet like a man disci-plining an unruly child. "Mr. Fangyu...to you, Chet."

"Mr. Fangyu!" Chet howled. "Fine! Whatever!"

"Good." Zhong leaned down slightly. "Now, say 'uncle.'"

A stream of agonized profanity flew from Chet's mouth but *uncle* wasn't any part of it. Chet's hand was turning purple.

Bolan spoke quietly. "Enough."

Grimaldi fell into rank beside Bolan. Highlander's hackles rose as he growled low in his throat.

Zhong turned his gaze on Bolan for several more long moments of squeezing and then released Chet's wrist. "We will speak in the bar in half an hour." Zhong turned and left. Qu went with him.

Chet clutched his swiftly blackening wrist. "Bruce Lee son of a bitch…"

Bolan sighed. "You just insist on learning the hard way."

Chet glowered. "Yeah, well, that bodyguard crack was cold."

"That man is as cold as they come, Chet. The only reason he let go was because I have something he wants." Bolan held out a hand and hauled Chet to his feet. "Next time you have a problem with him you better shoot him."

"Yeah, I copy that." Chet tried to squeeze his hand into a fist and failed. "But Qu isn't the only one who's called in some backup."

"Oh, yeah?"

"Oh, yeah." Chet took out his phone and dialed a number with a still shaking hand. "Yeah, you in town yet?" Bolan could hear a woman speaking, but he couldn't quite hear her words. "Great. Even better. I'm going to be in the bar in ten minutes. You see a guy who looks like the Chinese version of Clark Kent stay out of his way, for now." Chet laughed. "Yeah, he's even out of Terrell's league." Chet clicked the phone shut.

"What have you got?"

"I got Libby and Terrell on the job."

"You know them from the private security agency?"

"Yeah, Terrell I knew back in Iraq. He was my unit's designated marksman. The man can hit an ant in the ass at five hundred meters, and he can bench-press a truck. I got him a job with the agency. Only he didn't screw it up like me."

"Who's Libby?"

Chet grinned. "Libby's a real interesting girl. She's been a stuntwoman, an LAPD reserve officer, a bail bondsman, bodyguard and a private dick with the agency."

"Sounds like she can take care of herself." Bolan frowned. "But we need more soldiers, Chet. I need ten Terrells in assorted colors."

"She also speaks German. Figured that might come in handy." Chet shrugged. "Plus she's one of the only two people in L.A. who return my calls."

Grimaldi voted with his libido. "Hey! I want to meet Libby!"

"You're going to stay here with Israel and keep an eye on Ayala. I'm going to go size up the new recruits and have our second date with Zhong."

Grimaldi was crestfallen.

Bolan ignored his pilot. The flyboy from Stony Man Farm would have plenty of opportunities to work his wiles. "Chet, we're out of here."

Kurtzman had come through on equipment. Bolan tucked his Beretta 93-R machine pistol into a small-of-the-back holster and tucked two spare mags in front. He looked at Highlander. "Guard."

Highlander took a look at Ayala and sat resolutely on his haunches pointed at the door.

"Good boy." Bolan glanced at Chet who hustled to follow him out of the bungalow. "These friends of yours? Are they good people?"

"Hell, Terrell won the Distinguished Service Cross in Iraq. I've known him since I was young and stupid," Chet replied.

"And Libby?"

"Let's just say that short of this Zhong Fangyu asshole and you, there aren't too many more people whose bad side I don't want to be on. She's a woman in a man's world.

She fights dirty and has a mean streak. I've seen her take people down, plus when we were working cases, she could always go places we boys couldn't."

"Anything else I should know?"

"Yeah, she can hypnotize people."

"Really."

"Oh, yeah. I've seen it. You got someone who wants to talk? She can make it happen."

"I'm liking Libby already." Given that they were dealing with born-again Satan cultists, that might be an interesting skill set. Particularly on those death-sentenced people wanting to get out. "Any personal baggage between you two?" Bolan asked.

"Not that she didn't chop off at the ankles right quick," Chet admitted.

Bolan and Chet walked across the beach toward the bar. Playa Vista was a series of bungalows just north of Mazatlán. Privacy and quiet was their claim to fame. Their bungalow had a little pier for pleasure boats and the narco-sub was parked beneath it. A quarter mile up the beach lay the resort facility with a bar, restaurant and gym and a more substantial man-made marina. Bolan walked into the bar. It was summer and Playa Vista was doing good business, but he spotted Chet's friends instantly. Terrell was hard to miss. He was the only black, bald, built-like-an-NFL-linebacker badass in the establishment. He sat at one end of the bar wearing a 3XL Hawaiian shirt and shorts, and grinned from ear to ear while a couple of bikini and sarong-clad cougars hung on him and his every word. There was a lot of exposed flesh in the beach bar, but Bolan picked up Libby easily. She sat at the other end of the bar.

Libby was lanky. She had curves, but most of them had been sculpted onto her body in the gym. Bolan could tell at least two of those curves had been sculpted onto her with surgery. Her face was more striking than beautiful. She had a strong nose and chin, but warm lips and big green eyes softened her face. Her red hair was cut short around her head in a pageboy. Bolan suspected she wore a lot of wigs while working. The green men's dress shirt she wore with the sleeves rolled up and tied beneath her ribs brought out her eyes, and Bolan was pretty sure she was wearing a shoulder rig beneath it.

Bolan noted that between them they had the door and the terrace in a cross fire.

Terrell caught sight of Chet and disentangled himself. "Chet!"

The Bayou State boys bear-hugged each other like long lost brothers. "Terrell, this is Coop. Cooper, Terrell Smallhouse."

Bolan's hand disappeared in Terrell's paw. "Any friend of Chet's is a friend of mine."

Chet rolled his eyes. "I didn't say we were friends."

Terrell laughed again. "Well, any man who can beat Chet I wanna be on his good side."

"I didn't say he beat me," Chet protested. "I said he was better than me." Chet's brow darkened. "It's that Captain *Kung Fu Hustle* son of a bitch who beat me."

"'Bout time someone did." Smallhouse laughed.

Bolan retrieved his hand. "You're just about the happiest sniper I ever met."

"I'm not a sniper. I'm a designated marksman." Terrell pointed a sausage-sized finger for emphasis. "And there is a difference."

"Here he goes..." Chet sighed.

"You see, snipers slink around in the mud and the weeds, they're no-see-ums with a rifle." Smallhouse's finger came dangerously close to poking Bolan in the chest. At the last second the man happily jabbed himself with his thumb instead. "Designated marksmen fight from the front, supporting their little ducks."

Bolan was more than passingly familiar with both roles. "God bless them, one and all."

"Damn skippy!" Smallhouse agreed.

Libby approached the heaving sea of testosterone. In flip-flops she was pushing five-nine and looked well worth the climb.

"Coop?" Chet said. "Libby Oderkirk."

The woman looked at Bolan in open speculation. "Chet says you're the man."

"Chet gets it right once in a while," Bolan admitted.

The hint of a smirk ghosted across Oderkirk's lips. "Is he right about all this Satan stuff?"

"You know anything about it?" Bolan asked.

"Just what I've seen in the movies."

"Have you seen *The Exorcist? The Omen? Race with the Devil?*"

"I've been to the drive-in."

"As of now we're not ruling any of that out."

Oderkirk gave Chet a cold look. "Thanks for the invite, Chet."

"Hey!"

Smallhouse shook his massive head dismissively. "Don't matter what hoodoo they're up to. They all fall by rule Three-O-Eight."

The .308 was the caliber of U.S.-issue designated marksman weapon.

Oderkirk interrupted him. "Terrell and I are both legal-to-carry in Mexico, but we're going to need something heavier than sidearms."

Smallhouse nodded. "Definitely."

"Give me a list, anything and everything you could possibly want, weapons, armor, gear. Sky's the limit.

"I know you're both doing this for Chet, but whatever they pay you per day at the agency, I'm going to pay triple, plus bonuses."

Oderkirk's smile broke out like the sun. "Thanks for the invite, Chet!"

"What I need now," Bolan said, "is for you two to get back in position and cover us. We're expecting Captain *Kung Fu Hustle* in about five minutes. If he's half as good as I think he is, he'll pick you out of the crowd at a glance, but that might be enough to keep him from getting froggy if I end up telling him something he doesn't want to hear."

"We got your six." Smallhouse and Oderkirk got back on station. Bolan and Chet took a table in the middle of the bar and ordered a round of beers. Zhong walked in exactly on the half hour. He had traded his power suit for a black batik-print silk shirt and blindingly white linen shorts. The expensively tailored casual clothes made his physique even more imposing. He was carrying a black leather laptop case.

"Son of a bitch really does look like Superman by way of Shanghai," Chet muttered.

"He's Hong Kong connection, all the way," Bolan said. "But I bet he operates a lot on the mainland."

Zhong walked over and took a seat. He shot the waitress a startlingly friendly smile and ordered a French 75 cocktail, then turned the stone-Buddha look back on for Bolan and ignored Chet completely. Bolan didn't see any reason to bandy words. Barring certain names and addresses he told Zhong the story of Tijuana, Mexicali, the events in the Laguna Salada, the battle for the island and its aftermath, including the trip on the narco submersible. Zhong listened to it all while staring into the middle-distance without asking any questions.

He turned his gaze back on Bolan. "With minor variations Qu's account of the affair on the island is in line with yours."

"Two different warriors will see different things in the same battle, and Qu is a good man."

Zhong grunted at the wisdom of both statements. "That is why I am willing to accept the more, incredulous, elements of your narrative, for the nonce."

Zhong seemed to have a fetish for flexing his English vocabulary.

Chet was less impressed. "For the nonce? These guys are straight up for Satan and you had better start wrapping your melon around that."

Zhong broke character again and accepted his drink from the waitress with a grin and left her giggling as she left. Depending on your preferred base liquor a French 75 was just about the most expensive gin and tonic or brandy and soda you could order in a bar. Zhong ignored the drink and shook his head vaguely in dismissal at Chet. "I do not subscribe to Christian mythology, nor is any aspect of it in this affair of any interest to me."

Chet bristled again.

Zhong ignored him.

Bolan sipped his beer. "It doesn't matter whether you believe in it or not. They do, and it's a valuable insight into their motivation."

Zhong chewed that over. "I will admit there may well be some merit in that line of thinking."

Bolan held up his beer in a toast. "Your English elocution is brilliant."

For half a heartbeat a smile of pleasure tried to break

out across Zhong's face. He instantly crushed it down again. "Thank you."

He opened his case and laid a hatchet in the middle of the table. It was a simple tool. The head was painted black against rust. The edge was dull gray and the handle a simple piece of hickory. It was the product of a village blacksmith rather than any Chinese industrial tool line. Like the Ninja throwing star or the sawed-off shotgun in Sicily, it had been the trademark weapon of Chinese hit men since time out of mind.

"As I said previously, Juan-Waldemar Wang and Miss Sarah Tsui were people of some consequence. I am required to bury this within the skull of those responsible for their deaths."

"Cool." Bolan took another swallow. "But I'm in command."

Zhong didn't blink. "Unacceptable."

"Then we are rivals with the same goal. Good luck, but if at any point I detect you endangering my line of inquiry into this matter, I'll kill you."

Zhong regarded Bolan for several long, dispassionate moments. "I appreciate your candor."

"I'm in command. I tell you to take point? You take point. I tell you to watch my six? You watch my six. I tell you to stay behind and watch the prisoner? You're babysitting. Got it?"

"Very well, but once we have flushed out those responsible, I reserve the right to light out on my own and kill them my way."

"Fair enough, but I still stand by my previous statement."

"Noted." Zhong sipped his drink. "I fear I have little to add to our line of inquiry at the moment. How do you believe the enemy shall proceed next?"

Bolan had been giving that a lot of thought. "If they know we're here, which I'm betting they do, then like us they've had seventy-two hours to play with. Qu dropped a dime on you, and meantime we picked up two new team members—"

"So I noticed."

"I think if it happens it's going to happen soon."

"By your description each of their attacks had grown more bold than the last. You believe they will attack in overwhelming force?"

"They've tried that, bigger and badder each time and, despite our losses, we've kicked their ass and our latest prisoner is still alive."

"So what do you believe will be their next stratagem?"

Bolan leaned back in his chair. "Well, this time around, rather than a platoon of drug soldiers or manufacturing a magic show, I'd send someone like you."

Zhong raised his glass and his smile was genuine.

CHAPTER THIRTEEN

Ayala cringed beneath Zhong's scrutiny. The triad hard-
man had brought along a genuine Chinese doctor with two
suitcases full of medical supplies. The sniper's forearm had
been professionally set. Bolan had shattered that forearm
himself, and he would have sworn it would have required
a quiver of steel pins to put it back together. The doctor
had put the bones back in place, bound them, put the arm
in an air cast and sworn the sniper would regain full use
of it with time. Villaluz's dislocation wasn't good, but the
doctor had seen far worse. He had shoved it back into position, manipulated it and told the inspector to go easy on it
for a week or two. Qu's stump had been sewn shut, and he
was sporting a cup over it that Bolan was pretty sure was
the lining of some endangered animal's interior.

Everyone else had had their sprains and aches manipulated and their bruises liberally linimented.

Even the worst off among them was flying at least half-
mast and while they waited for Armageddon or the knife
in the night, attention was beginning to focus on their
charge.

"I can make him talk," Zhong ventured. Zhong had
buried his hatchet in the kitchen cutting board and left it
there. Ayala's eyes flicked to it in dread.

"I'm sure you can," Bolan said. "But can you get him
to say the things I want, or the things he thinks I want."

"It is a conundrum."

Bolan walked into the kitchen where Oderkirk was brewing another round of Mexican coffee. She was grinding her own nutmeg. "You think you can hypnotize him?"

"Ayala?" Oderkirk pursed her perfect lips in thought. "He's a sniper."

"That takes him off the susceptibility list?"

"No, it means he is capable of acute one-point concentration, which actually puts him at the head of the class."

"And?"

"And he's a member of a cult, which shows he's susceptible to suggestion. He's also on drugs, which always helps. He's scared out of his mind, and scared people are usually desperate to talk."

Bolan nodded. "So you own him."

"We do, except we've got one big hurdle." Oderkirk raised a vaguely taunting eyebrow. "Can you guess what that is, bright eyes?"

"We're the enemy. We put him in the situation he's in, and you can't hypnotize an unwilling subject."

"Check out the cranium on Cooper!" The woman grinned. "You're going to have to get me a ticket in."

"Pain," Bolan said.

Oderkirk's big greens flared. "Letting that guy Zhong go lumberjack on the subject will not be conducive to relaxation and one-point concentration."

"No, I agree, but doesn't hypnosis help with pain management?"

Oderkirk nodded thoughtfully. "Yeah, not always, but it's been useful in a lot of pain-management regimens."

"Good. Our boy Ayala is in a lot of pain despite the medication." Bolan glanced at the woman's Mexican coffee fixings. "Bring the man a cup of joe, go heavy on the

Kahlua, then tell him you can help him with the pain if he lets you."

"Ah, the old mothering instinct, nice."

"I'd call it a sugarcoated bit of Stockholm syndrome goodness, but yeah, charm him."

Oderkirk began mixing drinks. "I own him." She brewed up a triple, wrote a few things on a notepad and wandered into the living room. Ayala sat on the couch under the uncomfortable scrutiny of Highlander and a triad assassin. Bolan watched as she shooed away both canine and killer and gave Ayala the warming drink. She ran a hand across his brow and her big green eyes stared into his with infinite sympathy. Bolan could just barely hear her saying solicitous things very softly in Spanish. Ayala was a warrior, but he was mentally, physically and emotionally at the end of his rope, and there were just some things a beautiful woman could bring to that party that no one else could. Bolan smothered the smile on his face as Corporal Ayala began crying.

Bolan had to turn around when Oderkirk began crying with him. The woman was good. The soldier quietly spoke into his tactical radio. Terrell Smallhouse and a very large rifle were on the roof, and Grimaldi and the inspector were watching the front and back respectively. "Keep sharp. Libby's going to try something with the prisoner."

The current watch all came back in the affirmative.

Highlander stared up at Bolan and sighed at all the human goings on. Bolan pulled a wad of shredded beef from an uneaten taco and squeezed it into a ball. "Sit."

Highlander sat.

"Down."

Highlander went prone.

"Settle."

Highlander rolled onto his side, his eyes never wavering from the meat.

"Release."

Highlander snap-rolled back onto his haunches.

"Wait for it…" Bolan cautioned and placed the meat-wad on the bridge of Highlander's snout. The dog vibrated as he stared at it cross-eyed. "Get it!"

Highlander did a head-fake and snapped the treat out of the air.

"Good boy," Bolan said.

Highlander rolled onto his back and squinted his eyes in pleasure as Bolan scratched his stomach. The whimpering in the living room continued for about another five minutes. Then Oderkirk called softly from the living room. "Cooper?"

Bolan came out and handed Ayala a fresh brew. He had gulped the first one. The sniper was on pain meds, Kahlua and a liberal dose of sympathetic redhead. He looked about ready to spill. Oderkirk had turned off the lights and lit some candles. Chet and Zhong had pulled a fade into the shadows behind Ayala. The woman looked up at Bolan. "I want to do something for the young man's pain."

"If it keeps him quiet and comfortable—" Bolan shrugged "—I don't care."

Oderkirk produced a U.S. "Walking Liberty" silver half-dollar like a magic trick. It had been polished mirror bright, and she made it walk across the top of her left fingers with genuine sleight of hand. Ayala's teary and somewhat glazed gaze followed the coin. Oderkirk brought the coin to a rest between her thumb and first two fingers. The coin gleamed like quicksilver as she raised it level with Ayala's eyebrows about a foot and a half away to make him look slightly up at close range. She spoke so quietly in Spanish that Bolan couldn't make out her words, but he could guess.

Bolan knew a little about hypnosis, and Oderkirk was using the classic eye-fixation induction method. The closeness and height of the coin was calculated to induce maximum eyestrain while at the same time her voice and the concentration induced relaxation everywhere else. The half-dollar slowly began to turn between her fingers and in time with the cadence of her voice. One second flashing the Lady Liberty, the next the perched Bald Eagle. You could set a metronome to her voice and the achingly slow revolutions of the coin.

Ayala's eyelids fluttered. Oderkirk said something, and his entire body visibly relaxed. Chet shot Bolan a silent thumbs-up from the corner. Zhong watched the proceedings with keen interest. The coin kept turning.

Oderkirk spoke quietly. "How is your arm?"

Ayala's eyelids fluttered again. "Better, thank you."

"The doctor says it is healing fine. You will have far less pain when you wake up."

"Thank you."

"I want you to relax. Let any pain or anxiety fade. I want you to close your eyes and relax completely."

Ayala's eyes closed and he sagged into the cushions.

Oderkirk looked at Bolan and silently handed him a note that read "He's ready." Bolan nodded.

The woman spoke soothingly. "When I say the word *orange*, you will wake up relaxed and refreshed. Do you understand?"

Ayala spoke very quietly but clearly. "Yes."

"You still seem tense. Is there anything else I can do for you?"

"No."

"Are you frightened?"

"Yes."

"Can I help?"

"No." Ayala twitched. "He comes."

"Should we let you go?"

"It does not matter. He comes. He comes for us all."

"Who comes?"

Ayala twitched again. "Him."

"Him?"

Ayala shuddered in his somnambulistic state. Oderkirk shot Bolan a look. Even the deepest hypnotic state was precarious. People wouldn't answer questions they didn't want to already, and being told to do something they didn't wish to was usually enough to snap them right out of it. Then again they were running out of time and ideas and really didn't have much to lose. Bolan shot Oderkirk the sign of the horns.

She nodded and addressed Ayala. "You mean the Beast," she said. "*La Bestia*. He—"

Ayala went into violent convulsions.

Libby was shocked. "Oh, my God!"

Bolan stepped forward. "This normal?"

"No!" She put her hands on Ayala's shoulders. "I need pillows around his head so he doesn't hurt himself!"

"Snap him out of it!" Bolan ordered.

"Ayala!" Oderkirk had lost the soothing edge of her voice and it was rising in panic. "Ayala!" Chet and Zhong stepped forward to restrain him.

The room shook as Bolan's voice boomed like a Mexican drill sergeant. *"¡Corporal Ayala, atención!"*

Oderkirk yelped as Ayala suddenly sat upright. Chet and Zhong involuntarily stepped back. Ayala's head snapped around at Bolan. The sniper's dark brown eyes were as black as a shark's in the candlelight and just as dead as he stared at Bolan. His face split into a smile wide enough to expose his gums. Ayala's voice dropped an octave as he spoke in perfect, unaccented English.

"Corporal Ayala isn't here right now."

Oderkirk screamed and recoiled off the couch. Zhong's eyes flew wide. Highlander backed up growling in alarm. Chet slapped leather for his Magnum. "Son of a bitch!" Zhong had reflexively fallen into a fighting stance, and his fingers were curved into kung-fu tiger-claw conformations. Bolan's Beretta was already out and aimed at Ayala's face. A cold ugly feeling moved up Bolan's spine as he looked in Ayala's empty eyes over the front sight of the machine pistol.

Corporal Ayala wasn't home.

The click of the 93-R's selector lever was very loud as Bolan thumbed it from semiauto to 3-round burst. "Who is?"

Ayala's smile strained into a Joker-like rictus. The effort of maintaining that death grimace made the tendons in the man's neck stick out like bowstrings. Only the letter *M* forced his lips to move as he spoke. "You named me."

Bolan's skin crawled.

"I came."

Bolan looked at Oderkirk. She had scuttled all the way back to the wall. A Jericho automatic pistol had appeared in her hands. The laser sight in the grip was painting a red dot right over Ayala's heart. "Libby?"

Oderkirk was rattled. "Jesus…"

"Cannot help you," the thing on the couch intoned.

"That tears it!" Chet was wild eyed as he cocked his .357 and pointed it at the back of Ayala's skull. "Boss, you say the word and by God I'll pop goddamn Captain Howdy's head like a cyst!"

Bolan held up a restraining hand. "Hold that thought."

Zhong spun on his heel, went into the kitchen and came back with the triad hatchet in hand. "My way?"

"Hold that one, too." It took a lot of effort, but Bolan maintained his poker face as he returned the dead gaze of the thing on the couch without blinking. In the Caribbean, Asia, and a few other places he had seen examples of possession and trance. Most could be explained away, a few were anomalous. Conversations with Old Scratch à la *The Exorcist* was a new one even to him. Bolan put his initial revulsion away. He had declared his War Everlasting against evil long ago. If he had just met it at the source? Then so be it.

Smallhouse's voice exploded across the tactical radio. "What the hell, Cooper! I heard Libby scream!"

"Stay on station. We're under control."

Terrell wasn't buying it. "Lib?"

Oderkirk steadied down and clicked on her radio. "I'm all right. Stay on station, big man."

"Copy that." Smallhouse wasn't happy, but he clicked off.

Bolan continued the face-off with whatever was up with Ayala. The corporal hadn't blinked once since the visitation had started. Neither had Bolan, but his eyes were starting to sting. "You want Ayala?"

"This one already belongs to me."

"So why don't you come and take him?"

"I am already here."

"How about I have Mr. Zhong cut you out of him?"

Zhong took a step forward and showed Satan the ax. "I start with your toes and work up, demon."

The skull grin turned up another impossible notch. Ayala looked like a ventriloquist dummy whose jaw was about to snap off.

"You are all going to die. You are all going to burn. You are all going to be with me."

Chet was shaking. "Coop…?"

Smallhouse spoke low and urgent across the tactical radio. "I don't know what the hell you're doing down there, Coop, but I got movement in the trees!"

Bolan struck like a snake. He drove the butt of the Beretta between Ayala's empty eyes like the bolt at the end of the slaughter chute. Ayala went limp like a bull giving up the beef. Satan seemed to go with him. Bolan holstered his pistol. "Chet! Tie him up!" Bolan took a clone of the SCAR-H rifle he had used in Tijuana out of a rifle case and draped a bandolier of munitions across his shoulder and clicked on his tactical radio.

"Here they come."

CHAPTER FOURTEEN

"Well, why aren't they coming!" Chet asked.

Bolan noticed Chet's accent got thicker the more upset he got. They had been sitting in static defensive position in the bungalow for the past four hours and he felt Chet's pain. It was closing in on 4:00 a.m. Bolan shrugged from his position by the door to the back patio facing the trees. The bungalow was thirty yards from the beach and about a hundred from the trees. "Because they're screwing with us, Chet."

"Well, they're doing a jim-dandy job of it, too!"

Bolan scanned the tree line again. "Did you just say jim-dandy?"

"Goddamn it…" Chet glared outward over his gleaming shotgun. "So how'd you like Libby's hypno-therapy session turning into a séance?"

"I didn't care for it at all," Bolan admitted.

"You ever seen anything like that?"

"Not exactly."

"You buying it?" Chet asked.

"I don't know. What do you think?"

Chet stewed. "You said they went Mad Max on you and Bree in Tijuana?"

"Yeah."

"And full-on kamikaze when Villaluz took you into the Laguna Salada?"

"Yeah."

"They used submersibles against us on the island."

"So?"

"So what do you think they're going to do here in Mazatlán? Tactical nuke?"

"Whatever it is, they've had time to plan it." Bolan clicked his tactical radio. "What have you got big man?"

"I don't got nothing." Smallhouse was on the roof with a U.S. Marine Corps Designated Marksman Rifle with a night-vision scope on top and the Barrett just in case he needed something even bigger. "But I'm with Chet. It's too quiet out there. I don't like it."

Bolan called back to the living room. "Libby?"

Ayala was still on the couch, but he was bound and gagged and Oderkirk was babysitting him. Besides her Jericho automatic pistol, she now had her requested Micro Galil assault rifle across her knee. "You dropped him hard. He's still lights out but his breathing seems regular and nothing is leaking out of his eyes or ears."

"Inspector?"

Villaluz reported from the terrace facing the sea. "I have no movement, amigo. Unless they have frogmen the submersible remains unmolested beneath the dock."

Bolan wouldn't put it past them. "Jack?"

"North flank clear."

"Zhong?" Bolan called.

"South flank clear." Bolan heard Zhong talk to Qu in Cantonese and the assassin came forward. He dropped to a knee beside Bolan. "This has gone on too long. Allow me a perambulation around the perimeter."

Besides loving esoteric words in the English language, Zhong appeared to have a 10 mm Glock fetish, and had a briefcase full of them. He had assembled a Glock with a snap-in shoulder stock and add-on rails for a red-dot sight up top and a tactical light below. He carried another

10 mm Glock on his hip, and Bolan had seen him tuck a compact version into an ankle holster. Zhong was ready to top-ten someone into oblivion, if he didn't chop their head off with the hatchet tucked into the back of his belt or tiger-claw their throat out first.

"How you going to manage that?" Bolan inquired.

"Qu told me of your aqueous attack on the submersibles. I will use the bungalow for cover and go straight into the surf. I will swim a kilometer up the coast, insert into the trees and make my way back." Zhong gave a reluctant grunt. "Like you, I will take the parvenu Chet with me. Together, he and I will sweep south and flank the enemy. We flush them out and you attack directly."

It wasn't bad. Bolan had been considering that exact plan himself.

"You hear that, Chet?"

"Yeah, I heard." Chet made a disgusted noise of resignation from the next room. "And if you say the word, I'll go with him."

Zhong moved back and spoke quick words to Qu. Chet spoke lower and reluctantly to Bolan. "Uhh, Coop? Do you—"

"Parvenu means upstart or pretender," Bolan finished.

"Son of a bitch…" Chet muttered. "Zhong! Let's go light up these satanic sons a bitches!"

The enemy lit up first.

Smallhouse's voice came across the tactical radio. "Oh, my stars… You see that?"

You could hear Chet's jaw drop. "Oh, hell…"

Oh, hell was right.

The tree line became a Klansman cross-burning extravaganza. Biblical execution-size crosses lit up like a line of soldiers among the trees. The even more unpleasant aspect of it was that the crosses were upside down. "Everyone hold position!" Bolan ordered.

The soldier's eyes narrowed over the sights of his rifle. He counted five fiery atrocities. He didn't think Satan had a flaming cruciform in store for Highlander, but even barring the dog they were still three abominations short. Bolan did some fast math and the equation told him two things. The local Mazatlán Mephistopheles battalion had either run out of lumber, or they didn't know about Zhong, Oderkirk and Smallhouse. The people outside were all about getting their terror correct, and when Ayala had gone empty vessel, Oderkirk and Zhong had been in the room, and Satan didn't seem to have noticed.

Bolan spoke through the tactical radio. "Terrell, you got our firebugs in sight?"

"No, man! I didn't see anyone. Their shit just lit up by its lonesome as far as I could see. They got some kind of sleight-of-hand pyrotechnic ass-holiness going on."

Bolan was willing to give the bad guys the benefit of the doubt when it came to a little bit of pyrotechnic ass-holiness. If it was El Diablo's doing, he was going to have to step up and prove it.

Satan stepped up and the night erupted into tongues of hell fire arcing out of the trees.

Bolan shouted across the tactical radio. "Terrell, get out of there!"

Three streamers of liquid firehosed against the side of the bungalow. Bolan jerked back as the fire spattered the glass in front of him. Even with the doors and windows closed he could smell the reek of jellied jet fuel.

The enemy had flamethrowers.

Bolan's window went opaque in a curtain of orange fire and black smoke. He heard Smallhouse's boots slamming on the roof overhead and a second later there was a crash as he jumped and fell through the patio picnic table out back. "Terrell!" Bolan shouted.

"Motherfuckers!" Smallhouse responded.

The entire inland side of the bungalow became a wall of fire. The heat radiated through the glass of the windows and the French doors. The flames roared, and the heat pulsed into the house as the back wall took a second dousing. Bolan, Chet and Zhong were forced to retreat.

"Screw this!" Chet snarled. "We get in the submersible and extract!"

"No!" Bolan knew that was exactly what the enemy wanted. "Forward!"

Chet's voice went up a little. "You don't charge goddamn flamethrowers!"

"You don't run away from them, either!" Bolan shouted. "They want to drive us to the beach!" Despite the blast-furnace heat Bolan felt the cold certainty in his bones. "They're waiting for us to try it! We've got to take them out and take them out now!"

"He is right," Zhong said.

Chet waved his arm at the inferno before them. The adobe walls were turning into a brick oven. The French doors were a window into a solid mass of roiling flame. The wooden panes had turned black. "You wanna go through that!"

Smallhouse ran in breathlessly from his plunge to the patio. "The roof is on fire! We're—" He took a look at the inferno on the other side of the glass. "Jesus!"

The only way to break out of the trap was to go straight into its teeth. Bolan had done it before. The only problem this time was the trap was breathing fire. It was time to blow the fire out. Bolan reached into one of the goody bags the Farm had provided in Mazatlán. Bolan reached for the C-4. "Libby! Get Ayala up and ready to move!

Zhong, have Qu help her! Everyone else get back and get ready! Terrell, hang back! Most flamethrower units have three shots! We're attacking, and they'll have one salvo left! Kill the flame men! You understand! Kill the flame men!"

Smallhouse had just avoided being burned alive and jumped off a roof. His marksman's rifle was like an M-16 on steroids. He suddenly raised it like a holy talisman and his eyes narrowed in anger. "I got 'em!"

Bolan nodded. He got to work and worked fast. The standard U.S. military demolition charge was twenty pounds of high explosive, and he had one. Bolan clicked out his tactical knife and cut the block of C-4 down the middle to halve the charge. He inserted detonator pins and dropped the rest back in the satchel. Bolan checked the detonator pin and grabbed the remote, then slid the charge across the tiles. It bumped against the French doors. The plastic wrapping and tape around the bundle of blocks instantly began to blacken and burn.

"Fire in the hole!" Bolan retreated into the kitchen and pushed the red button on his detonator.

The walls shook like an earthquake and a searing hot gale blew through the bungalow, but the brimstone stench of burned high explosive was a godsend compared to the acrid burn of jellied aviation fuel. Bolan ran back. The French doors and a good section of wall had blown out and blown the clinging fire back with it. Bolan spun like a discus thrower and sent the second half of the charge out into the night. He hit the remote as the satchel hit the ground. Sand erupted sending ribbons of fire in all directions, but there were paths through the blaze. "Go! Go! Go!"

Bolan charged out of the bungalow. His rifle was shouldered, and he scanned for targets as he leapfrogged puddles of fire. Grimaldi was suddenly right next to him spraying his submachine gun from the hip-assault position. The crack of Zhong's carbine was unmistakable off to the right. It was joined by the blast of Chet's shotgun and the crack of the inspector's hot-loaded .38.

"Attack! Attack! Attack!" Bolan shouted. Highlander was a dark blur in the night as he streaked ahead toward the enemy. Bullets streaked back. Smallhouse's rifle sought muzzle-flashes. Between the bungalow burning out of control behind them and the burning crosses in the trees, the sands of Mazatlán glowed orange like the beachhead to hell.

Hell sent forth its fire once more.

The operator showed his lack of expertise. Instead of playing fire across the beach in an incendiary fan, he was aiming at individual targets as if he were shooting a rifle. He was wasting a lot of fuel shooting line of sight. It was cold comfort as the fire-snake hissed through the air trailing black smoke straight for Bolan, who hurled himself to one side. The fire started to follow but suddenly the snake shot vertical and lit the tree canopy as the gunner fell backward.

Smallhouse roared in triumph. "Got you, mother-fucker!"

A second spurt of fire shot from the trees, but it was suddenly cut short and fell into the no-man's-land like an act of premature immolation.

"Got you too!" Smallhouse whooped. Human screaming was wedded with canine fury in the tree line as Highlander got some of his own. Bolan closed the gap. He threw himself flat and rolled as a geyser of fire sought his life once more. He felt the sear as liquid fire dripped out of the stream and spattered across his leg. Bolan snarled and scooped up a fistful of sand. He slapped the sand across his thigh, smothering the puddle of clinging, coagulated fuel and scraping it away.

"Inspector!" Chet was screaming. "Inspector!"

Bolan looked back. Qu and Ayala were both flat on the ground, dead and folding up upon themselves like charred crickets as their bodies barbecued down to the bone. Someone had shoved Oderkirk aside, and she was screaming.

Inspector Villaluz was still on his feet, a flailing marionette of fire from head to toe, and screaming like the damned in hell.

Bolan brought his SCAR to his shoulder and punched three quick rounds into the burning officer's heart. The inspector collapsed dead and burning to the sand. Bolan spun. Despite the radiant heat all around, his heart went as cold as a grave. "Go! Go! Go!" Bolan hit the enemy line.

A man stood between two trees. He shrugged off the tanks of his flamethrower and drew the pistol strapped to his thigh to put a bullet in Highlander. His eyes flared wide as Bolan appeared before him. The would-be canine killer's eyes rolled back in his head as the butt of Bolan's rifle cracked across his jaw in passing and dropped him to the dirt. "Come on, boy!"

Highlander abandoned the dead man beneath his jaws and followed.

Bolan charged toward the sound of a turbo-diesel engine kicking over.

What Bolan guessed was a stolen Mexican military light armored vehicle was parked in a small clearing. The French-made VBL looked like a camouflaged, armored, Japanese SUV on steroids mounted on monster-truck tires. Gears ground. Unlike the majority of the Satanic suicide commandos Bolan had been meeting, the driver of the VBL seemed a bit panicked. The tailpipe suddenly shot blue smoke and all-terrain tires spit soil as the armored car leaped forward. Bolan pursued as the VBL smashed through saplings, his lungs burning as he raced after it. Once the VBL reached a road it would be gone.

Bolan sprinted flat-out to catch up as the all-terrain vehicle smashed against a sand berm nose-on and nearly went vertical. He leaped as the VBL began climbing the berm. The externally mounted tools, fuel cans and gear had been removed, but that left a lot of cleats and racks to grab for. Bolan seized steel and his boots bounced off the dirt. Whoever was inside had left the top hatch open. He clawed his way up the back of the vehicle as it crested the little hillock and began plunging downward.

A blond man with a short mustache and beard appeared in the hatch. He scowled at Bolan, smiled, and then pulled an automatic out of a shoulder holster.

"Attack!" Bolan shouted.

Highlander ran right up the back of the vehicle and sank his fangs into Blondie's throat. The killer collapsed back down the hatch. Highlander was firmly attached to his trachea and followed. Not surprisingly the VBL suddenly started swerving wildly. Bolan heaved himself up to the hatch and looked into the armored car's interior. Arterial blood had sprayed everywhere from Highlander's attack. Blondie had sunk into the passenger side foot well and Highlander was snarling and trying to get a renewed grip on his neck stem.

Bolan snaked down through the hatch on top of the driver.

"Gott im Himmel!" the driver shouted. The VBL went up on two wheels. Bolan slammed his fist into the side of the man's head again and again. The driver screamed as he tried to control the armored vehicle as it rolled down the hill and cover up at the same time. *"Nein! Nein—"*

The driver went limp beneath the battering ram of Bolan's fist.

The VBL rolled.

For the second time in a week Bolan was in the cabin of a vehicle that was going topsy-turvy. He ceased his assault on the wheelman and slammed his hands into the roof and rammed his boots down into both footwells. The driver wasn't belted in or particularly conscious, and Bolan grimaced as his weight hit him. The dog slammed into Bolan's chest and he spared an arm to hug Highlander tight. The VBL rolled twice and came right side up. The armored car came to stop against a tree. Highlander whimpered and squirmed in Bolan's grasp. He shoved the dog up the hatch, and Highlander didn't need any encouragement. He scrambled off the roof of the VBL and down the hood to find solid ground. Bolan clambered out and hopped down. He yanked open the driver's door and the driver nearly fell out. The Executioner's fist and the steering wheel had done a number on his face. He blinked out of a curtain of blood pouring down his torn scalp. He mumbled in German, *"Sie...sie sind—"*

Bolan slammed an uppercut into the man's jaw. The driver went as limp as a boned fish and fell out of the VBL to the ground. Highlander growled at him. Zhong and Grimaldi appeared at the top of the hillock. "You all right?" the pilot called.

"Give me a count!" Bolan called back.

"We got five dead bad guys back that away, three of them the flame-thrower gunners. One of the flame units has one squeeze left. There's a guy whose jaw you broke and there's another armored car back in the trees!"

Bolan looked over the VBL. The windshield was cracked and the interior was drenched with blood. "I have a prisoner! We load up the other vehicle and go!"

"Chet!" Grimaldi shouted back. "Bring the car around."

"And the man with the broken mandible?" Zhong inquired.

Bolan thought about that. A broken jaw would make an interview a little difficult. VBLs normally had a crew of three, and it was going to be a tight fit as it was. The bad guys had expected them to flee for the water. Bolan was betting that's where the main enemy concentration was, and since his team was a no-show they were most likely going to go D-Day on the Playa Vista beach any minute. "Leave him."

Zhong nodded. The second VBL crested the hill. Bolan strung the semiconscious German speaker over his shoulder in a fireman's carry. Chet leaned out of the VBL driver's window. "Coop! This rig has a police scanner, and it's blowing up! The *federales* are inbound, in force and they sound scared and pissed!"

Bolan flung open the passenger door and unceremoniously dumped his passenger into the seat. "Libby! You and Highlander in the back!"

Oderkirk was weeping. "The inspector...he pushed me out of the way. Of the fire...he—"

"He was a brave man, and he died going forward," Bolan acknowledged.

He jerked his head at the German. "Get in and get that guy tied up."

Bolan snapped his fingers. "Highlander!" The Doberman scrambled in and Oderkirk climbed in through the top. "Terrell, you're our gunner. Stand in the hatch." Terrell heaved his huge frame up the side and stood in the hatch. Bolan and Chet switched and Bolan slid behind the VBL's wheel. "Everyone else up top!"

Grimaldi, Chet and Zhong climbed onto the sloping sides of the VBL and grabbed cleats and tool racks.

Oderkirk had the prisoner bound, gagged and belted in. "What's the plan?" she asked.

Bolan pulled out his phone and enabled the GPS and mapping apps. "This rig is Mexican military and it's stolen. We can't afford to be seen in it."

"So what do we do?"

He killed the lights and pulled down his night-vision goggles. "We run dark, and we go cross-country. The Rio Presidio is about eight klicks south of here, and this ride is amphibious. We take the hill route and head upstream."

Bolan looked at the map inset on his phone. "There're three towns along the river, Villa Unión, El Robles and Siqueros. If we aren't followed we'll pick a town, ditch this rig and get some alternative transportation or arrange an extraction."

"Chet said these guys have followed you everywhere you've gone from desert sands to desert islands."

Bolan put the VBL into gear. "That's true."

"So what if they follow us now?"

"First, what they have is their sea assault, so they're going to have to unload, get in vehicles and follow us cross-country. Then we hit the Rio Presidio."

Oderkirk smiled tiredly. "And then we go amphibious and they have to find boats again to follow us."

"And?" Bolan prompted.

"And then we just drive up onto the shore and go cross-country again."

"That's the plan," Bolan said. "Then again I'm in a bad mood. We might just give them a fight."

Bolan called up the hatch. "Hang on! This is going to be a long ride, and rough one!"

He steered the VBL through the trees and aimed for the foothills.

CHAPTER FIFTEEN

Rio Presidio

It was a nice morning for a swim. The VBL puttered up-river under the power of its churning, over-sized tires at a steady 3.5 kph. The ride in the night had been hell. The eight klicks to the river had seemed like eighty, and it had involved some extensive offroading. Chet, Grimaldi and even Zhong had each been bounced off the back of the VBL repeatedly, and they had taken an unavoidable beating by tree branches. The sun was just starting to rise over Sinaloa and the VBL water-wheeled its way toward the golden glow growing behind the mountains. Bolan took his turn stretching out on the hood and made a call. "You got me on satellite, Bear?"

"We have your GPS signal, Striker," Kurtzman replied. His voice was a little quizzical as he looked at his screen back in Virginia. "Are you on the river or paralleling it?" Bolan enabled his camera and tracked it across the top of the VBL, Grimaldi, Smallhouse and Zhong and then the banks of the Presidio. The computer wizard made a bemused noise. "Interesting. Sitrep?"

"We lost Ayala." Bolan pointed his camera at the German through the passenger window. He sat bound and gagged, but he had stopped his whimpering and finally gone to sleep. "Picked up Fritz here."

"Fritz?"

"That's what we're calling him for now."

"Listen, the DEA is going ballistic over losing Agent Smiley, and FIA is ready to drop a litter of kittens. Inspector Villaluz hasn't checked in since—"

"Villaluz is dead."

Kurtzman's voice went flat. "That isn't good, Striker."

Bolan stared out across the Rio Presidio. "Tell me about it."

"Listen, somehow Hal is going to have to square this. How did—"

"They had flamethrowers."

Kurtzman was silent.

"That's how they got Villaluz and Ayala." Bolan sighed. "They burned Qu down, as well."

"All right, I'm going to try and see what the CIA can get me on what the locals are doing about what went down."

"We've been monitoring the law-enforcement band. So far they're calling the beach incident a battle between rival drug gangs. I don't know who's suppressing what, but there's been no mention of us and no mention of Satan or the Beast." Bolan looked over at two kids on the riverbank with fishing poles. They were jumping up and down and waving gleefully at the swimming car. Bolan waved back. "No APB on a missing VBL."

"I think you need to get out of Mexico," Kurtzman advised. "You keep getting slammed everywhere you go. And we keep losing people. Good people."

"I know." Bolan gazed across the water. "We need to stop playing defense. Chet was wondering if they were going to use a tactical nuke against us next. I'm not sure I'd put it past them."

"And?"

Bolan looked at the mapping app on his phone. The

dot representing their position was moving slower than the human eye could perceive. "We passed Villa Unión about an hour ago. El Robles is coming up and so is the sun. It's time to get off the river and ditch this ride. Can you arrange extraction?"

"Well…" Kurtzman was mildly reproachful. "Our best pilot happens to be sitting on top of a car in the middle of a river."

"I think the amphibious action threw the pursuit off slightly, but I need to get airborne. Mazatlán is infested with the enemy and we need to jump someplace new. The state of Sinaloa is full of cartel airstrips. Find me one, preferably with a plane on it."

"I'm on it."

Smallhouse's rumbled low from the hatch. "Somethin."

Bolan clambered up on the roof. "Can you get visual, Bear?"

Kurtzman grunted unhappily. "I have tracking on your signal but no eyes-on yet. Working on finding a satellite over your local with high resolution imaging and getting authorization."

"Get it ASAP, but keep finding me an airstrip your priority. I'll get back to you." Bolan took up his binoculars and looked where Smallhouse's designated marksman's rifle was pointing downstream.

"I make it two," Smallhouse stated.

Two speedboats were shadowing their progress upriver a little more than a klick back. Bolan made them for twenty-two-foot runabouts. The retro faux-wood construction implied they were tourist boats and probably stolen from one of the Mazatlán marinas. The VBL could do a max of 4.5 kph in calm water, and they were overloaded and heading upstream. Right about now a high school water polo team could chase them down. The pursuit disappeared as the VBL chugged around a shallow bend in the river.

Smallhouse momentarily lowered his rifle. "How you want to play it?"

The obvious answer was to take the current window of opportunity the bend in the river had provided and get their wheels on solid ground and leave the enemy behind. But Bolan was getting tired of running.

Chet echoed the sentiment up the hatch. "These sons of bitches need some payback!"

Smallhouse looked at Bolan hopefully. "Turn and fight?"

Bolan filled his lungs. "Hard to starboard, Chet, 180 degrees!"

"Oooh, yeah!" Smallhouse grinned. His voice rose happily as the VBL slowly swung around and picked up speed as it joined the current. "You want me to start the fun?"

"No, get down. Zhong and Jack, we're in the water. Grab yourself some bumper."

Smallhouse was crestfallen. "Then what do you want me to do?"

"First off hand me the flamethrower."

"Oooh, yeah!" Smallhouse folded his huge frame into the armored car's interior.

Bolan dropped off the side and joined Zhong and Grimaldi in the water. Four strokes brought him behind the VBL, and Bolan grimaced as he was forced to suck diesel fumes. Smallhouse handed down the flamethrower. Grimaldi and Zhong manhandled the flamethrower's pack straps onto a cleat and carefully handed Bolan the flame unit. His voice boomed in warning "Enemy reacquired! Here they come!" The big man's voice suddenly went wary. "Oh, shit! They've got machine guns!"

"Mounted?" Bolan asked.

"No, man! They're just slapped down across the dash!"

"Any other support weapons visible?"

"No! But they're all pigged up!" Smallhouse replied.

Pig was lingua franca for the M-60 general purpose machine gun in the U.S. military. "Get down! They're going to make a gun run! Let them do it! Let them think we've gone turtle and buttoned up! I'm going to nuke the starboard gunner! The rest of you hit the boat to port with everything you got when it passes!"

"Here they come!" Smallhouse called. The enemy outboards snarled as their drivers shoved the throttles full forward. Their machine guns opened up, and twin streams of bullets played over the VBL's armored hide. Bolan laid the vaguely riflelike flame unit across the VBL's rear fender. The Russian-made flamethrower had three tanks, each one good for one shot. Bolan pushed the selector to the third tank.

Chet shouted up through the hatch over the roar of the machine guns. "They're coming!"

Bolan leaned around the fender.

The runabouts roared in, spraying lead. The flamethrower's range was seventy meters. Bolan's target was at forty and closing. He gazed down the flame unit's crude sight and squeezed the trigger. The tank-pressurizing cartridge fired with a thump, the igniter pellet in the muzzle hissed into life and thickened jet fuel shot past the igniter pellet, lighting the high-pressure stream into a dragon's tongue of liquid fire. The stream hit the prow of the runabout, the impact creating a fireball. Bolan raised his aim slightly, and the fire smashed against the windshield and smashed over. He gave the enemy the last second of the burst directly amidships. The runabout shot past like a flaming comet and ran itself aground on the bank completely engulfed in flame. Bolan dropped the flame unit into the water and drew his pistol as the other boat flew past. They had no good way to traverse their M-60. Bolan and crew had no such problems. Grimaldi's MAC-10 ripped on full-auto and Zhong's 10 mm carbine slammed as fast as he could pull the trigger. Smallhouse's rifle began slapping out shots in rapid semiauto. Bolan shoved out his Beretta 93-R and punched 3-round bursts into the boat's stern. The enemy might have survived the barrage of pistol bullets and zoomed out of range, but Terrell Smallhouse lived up to his billing.

The marksman lowered his rifle. "All four hostiles down."

The boat swerved landward without a driver and brutally bounced off the roots of a willow tree hanging out over the water. The engine died and the boat bobbed among the roots. There was no sign of life in the open cockpit. Blood covered everything. The other boat sat stuck in the mud and was burning like a torch. "Chet, bring us around! Take us to the willow!"

The VBL turned midstream and achingly crawled its way upriver once more. The all-terrain tires grabbed mud in the shallows. Bolan, Zhong and Grimaldi dropped off the back and slogged their way to the enemy boat with weapons leveled. There was no need. The cockpit was a butcher's yard.

Grimaldi stated the obvious. "He's good."

Bolan turned back to the VBL. "Nice shooting."

Smallhouse nodded. "The designated marksman fights from the front. He supports his little ducks in their endeavors, however weird and wonderful those endeavors may be."

Bolan smiled wearily. "You'll do, Terrell."

"I do damn well actually," Smallhouse said, but he smiled at the compliment.

"Keep an eye out."

"Always do."

Bolan turned back to the boat.

All four men appeared to be Latino. They were all wearing civvies. The M-60 bore Mexican army stamps. The dead men bore gang tattoos, and they all bore the mark of the Beast behind their left ears. Their handguns were a hodgepodge of civilian semiautos. Zhong cradled his 10 mm carbine and kept an eye downriver. "Anything pertinent?"

"Nothing obvious." Bolan shook his head. "And we don't have the tools, time or qualified personnel to do any real forensics."

"And so?"

"And so we take that M-60 and we're out of here." Bolan trudged back up to the car and climbed on top. He took out his cell phone and punched a button. "Bear, tell me you have something for me."

Sierra Madre Occidental, Sinaloa

KURTZMAN HAD something for them. It required another fifty kilometers of cross-country driving with rotating shifts of people riding on top and taking the worst of inland Sinaloa's heat. With the VBL running on fumes and just short of sunset they came upon Kurtzman's gift. It was an airstrip, and two planes were parked on the tarmac. It also had a shack and a fuel station. The shack was a Vietnam-era U.S. military squad tent, but it had the slender gleaming spire of a radio antenna tower sticking up beside the chimney of a potbelly stove. The fuel station was a fuel truck parked next to a bunch of fuel drums, but the fact that they were operating so openly told Bolan that they had paid off the local police and military. The town of Concordia was just conveniently far enough away and with 4x4s, Road 40 was accessible to bring in supplies.

The VBL was parked behind a formation of rocks about 750 yards out. The team examined the airstrip through various optics. Bolan had counted four people coming in and out of the tent. One of them had a rifle, but they seemed to be on a very low state of alert. Drinking beer, smoking cigarettes and staying out of the sun seemed to be their biggest preoccupation.

Grimaldi nodded to himself. "The guy on the campstool playing solitaire is a pilot."

"Yeah?"

"Yeah, the other guys are bored out of their minds. He, on the other hand, is antsy. He wants to get in his plane and go. You can tell."

Bolan chalked it up as a pilot thing. He played his optics across the two planes in residence. "What about our ticket out of here?"

"Well, now!" Grimaldi was eyeing the larger of the two aircraft. "Socata TBM 700. That's a nice ride. The other is Cessna Skymaster. She's a grand old bird but she isn't going to get all of us out of these mountains."

Bolan eyed the larger, sleek single-engine turboprop. He counted four windows behind the cockpit. "Will it carry all of us?"

"Oh, hell, yeah. All six of us plus canine and captive, with leg room to spare."

Bolan configured his battle plan. "Chet, have you ever fired an M-60?"

"Wasn't my specialty, and it's been a while, but yeah."

"I want you in the hatch with the pig. Libby, you're

driving. All of you keep your phones on speaker mode. Zhong and I are going to go for a walk."

Smallhouse scowled. "What about me?"

"You and Jack are going to circle wide and secure our plane and the airstrip. You're also going to discourage anyone who makes a break for the skies."

"Gotcha."

"Libby, if any of these guys get past us and tries to run the other way, you sic Highlander on them. Use the word *fetch* instead of *attack*."

Libby nodded. "Right."

Bolan figured as an assassin Zhong had some skills at sneaking up on people. "Let's go for a walk. Don't kill anyone unless you have to."

Zhong nodded and the soldier and the assassin began making their way toward the airstrip. The sun was starting to go down, and Bolan and Zhong approached out of the long shadows. The sound of Tejano music coming out of a boom box hid what little sound they made. The pilot playing solitaire was wearing an MP3 player and oblivious to all but his boredom and his game. The other three men were back in the tent. Bolan and Zhong put the tent between themselves and the preoccupied pilot and literally walked right up. Bolan stepped in front of the pilot, Zhong behind him. The man looked like a Mexican weatherman gone casual. He was TV handsome with perfect teeth and not a hair out of place despite the heat. He looked up from his cards at Bolan, looked at his watch, and looked at Bolan again. "You're early for once."

"No." Bolan corrected. "I'm right on time."

"No, you're…" The pilot looked around quickly. "Where did you come from?"

Bolan pointed back at the VBL. Chet waved over his weapons.

The pilot goggled. "Oh, shit, listen—" The pilot suddenly found himself staring down a machine pistol.

The man with the rifle walked out of the tent. "*Que pasa*— Hey!"

Zhong's thrust kick sent the rifleman flying back into the tent as if he had wings. Zhong walked in after his victim. Bolan smiled amiably at the pilot as a rapid series of meaty thudding noises and one gasp came from within the tent. Zhong stepped back out and made a show of brushing some dust off one shoulder. The pilot shrieked as Zhong checked behind both of his ears. Zhong shook his head. "No mark, and neither those within."

"Status?" Bolan asked.

"They'll live."

Bolan looked at the pilot. "You're a pilot, aren't you?"

The pilot blinked. "How did you know?"

"You want to get in your plane and go." Bolan shrugged. "I can tell."

The pilot gaped. Bolan waved Oderkirk in, and the VBL began rolling forward. "So, what's your name, flyboy?"

"Nazareno." The pilot swallowed with difficulty as he stared up the barrel of the 93-R. "My friends call me Naz. I—" Nazareno suddenly noticed the door to his plane was open and a black man was standing beside it with a big rifle at port arms. Nazareno's shoulders sagged.

"When is company coming?" Bolan asked.

The man stared at the tips of his boots in misery. "After sundown."

Bolan spoke into his phone. "What do we have, Jack?"

"Good news is we got a Socata TBM 700 fueled and ready to go."

"Bad news?"

"They removed all the passenger seats and replaced them with what looks like 250 kilos of coke."

Nazareno sagged in his seat. The VBL rolled up. Chet jumped out of the top with the M-60 in the hip-assault position. Oderkirk kicked open her door and Highlander leaped out. He trotted up to Nazareno, sniffed him, instantly perceived who was the lowest in the pecking order and growled at him.

The pilot just held his head in his hands.

"You work for the Beast, Naz?" Bolan asked.

The pilot flinched and instinctively crossed himself. "Shit, no!"

"I believe you." Bolan took a look around the perimeter and spoke into his phone. "Jack, unload the Socata and take a can of fuel from the truck. Burn the H. Libby, give him a hand."

Nazareno's head sagged back into his hands. "Aw..."

"Chet, get some fuel and burn out the VBL. I don't want to leave any evidence."

"You got it, boss."

"Terrell, when they're done, blow the fuel truck."

You didn't need an open line to hear Smallhouse laughing. Lighting things on fire and blowing them up were near and dear to every soldier's heart. Bolan's team went to work. Individually wrapped kilo-sized packages of coke began sailing out the Socata's door. Smallhouse and Chet walked over to the fuel truck and began filling cans.

"Uh..." Nazareno began unhappily.

"Yes?" Bolan asked.

"You don't wanna do this."

"I don't?"

"No, man. You don't."

"Whose coke is it?"

"Federation Car— Oh, shit!" Nazareno rolled his eyes as he realized he was talking too much.

"Federation Cartel," Bolan finished. "And who are they taking possession from? The Colombians?"

"Aw…who do you think, man!"

Chet and Smallhouse came back. Smallhouse was pouring a thin stream of fuel to make a fuse. He took out a lighter and lit it with a grin. "Fire in the hole." There was a little poof noise and fire rushed down the one-hundred-foot rivulet back to the truck. Grimaldi and Oderkirk had piled the coke in a loose pyramid. The Stony Man pilot taxied the Socata away while Oderkirk poured gas on the blow. Moments later, Nazareno jumped as the fuel truck blew sky-high. The packages of coke were blackening and oozing black smoke into the air.

"Aw…c'mon!" Nazareno shouted. "I'm dead! You know that? Dead! You just killed me! Why don't you just shoot me right now?"

Bolan extended his Beretta. "You want me to?"

Nazareno flinched backward. "Aw, man! I'm just a pilot!"

"I think you have bad taste in passengers, Naz. And even worse discernment when it comes to cargo."

Zhong suddenly lifted his head and stared into the middle distance. "Discernment…"

Nazareno blinked at the Asian assassin.

Bolan shrugged. "Don't mind him, he just notched himself up a new noun."

Nazareno stared at nearly six feet of redheaded executive protection as Oderkirk walked up. His incredulousness grew as Smallhouse pulled the bound and gagged German out of the armored car, heaved him over his shoulder like a sack of potatoes and began marching him to the plane. The drug pilot looked at Highlander and flinched as the dog growled at him. He finally looked back at Bolan. "Man, who are you guys?"

"We're the good guys. Who are you?"

"I'm just the pilot."

"You keep saying that."

Chet dropped the emptied the fuel can down the VBL's hatch and leaped down. He lit a wadded rag and shot the three-pointer. There was a whump noise and flames began crackling behind the windshield. Chet sighed. "Gonna miss the old girl."

Nazareno visibly collected himself. "Mister? They're gonna kill me. Between Federation and the Colombians I'm dead anywhere south of the Rio Grande."

Bolan looked hard at Nazareno. It took a certain amount of guts and skill to become a pilot. He had met many who were fools, but few who were cowards. "You want a job?"

Nazareno gazed sadly at his Socata. "You already have a plane."

"Actually—" Bolan nodded at the Cessna "—I have two."

CHAPTER SIXTEEN

Berlin

The Beast reclined in his chair. The room was black on black with black leather furniture. He steepled his huge, scarred hands and contemplated the strange unfolding of events. The Beast wasn't pleased with them. The Americans used the term "blood and treasure" as a metaphor for the expenditure of men, money and matériel in warfare. He had parted with far too much blood and treasure in Mexico. The Beast regarded one of his bloodiest treasures. The man standing before him was huge. Not pumped up like a bodybuilder or an American football player. He was quite simply an oversize human being. He was well over two meters tall and had to be running at least 130 kilograms. Arms like fire hoses were crossed over a chest like a barrel. If anything, Bogac Krom bore a disturbing resemblance to Popeye's nemesis, Bluto. Right down to the shaggy black hair and beard. Anchor tattoos and a Greek fisherman's hat would have been frivolous excess.

The huge Turk shrugged and spoke in guttural German. "It would be best if I went to Mexico."

It was a very tempting offer, but Krom's propensities and the fear they inspired were far more important in Berlin at the moment. The Beast considered the other man in the room. Meinrad Gerwulf was the mighty Turk's polar opposite. He was a half a head shorter, but that still made him a big man by anyone's standards. His pinstripe silk suit was immaculate. Every single spike of his naturally platinum blond hair was artfully in place. As opposed to Krom's ogrelike mass, Gerwulf was as sleek as a panther. Krom was a brute. Gerwulf was a sadist and a sociopath who was always looking for a new distraction.

The Beast nodded at him. "Meinrad."

"Ya?" Gerwulf asked.

"The situation in Mexico desires resolution. It desires rectification."

"Rectification?" Gerwulf raised a mildly intrigued frost-blond eyebrow and savored the word. "How shall I proceed?"

"I believe Rudi is still alive."

"I am not surprised. Americans are too weak to kill a helpless enemy."

"Yet we have reason to believe not all of these desperados misbehaving in Mexico are Americans."

Gerwulf's pale eyes became serious. "By Satan's grace we had the Mexicali tongs cowed. Somehow the American gave them backbone, and somehow the deaths of Herr Wang and Fraülein Tsui have filled the Chinese swine with further resolve. This intervention of the Hong Kong triads is an unwelcome development."

The Beast inclined his head a fraction. "And how would you proceed, Meinrad?"

"I would say we should proceed with cat's paws. In their efforts to escape, these impudent slaves have attacked a Federation Cartel airstrip and burned a huge consignment of their cocaine. We know where they are. To inform the cartel where and how they can exact their revenge would only add to your prestige. Let their bully boys resolve the Rudi situation, and let them rectify these who vex our master."

The Beast regarded Krom. "What say you?"

Krom rumbled grudgingly from deep in his chest. "The quince is clever."

Gerwulf acknowledged the backhanded compliment with the barest of nods. "Shall I see to it?"

The Beast nodded. "Yes. Go at once."

"Very well." Gerwulf walked away sighing to himself. "Mexico, in June. Whatever shall I wear?"

The Beast turned to Krom as Gerwulf left the room. "And what are you thinking, Bogac?"

"I am thinking I am glad he is on our side." The Turk scratched his beard warily. "That one frightens even me."

Bolsón de Mapimí, Durango

THE SKYMASTER climbed into the night. Bolan watched as Grimaldi waggled the wings in farewell. Nazareno scratched his head. "Where are they going?"

"Not far," Bolan replied.

Nazareno looked around at the empty, high desert. "Not far from here is nowhere, amigo."

"I know." Bolan nodded and walked back to the mission. Kurtzman had gotten his imaging satellite and found them another place to perch. Bolan wanted someplace secluded, and where they could see the enemy coming from a long way. The abandoned mission fit the bill. It was little more than a tiny church with an attached cottage, but it had an adobe wall enclosure to provide cover. The mission also had a little belfry, and Smallhouse and his rifle were currently encamped on top.

The roads were dirt and had nearly torn off the Socata's wheels on landing. Grimaldi had managed to taxi the plane behind the mission, and he wasn't entirely sure he could get it back to the road again. The nearest village was ten miles away. The gangsters at the airstrip had had an ice chest with beer and sandwiches that Bolan had confiscated, but they were going to have to make a trip into town in the morning to get supplies. The soldier went in and contemplated the pile of weapons on the sawhorse table. They were running low on ammo. On the plus side they had confiscated one M-16 and three Glock pistols from the men at the airstrip.

"You shoot, Naz?" Bolan asked.

"Yes. I mean, I have shot a gun, not much, but I have."

Bolan picked up two of the Glocks and checked their loads. He handed them to Nazareno. "Here, each one has seventeen rounds."

The pilot looked at the loaded pistol in each of his hands. "Thanks."

Bolan looked at the prisoner. He sat in one of the ancient pews tied but no longer gagged, staring at nothing. "Libby, how's our boy?"

"He accepted half a sandwich and half a beer, but he was pretty robotic about it, and he still isn't talking." Oderkirk gave Bolan a leery look. "And if you ask me to hypnotize him, I quit. I don't do exorcisms. You want to talk to the beyond get yourself a Ouija board."

Bolan couldn't imagine any conversation with the Devil being productive. "Wouldn't ask you to." Bolan regarded the subject and flexed a little of his scant German. *"Wie ist Ihr Name?"*

The man stared unblinkingly. "Rudi."

"Sprechen Sie Englisch?"

Rudi nodded like a sleepwalker. *"Ja."*

"Rudolph what?"

"It is unimportant," the German replied.

Bolan shrugged. "Well, I care."

"*Das Tier* does not."

Bolan looked to Oderkirk. "The what?"

"*Das Tier.*" Libby looked at Rudi askance. "The Beast."

Rudi twitched but continued his somnambulant stare at nothing.

"*Che hombre,* I been hearing about this shit." Nazareno pointed a finger at Rudi. "They say La Bestia takes you? You're his. Forever. No escape."

Bolan had been hearing that, too, and a cold part of him had to admit that no matter what move he'd made he hadn't escaped the Beast. "You been hearing anything else, Naz?"

"Crazy shit. That El Diablo is alive and well in Mexico and La Bestia is his servant on Earth. That he grants power and protection to those who serve him. Some people believe it. Some people don't. But no matter what you believe, people are disappearing and reappearing all changed and shit, and all across Mexico this Bestia asshole is taking shit over and he can't be stopped. No bullshit. When I heard La Bestia was moving into the west coast operations, this was going to be my last job for Federacion. I don't want to bear that mark. Figured I'd move to Puerto Rico. They always need pilots, but then you showed up and…" Nazareno trailed off as he met Bolan's cobalt gaze.

"So, Rudi," Bolan said. "The Beast is coming?"

"Without fail."

"When?"

Rudi resumed his catatonic staring.

Bolan took up his rifle. "I'm going to go spell Terrell." He went outside and hauled himself onto the roof and clambered up the ten feet to the belfry. The bell was long gone, but even so Smallhouse's frame took up nearly all the space inside. The sniper had to fold himself up even more to give Bolan a bit of ledge to perch on. The belfry's elevation caught a blissful bit of wind.

"What up?" Smallhouse asked.

"We saved you a beer and sandwich. Go eat and get some rack time."

Smallhouse's smile flashed. "Don't gotta tell me twice."

Bolan half expected the man to plunge through the roof as he jumped out of the belfry, but the ancient adobe held. Smallhouse jumped off the roof and disappeared inside. Bolan scanned a 360 of the area through his night-vision scope, then turned off the unit. The batteries on the night vision and cell phones were all running perilously low. He just had to hope something in the village had an electrical connection.

Bolan turned his thoughts to his opponent.

The Executioner believed that weakness, temptation, hardship and pain were the breeding places of monsters, and were where human evil was birthed. Mexico was one of the most beautiful countries on Earth, but it had weakness, temptation, hardship and pain in abundance. It had more than its fair share, and the Beast was cleaning up in recruitment.

The Beast claimed to take souls. Bolan couldn't quantify that but the Beast sure did like taking heads. He inspired suicidal loyalty in his subjects and almost catatonic fear in those who had failed him. Bolan frowned. He had seen some very freaky and unpleasant things in his time. Watching Ayala's personality disappear while someone or something else spoke through him was definitely in the top ten. And there was no denying that as long as Bolan held something the Beast wanted, the Beast had reached out his hand and taken it.

Bolan was absolutely sure the Beast wanted Rudi back.

His eyes narrowed in the dark as he seriously considered Satan.

End-of-the-world types often disagreed on the exact date but most guesstimated right about now was when the fallen angel would rise. Drug gangsters as foot soldiers made perfect sense. Bolan smiled coldly. There had to be a joke lurking somewhere about Satan using Germans as his sergeants. Bolan's finger tapped his rifle's receiver in thought. The reoccurring German angle was a puzzle.

It might just be the key.

Bolan's musings were interrupted as Oderkirk swung herself onto the roof of the mission in athletic fashion. He caught the pleasing scent of sweaty redhead as she began climbing up the belfry. Bolan reached out a hand and hauled her up. The woman perched on the bit of ledge next to Bolan and sighed. "There's a breeze up here."

Bolan lifted his chin and spent a moment enjoying it.

Oderkirk pulled a bottle out of an empty magazine pouch. "There's a beer up here, too."

"I'm on duty."

"There's no potable water for miles."

"Well, since you put it that way."

Oderkirk cracked the sweating bottle and they passed it back and forth. "You think they'll hit us tonight?"

Bolan shook his head. "No. I don't know if I'm buying Old Scratch or not, but so far no matter what he's done, the Beast has done it in real time. He has to move his pieces into place. We skipped like a stone into the middle of nowhere. If his agents are going to hit us, they have to get themselves into one hell of a god-forsaken corner of Durango."

"But you're still up in a belfry with a rifle."

"The Prophet Mohammed said to put your faith in Allah but tie up your camel."

"Can I tell you something?"

"Sure," Bolan said.

"I'm scared."

"You should be."

"Can I tell you something else?"

"Shoot."

"I like having sex in weird places."

Bolan shrugged. "You take people out of their normal element and they tend to lose their inhibitions."

"I usually have sex with men I've been in danger with," Oderkirk stated.

Bolan was thinking that Chet and Smallhouse were lucky men. "Shared danger is a proved aphrodisiac."

"You ever done it in a belfry in Mexico?"

Bolan smiled in the dark. "What if I said yes?"

"Bet you have." Oderkirk snorted. "But with a red-head?"

"Got me on that one," Bolan conceded. "But I'm on duty."

"You're drinking on duty."

"There's no potable water for miles."

Oderkirk's voice lowered. "I just threw myself at you, idiot."

"Well, if you can think of something to do that still allows me to watch the perimeter, knock yourself out."

Oderkirk smiled.

Milagro

BOLAN AND ZHONG walked into the village of Miracle. Bolan was hoping for one. Short of that he would settle for beans, tortillas and bottled water. The village was a single dusty lane lined on both sides by whitewashed adobe buildings hunched against one another. Bolan half expected

a young Clint Eastwood to stride out into the street in a
serape with a pair of six-guns strapped to his hips. The
only nod to the twenty-first century, or even the twentieth
for that matter, were two very ancient-looking pickups
and an even more ancient-looking military-style jeep. One
building had the words *Mercado y Taverna* painted over
the door. Bolan suspected it was the center of most activity
in town. Three old men sat on a bench outside drinking
coffee, and they gaped openly at Zhong. Bolan nodded
politely at the seniors as he went in.

The interior was scrupulously clean, and the walls were
lined with merchandise. Tables took up the center. Cooking
and coffee smells came from the kitchen in the back. An
old woman stood behind a counter that served as the bar
at night.

Bolan smiled at the woman. *"Buenos días."*

The woman smiled back with about half the normal set
of teeth. *"Che guapo."*

Bolan smiled at the thought that he was handsome and
bought beans, dried beef, tortillas and coffee. There were
no tourists in Milagro, and no one needed bottled water
so he settled for two cases of Tecate beer and sacks of ice.
"Ask her who owns the jeep."

Zhong's Spanish was excellent. "She says Señor
Ansaldo. He is sitting outside."

"Translate for me." Bolan stepped outside and nodded
at the old men on the bench. "Señor Ansaldo?"

A weathered old man wearing a John Deere cap nodded.
"Sí."

"Tell him I need his jeep."

Zhong told him. "Señor Ansaldo says he needs it, as
well."

"Tell him I'll give him a thousand dollars for it."

Zhong spoke. Ansaldo waved a grizzled hand in

dismissal. Zhong translated. "Señor Ansaldo says five thousand."

"Done," Bolan said.

"*Sí.*" Zhong told the man.

Ansaldo cackled like a rooster and fished a key ring out of his pocket and tossed it to Bolan, who caught it and nodded respectfully. "*Muchas gracias.*" Ansaldo's eyes widened as Bolan began pulling American green backs out of his money belt.

"Ask him if he's seen any strangers in town." Ansaldo gave Bolan a look implying that he and Zhong were about the strangest thing to happen to Milagro in quite a while. Bolan took out a card. "Tell him I would like him to call me if any other strangers come. It's worth a thousand dollars to me." Bolan produced more bills. "Five hundred now, five hundred more if he calls."

Ansaldo took the money and the card with great seriousness. His two companions could only gape at the morning's transactions. Bolan looked up at the rising sun. "Let's load up. It's going to be a hot one."

CHAPTER SEVENTEEN

The Mission

Everyone looked up from their food as Bolan's phone rang. Nazareno had cobbled together a serviceable chili. An application told Bolan the signal was coming from Milagro. Bolan handed the phone to Zhong, who answered and began speaking in Spanish. He nodded at Bolan. "It is Señor Ansaldo. He says there are three strangers in town."

"Ask him if they're Mexican or Anglo."

"Mexican, but he says they look like dangerous men." Zhong raised an eyebrow slightly. "He also says these men walked out of the desert, out of nowhere."

"No vehicles?"

"No, they just walked out of the desert. Like you and I."

"Ask him if they looked like they had been walking for a long time."

"He says no, and that he is scared of these men."

"Have they asked any questions? Anything about us?"

"No. They haven't talked to anybody. He says he thinks they are waiting for something."

"Where are they now?"

"He says two of them are in the cantina. He does not know where the third is."

Bolan rose. "Zhong, you're with me." He tossed him the jeep keys. "You drive."

Zhong caught the keys and pulled his hatchet out of the table where he had stuck it.

Oderkirk frowned. "What about me and Terrell?"

Smallhouse boomed down the belfry. "Yeah! What about me and Libby!"

"You're VIP protection specialists." Bolan flicked a glance at Rudi. "Protect his ass. And be ready. We may be coming back fast. If you get in trouble and we're not back, call the number I gave you for Jack and tell him you need him ASAP. With any luck he can solve your problem and then extract you." Bolan looked over at Highlander, who was contentedly gnawing on a strip of rawhide Bolan had bought in town. "Walkies?"

Highlander snapped to attention.

Bolan laid the big Barrett Fifty across his shoulder and he, Zhong and Highlander went out to the jeep. The sun was setting. The bad guys had had a good forty-eight hours to play catch-up. Zhong slid behind the wheel and they took off down the dusty road to Milagro.

"Unless we are giving credence to the paranormal, I believe these men must have parachuted in last night from high altitude," Zhong observed.

Bolan had been thinking the same thing. "And unless Satan has infiltrated the state of Durango's skydiving association, that makes them Mexican Airborne Brigade."

"A logical assertion. How do you propose we approach them?"

"I say we walk right up and start bitch-slapping ourselves some satanists."

Zhong's eyes narrowed and a smirk twitched at one corner of his mouth. "Bitch slap…"

"It's fun to say," Bolan admitted. "Even more fun to do.

I imagine a man who has undergone iron-palm training could bitch-slap the Satan right out of somebody."

Zhong grunted in amusement. "I was considering decapitations."

"I'd rather you didn't," Bolan said. "That's what they do. We're the good guys."

"I must tell you that I do not consider myself…one of the good guys."

"Well, I consider you one of the good guys."

"That is kind of you. However, it is my still my opinion we must take a sterner stance with our opponents.

"I agree," Bolan agreed. "You can take ears."

Zhong pondered that as he drove. "I had heard it rumored that American soldiers took ears as trophies during your police action in Vietnam. I would rather suspect the practice was frowned upon then, much less in the milder emotional climate we live in."

"I'm not talking trophies. I'm talking line in the sand. Anyone coming at us bearing the mark of the Beast, we take it off them."

Zhong pondered that and appeared to find it good. "I see."

The jeep bounced down the road as the sun disappeared into the desert. The batteries on the night-vision gear were perilously low, but Bolan handed Zhong a pair so they could make a lightless approach. The few lights of the village began winking on and Bolan had Zhong stop about one thousand yards out. He left the big Barrett in the jeep and loosened his pistols in their perches. "I'm thirsty," Bolan stated.

"The cantina?"

"Why not?" Bolan, Zhong and Highlander walked into Milagro as if they owned the place. Ansaldo and his two constant companions were sitting outside drinking beer and taking in the evening. The old man jerked his thumb at the cantina and held up two fingers. Bolan nodded and palmed Ansaldo a wad of twenties in passing. Banda music from an old boom box washed over them as they entered. A bullfight was showing on the TV over the counter. The crowd was sparse. Locals drank beer at the counter. Three men sat at a table in the middle wearing jeans, boots and cowboy hats like just about everyone else in Durango. It wasn't a chilly night in the desert, but these men were wearing windbreakers. The larger of the two had a machete leaning against his leg. Machetes in Mexico were about as common as lawnmowers in America, but like Mexicans, most Americans left their lawnmowers outside when they went into a bar.

Bolan, Zhong and Highlander beelined straight at them. The man with the machete reached for it as he pushed away from the table. *"¡Mierda!"*

"Highlander!" Bolan ordered. "Attack!"

Man and machete tipped backward as Highlander flew across the table. The man to Machete's right shoved his hand beneath his windbreaker. Bolan swung his hand in a short arc. The knob of bone in the heel chopped into the man's nose, snapping the septum at its mooring and wiping the nose halfway across the man's face. His head snapped back and his cowboy hat went flying. Bolan grabbed the man by the hair and bounced his face off the tabletop. Bolan chopped his hand down into the man's neck and cervical vertebrae snapped in grim finality.

Zhong was one step behind and his bitch-slap was a top-ten of all time. Tiger claw kung fu stressed the hands, and adepts trained their hands to be lethal weapons in all sorts of exotic formations. Zhong literally slapped teeth out of the man's mouth. His open hand formed a claw that closed around the man's ear. The man let out an ear-splitting scream as Zhong took his ear from him.

The locals left the cantina in a flood.

Zhong closed his hand into a fist and punched his man between the eyes. Bolan heard bones crack and it wasn't Zhong's knuckles. The man's pupils blew and he slumped. Highlander stood over a man missing his trachea. Zhong peered at the ear in his hand and held it up for Bolan. A tattoo at the base proclaimed 666. Zhong tossed it to the table and drew his hatchet to harvest the rest. Bolan held up a restraining hand as he peered at the ear. "Wait."

Zhong's eyes narrowed with hawklike impatience. "What?"

Bolan picked up the bloody organ. "You see what I see?"

Zhong's eyes went to slits. "I see."

At the root of the ear among the torn flesh and cartilage something slightly shiny glistened. Bolan pinched it and pulled it out. The device was just short of an inch long and as big around as a flattened grain of rice. One end widened slightly into an equally flat lozenge the circumference of a pencil eraser. Through the blood and plastic Bolan could just make out a thin filament within and the darker dots of what had to be the integrated circuits. Bolan could see that the flexible device could be inserted to lie along the inner cartilage of the ear. No coroner would look for it. A full body scan could easily miss it. Only Zhong's violent avulsion of the organ in question had revealed it.

"Now we know why the Beast harvests the heads of his own fallen," Zhong said. "And that the white man's devil is not involved."

Bolan admired the device grudgingly. "If he is, he's using RFIDs."

"RFIDs?"

"Radio-frequency identification devices."

"You have encountered such things before?"

"Never this small, this sophisticated or powerful. Much less used on such a scale." Bolan shook his head at the enormity of the operation. "Someone is spending one hell of a lot of money to make this happen."

"I believe the drug trade is literally awash with currency." Zhong waggled his hatchet. "Shall I take the rest?"

"No, I don't want the bad guys to know we know, at least not yet."

Zhong scowled. "How do we do that?"

"Translate for me." Bolan stepped back out into the night. Ansaldo and several other locals were watching the cantina from the stable across the street. Bolan and Zhong walked over. "Ask him who owns the cantina."

Zhong asked. "He says he is the proprietor."

"Tell him I want to burn it down."

Zhong translated. Ansaldo's jaw dropped.

"Tell him I'll give him fifty thousand dollars to let me do it."

If Ansaldo left his jaw open much longer birds were going to nest in his mouth. He finally started speaking. Zhong gave one of his thin smiles. "He wants to know if you are going to burn it anyway if he says no."

"Frankly," Bolan answered, "yes, but I would still give him the money as well."

Zhong snorted the response. "He says he wants one hundred thousand. He says he has been wanting to renovate for some time."

Bolan considered what was left of his liquid war chest. "Tell him I'll have to send him the second fifty thou by courier in a couple of days. Will he trust me?"

"Strangely enough, he says yes."

"Ask him what he'll charge me for a can of gas."

Ansaldo laughed. Zhong translated. "He says he will throw that in for free as long as you let him light the match."

Bolan nodded. "Done."

THE DRIVE BACK was uneventful except for the roaring bonfire they left glowing behind them. Bolan had given Ansaldo and a crew of villagers time to remove as many goods and valuables as possible and asked Ansaldo to let it burn twenty minutes before he and the villagers began any firefighting efforts. He left instructions to tell anyone who came there had been a gun battle between strangers. There had been explosions like grenades and then the fire had broken out.

Bolan called in about a half mile from the mission. "We're coming in, Big T. No apparent pursuit."

"Copy that, Coop. I have visual on you," the rifleman responded. "C'mon in."

They arrived and Bolan waved up the belfry at Smallhouse. Bolan came in and piled the dead men's pistols and cell phones on the table. He removed the phone's batteries and passed them out to Zhong, Oderkirk and Nazareno.

"Naz, take one up to Terrell and tell him to come down. You're spelling him."

Bolan wolfed some chili while the lookouts rotated. Terrell came in and happily took the bowl Bolan passed him. "What up?"

The soldier pointed at the German. "We're going to have an intervention."

"Ooh, yeah!" Smallhouse nodded. "About time."

Oderkirk pointed at Bolan defiantly. "I told you. I'm not doing anymore séances."

"This isn't going to be an exorcism." Bolan regarded Rudi coldly. The German sat before the sawhorse table. His chili was mostly untouched. He did seem to be accepting beer, and Oderkirk had been liberally dosing the man. Wariness was starting to glimmer through his malaise of terror. Bolan smiled at him without an ounce of warmth. "This is strictly going to be a come to Jesus."

"Take him to the shed!" Smallhouse enthused.

Rudi stared at nothing. Zhong moved behind him like a shadow.

"Rudi, I know you've had a rough couple of days, but I need to talk to you."

"Talk is useless."

"You know, you're right. I do go on sometimes." Bolan nodded. "Zhong?"

"Hey!" Rudi yelped as Zhong seized him by the earlobe and pulled the organ taut. "*Was tun Sie—* Ow!" Rudi yelled as Zhong shaved off his ear on the upstroke with the edge of his hatchet and flipped it to the table in front of the German. Rudi's scream rose to a shriek as he clawed at the side of his head. Blood spurted between his fingers.

Oderkirk shot to her feet in outrage. "For God's sake, Cooper!"

Smallhouse stared back and forth between Bolan, Zhong, Rudi and Rudi's ear in open shock. "Cooper…"

Nazareno shouted down the belfry. "What's going on?"

Highlander perked his ears and lifted his snout toward the ear in interest. Bolan was mildly worried that the dog might be developing a fondness for human flesh. Zhong took out his pocket square and shoved it into Rudi's hand. Rudi instinctively held it against the hole in his head.

Bolan loomed over the German. "Do I have your attention now? Are you focused?" Rudi, like everyone else in the room besides Zhong and Highlander was still in shock from what had just happened, but it was clear Bolan did indeed have Rudi's undivided attention. The soldier stared down at the mutilated German. "Hey, Rudi. You want to see some real magic?"

Rudi recoiled in horror at what might get lopped off next. Zhong shoved him back down in his seat.

Bolan took out his Swiss Army knife.

"Cooper!" Oderkirk shouted.

Bolan took out the tweezers. He picked up the ear and turned it to show Rudi his missing tattoo. "Now, watch close, Rudi," Bolan said. "I'm only going to do this once."

Smallhouse looked like he might be sick. "Cooper..."

"And we say the magic words, six...six...six...and..." Rudi looked like he might throw up, too, as Bolan inserted the tweezers into the severed flesh and fished around for a moment. He twisted the tweezers with a flourish and dropped the ear. "Presto!"

Smallhouse squinted at the tiny dripping device Bolan held up in the firelight. "What in the blue hell..."

Oderkirk blinked. "Oh, my God, what is that?"

Zhong spoke smugly. "It is called an RFID."

Bolan took the scalpel sharp point of his knife and ran it down the device's minuscule length. The tiny length of filament antenna gleamed. His voice dripped contempt for Rudi. "You need a magnifying glass or a diagram or are you getting this?"

Rudi shook like a leaf.

"Let me guess," Bolan continued. "They made you an offer, promised you power, euros and fraüleins gone wild? Then there was what? An orgy? An initiation? They gave you some kind of sacred Satanic sacrament? Got you high as a kite and gave you the mark of the Beast? I bet you were proud of it the next day.

"They tricked you! They gave you a magic show and implanted you like an animal! And you fell for it!"

Rudi threw up.

"You didn't sell your soul to Satan!" Bolan was relentless. "You sold your brain to the Wizard of Oz!"

Bolan went Geneva Convention on the sobbing German. "Now! Name! Rank! And serial number!"

"Lahm, Rudolf, Obergefreiter!" Rudi bawled. Rudolph Lahm appeared to have been a lance corporal in the German Armed Forces. He rattled off a series of letters and numbers in German too fast for Bolan to make them out, but Oderkirk's pencil flew across her pad. She tore it off and handed it to Bolan. The pencil hovered as Rudi babbled and sobbed and slobbered.

"What's he saying now, Lib?"

"He's praying to God for forgiveness, calling himself names." Oderkirk rolled her eyes. "He wants his mother."

Bolan's voice went cold as he addressed the German. "All he gets is me."

Rudi's head sagged inches from his spewed guts. Zhong yanked him up by the hair to make him look at Bolan.

"Corporal," Bolan said, "I don't know what brought you to this state. You got in debt, got on drugs or just got bored and fell in with increasingly wrong people. It doesn't matter. You thought you were a knight in Satan's service, but the Beast just tagged your ear like an animal and used you."

Rudi couldn't meet Bolan's burning gaze.

"They're tracking you," Bolan continued, "but now we know how, and we can stop it at anytime. Two things can happen. One, I cut you loose. I'll even have you shipped to a hospital and have them sew your ear back on. After that you're on your own. You'd better pray the Beast doesn't have the resources to find you by conventional means, but I wouldn't bet on it. Option two? I'm going to Germany. I'm taking down the Beast, and you are my golden ticket in. They're going to come looking for you, and I'm going to be waiting."

Rudi had nothing left to heave up and he was back to shaking.

"You were a soldier once. You can run, or you can fight. Your choice. I'll give you exactly five minutes to think about it."

Bolan's phone rang.

"Hell, I'll give you ten."

Bolan initiated the connection. "What's up, Bear?"

"The good news is that I have you on high resolution imaging satellite for the next six hours."

"Great. And the bad news?"

"The bad news is you seem to have company coming."

"How much company?" Bolan asked.

"Literally truck loads."

"How far out?"

"A convoy just rolled into Milagro."

It would take them some time to make the ten miles to the mission. The question was whether to try and tow the Socata back from behind the mission and try to take off or fight. Grimaldi thought he might be able to take off from the dirt road at night. Nazareno had expressed some hesitance.

Bolan looked at Rudi. "I just ran out of time. You want the keys to the jeep or do you want a gun?"

Something like anger kindled behind the German's eyes. "Give me a gun."

"Bear, keep me advised."

Bolan tapped a preset number and Grimaldi answered. "Yo."

"I need you."

CHAPTER EIGHTEEN

"I can't believe you gave him a gun." Nazareno was looking over at Rudi. Bolan had professionally dressed his wound, and the German's ear was on ice. His catatonia and terror had distilled into ice-cold rage. He was carrying the AK Zhong had liberated from the airfield.

"I gave you a gun," Bolan observed. "In fact I gave you two."

"Yes, but…you cut off his ear."

"No, Zhong cut off his ear, and that was the best thing that ever happened to him."

"Yes, but…"

"But nothing, Naz." They had spent the past hour making all the preparations they could. Firing loops had been dug in the mission walls, brush was piled up in the four corners of the perimeter wall, and Bolan had a few more surprises in store. It was going to have to be enough. "We hold them. We hold them right here."

Nazareno swallowed a very large frog lodged in his throat. "Okay…"

Kurtzman's voice came across Bolan's phone. "They're almost on top of you. Still five vehicles."

Bolan slung his rifle. "Copy that."

"Hey!" Smallhouse called down from the belfry. "I see their lights!"

Bolan took up the twenty-eight pound Barrett.

"Naz, you're with me. Rudi, you stay inside. Use the

firing loops." Rudi didn't look happy, but he nodded in the affirmative.

"Libby," Bolan continued, "you're with Zhong."

Everyone acknowledged. Oderkirk doused the fire and everyone moved out into the night. Bolan had done everything he could think of, but certain realities had to be faced. They had been playing musical batteries, but now the only people with active night-vision were Bolan and Smallhouse and even they were still low. They were the two best marksmen, but neither man's optics could be counted on to last out any kind of protracted firefight. In the end they were going to have to play this one close to the vest.

They were going to have to let the enemy get close.

Bolan stepped out into the night. By the same token he and Smallhouse were the only men with open lines. Bolan had what was quite possibly the most sophisticated cell phone on Earth, and he still had a quarter charge and was at full bars. Smallhouse had the last battery with any juice at all. Bolan needed instant communication with his top gun.

The rest of the team was just going to have to get shouted at old-school-combat style.

Bolan walked up to the wall, Nazareno on his heels with a Glock in both hands. "Fire one dry, then draw the second one," Bolan suggested.

"Right." Nazareno tucked his second pistol away.

"Go get the third one off the table. You may need it."

"Right."

Nazareno went in and came back loaded with iron. Bolan dropped to a knee by the wall. It was low but of ancient conquistador construction. He felt sure it would take bullets, but it wasn't quite thick enough for his liking. He laid the Barrett across his shoulder, flicked on his night vision and looked for what the night had in store. The enemy was about four hundred yards out—five vehicles as reported, within RPG range but beyond his grenade launcher. No one had gotten out yet.

"Hey, Rudi," Bolan called. "You figure these are your master's servants?"

"No," Rudi snarled through a hole they had dug in the mission wall. "But they are most certainly his tools."

Smallhouse spoke across the line. "We gave the Federation boys some cause."

Oderkirk gave Rudi a look. "And somebody's friends tattled on us."

Rudi ignored her. Bolan sighted on the grille of a vehicle. "Everyone hold fire except Terrell. Terrell, you take targets of opportunity."

"Ooh, yeah!"

"Here we go…" Bolan slowly took up slack on the trigger. The Barrett's over the shoulder configuration made it much more maneuverable, but it took what was already unpleasant recoil and made it brutal. The Barrett bucked like a bronco against the shoulder yoke. The .50-caliber bullet punched through the grille as it would through paper and buried itself in the engine block. The trucks had driven a long way across the desert and the engines were burning hot. The radiator exploded and the hood flew up in a blast of steam. Bolan turned to the second and third vehicles and gave them the same. Doors and hatchbacks flew open and men leaped out in all directions.

Smallhouse's rifle began cracking in slow fire.

Pistols, rifles, shotguns and submachine guns began blasting back.

"I make it around fifty," Bolan said.

Smallhouse's rifle cracked again. "Forty-seven," he corrected.

"Watch for the rocket," Bolan warned.

"Copy the hell out of that," Smallhouse agreed.

Bolan blasted a hole in the grille of the fourth vehicle, and once more the radiator erupted in a pleasing fashion. Another hailstorm of not particularly accurate fire greeted the deed. Bolan deliberately left the last vehicle alone. The onslaught died down as no fire answered. Smallhouse's rifle cracked again and a man screamed. Another broadside of bullets spackled the mission. "They're starting to spread out."

Bolan could see them scurrying from sagebrush, to rock to cactus clump. None appeared to have night-vision equipment but they were in the high, deep desert of Mexico. The number of stars visible was shocking to the eye and there was a crescent moon, more than enough light to attack the pale white lump of the mission by. Bolan kept his eye out for the rocket.

It came streaking out of nowhere.

"Rocket!" Bolan shouted. "Get out of there!"

"Shit!" Smallhouse responded.

The launch lit up the night, and Bolan put three rounds each into the rocketeer and his loader. The rocket streaked across the desert. Smallhouse yelped and dropped down the belfry like one very big Santa. The belfry blasted apart into chunks of smoking clay. "Terrell!" Bolan shouted. "Terrell!"

Bolan could hear rubble sifting as Smallhouse responded. "I'm all right, I—"

The Executioner shouted over a new eruption of gunfire. "Here they come!" He began picking off bad guys as they came in screaming and shooting as if it were 1944 and the mission was Omaha Beach. Nazareno shouted and screamed and fired his pistol back. Zhong quietly plinked at muzzle-flashes. Rudi was screaming and swearing in

German as he fired bursts from his AK. Bolan didn't want a protracted siege. He decided to give the bad guys some enticement. "Fall back!" he roared. Bolan's team dropped below wall level and scuttled for the doors. They piled into the mission and Oderkirk and Smallhouse slammed the ancient doors shut and slammed the back of a pew they had chopped out for the purpose into the brackets to bar the door.

The bad guys whooped and yelled for blood as their enemy retreated.

Smallhouse slammed a fresh magazine into his rifle. "Hope you know what you're doing, man! This place just turned into the Alamo!"

Bolan knew exactly what he was doing. The question was, would it work? He spoke into his phone. "Where are you, Jack?"

"Circling at seven thousand," the pilot replied. "Waiting on visual."

"Copy that, hold position." People began pounding on the door. Bolan nodded. "Light them up!" He shoved a torch into the embers of the fire and shoved it out the firing loop. The torch dropped into the line of cold, plane-fuel soaked embers and Zhong, Oderkirk, Rudi and Smallhouse did the same. Four trails of fire snaked out from the four corners of the mission and hit the fuel soaked bundles of brush stacked in the corners and piled low against the wall. Outside men shouted in alarm as the narrow mission grounds lit up.

The pounding on the mission door slackened momentarily at the fiery interruption.

Grimaldi's voice instantly came across Bolan's open line. "I have visual. Dropping to firing altitude."

"I'm opening the front door. Be advised friendlies on north side."

"Copy that" Grimaldi came back.

Bolan pointed his rifle at the section of pew barring the door and fired. His antiarmor round blew the bar in half and flung the doors open in a shower of fire and splinters. Bolan flicked his selector to full-auto and fired. Oderkirk, Zhong and Rudi joined in the fusillade. Outside the Federation Cartel thugs had been caught flat-footed and they twisted and fell. Above them a pair of Continental 210 horsepower engines screamed over the mission.

"In position," Grimaldi announced. "Orbiting."

"Commence fire," Bolan ordered.

Chet commenced fire. A bare hundred yards overhead Chet's M-60 machine gun ripped into life and began raining lead. The mission grounds were lit up like a bonfire and the men clustered within were sitting ducks as Grimaldi circled.

The Stony Man pilot and Chet had flown out into the desert and landed in a saltpan Kurtzman had located for them on satellite. While Bolan and his team had been engaging in their activities at the mission and in the village of Milagro, Grimaldi and Chet had removed the Cessna's back seats and the passenger door. They had taken all the seat belts and rigged chicken straps for Chet and the M-60. It was a poor-man's gunship at best, but it had the element of surprise. Chet leaned out into the night and dispensed fire.

Men twisted and fell beneath the barrage.

Cartel soldiers trying to reach the safety of the mission met Bolan and his team's full fury. Those who tried to flee into the night had to dodge the scything fire from above and hurl themselves over the mission's low but flaming walls.

"I have multiple targets retreating toward the trucks," Grimaldi reported.

"Concentrate on the mission," Bolan ordered. He re-loaded his rifle and slid a frag into his launcher. "Scrub it clean."

"Copy that."

The only problem with scrubbing the mission clean was that Chet was woefully short on soap. He was keeping his bursts short, but he only had a one hundred round belt. Grimaldi made two more orbits. "We're dry."

"Copy that. Climb to safe altitude, give me eyes on." Bolan turned back to Smallhouse. "On the roof. Give me eyes on the ground."

Bolan stepped out front. Overwhelmingly the cartel killers were dead or hightailing it into the night. A few brave souls were firing up into night at the fleeing plane they could barely see. Bolan did a lap and burned the drug gangsters down without mercy. The rest of the team followed. Smallhouse heaved himself up on the roof and crouched in the shadow of the shattered belfry. He did a 360 with his scope. "I got ten, eleven…twelve headed back toward the vehicles on the double. You want me to take them?"

"No. Let them go." Bolan pulled down his night vision and scanned the night. "Let them go back to their bosses. Let them report back what a bad tip the Beast gave them and what a goat-screw it turned into. Let everyone know the Beast isn't infallible."

MEINRAD GERWULF LAY in the dirt. He wore the latest German night-vision-disruptive camouflage battle dress uniform, and he and a stand of mesquite had become as one. He played his optics over the burning vehicles, the bonfires, the battered mission and the large collection of corpses littering the desert. It was quite impressive. Everyone, including himself, had concluded that the enemy had sent the Cessna out for reinforcements or to get word out. Using it for air support and keeping it as an ace in the hole had been a stroke of genius.

He played his night-vision sight over the black man on the roof and the woman below. The man was clearly a soldier, the woman, though capable, clearly was not. He ran his sight over the Chinese man and his lip curled in contempt. The Chinese in Mexico had been cowed by Gerwulf's own plan. He considered the appearance of the Hong Kong killer a personal affront, and one he looked forward to addressing. He gave the Mexican shooter the most cursory of inspections. The man had blazed away with his pistols for the most part indiscriminately. Gerwulf was fairly sure the man had to be the pilot from the Federation Cartel airfield and was of no account.

Gerwulf bared his teeth at Highlander.

He didn't like dogs. Properly trained they couldn't be intimidated or turned. Correctly trained they were fearless, and twice when Gerwulf had been about his master's business in Berlin, dogs had nearly been the end of him. The Doberman sniffed the night, bristling. Its superior senses told it there were still enemies out in the dark.

He yearned to shoot it.

Gerwulf turned his thoughts and optics onto more pleasant things. He sighed as he took in the American. The man was magnificent. He was clearly in command, and he was clearly more than a soldier. He was a warrior. The man wore a cap pulled down low and he was wearing night-vision goggles, but Gerwulf would recognize the man's carriage and grace anywhere. Unless, of course, the man was skilled in role camouflage, which Gerwulf would bet anything he was. That would only add spice to the game.

He considered shooting the American.

The range was just under 150 meters, close to the maximum range of his HK PDW. It was night, and Gerwulf, despite his many skills, was only an indifferent marksman. He liked to work up close. If he missed, he knew the dog would be loosed and they would come for him in a hunting party. It was a situation in which he might very well lose. Gerwulf always stacked the deck in his favor, and his master's orders had been to organize the attack and then observe and report.

His orders.

Meinrad Gerwulf was a sociopath. However, like many functional sociopaths he didn't consider himself insane, he simply considered himself outside the rest of unwashed humanity's rules of social etiquette. Like most sociopaths he felt this made him clearly superior. For him to respect people they had to prove themselves to him. Gerwulf shuddered happily as he thought of his master. He would obey his master's orders. He would observe the enemy. He would report. And wherever the beautiful American warrior went?

Gerwulf would follow.

He played his optics over his Yankee superman with a sigh. He deserved flowers.

Berlin

THE BEAST RECEIVED the news of the Mexican mission battle with interest. He asked a few pointed questions and pondered his next move as he spoke into the secure link. "Very well, dearest Meinrad. We will track the American, and given opportunity, you will be vectored in."

Gerwulf's voice was a wistful sigh over the link. "Thank you, my master."

"Sleep well, Meinrad. Rest." The Beast clicked the link closed.

Bogac Krom flexed his mighty pecs in unconscious agitation. "I cannot believe that Meinrad has failed."

"Oh, I would not say that Meinrad has failed." The Beast smiled as he considered his pet maniac. "I would be tempted to say that our Mexican brethren failed him."

Krom rumbled low. "I do not like it."

"I must admit I had not foreseen these events." The Beast smiled once more. "Nevertheless, Meinrad seems quite keen for the hunt. Indeed, he seems to be quite enamored of this Yankee 'Man of Steel' of his."

Krom made a face and shuddered inwardly. He was a brutal man with no qualms about committing violence and relished using terror as a weapon. However, he'd had the personal misfortune of witnessing what passed for love and affection in Meinrad Gerwulf's world, as well as its aftermath. When Meinrad lavished his affections on someone he was smitten with, he required the equivalent of a machine shop and a mobile field surgery to bring the horror-movie love story playing in his head to fruition. And when he was finished what was left required a hose and a mop. Not for the first time Bogac Krom reminded himself to blow out his brains the day Meinrad sent him a dozen red roses. Krom twitched his shoulders in revulsion and changed the subject. "The enemy, they are still alive, and they still have Rudi."

"Rudi..." the Beast mused. "Well, no one likes an apostate."

"Well, machine-gunner specialist Rudi Lahm is still alive, and apparently his heart has hardened toward us. If the Yankee swine can bring Rudi back alive to Berlin, the Rudi Lahm apostasy will spread like the plague."

"I doubt that. His cell has been dispersed. Though I

admit it is something of a nuisance." The Beast was still smiling but his pale eyes grew cold. "And I admit his continued existence vexes me. I wish him extinguished in fire."

"Yes? Well? They are free as birds, while Meinrad lies beneath the Mexican moon, dreaming his dreamy dreams of an American Special Forces superman and jigsaws and wood lathes!"

Krom paused, and for a moment he thought he had gone too far.

The corners of the Beast's mouth slowly turned up. "Dear Bogac, you never told me you had a poetic side."

Krom shifted uncomfortably. "Yes, well…"

"They are indeed flying like birds, however," the Beast corrected. "As for being free? They have yet to cross the Rio Grande, and while they have flown the coop Meinrad constructed for them, they have yet to escape their Mexican cage."

"They are airborne. Meinrad cannot give chase until they land. They will not do that until they reach the United States, and then our exposure rises a hundredfold."

"That is indeed Plan B," the Beast agreed.

"And what is Plan A?"

"I realize it will hurt Meinrad's feelings, but I wish them all to die in fire before they reach the United States."

"But what can we…" Krom suddenly straightened. "The captain?"

The Beast steepled his fingers. "Why not?"

"We are already highly exposed in Mexico," Krom warned.

"I agree, perhaps so much so that an outward demonstration of our power is in order." The Beast pressed a button on his desk console. A woman's throaty voice answered immediately. "Yes, my master?"

"Activate Captain Rivera. I am patching my computer into your laptop. You will vector him in."

11th Military Airbase, Santa Gertrudis, Chihuahua

CAPTAIN MIRIAMO RIVERA dropped his cell phone and went into violent convulsions on his bed. His German girl, the woman he loved, had spoken German words to him he didn't understand, as she had done so many times before when they had made love, but these words were different—they weren't words of endearment, they were keys, and they unlocked lightning in his head. His consciousness became a maelstrom of utter blackness and blinding white flashes. Between the darkness and the light La Bestia manifested himself in his goat-headed glory lit by lurid, pulsing red fire, filling his mind to the point that it left no room for Captain Miriamo Rivera. The pilot's arms and legs drummed the bed and his mouth frothed as the Beast filled the core of his being and blanketed his existence in a spiritual ecstasy of personal obliteration. He hung suspended in dark and light and fire. Golden power filled his veins and he was uplifted in the embrace of his god.

Captain Rivera's seizure ended as abruptly as it had started. His mind was perfectly clear as he sat up and picked up his dropped cell phone. His free hand unconsciously went to the tattoo behind his left ear. "What is required of me?"

The woman spoke quietly and matter-of-factly in Spanish as she told him the first part of his mission. Rivera clicked his phone shut and rose. He put on his dressing gown and checked the loads in his issue 9 mm Beretta. The Mexican Air Force had only about a dozen supersonic jet fighters. Two were always warm in their hangars for

emergency interdiction-interception duties. He climbed
into his personal jeep and drove from the on-duty officer's bungalow to the pilot's ready locker room next to the
tarmac. He opened the locker room with his personal key
and changed into his flight suit. Rivera took up his helmet
and went out to the ready hangar. Ortega, the hangar guard,
looked up with vague interest and saluted. Rivera leveled
his Beretta and shot the man in the face.

Rivera took up Ortega's G-3 assault rifle and went to the
two ready fighters. Mexico's fighter force was minuscule
compared to even some of the most impoverished nations
in Central and South America. Her main air-to-air and
interception asset was the Northrop F-5E. It was a 1960s
design. Antiquated in the extreme, it had been tiny compared to most contemporary fighters at the time. It was a
mosquito in comparison to the last three generations of
fighters. The F-5 had been deliberately pushed as a plane
the United States could give to friendly nations with "primitive" air forces in the Military Assistance Program.

Rivera loved them.

Primitive she might be. Her radar was a joke. Despite
massive upgrades to her avionics, they were even worse.
There was only so much that could be done to upgrade the
antiquated package. But the little fighter was twin-engined
and had a fantastic thrust to weight ratio. Her airframe was
beautifully clean and she was extremely nimble. The F-5E
Tiger was a joy to fly.

Two of them sat in the hangar fully fueled, spare cen-
terline tank attached in standard interdiction configuration. Rivera walked up to the first fighter and emptied ten
rounds from his rifle into one engine and walked around
the fighter to put ten rounds in the other so it couldn't
follow him. He dropped the rifle and clambered up the re-
movable ready ladder into his personal bird. Rivera kicked

away the ladder and took a seat. He put on his helmet, heated up his engines and armed his weapons console. He would have liked a pair of rocket and gun pods but coercing airmen into doing it was problematic, and there was no time. He would have to make do with the bird as she was. Rivera pushed his throttle forward slightly and taxied his green-and-brown camouflaged F-5E out of the hangar and onto the tarmac. The tower began making rapid, alarmed inquiries over the radio.

Captain Rivera switched to the radio frequency Cordula had given him as he pulled onto the main fighter runway. F-5s were known as Freedom Fighters or Tigers depending on their age, but the narrow little fighter with its short wings had always reminded him of a dagger. Rivera knew he was the sacrificial knife in La Bestia's hand.

People and vehicles began scrambling across the airfield, but they were far too late.

Captain Miriamo Rivera shoved his throttles forward and his engines roared in response as he picked up speed. He pulled his stick up and his landing gear left the ground. Hell was his welcome destination, but at the moment over Chihuahua he owned the heavens.

The pilot kept his fighter low as he left the airbase behind him and streaked eastward. He rammed the throttles all the way forward and "kicked the can" to light his afterburners and ten thousand pounds of thrust rammed him back into his seat. Rivera broke the sound barrier as he streaked across the Mexican sky to do the Beast's bidding.

Aguila airstrip, Coahuila

GRIMALDI REFUELED the Socata. The Cessna was geared to go, and Nazareno sat in the cockpit with both engines running. He had taken them to another desert airstrip to refuel their woefully thirsty birds. Aguila was in terrible shape. It was almost indistinguishable from the surrounding desert except that one hopeful patch had been delineated with white painted rocks. According to Nazareno, on night landings they used tiki torches. Grimaldi was pretty sure one more potholed strip of Mexico would rip the landing gear right off the Socata. The luxury turboprop had never been designed for unprepared airfields. The good news was all they needed was one more landing, and with any luck that would be in the United States on a glass-smooth concrete runway. Aguila did have one luxury. While the Federacion Cartel didn't seem to be big on airfield maintenance, they had sunk in a fuel tank and pump and it was currently three-quarters full of aviation fuel. A corrugated shack offered shade but little else. Bolan ate cold leftover chili and drank warm beer for lack of any other refreshment.

He'd had worse breakfasts, and dawn over the desert was beautiful as the sun rose over the Sierra Madres.

Chet and Smallhouse took the opportunity to clean their weapons. Oderkirk catnapped on a blanket in the corner curled up with Highlander. Rudi was a mess. Flying wasn't doing his mutilated ear any good and, he had taken the last of the painkillers from the medical kit and was sleeping fitfully.

Zhong had stripped to the waist and was doing his morning calisthenics. His muscles rippled, tensed and released with dynamic tension as his hands hooked into claws and closed into fists. He performed the tiger claw set in a slow-motion dance of death. Bolan had to admit it was impressive.

"I hate that guy," Chet opined.

Smallhouse laughed as he ran a rag over his rifle. "I

recommend you hate him from at least three hundred meters and preferably from behind something thirty caliber."

"Whatever…"

Bolan's phone vibrated. He took it out, saw Kurtzman's icon and took a short walk away from the shack. "What have you got, Bear?"

"You about ready to take off?"

"Jack is topping off the Socata as we speak, why?"

"Well, as you know I've been tracking your progress, when you decide to let me know where you are or where you're heading that is."

Bolan ignored the mild reproach. "I always feel safer knowing that."

"Yeah, well, given what's been going on I also have the team collating any news in your projected area that might seem relevant."

"What do you have, Bear?"

"About half an hour ago, Mexican air force Captain Miriamo Rivera went to the fighter hangar of the 11th Military Airbase, shot the guard on duty in the face, disabled one of the two ready-intercept fighters and stole the other one."

"Where's the base?"

"Santa Gertrudis, central Chihuahua," Kurtzman replied.

Chihuahua was the state next door to Coahuila to the west. "We got a bearing on the captain?"

"Striker, Mexico doesn't have much of an air defense net. What little they have is based on their northern border and the Gulf. They've got three Brazilian R-99 Airborne Early Warning and Control aircraft. They've launched them, but they're located on either coast and their southern border with Central America. They've got nothing looking inward on the Mexican central highlands, and we believe they are holding station to see which way Rivera tries to break out. If he's trying to break out, that is."

"We got anything eyes on?"

"I'm trying to get a satellite. Nothing yet, and if this info is relevant to you I won't have anything in time."

"What's he flying?" Bolan asked.

"Northrop F-5E. If he puts the hammer all the way down and is on afterburners, he can do Mach 1.6."

"Assuming he's doing that and someone is vectoring him in straight at us, what's his estimated ETA?"

"Minutes or less, Striker. You'd better get out of there."

"What's his weapons fit?"

Kurtzman clicked keys. "If he's in standard intercept configuration, then he has two Pontiac 20 mm cannons in the nose with 280 rounds each and a Sidewinder air-to-air missile on each wing-tip."

"Right, Bear I…" Bolan's eyes flicked to Grimaldi. The pilot was staring westward. "Jack!" Bolan shouted. "What have you got?"

"Fastmover! Coming in right on the deck! Looks like—"

"Get out of there!"

Grimaldi waved at Nazareno and pointed. The man was horrified. Both pilots took off running. Bolan began to hear the warbling thunder of the approaching Tiger's twin turbojet engines. He'd dropped to low subsonic for his ground attack run. Bolan sprinted back to the shack. "Fastmover! Scatter!" Chet yanked up Oderkirk and thrust her rifle in her hand. Smallhouse pulled up the half-comatose Rudi and hauled him along.

Smoke puffed as a Sidewinder missile hissed off the Tiger's starboard wing rail. The Cessna Skymaster sat at the head of the strip with both its props turning. It wasn't a huge heat source, but in the early chill of the desert dawn the twin turboprops glowed like red suns in the Sidewinder's infrared seeker. The missile slammed into the Cessna's snout. The blast lifted the aircraft's nose up in a flaming wheelie, sending the propeller and the nose gear flying in separate directions. At the same time a continuous-rod fragmentation warhead sent its expanding, zigzag ring of welded rods buzz-sawing through the fuselage. The Cessna dropped its burning nose to the ground and sagged open in two smoking directions like a ragged steel wound.

The fighter jet streaked overhead with a thunderclap.

Chet and Smallhouse sent rifle fire after it, but it was out of range within seconds. The jet climbed into the sky and turned hard. Bolan ran for the Socata. "Cooper!" Everyone was screaming at him. "Cooper!"

Bolan leaped up through the Socata's cabin door as the fighter began its attack run. With its engine off and presenting its tail, the executive private plane didn't offer much of a target to a heat-seeking missile. Bolan could hear Smallhouse firing as fast as he could pull his trigger and everyone else's weapons chattering on full-auto. The F-5 was a light jet. Head on was the easiest angle to hit a plane in the air, and small arms fire might take it out. Bolan and his people had no time to slug it out. The pilot would knock out the Socata and then turn his attention to reap them with strafing runs as they ran.

The Executioner grabbed one of the RPGs they had taken from the mission fight and the Barrett Fifty. He lunged out the door of the Socata and hit the desert hard as he rolled under the turboprop's wing. It would provide no cover at all from the 20 mm cannons, but it would give him a precious few seconds of hiding time as the pilot began his gun run.

Bolan's people began shooting again, and as the soldier crouched beneath the wing he knew the storm was coming.

The twin Pontiac 20 mm cannons began tearing chunks out of the airstrip as the pilot began his gun run on the Socata. Bolan stepped out from under the wing with the RPG-7 shouldered and fired. Even head-on he had almost no chance of hitting the plane as the antitank rocket had no proximity fuse.

But whatever satanic bug Captain Rivera had planted in his head, he was still a pilot and all he saw was a man pop up and launch a shoulder-fired rocket at him. He ended his gun run and broke hard right away from the smoking rocket trail. Bolan dropped the smoking tube and heaved the Barrett onto his shoulder. The F-5 flashed overhead and its passage was like a slap to both of Bolan's eardrums.

The soldier swung around like a human turret and dropped to a knee.

The only attack profile on an aircraft better than head on was pulling straight away. Pulling away from small-arms fire was one thing. Pulling away from a rifle that fired .50-caliber machine-gun bullets was another, and the Barrett .50 was just short of being a crew-served weapon. Long ago Bolan had been trained as a sniper, and he had been one of the best. The hard, ugly years of his War Everlasting had arguably turned him into the greatest rifleman currently living on Earth. Bolan put his crosshairs directly between the Tiger's exhaust nozzles. They were flaming owl's eyes in his optics. Bolan started pulling the trigger. The armor-piercing incendiaries flew through the nozzles and tore through the mixers and buried themselves, burning, in turbines, compressors and combustors. In his scope Bolan saw one engine flame out and then the other.

The F-5E suddenly dropped from the sky like a stone tiger.

Bolan watched as exploding bolts blasted the cockpit canopy away and the ejection seat shot skyward. The pilot-less plane tipped over and fell toward the Coahuilan desert like a giant lawn dart. The jet punched a hole in the sand a mile away and exploded in a fireball. Bolan eased the Barrett off his shoulder and rose. He never took his eyes off the pilot as his seat fell away and he drifted down on his parachute.

Smallhouse appeared at Bolan's elbow. The huge marks-man looked out at the smoking hole in the desert, then Bolan, then back at the downed fighter and then Bolan again in open awe. "Dude...teach me."

"You want to know the secret?"

"Yeah!"

Bolan drew his pistol as Rivera landed about five hundred yards away. "Practice."

Smallhouse snorted in disgust. "Dude! I knew you were going to say that!"

"Keep your crosshairs on him, but don't shoot him unless you have to."

"Right." Smallhouse dropped into a rifleman's crouch. "On it."

"Everyone else all right?" Bolan called.

The team sounded off and came back together. Grimaldi stared at the noseless, sawed-open Cessna smoking on the strip. "What kind of a man desecrates a defenseless Skymaster?"

"One who worships Satan?" Oderkirk suggested.

Grimaldi folded his arms across his chest and shook his. "It's the only explanation that makes sense."

Chet pumped his shotgun. "And here comes the spawn of Beelzebub now."

Captain Rivera was charging across the desert and firing his pistol as he came. Smallhouse heaved a huge sigh. "Oh, for God's sake! Five hundred yards? With a Beretta? Tell me I can cap his ass and end the idiocy."

Rivera tossed away his empty pistol, drew his pilot's survival knife, held it overhead in both hands and continued his screaming charge.

"Please?" Smallhouse pleaded.

Bolan shook his head. "Zhong, take him but don't kill him."

Zhong strode out across the desert to meet the captain. Rivera charged the triad killer with his knife overhead like a matador going for the kill on a bull. Zhong just waited. The pilot screamed in bloodlust. The Chinese assassin suddenly turned, bent and shot out his right foot in a back thrust kick. Bolan wasn't a martial artist per se, but at the Farm he sparred and had learned techniques from men who were. It was what in kung fu was known as a "tiger-tail kick." Zhong's right heel met Rivera's left iliac crest and snapped the left wing of his hip in two.

The pilot's left leg collapsed beneath him, and he fell screaming to the sand.

Bolan's blood went cold. Zhong could have taken the pilot with a throw, lock or nerve hold with childlike ease. He'd crippled Rivera because he'd wanted to.

Smallhouse muttered as he kept his eye on his optics. "That was messed up. Remember what I told you, Chet."

Chet clutched his shotgun white-knuckled. "Loud and clear, brother."

Zhong drew his hatchet from the back of his belt, took a knee and shaved off an ear. Rivera screamed and flailed. He didn't notice as the assassin held it up and shrugged at Bolan. The soldier waved his hand beneath his chin in the negative. Zhong flipped the ear into the dust beside Rivera and walked away.

Bolan turned to Grimaldi. "I want to be airborne before they send the cavalry after us."

"Ten minutes."

Bolan looked at the fallen pilot weeping and clutching his shattered hip in the dust. "We got room for him?"

"We'll make room."

Grimaldi shouted at Nazareno. "Naz! Let's get that girl prepped!"

"Terrell, Chet, grab the blanket from the shack. Put our friend on it and take him to the plane. Try and be gentle about it. Libby, we got any painkillers left?"

"No, Rudi took the last of them."

Bolan frowned. "Pour a few beers down him. It's the best we can do until we get him stateside."

"Right."

Bolan pulled out his phone and hit Kurtzman's icon. Kurtzman answered instantly and he was pretty frantic. "Striker!"

"We're all right."

"What happened? Was it Rivera?" Bolan activated his phone's camera and played it on the crashed fighter in the distance and the captain being loaded into a blanket.

Kurtzman paused for a moment. "You shot him down and took him captive?"

"Yeah," Bolan admitted.

Every once in a while Kurtzman came to the conclusion that Mack Bolan could no longer do anything that surprised him. He was always wrong. "What do you want on my end?"

"I need to get out of Mexico. The Beast is hurling every asset he has at us, and it keeps getting nastier. Frankly I'm worried about what kind of assets he might have in the States. My people need rest, and then we need to get across the pond and hit Berlin. Twenty-four hours without being attacked would be nice."

"What's the range on your plane?"

"Jack says about seventeen hundred miles."

"All right, I have an idea. It'll be right at the edge of your range, but once you get there it's tropical breezes and nothing satanic in sight."

"Good enough."

"I'll get on the horn with Jack," Kurtzman said.

Bolan clicked off wearily. He looked down to see Highlander staring at him as if the dog felt he needed a job, as well. "You just watch my six, that's your job."

Highlander wagged his tail. He understood his job perfectly.

CHAPTER NINETEEN

Pensacola Naval Air Station, Florida

F-18 fighter jets screamed overhead. Jack Grimaldi sighed as he watched them. Bolan had to smile. Grimaldi was in the running for greatest living pilot on Earth, but U.S. naval carrier pilots were the best of America's best. Bolan knew Grimaldi's heart was up there with them as the fledgling fighter pilots trained to make the grade.

The soldier went back into the empty hangar they were calling home. He was giving his team twenty-four hours' rest and recuperation before they invaded Germany. If Satan and his servants wanted to come after them, they would have to take on an entire U.S. Naval Air Station to do it.

A base surgeon had successfully reattached Rudi's ear, sans tracking device, but he was still carrying it on his person. Rivera was still in the station hospital having his hip pinned back together. Just about everyone else was taking the opportunity to eat and clock nap time. The side of Rudi's head was swollen like a balloon. He was on some serious painkillers and sleeping on a cot in the corner. Chet and Zhong were sleeping next to him. Nazareno was out admiring aircraft, and Oderkirk and Smallhouse were at the PX getting some fresh clothes and personal supplies that everyone was in dire need of. Everything they needed for the next phase would be prepositioned in Berlin, but at the moment the team was beaten, bruised and exhausted and in the limbo of transition. No one was looking forward to catching that transatlantic flight to Europe.

Bolan would sleep on the plane. He had been working, as had Kurtzman.

The soldier went into the hangar office. Highlander looked up and thumped his tail on the floor. "Good boy," Bolan said. He sat down in front of his satellite link and laptop and hoped his labors had achieved something. He had sent Kurtzman photos of the transmitter up close and from every angle. X-rays of the device had been taken at the base hospital and blown up. During the examination it had come to light that the 666 tattoo had a barium marker in the ink. Using the right illuminator, someone could scan the mark to see if it was legitimate or not. Included were photos of Rudi's ear before it had been reattached and notes about the placement of the device by the surgeon who had done Rudi's ear reattachment. It was scant. Kurtzman was dying to get his hands on a real specimen, but the only weapon Bolan had against the Beast was one big bluff. Rudi and Rivera were their prisoners, but the Beast had no clue that they knew about the transmitters they had carried inside their bodies.

Bolan clicked a key and Kurtzman's craggy face appeared on an inset in his screen. It was a good sign that the man was smiling and sipping a mug of the battery acid he liked to refer to as coffee.

"So," Bolan said. "We're talking RFIDs?"

"Oh, we are indeed," Kurtzman replied. "The most sophisticated I've ever seen."

Bolan almost regretted his next sentence but he needed info. "Tell me about it."

Kurtzman stopped short of cracking his knuckles. "There are basically three kinds of radio-frequency identification devices or tags. The first are active tags. They contain a battery and can transmit signals autonomously. Those are like the kind they use to track whales and polar bears and wolverine populations in the wild. Until very recently those devices tended to be rather large. You had to attach them to the subject with a collar or in the case of a whale embed it in their skin."

"Number two?" Bolan asked. So far it was pretty painless.

"The second is a passive tag. It doesn't have a battery so it can be a lot smaller, but then you need an outside source to provoke a signal transmission. That's like the tags veterinarians put in your dog's ear or the tags the European Union and a number of other nations are starting to put in passports. Animal control or your friendly customs agent hits the tag with a scanner and it gives back information about who the dog's owner is, address and contact info and even medical history."

"And number three?"

"Number three is the magic number," Kurtzman stated. "What we're talking about, and what I think you have there, is a BAP, or battery assisted, passive tag."

Bolan sensed it was about to get technical. "And so…?"

"And so a BAP requires an outside source to wake up, but they have a much higher forward link capability for modulating and demodulating radio frequencies."

"Bear…" Bolan cautioned.

"Range." Kurtzman sighed. "We're talking incredibly small and incredible range."

"We're talking satellites."

"Indeed, possibly more than one, but remember all we're doing is transmitting and receiving radio frequencies. You wouldn't need a military-grade orbiter. Any commercial telecommunications satellite could do it, and there are well over a thousand of those currently circling the globe."

"So Satan has his own bar-code scanner in the sky."

Kurtzman grinned over his coffee. "Not bad. Listen, the technology isn't that sophisticated, but it's the size of the device that's remarkable, and the way they're deploying it is incredible, but you've got to give them credit for cleverness."

From long-ago Sunday school, Bolan recalled the Book of Revelation. "'And he causeth all, both rich and poor, free and bond, to receive the mark…'"

The computer expert sobered slightly from his earlier enthusiasm. Bolan stared at the tiny device on the table before him like it was a spider. "How long can a battery that size last?"

"Don't know, and won't until I can take it apart, but it doesn't take much energy to generate a radio signal."

Bolan frowned at the tiny thing before him. "That's going to be one weak-ass signal."

"Oh, undoubtedly, but the real question is not how weak the signal is, but how close and or how powerful the ear listening for it is."

"Can he really be tracking hundreds of people at once?"

Kurtzman had been giving that a lot of thought. "I could be wrong, but I don't think so. Unless the Beast has his very own dedicated satellites, which I doubt, he is using someone else's, or even a string of someone else's under the guise of some other telecommunication activity. If that's the case, he'll want to keep his exposure to a minimum."

He leaned back in his chair. "Then again, from everything you've told me he doesn't have to keep tabs on his flock all the time. The Beast seems to be doing a fine job of keeping his little droogies in line with pure terror, so most of the time he doesn't have to track them. He would really only need to go active, say, during an operation when he wants to keep track of the participants."

"Or if one of his little acolytes happens to leave."

"Exactly. During an operation, a satellite sends down a signal and the RFIDs go active. The microchip is tiny, but the functions he requires are extremely simple by processing standards. All he really needs is to have the equivalent of a tracking number to ID everyone in range and track them. There would be plenty of room on the chip to have different frequencies and different activation signals for different individuals, groups or even situations. For example, if one of his guys dies without anyone else knowing about it, it would take almost nothing to have a tiny sensor in that device that would tell it to go active if the body temperature of the wearer went, well, since the ear is an externally mounted organ, say twenty degrees below body normal. The signal only has to last for a couple of days. He swoops in, takes heads and he's gone. If for some reason he needs to reimplant someone after the device wears out, pick your satanic ritual. We're dealing with a cult. There's a million ways to make it work."

Kurtzman shook his head in admiration at the scope of the scheme. "Keep this in mind, too. He doesn't necessarily have to rely totally on satellite windows. It's very possible, and I'd say likely, that he has mobile, ground-based sending and receiving units as well to communicate with the implants, and the rig wouldn't be any larger than the one you're talking to me with now."

"It's slick," Bolan admitted. "So, we're figuring the Beast is based out of Germany. Probably Berlin is home base. He has some pretty wide-open access to telecommunication satellites, has staff or access to people working on the latest RFID technology and has the capacity

to mass produce the devices on at least a limited scale.
That's going to take real money. Figure he some initial
seed money to get started and then garnered more in the
German criminal underworld. Narcotics would be his fast-
est money vector."

"Barring direct intervention from the beyond?" Kurtzman said. "That's my best scenario, too."

"Then I need a shortlist of likely suspects by the time
I hit Berlin, and something with a barium marker so I can
fake the mark of the Beast."

"I'm on it. What route do you intend to—"

"Boss!" Chet ran up to office breathlessly. "We got a
problem!"

"To be continued, Bear." Bolan cut the link. "What kind
of problem?"

"We got three individuals in full Navy dress uniform
comin' this way across the tarmac. Grimaldi makes them
out as JAG officers."

Bolan refrained from swearing. Kurtzman had chosen
Naval Air Station Pensacola because the chances of Satan's
minions considering a suicide attack much less even stag-
ing it were astronomical. The doctors, nurses and liaison
officers Bolan had worked with had sworn themselves to
secrecy, but the fact was he had commandeered a hangar,
engaged in some very anomalous activity and brought
some very strange guests onto the base. Someone along
the line had shot his or her mouth off, and officers of the
military's Judge Advocate General wanted to know what
the hell was going on.

"Jack!" Bolan shouted. "Stall them! Charm offensive!"

Grimaldi nodded and leaned nonchalantly against the
hangar door.

"Chet, wake up Rudi and hide him in the bathroom!"

"Boss, he's all hopped up and out like a—"

"Then carry him!" Bolan slapped his hands together like a gunshot. "Zhong! Naz! Hide. We have company!"

Zhong leaped to his feet like a cat. Naz looked up sleepily. Rudi continued to snore away.

"Zhong, get on the horn with Libby and Terrell! Get them here ASAP, but tell them to come in through the back and lie low!"

Chet charged over to Rudi's cot. The German made a few somnambulant noises as Chet slung him into a fireman's carry and hustled him toward the john. Zhong got on his phone. Bolan squared his shoulders. He had shaved, bathed and gotten a square meal into himself, but he was still bruised, somewhat flash-burned and knew he looked as ragged around the edges as he felt. He tucked his Beretta into the back of his belt and untucked his shirt over it. "Highlander, stay." Bolan walked out of the hangar office.

Grimaldi stood before the door chatting with two men and a woman in full Navy dress blue uniforms. The woman was a shorter, harsher version of Oderkirk. All were carrying briefcases and wearing sunglasses. The Stony Man pilot was smiling amiably.

The lawyers weren't.

Bolan checked the rings on the lead JAG officer's cuffs and eyed the patchwork of service decorations on his chest. Grimaldi tilted his head at their gentleman caller and his associates. "This is Captain Gerwulf, Lieutenant Vance—" Grimaldi gave the woman in uniform an extra bit of wattage in his smile "—and Lieutenant Smythe."

The captain smiled disarmingly and shoved out his hand. "My friends call me Manny. And you are…?"

Bolan shook the offered hand. "How can I be of help, Captain?"

Gerwulf sighed. "Listen, I'll be frank with you. Word is you have a German citizen here under some very suspicious circumstances and that there are some pretty peculiar guests in this hangar. Word is the situation is don't ask don't tell, but my superiors are not in the loop and they are not happy about it. Any cooperation at all you can give me would go a long way to smoothing over this situation."

Bolan took out a business card and handed it to the captain, who stared at it. There was nothing on it but a number. "What am I supposed to do with this?"

The Executioner kept his initial response to himself. "You can call it." Bolan looked meaningfully at the captain's rings on the man's sleeves. "All it will do is probably get you ripped a new one."

The captain stiffened. "I can take this to the base commander."

"You could do that." Bolan nodded. "But I already gave him one."

Gerwulf spun on his heel in a rage. "We're out of here."

Grimaldi shrugged. "Have a nice—"

Lieutenant Smythe tore a stun gun out of her satchel and shot Grimaldi in the chest. Bolan slapped leather for his Beretta. Gerwulf bowed at the waist and his back thrust kick slammed the air out of Bolan's lungs and knocked him backward. The soldier fell back with the force of the blow into a back roll. He came up on one knee with his Beretta in hand. Gerwulf fired his stun gun. One probe hit Bolan in his gun hand and the other spiked into his chest. Gerwulf's smile was sickening as he gave Bolan the juice.

The gun pumped 50,000 watts into Bolan's body. His body seized and his muscles tried to lock. He involuntarily fired a burst into the ceiling, and then the machine pistol

slid from his spasming fingers. Bolan had been hit with a
stun gun before and he didn't care for it. From the pit of
his gut a roar like a lion's ripped its way out of his throat.
Bolan seized the wires and tore the barbed probes from
his flesh.

Gerwulf smiled delightedly as he tossed the spent stun
gun away. "Impressive."

Bolan clawed for the snub-nosed pistol in his ankle
holster, but his twitching, overloaded nervous system
made him a heartbeat too slow. Gerwulf kicked Bolan in
the chest and sent him sprawling backward again. Bolan
couldn't manage a second back roll and he hit the concrete hard. "Smythe" already had Grimaldi zip-tied like
a hog.

Gerwulf's counterfeit JAG officers came in with silenced Heckler & Koch Personal Defensive Weapons in
hand. Then he opened his briefcase and took out a PDW
of his own. He spun a sound suppressor onto the muzzle
of the compact submachine gun and looked around the
hangar.

"I am pleased to inform you that Captain Miriamo
Rivera has paid for his failure." Bolan saw stars as Ger-
wulf kicked him in the face. "Now, tell me, where is young
Rudi?"

Chet's shotgun blast smashed "Vance" off his feet.
"Come and get him!"

Smythe snapped her weapon to her shoulder and for half
a heartbeat Chet balked at shooting a woman. Sparks flew
off Chet's shotgun and he staggered back and sat down as
she rewarded his chivalry with a burst to the chest. Zhong
had no such qualms. His hatchet spun through the air. The
redhead's feet flew out from underneath her as Zhong's
blade sank into her skull. Zhong beckoned Gerwulf in
with his empty hands. "Come. Contend with me."

Gerwulf sighed like a man who was genuinely regretting a missed opportunity as he raised his weapon. "I would love to, but—"

Highlander hit Gerwulf like canine lightning. The German staggered back, swearing a blue streak as Highlander's fangs sank into his arm. The dog ripped his head back and forth, flaying the flesh to the bone and lunged, snapping for the throat. Gerwulf pressed his pistol into the Doberman's side and pulled the trigger. Highlander yelped piteously and collapsed to the concrete. Zhong charged across the hangar, but he was empty-handed and ten yards too far away as Gerwulf swore, bled and lifted his weapon.

"Hey."

Gerwulf's eyes snapped to the man at his feet. Bolan was still shaking from the current but his pistol was in his hand. He pulled the trigger four times. Gerwulf jerked and flinched, and Bolan knew the man was wearing armor beneath his uniform. The Executioner put the front sight on Gerwulf's chin and squeezed. The German's head rubbernecked as he took a 9 mm uppercut to the jaw.

Zhong's flying butterfly kick was extraneous but still spectacular as he sailed over Bolan and separated what was left of Gerwulf's mandible from his head. The German dropped jawless to the hangar deck.

Bolan holstered his empty revolver, rose shakily and retrieved the Beretta. "Chet!"

Chet grimaced. There was blood on his chest, hands and face. "I…think I'm okay."

Bolan dropped to a knee beside him. Chet's shotgun lay on the floor, and its gleaming finish was scratched and scored where the PDW's burst had hit it. The needle-pointed bullets had broken apart and scored Chet like shrapnel. The wounds looked mostly superficial.

"Holy hell!" Smallhouse's voice echoed in the hangar. He and Oderkirk were breathless from running across the tarmac, and they had pistols drawn.

"Zhong—" Bolan nodded toward the lavatory "—go get Rudi."

Zhong took up a fallen PDW and went.

Smallhouse looked around at the carnage. "Is everyone all right?"

"Highlander!" Oderkirk cried. She ran to the fallen dog. "Highlander!"

Chet shook his head. "Go see to him. I'm okay."

Bolan pushed the selector on his machine pistol to semi-auto. He walked over and knelt beside Highlander. The dog lay in a pool of his own blood.

Oderkirk was close to tears. She bit her lip. "Is he okay?"

"Good boy," Bolan said. "You had my six." Highlander wagged his tail weakly. Bolan grimaced as he gently touched the wound. "He's shot."

"But he's not, I mean…" Oderkirk burst into tears as she looked at the gun in Bolan's hand. "No, you're not, you're not going to…"

Bolan gave Highlander's wound a closer look. For all the talk of the tremendous yawing and tumbling damage the new breed of subcaliber armor-piercing rounds inflicted on human flesh, it was Bolan's experience that most of the time they zinged straight through people, and luckily in this case dogs, like ice picks.

"Lib," Bolan said, "the U.S. military employs more veterinarians than any other organization on earth. I give you my word I'm going to get Highlander the medical care he's earned and deserves."

"And then what?" Oderkirk sniffed and pushed at her face. "We can't take him to Germany with us."

"No, not in this condition." Berlin was the final haul on this one. Bolan was missing Highlander already. "But I know a little place up north where he can rest and recuperate."

"What kind of place?" She looked at Bolan defiantly. "He's a hero. He doesn't belong in some stinky kennel somewhere."

Bolan smiled as he thought of the Farm and the surrounding Blue Ridge Mountains of Virginia. He looked Oderkirk in the eye and spoke the truth. "It's a place where the men are men, the women are women, and a dog can be a dog without being hassled by anyone." She giggled and pushed at the tears on her cheeks. Bolan nodded at her. "Get the medical kit. We need to staunch the bleeding."

Nazareno stopped dead as he walked into the hangar and stared around slack-jawed. "What happened here?"

Bolan looked over at Grimaldi. The hog-tied pilot rolled his eyes heavenward. "Naz, cut Jack loose."

Zhong ushered Rudi out into the hangar. He pointed at Vance. "You are acquainted with this individual?"

Rudi shook his head in a daze. *"Nein,* I mean no."

Zhong walked him past Smythe. "Perchance this one?"

"No."

"And what of—"

Rudi went white. *"Ach, mein Gott!"*

Even without a jaw Rudolph Lohm recognized the dead man and it rocked him to his core. "He said his name was Meinrad Gerwulf," Bolan said. "Is that true?"

"Yes." Rudi couldn't take his eyes off him. "He is Meinrad Gerwulf."

"And who is Meinrad Gerwulf."

"He is the man who recruited me." Rudi shuddered. "He is the hand of the Beast."

CHAPTER TWENTY

Berlin

"Where in the nine hells is Gerwulf?" Krom growled.

The Beast steepled his fingers. "I fear the worst for poor Meinrad."

Cordula Schön leaned in behind the Beast and began rubbing his temples. Krom watched in open envy. "Exotic" only began to describe the woman. Schön was tall and her skin was chalk white. Krom wondered if she had seen the sun at all in the past ten years. Her black hair fell to her waist. She looked like a Playboy bunny who had been buried alive then returned from the dead and turned Goth. She was tall and broad-shouldered. Her face was just short of emaciated, but her lips were red and generous and her dark eyes huge. Her breasts and hips were lush curves in stark contrast to the rest of her body, which almost spoke of starvation. Cordula Schön wasn't a beautiful woman, but sexuality seemed to glow from within her like an obscene hunger. It hit most men and many women like a left to the jaw and left them reeling, and often following. It was particularly effective among those the Beast sought to control. Her voice was a low purr. "Meinrad is in America. Retrieval will be difficult."

The Beast frowned and made a call he didn't wish to make. There had been far too much exposure already. He pushed a button on his desk. A nervous voice answered immediately. "Yes, my master?"

"Activate tags 2, 29, 32 and 47."

"Immediately."

The Beast watched as a geopolitical map of the United States appeared on the Yalos Diamond television screen on the wall. It was an extravagant screen, but opulence was something he believed he needed to project. Everything the Beast wore, drove, fired or inhabited was of the absolute highest quality and of ridiculous cost. The rewards to those who successfully served him were equally extravagant, just as the cost of failure severe in the extreme. The state of Florida highlighted and took up the screen. Four dots appeared in the upper right-hand corner of the state. The Beast frowned at Krom. "I was given to believe Meinrad and his team were in Pensacola."

The giant Turk shrugged his mighty shoulders. "As was I."

The screen zoomed on the blips. The voice on the intercom spoke. "Rivera, Gerwulf, Becker and Klose are currently in Jacksonville."

"Meinrad reported Rivera was dead. Give me a city grid and a location," the Beast demanded.

The screen zoomed again and a grid of city streets appeared. The blips were on the east side of the city. "What is their location?"

The voice spoke fearfully. "They appear to be located in Mayport Naval Station."

"Why would they be there rather than at Naval Air Station Pensacola?"

"I suspect because that is also the Southeast Field Office of the U.S. Naval Criminal Investigative Service."

"NCIS," Krom rumbled. "This is not good."

Schön narrowed her huge dark eyes. "Then they are

either incarcerated or their bodies are downstairs in forensics."

The Beast smiled dryly. "I believe incarcerating Meinrad would be an uncertain proposition at best."

"Then he, Klose and Becker are dead, and retrieval or disposal will be very difficult." Schön ceased her massaging and poured wine. "With one naval station already attacked they will be at the highest level of alert."

Krom chewed his lower lip. "And with an NCIS forensics pathologist examining the bodies, there is a genuine possibility of the RFID tags being detected."

"We always knew someday our ruse would be discovered." The Beast rose. His blue eyes gleamed with amusement. That gleam made Krom nervous. It even made Schön somewhat wary. "And if and when it was? We knew it would most likely be Americans who discovered it."

Krom scratched his beard. "So what do we do about Meinrad?"

"Nothing."

"Nothing?"

"Meinrad is refrigerated meat. I am not currently willing to expend any more assets in the United States. If the Americans discover our ruse, then so be it. It will take them years to dispel our mythology in Mexico, if ever."

Krom shook his head. "So it is business as usual? We do nothing."

"Business will never be the same," the Beast corrected. "And I said we would do nothing about Meinrad for the present."

"And the Americans? And the Chinese?" Krom shrugged again. "Rudi?"

"We kill them."

The Beast spoke into the intercom. "Where is Rudi now?"

The huge screen shifted to a world map. A blip appeared off the coast of France. "Rudi is currently over the North Atlantic, traveling at 300 knots. Given his current course, he will be in German airspace in approximately three hours."

"I believe it is time to put young Ernst to work." The Beast looked at Schön. "Do you believe he is ready to serve me?"

The woman's scarlet lips twisted into a smile of genuine evil. "His zeal would make a samurai blush." She crooked her little finger. "If I ask him to leap into a volcano he would do so, your name upon his lips and thoughts of my flesh engorging his groin."

The Beast threw back his head and laughed. He tossed back the glass of burgundy in a gulp. Krom took a moment to savor the glass Schön handed him. The Beast began giving a series of short, concise orders over the intercom. Krom smiled as the wine blossomed into pleasing warmth in his stomach. Whatever the Americans thought they might meet in Germany, this was certainly not going to be it.

Twenty thousand feet above Germany

"So it's all a scam?" Oderkirk asked.

"It appears that way," Bolan replied.

"Then how do you explain the *Exorcist* moment back at the bungalow?"

"You're a hypnotist."

"Yeah, but I have never seen anything like that. You can even imprint suggestions in the subconscious that will only emerge during certain triggers, but that was a full-blown—" Oderkirk searched for words "—event."

"I think that event was scripted, and designed to come out during an interrogation."

"That's stretching the powers of hypnotism, Coop."

"You said it yourself, you can't make anyone say or do anything they want to. These guys want to believe in Satan. They want to believe in his power. I don't think they would reject the script subconsciously."

"How do you implant the script?"

"Drugs," Bolan answered. "Very powerful drugs."

"That's horrible."

"There was talk about the Russians programming sleepers to commit assassinations and terror activities. But taking Americans, even ones sympathetic to the Red cause, whisking them off to Russia, conditioning them and sending them back wasn't cost effective. It was most effective locally. Emplacing East Germans in Germany."

"Or Mexican drug dealers in Mexico."

"Right."

"You ever seen anything like that?"

Bolan thought of a few minds he'd seen controlled, and an attempt or two that had been made on his. "Yeah, not exactly the same, but yeah, I have."

Jack Grimaldi's voice spoke over the cabin intercom. "Sarge, we have a bogey."

"What kind of bogey, Jack?"

"Not sure, but it's closing in fast."

Bolan went forward to join the pilot, copilot and Grimaldi in the cockpit. The Globemaster's pilot was pointing at something in the distance. Bolan squinted out the windshield. "Looks like some kind of small plane, coming head on."

The copilot was shaking his head. "He's not answering on any frequency."

The pilot was shaking his head, as well. "He's coming in fast. He— Jesus!"

Flame strobed from beneath the oncoming plane's

wings and raked the cockpit. Glass shattered and a wind-storm cycloned the cockpit interior. The emergency oxygen masks dropped from the ceiling as the cockpit lost pressure. The enemy plane streaked by and Bolan saw some kind of turboprop with a gun pod mounted under each wing. The pilot groaned and slumped his seat. Grimaldi hauled the stricken pilot out of his seat and shouted at the copilot. "Take care of your buddy!"

Grimaldi slid into the pilot's bloody seat and called out on the radio. "Mayday! Mayday! Mayday!" He shoved his wheel down and took the gigantic transport plane into a precipitous dive for the deck.

"What was that?" Bolan demanded.

"Looked like a T-6 Texan II. Luftwaffe issue! It's a primary trainer and someone has strapped some guns on it!"

"Can you outrun it?"

"Normally yes! But we got a belly full of armored vehicles!"

"Can he shoot us down?"

"The good news is it looks like he's got two .50-caliber guns and this is one gigantic airplane! Structurally we could take machine gun hits until doomsday. I don't think he knew we were in a C-17! I think he was just vectored onto us by that signal you dug out of Rudi's ear."

"Can he shoot us down?" Bolan repeated.

"He can make another run or two on the cockpit." Grimaldi flashed his grin. "That might do it! But it will take him a lot of time to get ahead of us, turn and attack again and again. If I were him I think I'd be better off in a stern chase and carefully shooting up our engines one at a time."

"So what are you going to do about it?"

"I can try and set her down if you like!"

Bolan gazed down at the snowcapped and rapidly approaching German Alps. "You mean crash."

"Yeah!"

"With a belly full of armor?"

"Yeah!"

"Naw!" Bolan pointed down. "Take us down to the deck but hold us steady! Hit the chaff flares when I tell you!"

"He isn't using missiles!"

"I know! Just do it!"

"What are you going to do?"

"I'm your tail-gunner!"

Grimaldi spared a glance at the pistol strapped to Bolan's thigh. "That would be a daisy!"

Bolan left the maelstrom of the cockpit. His team was all up and staring intently. The loadmaster was appalled. "Did we just hit something?"

"We just got shot up. The pilot's hit. They'll be coming around to chop us up from behind."

"Jesus! Can we outrun him?" the loadmaster asked.

Bolan looked at the line of tanks filling the hold. "Not with these bad boys on board. On my signal I need to open the loading ramp."

If the loadmaster had been appalled before, he now went apoplectic. "You are *not* going to rain armored vehicles on the Alps! I will see this plane go down first!"

"I'm not going to do that. All I need you to do is turn off the interior lights and open the ramp when I say."

The loadmaster stomped to the intercom. "Sir! Our passenger wants me to open the ramp!"

The copilot shouted over the hurricane in the cockpit. "I'd do it if I were you!"

"Fine!" The loadmaster looked about at Bolan's motley crew. "You all better fold down a seat and strap in!"

"Chet!" Bolan ordered. "With me!"

Bolan ran back to a tank, opened a spare ammo box and was pleased to find a belt of .50-caliber ammo.

Chet scrambled on top of the tank and loaded up the machine gun. Bolan took a seat at the weapon operator's position and fired up the interior remote control station for the Protector M151. The Stryker's .50-caliber gun was mounted on an exterior, unmanned turret slaved to an optical fire control system. Bolan punched a few keys and was pleased to see the hold of the C-17 appear on his targeting monitor. He heard the telltale "clack-clack!" above, and Chet slid down the hatch. "You're hot!"

The remote station agreed with Chet's assessment. Bolan took the joystick in hand and with the press of a button a pair of red crosshairs appeared squarely on the loading ramp. He panned left and right to make sure everything was working properly and then brought his sight picture back to the ramp. "Tell the loadmaster to turn the lights out and open it up on your signal."

Chet stuck his head out the commander's hatch and shouted back into the hold. Bolan set his phone for hands free. "Jack!"

Grimaldi's voice came back in a garble past the wind. "We're flying level! I don't know if you can hear it but we just lost the port outboard engine!"

"Hit the flares!" Bolan ordered.

He shouted up at Chet. "Now!"

"Lights out!" Chet shouted. "Open the door!"

The hold of the C-17 went dark. The fuselage vibrated with the dull pops of the infrared flares as they burst out of their boxes and turned the sky on either side of the C-17 into the Fourth of July. The huge ramp began to whine downward and the wind howled into the hold. They were below the clouds, and the gray light of the overcast day spilled inside. Behind them dozens of glittering flares filled the sky trailing smoke. The enemy plane suddenly appeared on Bolan's screen. He had instinctively jinked aside from the eruption of flares and was banking back onto his firing station. Whatever he saw in the open ramp didn't rattle him. Flame chattered beneath his wings as he went for another engine.

Bolan put the red crosshairs squarely on the turboprop's glass cockpit and squeezed the trigger on his joystick.

The .50-caliber gun spewed armor-piercing incendiary into the enemy plane at ten rounds per second. Bolan held the trigger down. The Texan II bubble canopy burst apart and so did the man inside it. The trainer's gun fell silent. The plane slid sideways through the sky with no one on the stick, then turned over into its death dive.

Chet rebel-yelled after their fallen enemy. "Yeee-haw!"

"Tell the loadmaster to button her up." Bolan got back on the phone with Grimaldi. "Get on the horn, get us down at the first airfield that can handle this bird."

"I'm on it. The Luftwaffe says we have fighter escorts inbound, ETA fifteen minutes."

It was fifteen minutes too late and a euro short, but Bolan had to admit a dogfight had been an unexpected development. "Tell them thanks."

"You know something?"

"What's that, Jack?"

"I believe that was the first air-to-air kill for a Stryker armored vehicle."

Bolan was pretty sure it was the first air-to-air kill for any armored vehicle. "Couldn't have done it without it you, Jack." Bolan powered down the remote station as the ramp clanged shut and a modicum of normalcy returned to the Globemaster's cargo hold.

CHAPTER TWENTY-ONE

Ramstein Air Force Base, Germany

Grimaldi stood away from his work. "What do you think?"

The Stony Man pilot had painted an excellent silhouette of a T-6 Texan II on the sand-colored hull of the Stryker vehicle confirming its shoot-down. The Strykers had been rolled off the C-17 while she was checked over for damage. The pilot had been rushed to the base hospital, and the doctors were confident he would regain the use of his arm and fly again. Bolan's team was once again calling an air hangar home. Bolan gazed on Grimaldi's artwork admiringly. "Very nice."

The pilot grinned happily. "You know, four more and you make ace."

Bolan snorted.

Both men looked over as a black van with U.S. Air Force markings drove up. Smallhouse's voice came across the com clipped to Bolan's shoulder. The marksman was perched up in the superstructure of the hangar with his rifle. "I have him."

The van driver waved and pulled into the hangar. A man who could have been Oderkirk's brother piled out of the van. He wore an Air Force uniform with silver Lieutenant's bars and sported a spectacular head of red hair that was threatening to riot out of regulation Air Force grooming standards. He looked at Bolan and stuck out his hand. "Lieutenant Bryan Krebs."

"Guy in lieutenant's uniform, German last name?" Grimaldi muttered under his breath. "This is how it started last time."

Bolan shook the hand. "Cooper. You our C3 guy?"

C3 was Command, Control and Communications. Lieutenant Krebs allowed himself a smirk. "Electronic Warfare specialist, actually, but yeah, I'm all C-cubed up."

"Even better. Follow me." Bolan led the lieutenant into the hangar. "What's your status, Lieutenant?"

"As of 0800 I am on detached duty to..." Krebs looked around at Bolan's team. Something made him look up in the rafters. Smallhouse waved down at him. "The secret world government?" Krebs concluded.

Bolan waved at a folding table. "What do you make of that?"

Krebs peered at the tiny almost gelatinous strip. "Some kind of dead bug?"

"Oh, it's a bug all right, and as of this morning we knew it wasn't dead yet." Bolan picked a magnifying glass off the table and handed it to Krebs. "Look closer."

Krebs took the magnifying glass and looked closer. "Wow." He leaned back in surprise and then leaned back in again. "Wow."

"Yeah."

"Where did you get it?"

Bolan pointed at Rudi. "I pulled it out of his ear."

Krebs blinked at the mutilated German. "You know I think I saw this on *The X-Files* once."

"We believe it's an RFID of the Battery Assisted Passive tag variety."

"Wow," Krebs repeated.

"We're pretty sure a satellite transmission triggered activation, and it's being tracked as we speak."

Krebs leaned over the device again. "Wow."

"I want you to determine what the signal was that activated it, and what signal it is giving off for tracking."

Krebs shrugged confidently. "Simple enough."

"And without tearing it apart or destroying it."

A little confidence oozed out of the lieutenant. "Uh, okay."

Bolan handed the Electronic Warfare warrior the rather thin report he and Kurtzman had compiled. Krebs quickly scanned the few pages of theory and scant data. "Wow. Interesting."

"Can you do it?"

"I can do it. Could take fifteen minutes. Could take all day. Could take all week. But yeah, I can do it."

"I'll give you all day. Then I have to move."

"Okay, first thing is to identify its tag. That's the easy part." Krebs went to the van and started pulling out olive-drab suitcases of electronic equipment. Within minutes he had what looked like God's own ham radio station set up on the table along with two laptops and several devices that could only be described as weird and wonderful-looking. Bolan had to admit that the little squib of the RFID looked helpless before Lieutenant Krebs's mighty array. Krebs sat down and put on a pair of headphones as he began flicking switches, twiddling dials and typing data.

Grimaldi cracked a grin. "Always a pleasure to see an expert at work."

Bolan nodded as Krebs's eyebrows raised and lowered, his brow wrinkled and cleared, and his eyes flared and narrowed in remarkable facial contortions as he processed what he was hearing and seeing from his equipment. "Got it."

Chet nodded. "That was fast."

Krebs hit a button and his printer reeled out a few inches of paper with a single line of text. "There's your tag by designation, frequency and wavelength." Krebs sat back and cracked his knuckles. "Now to find out what sets this girl off."

Grimaldi whispered low. "Lieutenant Krebs just called the RFID girl…"

"How do you do that?" Bolan asked.

"I want to turn the RFID off and then hit it with just about the entire radio spectrum until I find its trigger or triggers."

Bolan wasn't a communications guy, but he knew a little about the radio spectrum. "Isn't that a bit large?"

"Huge," Krebs agreed. "But I am going to start with what is likely, based on the nature of the device and that the enemy is using commercial communications satellites and trying to be sly about it. I'm going to start with how I would go about it and work outward from there."

"Good enough." Bolan nodded.

Krebs looked at the anorexic report. "You know, if I could get a line on German communication satellites and their windows cross-referenced with your movements that would be helpful."

"Done," Bolan said.

Krebs blinked. "That would require a lot of NSA cooperation."

"Done," Bolan reiterated.

Krebs looked at Bolan suspiciously. "Okay, then while you're at it would be nice if the NSA tasked some satellites to listen to what the German communication satellites are broadcasting."

"Done."

Krebs regarded Bolan patiently. "That would require

an NSA satellite priority realignment. That takes an order straight from the top. You walk with that kind of wampum, big man?"

"I do." Bolan took out his business card. "And now so do you. Call that number, and tell the operator exactly what you need and who you need to talk to. It'll be arranged."

"Uh, okay." Krebs looked like a man very nervously calling a poker bluff. He unhooked a phone from part of his array and began punching in numbers.

"Hey, Krebs?"

Krebs looked up distractedly. "Yes?"

"Did you bring me something?"

"Oh, yeah, your packages are in the back of the van."

Bolan went to the van and looked in on black equipment cases of various sizes. He began cracking cases and trunks of German steel. Everything he'd asked for was there. Bolan returned to his work space in the corner of the hangar and got on the link with Kurtzman. "Tell me you have something."

"I do. It's not much, but I do."

"Like what?"

"Like I raided Interpol's database on organized crime in Berlin."

"What'd you get?" Bolan asked.

"Rumors of someone or something called *Das Tier.*"

"The Beast." Bolan nodded to himself. "Shadowy, lurking figure? More rumored than fact but criminals in Berlin are being found without heads and getting their territory stepped on? But barely a blip on anyone's radar?"

"That about sums it up," Kurtzman confirmed.

"Listen, I have an Air Force lad breaking the Beast's activation frequencies. I want to use *Das Tier*'s own strategy against him. I'm going to have the lieutenant work me up a portable, land-based rig that can send out an activation frequency and then track the responses. By the same token I want an NSA satellite ready to do things on a much bigger level from space."

"That can be arranged."

"One problem," Bolan said.

"What's that?"

"Lieutenant Krebs wants to turn the RFID off and then turn it on again."

"So the enemy will stop tracking it, and it will let him bombard it across the radio spectrum," Kurtzman concluded.

"Yeah, what do you think?"

"The only way I can think of doing that would be by disconnecting the battery and then reconnecting it. That shouldn't be too hard."

"My problem is with exposure. You think the Beast will know we did it?"

"There's no guarantee on that one, Striker. But honest assessment? I'm surprised that RFID is still transmitting. Unless there has been a huge advance in microbatteries I haven't heard about then it's already got to be close to its limit. I think it's worth the risk."

Bolan looked over his laptop. "Krebs!"

The lieutenant looked up from his labors. "Yeah?"

"Cut the power. Bombard that son of a bitch across the spectrum!"

Krebs stopped short of jumping up and down and clapping his hands. "On it!"

Bolan returned his attention to Kurtzman. "With any luck I'm heading to the capital tonight. I want to go in with a better plan than just randomly bombarding Berlin with radio waves neighborhood by neighborhood."

"I do happen to have one interesting lead for you."

"What's that?"

"A German gangster, pretty high up. A guy by the name of Edmoore Strauch, right before he died he was having problems with the Turkish Berlin Mob."

"What about him?"

"Rumor is the Turks killed him."

"Let me guess. His head is missing?"

"Yeah, the Turks shot him to death, but the very same night someone got into the morgue and stole his head. Even more interesting, is that two days later three dead Turks were pulled out of the Spree River all without heads."

"The Beast takes care of his own. What else have we got on Strauch?"

"I think the most interesting thing about him at the moment is that he owned a place called Die Höllenfeuer-Verein."

Bolan searched his German again. "The Hellfire Club?"

"That would be it."

"Find out who owns it now, Bear."

"I did." Kurtzman pulled a picture up on the screen. "Cordula Schön."

Bolan beheld a woman who looked as if she should have her own late-night cable TV program running horror movies. "I'm going clubbing."

"You know? I just knew you were going to say that. What we have on her so far is pretty sketchy. I'll have more by the time you hit Berlin. Meantime, this place has a reputation as a real Sodom and Gomorrah. Lots of criminal types, lots of drugs, and lots of models, athletes and celebrities who want to feel dangerous and rub shoulders with the tough crowd."

"Sounds like a perfect recruiting ground."

"Yeah, and it's also very exclusive."

"I'll need some exclusive gear jet-couriered to Berlin ASAP."

"I figured. It's already on its way. I also got you an apartment overlooking the club building."

"Excellent."

"I got one!" Krebs called out.

Bolan shot him the thumbs-up. "Bear, I want to put you in contact with Krebs. I want to be able to walk into the place and have him tell me whose RFID is active and where they are around me."

"That shouldn't be a problem. Patch me—"

Krebs's voice was triumphant. "I got two!"

"He's got two." Bolan nodded. "When—"

"Oh, shit!"

Bolan looked up. "Don't say that, Krebs."

Krebs looked over at Bolan guiltily. "The RFID's dead."

"Did you kill it?"

"No, the battery died."

Back in Virginia Kurtzman shrugged. "Well, at least we know we were in the window. With any luck the Beast will chalk it up to natural causes."

Bolan rose and walked over. "I need a portable rig to activate RFIDs on those two frequencies you captured. I'm working on a satellite but I want one in a van with us."

Krebs spread his hands expansively at his array. "Shouldn't be a problem. I can set you up with all you need."

Bolan found himself liking the redheaded lieutenant. "You want to run that rig for me?"

"A field mission in Berlin?" Krebs nodded eagerly. "Cool!"

Bolan got the distinct feeling Lieutenant Krebs was

chafing at spending a lot of time in windowless rooms. "Can you shoot?"

"Well, I qualified on the M-16, and the .45, in basic." Krebs eyes narrowed in sudden suspicion. "Why?"

"Lieutenant, we're going after murdering, drug-dealing Satan worshippers who take heads."

Krebs's face went blank. "We are?"

"Oh, yeah." Bolan nodded. "If I were you, I'd go to the armory and get yourself an M-16."

"Right…"

"You still want the job?" Bolan asked.

"Uh, sure?"

"Then if I were you I'd go to the armory and get yourself an M-16," Bolan repeated. "And get yourself a .45 while you're at it."

"I'll…go do that."

"This is going to be a plainclothes operation. Get yourself some civvies and anything else you might need for a week."

"Right."

"Then I am going to patch you in with a friend of mine and you can coordinate."

"Gotcha." Krebs walked off to gear up, his brow furrowing as he considered the way his day was going.

Grimaldi leaned against the wall and sighed. "Techies."

CHAPTER TWENTY-TWO

Berlin

"Nice crib." Krebs whistled. The apartment building was new construction in what had once been East Germany. Even today the difference between East and West Germany was still very much apparent. The Hellfire Club was in a very bad part of town but gentrification was in effect, and the apartment building and others like it sprang up like beacons in the midst of rundown, post-Communist squalor. The team began spreading out, claiming beds and unloading gear. Rudi Lahm looked at the H&K M-4 light machine gun Bolan had acquired for him. He swiftly attached a bag with a 100-round belt to it and stored it in the closet by the front door. Bolan secreted hardware of his own around the place, then called for a team meeting.

Bolan's team dropped themselves into chairs and sofas.

"All right, first order of business, Highlander is expected to make a full recovery and is resting quietly in the country." This drew a round of applause.

"Wish he was here now," Smallhouse said.

"In his absence—" Bolan gestured toward their guest of honor "—we have Rudi and an M-4."

"I'd rather have the dog," Chet said.

Rudi gave Chet a rueful look. The swelling on the side of the German's head had gone down, and except for the railroad of stitches his ear almost looked human again. "I am willing to switch places with him."

"That brings us to the matter at hand, Rudi. I know you've had a rough few days, but we're going in. The Beast is going down. You're going to spill for me. Everything you know. Right now."

For a young man the German had a tremendous scowl. His voice was angry, but controlled. "You were right in your assessment. I came back from a tour in Afghanistan. The German coalition troops are not allowed to engage in combat. Our area is mostly pacified. Besides patrolling, there is very little for a jump-qualified machine gunner to do."

"And the Beast finds work for idle hands?" Bolan suggested.

Rudi made a bemused noise. "I came back to Berlin with gambling debts and more knowledge of the heroin trade than I had when I left. A friend told me of a way to make some easy money. I did a few jobs for a German syndicate. Mostly driving, security, a little muscle-work, but nothing serious."

"And then?"

"And then I heard there was a woman who liked soldiers." Rudi's eyes went far away in memory. "And who could find them big money work."

Bolan took an easy shot in the dark. He held up a picture of the woman who now owned the Berlin Hellfire Club. "Cordula Schön?"

Rudi went rigid.

Bolan nodded. "Figured."

"How do you—"

"Never mind, go on."

"I met her. She and I…"

"Yeah, I can imagine she and you. Then what happened?"

"She said she knew people who were organizing a—" Rudi sought for a word "—realignment of Turkish assets in Berlin."

Bolan nodded. Turkey was a gateway for heroin and human trafficking into Europe out of Asia. Turkish criminal organizations functioned primarily as coordinators, financiers and facilitators. The hard crimes they committed in Europe were mostly against their own immigrant populations, but if you wanted to make an inroad into the drug trade in Europe, you had to deal with them, one way or the other.

"And you signed up?"

"I was already in." Rudi looked at his boots. "Too far. There was an initiation. I saw things. Felt things. I was—"

"You were drugged and marked." There was no mercy in Bolan's voice. "And you saw what became of those who crossed the Beast."

Rudi's eyes dropped back to his boots.

"Tell me about Die Höllenfeuer-Verein, the Hellfire Club."

"I never heard of it, but I was told that like the Nine Circles of Hell, the Beast has his circles. If you serve well and faithfully you rise, you fail, you fall."

Bolan detected no lies in the young German gunner. Rudi just hadn't risen up to Satan's VIP room privileges yet. "Tell me about the organization."

"I can tell you little. We were organized into small circles, called upon when needed. Provided for, anonymously, with whatever our mission required and rewarded generously."

"Circles." Smallhouse shook his head. "Sounds one whole hell of a lot like terrorist cells to me."

"Tell me about your cell mates."

"We all had nicknames. We did not know each other. We did not contact each other unless directed to."

Chet leaned in. "Yeah, well, what about your satanic orgies and human sacrifices?"

Rudi's shoulders slumped. "We wore masks."

"Great!" Chet threw up his hands. "Rudi here is all *Eyes Wide Shut?* What good is he again?"

"He rated expert with his squad automatic weapon in the Bundeswehr. So he's got that going for him," Bolan admonished. "Now so do we."

A tiny thing that resembled pride almost moved behind Rudi's eyes.

Zhong let out a long sigh. "We lurk in our aerie above the Hellfire Club. How shall we descend upon it?"

"Simple. Krebs, you're in the van. You light the place up with radio waves. Naz, you're driving. Rudi, you're the van gunner. We may be coming out fast. You cover the extraction."

Rudi wasn't happy. "But—"

"But nothing. Jack, you're going to drop Terrell on the roof. He's our guardian angel. If anyone can't make the van you are extraction plan B."

Grimaldi nodded. "You got it."

"We're going to be inserting into an exclusive club. We need pretty people. That's me and Libby." Bolan grinned. "We'll just have to pretty Chet up as much as we can."

Chet rolled his eyes.

"We're going to use the barium marker and give ourselves tattoos. Rudi says these people work in cells, so with any luck security will simply scan our Beast marks and wave us through. Chet and Libby will keep an eye out while I try to take a look around. When I give the signal, Krebs will light the place up." Bolan held up a pair of designer-looking black plastic glasses. "We'll be wired for sound and video, and giving off a recognition signal of our own. Krebs will be able to track us inside, overlay our video with his radio tracking and with any luck let us know who around us is marked and who isn't. Unfortunately they all look the same, so I'll go in wearing mine. Chet and Libby, you won't put yours on until you're inside."

Zhong raised one hawklike eyebrow in question.

"Zhong?" Bolan said. "You're floating. You crash the party inside, start kicking ass outside or support extraction depending on how the situation develops."

"Very well."

Oderkirk raised a speculative eyebrow. "So what are you, Chet and I going in with besides determination?"

"I'm thinking if this really is one of the Beast's fronts, he has to have metal detectors at certain points. It wouldn't surprise me if they wand guests on the way in. We're going in with these." Bolan opened a case. Inside were what appeared to be three smartphones. He picked one up and pressed the click-wheel firmly. The phone came apart into two pieces. He held up the top piece and the brass gleam of the base of four .22-caliber bullets were evident. "You have four shots. The bullets blow through the top covering the barrels. It's designed for right-handed shooting. You press *Q, W, E* and *R,* right across the top of the keypad, one letter for each shot."

Chet shook his head. "Feeling a little undergunned, Boss."

"The whole point is surprise. If you have to use it, you surprise their guys and then take their guns."

"Yeah, yeah." Chet took one of the murderous mobile phones and eyed it curiously. "I feel you."

"These aren't silent. They go bang. So we're also going in with these." Bolan opened a tray in the case and took out a black plastic push dagger. "The grip is Kraton. The blade is Grivory. They aren't shaving sharp, but they will penetrate. Punch for the throat or kidneys for the silent kill."

"Eew." Oderkirk wrapped her hand around one and eyed the three-and-a-half inch blade with the reinforced point. "Cool." She tucked the weapon away, picked up a smartphone and checked its lethal payload.

"Everyone try to get some nap time. Terrell, Chet, take the first watch."

Krebs went into the kitchen and started brewing coffee. The man was looking a little nervous and Bolan followed him. "You all right, Lieutenant?"

"Yeah, I'm all right. That friend of yours, the Bear? He's incredible. I mean I knew I could light up anyone wearing an RFID and track them like a GPS signal, but overlaying that with the video feed? I'll be looking at these guys and tagging them. It's pretty James Bond."

"Yeah, the Bear knows his stuff. So tell me what's bothering you."

"This is my first, like, combat mission."

"You passed marksmanship in basic?"

Krebs's chest puffed with pride. "Head of my class."

"Then you know what to do. Put the front sight on your opponent, shoot him until he falls down, then shoot the next one until he goes down. You keep shooting until no one is standing but you."

"Sounds simple enough."

"The simplest things are the hardest. Don't worry about it. Concentrate on your part of the mission. You light them up, we take them down. If it gets hairy, you'll have one pissed off German machine gunner in the van with you and Naz has proved himself. And for that matter—" Bolan pointed at Zhong, who sat in the living room running a honing steel over the already gleaming edge of his hatchet "—you see that guy?"

Krebs swallowed and nodded. "Yeah."

"Zhong will be lurking at ground level, and I kid you not. That man is the Angel of Death, and I'm making him your guardian angel."

Zhong looked up and waggled his hatchet at Krebs. The lieutenant waved back at Zhong nervously. "Uh, thanks."

"No problem."

"So which watch do I take?"

"That's the good news. Since you're the man with the magic mission specialty, you get to sleep through the night. We want you bright-eyed and bushy-tailed come game time."

"Gotta take care of the talent!" Krebs agreed.

"See you in the morning, Lieutenant."

CHAPTER TWENTY-THREE

The Hellfire Club

Bolan went to the head of the line. The line went around the block and Berlin's bright and shiny were eager to get in. The team had spread out into their positions. From his aerie Smallhouse had reported those going to the front of the line had all innocuously put a forefinger behind their ear and the doormen had let them in without question. Bolan eyed the bouncers as he approached. The doormen looked like members of the Turkish National Powerlifting team jammed into designer warm-up suits and wearing earpieces. Bolan walked up to the velvet rope and slid a finger behind his ear as if he had an itch. One of the two doormen gave Bolan a slight nod and unhooked the rope for him. People in line sighed or glared in envy.

Inside were two more doors. One was open and American rap music played loud enough to rattle Bolan's bones with the bass. The other door had a red curtain across it and was flanked by another couple of trees in tracksuits. One guard led him behind the curtains and up a flight of stairs. *"Amerikanisch?"*

"Nein," Bolan replied. *"Englisch."*

They came to the landing and the security man nodded. "Close your eyes." Bolan closed his eyes. First he was professionally patted down. The reinforced plastic push-dagger was riding just below his belt buckle and the security man neglected to give him a cup-check. Bolan felt his ear being bent back and he heard a short electronic whine as his counterfeit Beast mark was scanned. The bouncer spoke to someone unseen. "Open."

An opaque glass door hissed open and the bouncer on the other side of it beckoned Bolan in. He found himself looking in on a VIP balcony full of Berlin's glitterati. The giant nodded. "Enter, and be welcome."

"Thank you." Bolan walked over to the rail and looked at the sea of writhing bodies on the dance floor below. Giant video screens showed vaguely satanic images timed to the throbbing beat of the music and the light show. Bolan subvocalized into the mike hidden beneath his hand-painted Italian silk tie. "This is Striker, I'm in."

Krebs's voice vibrated through the earpiece of Bolan's glasses. "Copy that, Striker. Control, sending in Bodyguard and Bounty Hunter."

A gravity-defying cocktail waitress who was naked except for a baroque mask beelined for Bolan. Someone in the intervening fifteen seconds had tipped her off to speak English. "I am Yvo. I am at your every pleasure."

Bolan put just a hint of London in voice. "A pint of bitter would be lovely."

"Regular or imperial?"

"What do you think, love?"

Yvo's lips quirked beneath her mask and she went to fetch Bolan his ale.

Chet spoke in Bolan's earpiece. "Bodyguard and Bounty Hunter. Inside without incident." Chet and Oderkirk walked by arm in arm. Her little black dress was something to write home about. Chet was dressed in off-the-rack, but it was some of the most expensive off the rack you could buy in Berlin. They were two good-looking people and they looked and acted like they belonged.

"Perimeter," Bolan whispered. "Status."

Zhong came back. "Perimeter, in position. Have eyes on Control and frontal access of target site."

Smallhouse's voice spoke urgently. "Christ! Striker, this is Eagle-eye. We got company! Chopper's landing on the roof!"

Bolan watched Yvo come back with his imperial pint of Bass ale. "Copy that Eagle-eye, hide!"

"I'm behind the ventilation unit! I don't think they saw me!"

Bolan took his pint and reached into his vest pocket for his money clip of euros. Even behind her mask Bolan detected a strange look. Apparently the Beast's beautiful, VIP people didn't pay or tip, and Bolan was pretty sure he had just breached some kind of etiquette. Yvo sauntered away without a word.

"God…damn," Smallhouse muttered.

"Talk to me, Eagle-eye," Bolan said behind his mug. "What do you see?"

"You know those XXL Turks they got on the doors?"

"Yeah?"

"They're shrimps compared to the guy who just got out of the chopper. Guy's a brick shithouse of a human. Big, like I'm letting Perimeter have first crack at him big."

"What's he doing?"

"Throwing off a real heavy head-of-security vibe."

"He alone?"

"Yes, no, wait…oh, hell, yes!"

Bolan detected some enthusiasm in the big man from Louisiana's voice. "What?"

"We got Cordula Schön in the house."

"This party is heating up. Do you—"

"God…damn it." It was clear Smallhouse saw something he didn't like.

"Talk to me, Eagle-eye."

Smallhouse's voice dropped a dangerous octave. "Well, you do know the Devil is a white man with blue eyes, don't you?"

Bolan had read the autobiography of Malcolm X. "Heard it rumored."

"Well, he's here."

"You saying we have a Beast sighting?"

"I'm saying if this guy isn't Satan himself, then all my Junior College black militant years were wasted. You want me to try and shadow him downstairs?"

"What's the chopper doing?"

"Sittin' hot on the pad. Pilot isn't going nowhere."

"Hold position. We're going to try to work our way up."

"Copy that."

Bolan gazed off the balcony. Chet and Oderkirk were down on the dance floor shaking what their mommas had given them and shaking it well. Both were now wearing identical glasses with thick plastic frames. It made them an even cuter couple. "Bodyguard, Bounty Hunter, do not attempt to pay for drinks. Finish your dance and head back upstairs. Take the other side of the VIP area from me."

"Copy that."

Bolan sipped his beer and people watched while Oderkirk and Chet moved back upstairs via the opposite staircase. The bouncers at the foot of the stair parted for them without any need for ID. The whole place was wired. "Control?"

"Striker?" Krebs came back.

"Status on video feed."

"Video Striker, Bounty Hunter and Bodyguard crystal clear."

"Control."

"Yes, Striker?"

"Light this place up."

"Shit howdy yes!" To the visible eye nothing happened. In the radio frequency spectrum things got interesting fast.

"What do we have, Control?"

"We got active RFIDs! Oh, man, we got a shitload of them!"

Bolan took out his phone and touched an application. The rig in the van picked up the video feed from his glasses. Software connected the video feed with the radio signal location and overlaid them. Krebs could position the signals in space with the video feeds Bolan, Oderkirk and Chet were sending. Given a week Kurtzman and company would have worked up a pair of glasses that projected the data right against the lens, but there had been no time.

To see what Krebs was seeing Bolan had to patch in with his phone. The software put a visual marker on the video feed. Krebs had found two signals on the RFID they had dug out of Rudi. One he had decided was the primary identification and tracking routine. The purpose of the other he hadn't figured out before the battery had died. Every human in the VIP room was giving off the primary tracking signal, and Kurtzman's software overlaid an LED-looking red exclamation point on their video image. Those also giving off the secondary signal bore a Riddler green question mark, as well.

The exclamation-point-only people outnumbered the question markers ten to one. All of the employees, bouncers, bartenders and cocktailers were questionable green. Something else besides the primary identifying and tracking routine had definitely been activated. In Bolan's imaging Chet and Oderkirk were conspicuously absent of any punctuation.

Bolan sipped his beer. "Give me a count."

"I have 250 exclamation points throughout the building. I've got seventy-five tags showing question marks, as well." Krebs's voice rose. "Got one coming up straight behind you!"

Bolan casually turned, apparently gazing out over the dance floor. A beautiful blonde who was wearing clothes approached. Bolan gave her an open up and down and a big smile. The woman smiled back. German was clearly her first language. "This is your first time?"

Bolan nodded happily. "Yes."

"'He maketh fire come down from the heaven on the earth in the sight of man,'" the woman quoted.

Bolan smiled. It had been some time since he had gone to Sunday school and he struggled to produce the Revelation of St. John from memory. The woman stopped smiling and produced a small, Italian pistol. "And?"

"And..." Bolan shrugged. "Well, hell."

The woman blinked. "What?"

Bolan snapped his wrist and sent half a pint of ale into the woman's eyes. He shattered the heavy mug across her gun hand and the pistol fell to the floor. Bolan upended the satanist over the balcony and dropped her screaming into a fountain below. Bolan spoke into his tie. "I'm made."

"No shit!" Krebs acknowledged. "Here they come!"

There was no time to go for the fallen pistol. A Turk the size of a refrigerator loomed up out of nowhere. He drew a knife big enough to skin a bear and twirled it between his fingers like a circus performer as he came in to carve Bolan like a Christmas turkey. He raised one sneering, bushy eyebrow as Bolan produced his smartphone and brandished it like a cross at a vampire. Scorn turned to white-faced shock as Bolan hit the keys with his thumb and the concealed weapon spit four times in rapid succession.

People screamed and scattered at the sound of the gun-shots, and the guard fell to his knees clutching his chest.

A second Turk came at Bolan with a stun baton crack-ling in his meaty fist. Bolan hurled the spent phone at the Turk. He barely flinched as it hit him in the face, but it was enough. Bolan ran three steps forward and baseball-slid across the marble floor beneath the sparking sweep of the baton. The stacked leather heel of Bolan's Italian loafer crunched beneath the big man's kneecap. He groaned and Bolan rolled aside as three hundred pounds of muscle toppled. Bolan snatched the baton and rammed it into the side of the Turk's neck and held the button down. The big man's body clenched like a fist as Bolan juiced him long and hard in the carotids. Bolan did a back roll and came up on one knee with the German woman's fallen .22 in hand.

Chet shouted as he discharged his smartphone into the face of a huge blond man in bouncer apparel. "How do they see us?" he snarled.

Bolan suspected the Beast had his own video security with overlaid RFID imaging, and all his security guys were wearing earpieces. Someone was directing traffic. Half the people in the VIP area were running screaming for the exits. The other half ran screaming toward Bolan and his teammates. Luckily a lot of them were getting in one another's way. Bolan swung his pistol toward the bar. Normally he would have cut the bartenders some slack, but not when the guy bore the mark of the Beast and kept silenced Uzis behind the bar. Bolan aimed his comman-deered pistol and printed three rounds in the bartender's sternum. The man sagged back into the premium tequi-las and disappeared from sight. Oderkirk snap-kicked a barman in the groin and did an impressive limbo-slide over the bar after the fallen automatic weapon.

The battle was turning into a brawl and any second the numbers game was going to tell the tale. "Perimeter!" Bolan shouted. "I need you inside now!"

"Understood."

Bolan emptied his pistol into another bouncer and ripped his push-dagger free. "Control! What is the status outside?"

"The doormen closed the doors without a word! Line outside is angry but dispersing! You want us to come in?"

"Negative! Hold position!"

Chet shouted over the tumult. "Shit! We've got company!"

A six-man goon squad charged up one of the sweeping staircases to the VIP area. They weren't Turkish muscle. They were in suits and brandishing the FN Personal Defensive Weapons so prized by the Mexican cartels. Their weapons had laser sights, and the green beams played over the milling, screaming throng searching for their target. Bolan gave each of the two men leading the charge a double tap to the chest to no apparent effect. The men were armored. Bolan's pistol racked open on empty, and he threw himself flat as the enemy returned fire. Their weapons snarled on full-auto and scythed through bystanders as they sought Bolan.

Libby stood up and put a burst into the lead shooter as he reached the landing. She yelped and dropped down as the PDWs shattered the mirror behind the bar and assassinated bottles of very expensive liquor. Bolan pulled his push-dagger and prepared to die going forward.

The gunman at the back of the pack flew off the balcony as if he had wings. The man beside him took two faltering steps to reach the landing and fell clutching his throat.

Arterial blood sprayed between his fingers as if his throat had been ripped out by the fangs of a wild beast.

Or a tiger's claw.

Zhong was suddenly among his enemies. He sank his hatchet into the side of one man's head. He abandoned the weapon and clapped both palms over the ears of the next man in front of him. The shooter screamed as both of his eardrums were ruptured. A gunman whirled with his weapon ready. Zhong's hands fell upon the gunman's, and the man howled as Zhong crushed his finger bones around the weapon. The man shrieked as the Chinese assassin shot both thumbs forward and gouged out his eyes. The remaining two men realized something was desperately wrong behind them. They both spun and shoved their guns forward. Zhong casually stepped between them past the muzzles of their guns and put his hands upon their necks.

Bolan had heard of tiger claw experts who could rip out a man's throat. He had never seen it done, much less in stereo. Zhong's fingers sank into flesh and he roared like a tiger as he heaved. The two killers fell with their throats open to the sky. Zhong flicked blood and bits of trachea from his fingers. Everyone left in the VIP area ran in the opposite direction for the curtained exit.

Zhong smiled at Bolan and retrieved his hatchet.

Bolan joined him on the landing. Chet ran forward and they relieved the dead of their weapons and spare magazines. Zhong eschewed the PDWs and held his hatchet in one hand and his personal 10 mm Glock in the other. Bolan slung a spare weapon. "Eagle-eye, what's going on up top?"

"Chopper still hot on the pad! No other activity! What do you want me to do?"

Bolan came to his decision. The Beast was here. The

building was sealed. This was no longer a recon mission. The final battle was now. "Eagle-eye, disable the chopper."

"Copy that!"

Krebs came across the line. "You want us in?"

"No hold position. I—"

The music in the Hellfire Club suddenly went dead. Every video screen and TV suddenly showed a blond man with a short blond beard and mustache. His blue eyes were as cold as death. His smile was just as cold as he spoke across the sound system in German.

"Töten Sie. Töten Sie die Eindringlinge." He smiled to show blinding white teeth with unpleasantly pointy canines. *"Töten Sie für mich."*

Chet snarled at the nearest screen. "Son of a bitch has subtitles!"

Beneath the Beast block script scrolled across the screen as he spoke.

The text read Kill them all. Kill the intruders. Kill them for me. The camera angle switched from the Beast and showed Bolan and his team on the landing.

The Beast concluded with a laugh. *"Lassen Sie keine entgehen."*

Let none escape.

Howls of bloodlust rose from the dance floor and the balconies on the other side. The security cameras kept Bolan and his team's position on the screen.

"Striker!" Krebs shouted across the line. "Striker! Sitrep."

"Control, Payback, Jack." Bolan watched as a mob surged up the stairs. "I need you now."

CHAPTER TWENTY-FOUR

"Ottokar von Saar!" Kurtzman shouted over the link.

Bolan finished barricading the door. It wasn't going to hold long. "What?"

"Blondie!" Kurtzman replied. "I ran his face through our recognition software! He's Ottokar von Saar, make that Baron Ottokar von Saar!"

"The Beast is German royalty?"

"He was also a lieutenant in Airborne Brigade 31!"

"Chet!" Bolan shouted down the hallway. "What do you have?"

Chet trotted back. "The door's solid steel! And the explosives are in the van!"

The Beast's voice spoke like God on high from hidden speakers. "Allow me."

The electronic lock on the security door buzzed and flung open under the pressure of the people behind it. Chet's jaw and the muzzle of his weapon dropped. "Jesus…"

A dozen women in varying states of mostly undress came boiling out of the door. Whether they were call girls, strippers or go-go dancers Bolan didn't know, but they came shrieking like harpies into the hall. Their eyes literally rolled in their heads with blood lust.

"Aw, hell!" Chet was appalled. "How do you fight naked chicks?"

Even Zhong shot Bolan a questioning look.

Bolan knew his team was on film, and the Beast would love to release video of them blowing away a baker's dozen of beautiful screaming women. Bolan had no time to go hand to hand with them. The team had to keep moving, and moving toward the Beast. Bolan drove his elbow through the glass covering the floor's antique emergency fire hose and yanked the brass nozzle and a length of canvas hose free. "Libby! Give me full pressure!"

The redhead cranked the pressure wheel. "Hose those sluts of Satan!"

Bolan hosed them. He threw the valve and the fanatic, screaming zealots met 250 pounds per square inch of hydrotherapy. Wildcats went flying, slipping and sliding and screaming. Bolan strode through them hydraulically hammering the women into point-blank, sodden, shuddering submission.

The Beast's voice reverberated in the hall. "Interesting…"

The last woman ceased her struggling and went fetal under the high-pressure hosing. Bolan dropped the valve and filled his hands with plastic, lead and steel. He strode through the shuddering women to the security door. In their bloodlust none had seen fit to shut it behind them. Bolan glanced around a suite of cubicles. His team came in and locked the door behind them. Zhong was thinking the same thing as Bolan. "Where did the women come from?"

"This asshole can't have half-naked psycho-bitches on tap 24/7," Chet stated.

Bolan smiled thinly. Being the Beast, maybe he could. "Hey, Baron!" Bolan called out. "Where you keeping your psycho-bitches?"

The hidden speaker system was conspicuously silent.

"Paging Baron Ottokar von Saar. Repeat, paging Ottokar von Saar," Bolan called.

"So," the baron said bemusedly. "You know who I am. But then if you knew who I was, this would not be the first place you would come to gird me."

Zhong lifted his chin with interest. "Gird…"

"In this usage it means to encircle or entrap," Bolan said.

"Ah." Zhong nodded as he filed that one away.

The baron continued. "I deduce you did not know my identity before you entered the Hellfire Club. This tells me someone has been talking to you. Let us put an end to that."

"Control! This is Striker!" Bolan called through the link. "I think we got—"

Chet suddenly snarled and Oderkirk cried out in pain. Bolan ripped off his glasses as a blast of feedback through the earpiece threatened to shatter his eardrums.

"Better," the baron declared. "Now, tell me, who are you?"

Bolan moved through the empty cubicles. "Those women weren't in here exchanging lingerie or bikini-waxing tips. They got sent in from somewhere else."

The baron's voice continued to echo from nowhere. "What is it you hope to accomplish? You know that the blackie on the roof is dead."

Bolan noted the racism but otherwise ignored the baron. Anyone who wanted to take Terrell Smallhouse when he had a precision rifle in hand and was behind cover would have to blow up the building, and Bolan was pretty sure he would have heard about it by now.

"Did you think I did not know about your surveillance van?" the baron chided. "I hope for your sake you do not expect them to effect your rescue."

That was a little more worrisome. Krebs was a C3 warrior, Nazareno was a narco-pilot and Rudi was an ex-satanist machine gunner bent on revenge. Bolan whipped out his phone. No calls were going out. Just as he had at the beach house, the Beast was jamming all communications. Bolan called up the blueprints of the Hellfire Club's old Communist-bloc structure Kurtzman had already given him. The building had been gutted and modified, but in other respects the old blueprints still told him a few things. Like where the hidden elevator might be. Bolan was betting it had never been moved, it had just been covered up in this modern office suite.

There. Bolan strode to the far wall. It had been paneled in blue fabric. Bolan put a burst through the paneling and then drove the butt of his weapon through the weakened area. He put his hand through the panel and tore it off its track. Elevator doors gleamed.

"Clever," the Beast commented. "What do you intend to do now?"

Chet sighed. "The explosives are in the van."

Bolan contemplated the flush seam between the doors. "Zhong?"

The killer from Hong Kong stepped forward. He stared at the doors as if his eyes could burn holes through it. His breathing became very deep and made a low hissing deep in his throat. His hatchet hung loose in his fist. "Cover your eyes." Zhong roared like a beast. His blow was like a baseball pitch and almost too fast to follow. Sparks ricocheted off the doors and metal shrieked. The force of his blow wedged the hatchet blade between the doors up to the bit. Bolan and Chet flanked Zhong. They forced their fingers into the narrow gap and heaved against the ancient hydraulics. The hatchet fell to the carpet as the doors gave a few inches. Chet hissed through clenched teeth. "Wish Terrell was here…"

Bolan groaned with effort. "Zhong!"

Zhong clapped his hands three times like gunshots and stepped to the narrow breach. The hatchet man's hands curled around the edges of the doors. His shoulders bunched and a sound like that of a wounded bull tore from his throat. Chet nearly fell over as Zhong slid the doors open with one smooth motion.

Oderkirk spoke quietly behind them. "Wow."

"Very impressive," the Beast agreed.

Bolan and his team piled in. Chet glanced at the buttons. "Up or down?"

Smallhouse was upstairs. Krebs's team, the Beast and most likely hell itself were all down. "First floor."

The abused doors groaned in their tracks but closed, and the car started down. Bolan and Zhong pressed themselves against one side of the car and Oderkirk and Chet the other to take what little cover the car provided. A bell pinged as the car hit the ground floor.

The door opened on a siege.

The dance floor had been cleared of everyone except the dead. Krebs's communications team was barricaded ten yards away behind the surveillance van. Nazareno had apparently driven it through the front door and it was filled with hundreds of holes. A half dozen security men with PDWs ringed the dance floor taking cover behind overturned tables and fountains. An equal number of track-suited Turks were aiding them, and they were wielding shotguns instead of clubs and knives. Krebs fired around one corner of the van and Nazareno the other. Rudi lay on the floor. The German was a bloody mess and unmoving.

Two Turks with shotguns were moving through the

shadows along the wall and about to flank Krebs. Bolan gave each a burst through the chest and dropped them. Nazareno whirled at the sound of gunfire behind him and nearly shot Bolan, who ran forward. The Executioner had equipped the surveillance team with armor. The fabric covering Rudi's armored vest was shredded. Buckshot had shredded his unarmored shoulders and face. Krebs looked back over his shoulder. "Is he?"

"He's gone. Grab the gear." Bolan dropped his PDW on its sling and took up Rudi's squad automatic weapon and two spare belts of ammo. "We're out of here!"

Bolan held position as Krebs and Nazareno made for the elevator. The security men sensed something was wrong and charged. Chet, Oderkirk and Zhong gave it to them as they left cover. The Turks appeared to be hired help rather than true believers and had the good sense to drop flat. Bolan ran back to the elevator car and Chet hit the emergency close-door button. Buckshot rattled off the doors but the lead pellets failed to penetrate steel.

The elevator car shuddered as something heavy slammed into the roof.

Every weapon pointed up into the lighting. Bolan had a sneaky suspicion just who would be foolhardy enough to slide down an elevator cable and have enough mass to hit that hard. "Terrell?"

The big man's muffled voice came back questioningly. "Coop?"

"Clear!"

The access hatch opened and Smallhouse's head stuck down and his eyes flicked from face to face. "Hey, what are you guys doing?"

"We're on the elevator to hell," Bolan said. "Going down. Want a ride?"

"Oh, hell, yes." Smallhouse squeezed his massive frame down the hatch and into the already crowded car.

Chet's finger hovered over the button for the basement. "Speaking of hell, I think the next time this door opens we're gonna be in a world of hurt."

Smallhouse pushed his way to the front. "I got full armor. I'll take point."

Krebs handed Zhong the gear bag from the van and shoved in beside Smallhouse. Bolan had insisted everyone in the surveillance van wear vests. The C3 man was heroing up. "I'm right behind you, big man."

Nazareno pushed forward to complete the armored wedge in front of the door. "Let's do it."

Bolan took a flash-bang grenade from Zhong's bag and nodded at Chet. He pushed the button and the car lurched down toward destiny. Smallhouse was whispering to himself. His words were almost a mantra. "Here we go…here we go…here we go…" The car stopped and chimed. The damaged doors began to rattle open. "Here we go!"

A hand grenade bounced off Smallhouse's chest and clattered to the concrete floor of the basement. "Shit!" He threw himself on it as automatic weapons in ambush ripped into life. Nazareno staggered backward as he took a dozen hits. Krebs sprayed with his M-16 and Bolan tossed the flash-bang. Smallhouse jerked as the grenade beneath him detonated. A second later thunder echoed in the basement as the flash-bang blew.

Bolan shoved Krebs forward and followed. "Go! Go! Go!" The elevator car was a ready-made meat grinder for the enemy. The only way to go was forward. Krebs charged forward like a howling commando shooting at muzzle-flashes. Bolan followed with the M-4 light machine gun firing from the hip-assault position. The second he was

out of the elevator he took one step to his left and dropped
to one knee.

Everyone was firing. The space was a concrete ante-
chamber and everyone was exchanging fire at point-blank
range. His team was outnumbered and outgunned, but the
enemy had expected them to be slaughtered the second
the doors opened. Instead they took the hits and exploded
out of the death chamber like Butch Cassidy and the Sun-
dance Kid, suicidal and crazy brave. Bolan rattled off the
M-4 squad automatic weapon's 100-round belt in 10-round
bursts swinging his muzzle from target to target and picking up lives like spares in bowling.

Bolan's machine gun racked open on empty, and he
instantly dropped it on its sling and pulled up a locked
and loaded PDW. There were no more enemies. A dozen
of the enemy lay dead or dying. Bolan looked back at his
team. Oderkirk was sitting against the wall as pale as death
with two red pinholes in her bare right shoulder drooling
blood. Nazareno had been wearing a vest, but the PDWs
had been designed from the get-go as armor piercers. He
lay on his back clutching the tufted shreds of the armor
covering his belly and praying in Spanish. Bolan dropped
to a knee beside him. Nazareno's armor was keeping his
guts in but had failed to stop three rounds.

"Naz."

"Pendejo!" the wounded Mexican snarled.

Bolan smiled. Nazareno was wounded, but he was still
salty. "Listen, you're gut shot. You're going to feel really
bad for a while, but you're not going to die. Libby will take
care of you."

Oderkirk clutched her shoulder but slid over to Nazareno. "You're gonna be all right. I'm staying right here
with you."

Bolan turned to Smallhouse. The big man suddenly

sat up. "I'm fine, man. I'm…" Smallhouse was about as black as they came, but his face took on an unhealthy, gray, acidy look. The whites of his eyes went wide with shock. He was wearing full Ranger armor, and it had smothered the shrapnel that had tried to blast through his chest, belly and groin. His arms were scored with cuts, but the blood spurting from his right thigh was the culprit. Smallhouse was geared up for a day in Afghanistan. Bolan tore a field dressing from the marksman's fanny pack. The wound was spurting, but from long experience Bolan knew the femoral artery had been nicked rather than severed. Bolan slapped the dressing against the man's thigh and put the sharpshooter's hand over it.

"Keep the pressure on it. Listen, you guys. You're going to have to take care of each other while we finish this. You got it?"

Smallhouse leaned back against Oderkirk and dragged his rifle to him with a shaky hand. "Yeah, we got it. This elevator isn't going anywhere, and no one gets past us. We'll see you in a few."

Bolan opened the action of his machine gun, put a new belt into the feed and slapped it shut. "See you in a few."

CHAPTER TWENTY-FIVE

"Jack!" Kurtzman was getting a tad frantic. "Jack!"

The computer wizard sagged in his wheelchair in relief as the pilot came back. The thrum of rotor blades came through the link. "I read you, Bear."

"I've lost contact with all units in the building!"

"I have no joy on any frequency either," Grimaldi responded. "I lost contact with you until I took her up to five thousand feet."

"Sitrep?"

"Terrell pounded the engine cowling of the enemy chopper into ruin, and then he pounded on the pilot when he objected. When communications went out, he gave me the high sign and went downstairs after Blondie, Bluto and the babe. A couple of minutes later Krebs drove the van through the front door, which I thought was pretty creative."

"Anything since?"

"All quiet. No lights, no sirens, nothing on the emergency channels. Whatever is happening in there is being contained. What's new and different on your end?"

"This Baron von Saar is bad medicine. The Mexican government had U.S. Special Forces train a bunch of their guys to fight the drug cartels a few years back. The men we trained ended up working for the enemy, and even organizing their own cartel. That soured the Mexicans on U.S. trainers and training. Rumor is the Mexican government still realized they were being outclassed but even more so, so they brought in some German Special Forces operatives. Rather than training platoons of soldiers ready to turn they made up small fast reaction units out of people they considered 'untouchables,' who had real grudges against the cartels. Most of the units were small, usually no bigger than a four-man fire team and their leader. Rumor is these guys ended up acting more like hit teams than drug interdiction enforcement. Apparently they were a little too good at their job and the program was canceled after a year."

"Von Saar was one of these advisers?"

"It was top secret in the German military, and officially denied, but we hacked their records enough to know von Saar was on unspecified 'detached duty' during the year and a half the program was in place."

"So what about the widgets in people's earlobes?"

"Would you believe his brother Hans is an electrical engineer working for a company specializing in communications that has done contract work for the German military?" Kurtzman asked.

"So our Otto goes to Mexico, sees how bad things are, sees his little protégés turn into vigilantes."

"He sees the satanism and Santeria percolating around the fringes of the cartels," Kurtzman continued.

"And comes back to his brother Hans with one grand plan."

"And it expands to both sides of the Atlantic."

Grimaldi whistled in appreciation. "I love it. I love this von Saar guy. I think I'm going to land on his club and blow his brains out if Sarge hasn't already."

"Terrell took out their helicopter after it landed, and he is no longer on the roof," Kurtzman warned. "I strongly recommend you stay airborne until the man tells otherwise or you have visual confirmation they need help."

The ace pilot made a rude noise but he came back in the affirmative. "Copy that, Bear. Holding tight."

THEY WERE in an ancient section of the East Berlin sewer system. It had long ago been blocked off, but the Beast had reopened it. The tunnel complex was a ready-made set for a horror movie. The walls were ancient, blackened brick covered with cobwebs. Rusted iron bars covered smaller drainage sections. Torches burning in iron sconces threw off lurid and insufficient light. Seepage created foul-smelling puddles and slimed the walls in streaks.

"Coop?" Krebs whispered.

"Yeah?"

"I'm scared."

Bolan glanced back at Krebs. Except for a canteen and pack, he was wearing a full infantryman's load of web gear on top of his armor. "Fix bayonet, Lieutenant."

"What?"

"You heard me."

Krebs pulled the M-7 black dagger blade from its sheath and clicked it onto the end of his rifle. He gave Bolan a happy grin. "Haven't done that since basic!"

Bolan nodded. "Stay frosty."

A high despairing scream echoed down the filthy passage out of the dark. Bolan snapped down the left leg of his machine gun's bipod for an assault grip. Chet filled his hands with a PDW apiece. Zhong put away his hatchet and produced a second Glock. Krebs stared back at the three men eyeing him. "What? I'm down with this!"

"Give me some light," Bolan said. Krebs took a tactical light from the gear bag as Bolan moved forward on point. The scream echoed out again. It was a scream of fear and despair as opposed to genuine agony.

"Again with the sound and light show?" Chet whispered.

Bolan ignored the question. They came to another drainage grille. Beyond the rusted brown bars nothing was visible. Something beyond sight was making a gobbling noise. Bolan stepped past the grate. "Chet, put it in a cross fire. Krebs, give us some light." Bolan and Chet pointed their guns down into the darkness. Chet played the tunnel with light.

"Jesus!" Chet snarled.

"No fucking way!" Krebs shouted.

A pale shape behind the bars shrieked in the glare of Krebs's tactical light. It was a man. He had been fat until recently and was naked except for filth. He babbled and cringed in a corner against the light. Bolan grimaced at the grate. The bars had been recently removed from their mortar and nailed back in place with a pneumatic bolt gun. The prisoner within could lick the walls for a grotesque source of moisture and the grime caking his lips showed he had. He had been condemned to death by starvation in the dark.

Chet's voice was low and ugly. "You know, this Beast guy is taking his role just a little too seriously."

Zhong spoke softly. "A man may not assume the mantle of evil without being corrupted by it."

"We'll break him out on the way back," Bolan said coldly. "First the Beast goes down."

Krebs gazed at the captive in horror. "Amen to that, brother."

The captive in the shaft made a mewling noise as the party passed by him. The team approached a bend and the light got brighter. Bolan eased around the corner machine-gun muzzle first and found the gate to hell. The gates were huge, oaken and bound with black iron like the gates to a castle.

Chet smirked at Zhong. "You gonna kung fu those ones open, too, Zhonger?"

Zhong seemed to consider the proposition. "I believe that is beyond my skill."

Bolan scanned the section of corridor. There were a lot more torches burning, and two more elevated, barred drainage tunnels to either side. The stench of corruption came out of the closest. Bolan lifted his chin at the ceiling. "Zhong, security cameras."

Zhong's 10 mm Glock barked three times, and the cameras in the ceiling exploded in electronic ruin.

"You know something?" Krebs said.

Bolan took an explosive charge out of the gear bag and pushed a detonator pin into it. "What's that?"

"I think when that door opens, things are gonna get steep and deep real fast."

"I agree. Why don't you take one of the spare shotguns and blast those grates open."

"Blast them open?"

"Shoot the bolts," Bolan advised. "That should weaken them enough for Zhong to rip them out of the walls."

Krebs unslung a shotgun. "Right!"

Bolan took a C-4 charge, stripped off the adhesive backing and pressed it into the center of the double-doors. Krebs's shotgun slammed and mortar crumbled. Grates clanged to the stone floor as Zhong tore them free in his fists.

Bolan passed out the last four grenades. "Krebs, keep yours in reserve." Bolan clambered up into the drain and was confronted by a rotting, emaciated body. "Zhong, across from me. Chet, Krebs, same-same."

Bolan's team clambered into cover while Bolan took

out his remote detonator. "Fire in the hole!" The air in the sewer shuddered with the blast. The doors sagged and fell in a collapsing curtain of smoking, broken beams.

Hell unleashed its fury.

Bolan heard the crumping of Claymore mines going off in a chain. The corridor cracked with the flight of several thousand ball bearings expanding outward in a supersonic cloud. Bolan crouched in the drain and pulled the pin on his frag.

Krebs shouted over the tumult. "Shit!"

Gunfire and tracers began streaming into the sewer section.

"Chet! Zhong! Grenades, now!" Bolan looped his grenade over the broken doors. The fragger whip-cracked and sent out its own, smaller, deadly cloud of steel. Zhong's flash-bang boomed like a cannon in the stone chamber and Chet's frag blasted on its heels a heartbeat later. Bolan leaned around the lip of the drainage tunnel and cut loose with his machine gun. "Chet! Zhong! Go! Go! Go! Krebs, with me!"

Bolan dropped to the center of the relatively dry sewer bed and fired off bursts into the smoke-filled chamber beyond. Chet and Zhong charged past and stopped on either side of the shattered door to put the occupants in a cross fire. The Executioner rose and walked forward, walking fire into the room ahead. Fire streamed back from a light machine gun with the same firing signature as Bolan's. Smoke filled much of the chamber but the muzzle-flashes showed someone firing from cover in the middle of the room. "Krebs! Muzzle-flash!"

The cotter pin pinged away from Krebs's grenade and he softball pitched it like a pro at the offending bursts of fire. Bolan and Krebs plastered themselves next to Zhong and Chet as the fragger flashed.

Bolan slapped his last belt into his machine gun and entered the Beast's church.

The Executioner coldly stood and took in the twenty-foot golden pentagram dominating the black basalt floor. The red-eyed head of a painted, malevolent golden ram filled the five points.

"The Goat of Mendes…" Krebs whispered. "The Devil himself."

The chamber was a pentagon. Stone benches ringed the unholy stage on all sides. There were no cultists wearing goat masks, club goers, frenzied strippers or titanic Turks within. A dozen heavily armed men who looked suspiciously like soldiers lay dead and dying on the black stone floor. The twisted frames of the spent Claymores lay on their sides smoking. Bolan looked at the chunk of black stone that made up the altar. The brass shackles bolted to its sides were crusted with dried blood. A German M-4 light machine gun lay on the altar like a sacrifice. The gunner lay dead behind the altar, shredded by Krebs's grenade. Open doorways led in opposite directions on the two sides of the pentagonal walls ahead of them.

Zhong lofted an eyebrow. "The Lady or the Tiger."

"Nice reference," Bolan admitted.

The Beast's voice throbbed through a hidden speaker. "You are becoming a serious annoyance."

Bolan stopped by a dead man with a ditty bag and pulled out two Claymores, wire and a squeeze detonator. He put them in his own bag and took the shredded machine gunner's spare belt of ammo. "What are you going to do it about it, Otto?"

"This."

A steel door unsheathed down out of the ceiling behind them where the medieval portal had been. The doorways ahead clanged down like castle portcullises with similar finality.

"Man!" Chet's eyes flicked around the room warily. "This guy is going from Beast to Bond villain! What's he going to do? Fill the room with water and release the sharks?"

Krebs shook his head. "You saw the guys locked in those drainage tunnels. Maybe he's just going to leave us in here and watch us eat each other."

Zhong stood by the altar with his hatchet in one hand and his Glock in the other, waiting for the other shoe to drop. "Cooper's people know we entered the building above. The Beast does not have the time for theatrics. He is making his move."

Bolan silently agreed as he began attaching leads to the two Claymores and began unspooling wire.

Chet and Krebs laid the spare shotguns and PDWs on top of the altar and took cover behind. Chet filled his hands with PDWs again. He dropped to a knee beside the altar and aimed his weapons at the doors. "Bring it on you son of a bitch!"

Bolan put the Claymores on the other side of the altar, one facing either door. He deployed both legs of his squad automatic weapon's bipod and took a firing position over the huge square of basalt.

"Waiting game!" Krebs was getting agitated. "Asshole called timeout and is trying to freeze the kicker!"

The football analogy was a good one, but Bolan agreed with Zhong. The Beast was running out of time. He was already making his play. Bolan's face tightened as a knife started screwing through his temple. "Anyone else getting a headache besides me?"

"Well, goddamn it!" Chet snarled. "I thought it was just me."

Krebs rubbed his forehead. "Oh, hell, yes."

Zhong stood impassive as stone. "I feel nothing."

Bolan looked back at a rustling behind them. The three wounded men lying on the floor were going into convulsions and their skin was turning ruddy. "Carbon monoxide!" Bolan shouted. "Everybody up! On the altar!"

The team leaped up and crowded onto the rock slab.

Carbon monoxide was invisible, odorless and the number-one cause of poisoning deaths among humans. Usually there were a whole lot of combustion-engine emissions accompanying it, but in its pure form it was an unseen killer. The Beast was filling the chamber with pure CO. Lighter than air, the gas was slowly rising from vents in the floor. That was why the men on the floor were dying and his team, who were kneeling, had started getting headaches while Zhong had felt nothing; but the CO would force its way upward until the team was engulfed in an invisible sea of death that would proceed in rapid onset from headaches to dizziness, nausea, confusion, convulsions, unconsciousness, respiratory arrest and then death.

Chet's weapon snarled as he fired a useless burst into a steel door. "Son of a bitch is giving us the Nazi bus ride!"

"We have to bust out of here," Bolan said. "Now."

"Yeah?" Chet's eyes were widening in panic. "How?"

Krebs shuffled through the gear bag. "We're out of HE!"

Bolan glanced around the church of hell. Three corners of the pentagon were sealed with steel. A fourth was blank. The fifth corner had a small apse with a second altar adorned by a chalice and black candles. Bolan looked down at the floor. Death was rising in an invisible cloud to engulf them. The Goat of Mendes stared back up at Bolan out his pentagram. Outside the upside down Satanic star there were scratches in the black marble floor that led to the right hand door ahead of them. The black altar had been moved in and out of the room before. Past the dais the floor sloped slightly downward toward the door. Bolan's brows drew down in thought.

Chet whooped. "I've seen that look! He's gonna rig something!" Chet's face went serious. "You're gonna rig something, right?"

"Yeah." Bolan jumped off the altar.

Krebs was horrified. "Dude!"

"Claymores! Duct tape! Right hand door! High and on both sides!" Bolan ran to the altar in the apse.

"What the hell?" Chet shouted.

Bolan jumped up on the altar in the apse. "How'd you force entry in Iraq, Chet?"

"With shotguns! And no shotgun is gonna crack these steel sons of—"

"What's a Claymore?"

"Goddamn!" Chet grabbed the mines. "A giant shotgun shell!"

"Right!"

Bolan took a deep breath and jumped down. He yanked open the doors of the altar cabinet and once again his instincts were correct. He didn't know that much about Satanism, but he knew most of their rituals were evil reversals of Christian doctrine. Christian Mass became the Black Mass. And there beneath the apse altar was a giant, three-liter ornate silver chrismarium of unholy oil. Bolan grabbed his prize and ran back with his lungs burning on his held breath. Bolan jumped up on the altar and took a few ragged breaths. He hopped back down and uncorked the gothic bottle of oil and began pouring it liberally in front of the altar stone and down the scratched path it had made to the door. Chet and Krebs looked at him as if he were insane as they ran back red-faced from holding their breath and reeling wire out from the two Claymores duct-taped to the door. Bolan spilled the last of the oil along the path and ran back. His head ached like a migraine and his vision was starting to skew. Bolan jumped on the altar and his chest heaved as he breathed. All he could hope was that the air up high was ugly rather than acute. Bolan jumped down behind the altar with the rest of the team for cover. "Hit it!"

Krebs pumped the detonator unit.

The Claymore was an antipersonnel mine, its job was to send its payload of ball bearings out in a cloud of death. The good news was that it used 680 grams of C-4 to get those ball bearings in motion. The Claymores thumped and 1400 steel balls broke apart and screamed away in all directions. The top of the door was blackened and looked as if it had been punched by two giant fists and hung askew in its frame.

"Push!" Bolan roared.

The four men pitted their strength against the huge black stone. The rock was the immovable object, and Bolan's slowly dying team was far from the irresistible force. Bolan's muscles and bones creaked with strain.

"Wish...Terrell...was here!" Chet gritted.

So did Bolan. A strange hissing noise came out from between Zhong's clenched teeth as he called on whatever ancient discipline of power he had learned in the training halls in Hong Kong. The black altar shifted. Bolan bellowed and heaved with all of his might. Basalt grated on marble as the stone moved. Marble was a slick surface to begin with, and it became easier as the altar slowly shifted into the oil slick. The team heaved the stone a foot, two feet, three, and suddenly hit the sloping path down from the dais.

The giant piece of stone suddenly took on a life of its own.

"Heave!" Bolan snarled. The team heaved. The altar stone picked up momentum. The team was now running with the rock adding to its speed. "Weapons!" The team snatched up their weapons from the top of the altar and jumped to either side.

Stone met steel in a rending crash.

The damaged door tore from the frame above and clanged to the floor, and the altar stone sailed onward with oiled momentum. Bullets instantly began seeking out Bolan and his teammates. The Executioner held his machine gun by its grips and one bipod, shoving it around the shattered door frame. The weapon shuddered and squirmed in his grasp as he fired it dry around the corner. He dropped the spent weapon and dived through the door.

He was in another sewer section. Four men were firing from the opposite end. Bolan rolled up behind the cover of the stopped altar stone. Krebs and Chet gave him covering fire. Bolan dropped prone with his PDW, his thumb flicking the selector to semiauto. His trigger finger squeezed off four rapid double taps. The four shooters fell like bowling pins. Bolan rose and moved forward. "C'mon."

"Well, just, shit…" Chet put hand to the wall to steady himself. Blood was soiling the left side of his Berlin haute couture.

Bolan knew the gas was silently expanding through the door behind them. "We gotta move. Can you walk?"

"I can walk." Chet took two steps, coughed and fell to his knees.

Zhong slung Chet unceremoniously over his shoulder. "We go."

A voice spoke quietly behind them. "You are going nowhere."

Bolan whirled and too late realized the trap. The Beast wasn't behind them. He had simply turned off the intercom in the sewer section and turned down the one in his temple. Bolan spun. Von Saar and Bogac Krom were at the end of the tunnel, their weapons firing. They faded back around the corner. Chet yelped as Zhong toppled like a tree. Bolan hauled Chet off him. Zhong had taken a burst through the chest. He'd been dead before he hit the ground. Bolan took his hatchet and his Glock and shoved them under his belt. "Krebs, drag Chet out here."

Bolan loped forward. He knew he was being drawn into a trap. He came to the bend and put a burst around it, but no answering fire came. A wrenching coughing fit tore through Bolan's lungs, and he nearly threw up. His vision smeared and his knees suddenly went rubbery. The soldier shook his head and tried to suck it up. What he needed was forty-eight hours' rest in an oxygen tent. Unfortunately he was going to have to earn it the hard way.

Bolan moved.

The section of sewer was another horror film production. Niches lined the walls on either side. Dead bodies in chains filled them. The smell told him they weren't props. The door at the end of the section was open. Ottokar von Saar peeked around the door and fired off a burst. Bolan fired back and drove the Beast back behind cover. He took a deep breath and broke into a run.

Bogac Krom blindsided Bolan out of one of the niches and sent him flying.

Bolan hit the niche on the other side and the withered corpse within broke apart around him like kindling. The Executioner clawed for Zhong's Glock but a fist like a freight train hit him right over his heart and crumpled him. Krom loomed over Bolan wearing full tactical armor. His PDW was slung and a 9 mm Beretta was strapped to his thigh. The killer hauled Bolan to his feet, ripped away the pistol and hatchet, and delivered a blow that nearly unhinged Bolan's jaw. The soldier's vision went white as Krom punched him brutally in the side of the neck. "The baron is ready to speak to you now."

Krebs's outraged voice was a welcome addition to the party. "Speak to this, Bluto!" Krebs unloaded ten rounds into Bogac's chest and his M-16 racked open on a smoke chamber. Krom peered down at his armored chest and gave Krebs an ugly look. They both knew he would never live long enough to reload or draw his .45. Krebs leveled his bayonet and charged. "Geronimo!"

Bolan took the opportunity to throw a punch. It was a weak one, but it slammed into Krom's bearded chin and distracted him slightly. The Turk threw an elbow into Bolan's breastbone that crumpled him to his knees again. Krom held up a warding hand as Krebs lunged. The lieutenant ran the hand through. The killer roared in rage and closed his huge fist around the muzzle of Krebs's rifle. He held the weapon immobile while he reached down to draw his pistol.

Bolan had drawn it for him.

Krom's eyes went wide in alarm. The Executioner shoved the gun up and pulled the trigger. The bullet punched through Krom's beard and traveled on to blow out the top of his head. He fell to the floor dead as a doornail. Bolan tucked away the Turk's pistol. "You'd better reload."

Krebs patted the limp magazine pouches on his pistol belt. "I'm out."

Bolan reached down and relieved the Turk of his PDW. "Take this." He set it on semiauto. "You've got fifty shots."

Bolan wearily retrieved his own weapon and Zhong's pistol and hatchet. "Where's Chet?"

"He's coming along as quick as he can. He took three hits high and wide to the left side of his rib cage. They're messy with a lot of splintered rib in them but they aren't deep. I think it's the combination of blood loss and gas that has gotten to him. He sent me ahead. Said you might need my help."

"I did. Thanks." Bolan took a breath past creaking ribs of his own and broke into a fresh fit of coughing. "Let's… finish this." Bolan and Krebs limped forward toward the open door.

"If the son of a bitch has any brains he's long gone," Krebs remarked hopefully.

"He's still here." Bolan gazed at the open portal ahead. Despite a brutal beating and a heavy duty gassing, Bolan's instincts were still on point. "He's waiting for us."

"I'm wearing armor, and except for feeling a little light headed I'm fine." Krebs squared his shoulders. "You want me to go in first? Draw his fire?"

Bolan took a breath and broke into another coughing fit before he could tell Krebs no. Blood speckled the back of Bolan's hand as he hacked, but he didn't know whether it was toxin or fist related. "You don't mind?"

Krebs shrugged. "Naw."

"You know, if he's got another Claymore in there it's going to erase every part of you that isn't armored."

"Yeah…but I'm wily," Krebs countered.

Bolan smiled wearily. "You'll do."

"Give me the other carbine."

Krebs slung his PDW and took up the one Bolan gave him. "Okay…"

Bolan filled his hands with Zhong and Krom's pistols. "One, two, three…go!"

"Bring it on!" Krebs bellowed. The C3 man went through the door with his weapon blazing on full-auto. He sprayed the P-90 in an arc. When it ran dry he dropped it and brought up his second one. "Coop? I don't see shit."

Bolan leaned around the door. Krebs stood in a warehouse-sized, barrel-shaped section of ancient sewer. The bricks had been floored over with wood and overhead lighting installed. A dozen workspaces with chairs, desks and computers sat empty. Bolan raised an eyebrow at the gleaming black Panoz Esperante convertible and the pair of BMW motorcycles parked at the far end. The work spaces were separated by a maze of low partitions. One corner suite was security. Dozens of video screens gave the Beast visual on every inch of his club. Bolan was most interested in the suite opposite. Military-grade telecommunications equipment stacked roof high. "Krebs, you see the C3 station?"

Krebs couldn't contain himself. "Oh, man, that is a sweet set-up!"

"You figure that's where communications are being jammed?"

"Most definitely."

"Kill it. I'll cover you."

"Damn shame." Krebs sighed. Shame or not he raised his PDW to his shoulder—then gasped as his right leg was kicked out from underneath him in a spray of blood. He landed hard on his side. "Son of a bitch!"

Bolan searched for the shooter, but he hadn't heard the shot. Krebs slapped a hand over his wounded leg and tried to bring up his PDW. Blood misted out of his shoulder and the weapon clattered to the floor.

"Motherfucker!"

Bolan searched, but the Beast was nowhere to be seen and had a truly silenced weapon. One that didn't cycle

with each shot or eject brass until it was manually operated; and he was pulling the sniper's draw. He was going
to keep shooting Krebs in nonvital areas until he forced
Bolan to charge in. Bolan was betting the partitions were
fabric on frame. The Beast was firing through them, and
moving after each shot.

Bolan smiled coldly as he heard a wheeze and scrape
behind him. Chet's voice was a whisper. "Right behind
you, boss."

"Fuck!" Krebs writhed as a bullet hit his other leg.
"Fuck!"

The Beast spoke, but it came from the concealed speakers he seemed to have everywhere. "If you don't drop your
weapon, I am going to shoot your friend in the balls."

Krebs shouted out in defiance. "I've already had two
kids! I've led a full life! Jack him up, Coop!"

Bolan nodded. "You heard the man."

Bolan and Chet came through the door. Chet put pat-
terns of buckshot through partitions. Bolan did the same
with Krom's pistol. Krebs managed to yank out his .45
left-handed and joined the party. Bolan ran straight for the
nearest workstation. Krom's gun racked open on empty,
and he kept the pressure on with Zhong's Glock. Bolan
reached the workstation. Krebs suddenly went limp as he
took a hit someplace vital.

"Son of a bitch!" Chet dropped his empty shotgun and
started firing his PDW. Bolan jumped on top of the desk.
Chet suddenly staggered. "Son of a…" The man fell. But
Bolan had seen the slight vibration of a partition as the
bullet had passed through it. The Beast was six work-
stations away. Bolan leaped down and charged. He fired
the 10 mm pistol as fast as he could pull the trigger, and
the partition shredded. The Glock locked open on empty.
Bolan tore Zhong's hatchet out of his belt.

The Beast rose. He held a silenced Russian pistol with a custom shoulder stock attached. The ruby beam of the laser pointer winked into life. Bolan hurled Zhong's hatchet. It spun once and hit the Beast blunt end first and bounced off, but it was enough to spoil his shot.

Bolan hurled himself over the partition and tackled the Beast. They hit the desk and the two men, the chair and the monitor fell in a tangle. The Executioner came up on top, and the Beast grinned at him. He shot one hand around Bolan's throat. His tactical knife clicked open, and the soldier felt the burn as it grated against his ribs. He ignored both. The Beast's eyes went wide as Bolan raised the twenty-four-inch flat screen monitor overhead in both hands. He let go of Bolan's throat a second too late. The Beast brought up his arm to block, and Bolan slammed the monitor edge on and broke it. The Beast cried out as he tore the knife out of Bolan's side to stab him again.

Bone crunched as Bolan smashed the twenty-three-pound screen against his adversary's skull.

Bolan dropped the shattered screen. "Chet?"

"I'm still here," he rasped.

"Krebs?"

Krebs groaned. "Tell me you killed that sack of shit!"

Bolan rose and shambled over to the communications suite and sagged into the chair. He wasn't a professional C3 guy, so Bolan just shut off everything except what was clearly the radio. He turned the dial to Grimaldi's frequency. "Jack?"

"Sarge! What's your status?"

"Zhong and Rudi are dead. Everyone else is wounded. Libby, you read?"

"I read you. Naz is in real bad shape."

"You're going to have to get him in the elevator. Go to the roof. Jack will extract you."

"What about you?"

"Krebs is shot up bad. Chet isn't much better." Bolan broke into another ragged fit of coughing. "I've felt better myself. I don't think we can walk back, and even if we could there's an ocean of poison gas behind us."

"Don't tell me you're going to wait for the authorities," Grimaldi warned.

"One or more us will most likely bleed out before they get here."

"Tell me you have a plan," Grimaldi begged.

Bolan eyed the shark-shaped Panoz in the back and the automatic rolling door behind it. A sewer was a funny place to park a premium sports car unless you had some way out. "We're going for a ride."

EPILOGUE

Stony Man Farm, Virginia

Bolan watched the sun set. He sat on the farmhouse's porch with a cold lager sweating in his hand.

It had been a rough ride back.

Krebs had nearly bled to death on the ride out of the sewers. They barely made it to a CIA-provided safe house and the waiting medical team. Nazareno had been taken off the critical list only yesterday. Both men were still in Germany at Ramstein. Chet and Smallhouse had been cleared and returned to the States. The two wounded warriors were getting some well-deserved rest and recuperation at a five-star hotel in Miami on the Farm's dime. Bolan had sent Zhong's blood-covered hatchet to Wang's restaurant with a simple note a contact had written in Chinese characters. "The White Devil is dead. Miss Tsui is avenged." Bolan was pretty sure the weapon would find its way back to Hong Kong.

The slaughter at the Hellfire Club had made international headlines. The German state police were dismantling von Saar's organization and were in direct communication with the Mexican authorities. Von Saar's brother had been arrested. Cordula Schön was still at large. Bolan looked down at Highlander. The dog's side was bandaged, and he was mastering the American canine art of lying on the porch all day with great aplomb. "Good boy."

Highlander thumped his tail against the deck.

Bolan considered himself. The bruises had gone from black to yellow. He had ten stitches in his side. He had stopped coughing a day ago. The headaches were far less severe and becoming less frequent. The doctor had warned him that the worst effects of acute carbon monoxide poisoning were neurological, including depression, amnesia and Parkinson's-like symptoms, and could manifest themselves days and even weeks afterward. Except for a little short-term memory loss he seemed to be making a speedy recovery.

All in all, the Executioner felt lucky to be alive. With a final salute to fallen friends, Bolan drained his beer and stood.

"Walkies, Highlander?" he said, and stepped off the porch, heading for the orchard.

* * * * *

The Don Pendleton's
Executioner®
CRUCIAL INTERCEPT

Black ops assassins turn Virginia into a war zone...

A series of high-profile shootings in Virginia exposes a deadly scavenger hunt with numerous factions competing for the prize. An ex-CIA cryptologist who created an unbreakable code has unwittingly been sold out to whichever terrorist group can get to him first. It's up to Bolan to intercept the human bounty and keep the code from falling into enemy hands.

Available January 2011 wherever books are sold.

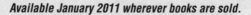

GOLD EAGLE®

www.readgoldeagle.blogspot.com

James Axler
Outlanders®

CRADLE OF DESTINY

The struggle of the Cerberus rebels stretches back to the dawn of history…

When millennia-old artifacts are discovered in the Middle East's legendary Fertile Crescent, they appear to belong to one of Cerberus's own. It's not long before Grant is plunged back through the shimmering vortex of time, forcing the rebels to lead a rescue party across a parallax to destroy a legendary god beast—before Grant is lost forever.

Available February 2011 wherever books are sold.

TAKE 'EM FREE

2 action-packed novels plus a mystery bonus

NO RISK
NO OBLIGATION TO BUY

JAMES AXLER

DEATH LANDS®

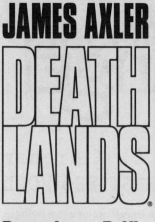

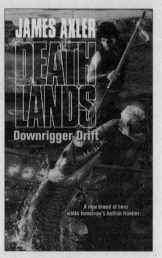

Downrigger Drift

A new breed of hero walks tomorrow's hellish frontier...

In the nuke-altered region of the Great Lakes, Ryan and his group face the spectrum—from the idyllic to the horrific—of a world reborn. Against the battered shoreline of Lake Michigan, an encounter with an old friend leads to a battle to save Milwaukee from a force of deadly mutant interlopers—and to liberate one of their own.

Available January 2011 wherever books are sold.